Cradle Crow

A Novel
By S. L. Schultz

Published by
Yellow Horse Books

ISBN: 979-8-9885918-2-5

Printed in the United States of America

For Mom

The crow on the cradle
The black and the white
Somebody's baby is born for a fight
The crow on the cradle
The white and the black
Somebody's baby is not coming back
Sang the crow on the cradle

"The Crow on the Cradle"
Sydney Bertram Carter

Prologue

American Midwest – October 1981

Show of Force

He pulls Jeanine into the car by her hair across the cold, shiny vinyl. She does not scream, moan or utter any sound, for the rough and cruel draw steals her voice away as well. Her eyes dart frantic, up at the interior of the roof, where the centered light, a small sun or maybe a moon shines in the darkness. Her hands, those hands, so lily white, do not strike out in fists but weigh heavy in terror by her sides. She neither asked nor prayed for this abduction. Somehow, someway he found her, by chance or through intention, she cannot say.

A ghost, a ghoul, a monster of some kind? Clearly not an emissary from heaven. Yes, she wanted out. Out of that house. Out of that life that robbed her of so much inspiration. Out from under the scrutinizing of *his* eye, the moldering of *his* hands, and the stinging of *his* words. She felt free of there at last.

Only to be manipulated by another.

After he pulls her in, he rolls her over on her belly, and then walks over to the other side of the car to tie her hands behind her, those hands so delicately scarred with small nicks from quick sharp kitchen knives. He does not fasten them with rope, plastic, or metal cuffs, but something soft, like cloth but tight, so tight the palms chafe. Please, she wants to plead, not so tight. Another cloth, maybe the same – a scarf, a hanky, a cotton hand towel? This one gags her. He pulls her over onto her side now and curls her legs behind her. She rests her head on that cold vinyl and shuts her eyes, her heart beating like a bird in hand. He slams the door, then stomps around the car to shove the other closed too, then opens his own and drops his body in.

Where will he take her?

She follows several turns and stops in her mind's eye, but soon loses direction, her body jolting forward and backward and forward. She fears a toss onto the floor, a small space really, between the seats. Although that space lies shallow, she fears it may become fathomless instead. She will fall into a pit, her skin scraping the jagged stone sides. That fall will never end, but perhaps preferable to what he has planned.

At one point, music shatters the silence. The beat drives, insists, and abuses. The vocalist screams and growls words that sound foreign, and occasionally punctuates the ruckus with a "fuck." The guitar line pulses, pounds and rips the air into ragged shreds.

The man wearing the stocking cap pulled down around his chin must be young. She could not tell looking for one moment into eyes peering out of the frayed cut circles, or from the voice hissing through the knitted black wool. If only she had not opened the door. If only she had looked out of the window first.

Her children were alone now. Brenda, at fifteen, hardly a child. But her boy, only ten, a sensitive, sometimes clinging child, whom *he* beats down as much or more than she. If the boy awakens and tiptoes in to see her abandoned bed... In her heart, she hears him cry already. If only *he* did not travel away from home so often to play golf, attend conferences, go deep-sea fishing in the waters south.

Who knows, maybe *he* arranged this. To this day, *he* still believes that she talks to, even steals away to visit a man she has not seen in more than a decade.

That man's guitar never sounded like this. His guitar purred and soothed, and he sang the sweetest melodies. His voice, the voice of the man she did indeed once love, set all the girls on fire. He, too, played rock and roll, but not the type of dredge playing now that extinguishes the spirit, shifting light into dark within the first two bars.

Jeanine feels cold. Her nightgown, cotton, splashed with little red flowers, three-quarters length, now accordions up above her knees. Is she wearing underwear? She cannot remember. Her body shivers, even shakes, as her restrained teeth tap a tiny Morris code of fear. She dares not move, especially her hands, chaffed now and burning from the turns and jolts. Will he rape her? Kill her? Where the hell are they going?

And then, the car stops. The incessant nerve-shattering gallop of rhythm, the screeching of voice seemingly too high to be male, and the guitar chords that sawed into the night stop too.

Her abductor opens the car door and steps out. He slams the door shut. He stomps around again and pulls the back door open, grabs her feet to straighten her legs, and with a jerk flips her over onto her belly and draws her out. His gloved hands feel rough against her freshly shaven legs, and feet buffed smooth and soft with pumas. She hears her heart pumping blood with a roar inside her ears. Surely, one could witness the mighty muscle of the organ lifting her ribs and flesh.

Her feet reach the cold ground of dirt, not grass, and the masked man huffs and puffs as he draws her upright by her hair and her hands. He shoves her forward and commands, "Walk!"

The October night feels cold with a wind blowing in from the west. She looks up and around to see the stars cast against the deep dark indigo and the sliver of a moon. Jeanine wishes she could remember what Martha, her mother-in-law, told her about the moon in its early cycle. The beginning or the end of something. Yes. Yes, that's right. The beginning or the end, but which one? On the distant horizon, the dark mass of a storm moves in.

Her captor shoves her from behind, "Faster!"

Little rocks and occasionally sharp, hard weeds threaten to puncture her tender feet. Where are they? In a field barren of crops, dotted with trees, leafless skeletons silhouetted by the moon, and rocks, even boulder size rolled in by a glacier from another time. Perhaps a half mile away she sees but does not recognize a house. The gathering wind blows her hair back, and the hoot of an owl echoes. The bringer of the dream, the owl. The bringer of death. Which one this night?

She could run. Take off like a rabbit across the fields, but she cannot, held hostage now by him but also through cold and fear. Besides, he could have a gun tucked down into the rear waistline of his pants, or cropped down into a pocket of his jacket. She caught one glimpse of that denim jacket trimmed in suede by the light on the porch, when she answered that pitiful plea for help.

"There's been an accident. My wife is lying still and bloody. Please help me. Please!"

The knock did not awaken the kids. Good. Thank God. If they had stumbled down the stairs, sand in their eyes, yawning, would this predator, this monster, have taken them as well?

If she could break this cast of icy fear, gun or not she could run, but now as she zigs and zags across this barren field, she feels her energy begin to drain, starting from her womb, then pulled into Mother Earth with a gulp.

If she possesses only a short time to live, then she wills the sweetest memories to rain over her.

The faces of her girl and boy. The trust of her always present in their eyes. Their smiles so bright when she points out the things they do correctly, the cleverness of their words, the simple beauty of their hearts.

The world around her looks blurred now. Tears have sprung, pooled, and roll slowly down her cheeks. They hesitate for a moment on the cliff of her chin then fall, some hitting the ground with a tiny unheard splash, but others sinking into the thin cotton of her gown to feed her freeze.

He shoves her from behind, one hand against her back.

"I told you to hurry, bitch."

Jeanine pushes herself to pick up speed, though her feet are practically numb. As her toes graze, bump, and sometimes roughly stub, she feels only a shadow of the pain.

"Faster! I haven't got all night!"

Now she begins to trot, well, hobble really, hoping to reach the place that this wicked man has in mind. Her hands raw in that one spot where the tying together captures them tightly enough that they cannot move at all. That place where the thumbs meet, palms together, perhaps looking from behind like an awkward prayer position.

But it feels too late for that.

On she stumbles with him behind her, in his long hard strides. The earth, the pebbles, the stubble, and the weeds cruelly grind beneath his feet.

She sways, and her torso lunges forward, propelling her onward. Her body grows stiffer with the cold. If there were no cloth, scarf, or towel in her mouth, that Morris code of fear would echo through the field, as the darkness of night closes in. The stars, those still showing as the storm mass approaches, look much farther away than before. No hoot of an owl now, just the sound of a dog barking somewhere across the field.

One last shove at her back does her in. She teeters on one leg as she lifts the other to take a step, places that foot down and lifts the other. The foot just placed rocks on top of a small pile of loose stone; she loses her balance and falls face down.

He kicks her over onto her back, which arches towards heaven above her hands and arms, and he begins to pull her by her hair again. He drags her across the stones, the sharp, spiky blades of weed, the cold, rough skin of the earth she has called her mother. The petite red flowers of her gown shred, exposing her tender, ivory flesh to the ground, ivory as the single strand of pearls around her throat. The only piece of jewelry besides her wedding band that she ever wears. Suddenly, the sharp spikes of a weed pull upon, strain, and break the string of pearls. From one corner of her eye, she watches as they roll away and disappear, not into the darkness, but as if suddenly swallowed into the earth whole, lost forever from the human eye. A whimper rises.

She feels little in terms of pain, though her body bumps and the earth scrapes a layer or two of skin away. But her hair. She does feel the pulling of her flesh from the bond of her head, and her neck straining, the muscles stretching, surely they will snap and break. She feels the vertebras separate like the cars of a train wrenching apart.

He moves in longer strides, with an urgency she can sense, huffing and puffing punctuated occasionally with a "fuck." The star, only one alone now, jerks and dances with her body below. From the corner of her eye, she watches as a fork of lightning flashes out of a cloud. She can feel, she swears she can, as her life or spirit perhaps, begins to seep out.

Then, he stops.

Her head falls loosely to the side. She cannot move the globe. Her eyes stare deeply into the night as he walks away. The eyelids flutter, conjuring in memories that she holds dear. Peter's head of shiny dark curls. Brenda's full lips turned up in a smile. *His* well-toned, rippling muscles when they were teens. Her mother's sweet voice when she sang to her. Her father's cloak of protection that cannot help her here. Brenda and Peter when they were babes, like tiny birds, helpless in the nest. Her children's tiny hands clasped in hers tightly as they walk through a field on a sunny day.   That other man she did love standing on the stage with his guitar.

The man, the boy, whoever, whatever returns. She hears those cruel steps stamp their print upon the land. For one moment, she feels ashamed of her nakedness, lying on the cold hard ground.

Almost every shred of her nightgown left behind.

He kicks her legs open and she feels, yes, this she feels, as he plunges something deep inside her. Her mouth strains to open to emit some sound, some scream, a shriek, or moan. Instead, through the small gaps of cloth that hold her voice at bay, her very last breath escapes.

Part I
Crows Gather
American Midwest – October 2002

2

Tattletale

Friday 4:23 p.m.

Jeff Tillman drives into Willis in his lead-colored Lexus, feeling as if he has driven into a shell. He has been gone for over twenty years, and the town reflects all of the changes that he has read about. Small industries closed. Once-successful farms auctioned off. Men and women moved into occupations they never dreamed. Farmers work as custodians and sales clerks, factory men as cab drivers and baggage loaders, factory women as house cleaners or aids in convalescence homes. Many drive the big commute into nearby cities, eating up time otherwise spent with family. People of all ages attend college, racking up debt and pursuing programs out of need. Staying alive and living the American dream takes two incomes, if not three, so farm girls and homemakers work in offices, or as cooks and servers. Some work in the health fields or teach, though school systems also suffer. Boarded-up buildings and storefronts for sale tell the story. Willis reflects a past, truly American in roots, crumbling now through corporate takeovers, outsourcing and improved technology, but none of that matters much to him. He has no plans to stay. He knows that the secure family life that the American Heartland once offered sits compromised forever.

Jeff has travelled back to his supposed homeland, or what remains left of it, to reconcile with his conscience. Negotiate his redemption. Make his amends.

And to escape from her, that woman, Desiree.

Six months ago, he contacted Jack, his eldest brother and the only one left alive out of three. Tracking him down took time. Last he knew, Jack was in prison, serving time for Assault with

8

Intent to Commit Murder. In this town, like many small towns, weak minds guided by skewed convictions contributed to darker times, when a stray bullet from a hunter's gun killed his brother Jordan, an impaired old man struck his brother James' car on a warm summer night, and Jack's beating of a pedophile led to twenty years behind bars.

Let it go. Let it go now.

Attend to the task at hand.

He pulls a cigarette out of a pack with his teeth and lights it. His right hand begins to shake with the palsy gained from years of head bashing and neck strain. With a shaved head and a body covered with provocative ink, his social outbursts took a toll. Now hiding the tattoos beneath his clothes, he grew his hair out, letting it hang down freely, not too long, carefully and conservatively cut really. The outbursts, well, Tom Washke took care of those.

"I've got big plans for you, Jeff. I'm going to clean you up, educate you, and send you out into the corporate world."

"You're kidding, right?"

He was not. Washke discovered that Jeff had a gift with numbers and enthusiastically fed his prejudices. Two weeks of vigorous hand washing removed the grease beneath his nails, from all those years of fixing cars so they sped around the tracks like cheetahs. Behind him now. All gone.

Jeff mashes down on the butt of his cigarette, with his fingers, freeing any stray tobacco or fire to fly away with the wind, and then pulls a cell phone out of his shirt pocket. Holding the wheel of his car with his left hand, he punches out Jack's number with his right index and listens as the other end rings and rings. Finally, he hears his brother's voice.

"This is Jack."

"Hey, I'm here."

"So you made it. Well, I'm still at work. You can go by the house, if you like…"

"No, I'll nose around town for a while."

"Should be there by 6:30 or so. Did I give you the address?"
"Yep. Got it."

With time on his hands, he turns around and drives back through town looking for something. Maybe a connection. Some proof that he grew up here. Journeyed from a smudge-faced boy dressed in hand-me-downs, neglected and often hungry, to a rebellious teen determined to stir things up.

In those early days of rebellion, beyond a few fistfights, Jeff never physically harmed anyone. His revenge upon the world took the form of thievery.

Eric Thompson was Jeff's comrade in crime, a onetime high school football star with a nasty reputation. Good looking, friendly enough dude to the face, even what some might describe as charismatic, but one mean-ass dog behind the back. Tall and big, muscular, hard hearted, and shrewd beyond his years. They started their spree of crimes lifting small items off shelves, including bubble gum, jawbreakers, Twinkies and lighters. A sleight of hand into a deep pocket. A wink around a corner by his comrade, signaling the coast is clear. They would buy a stick of gum and carry out a half of bag of goods on their bodies.

Clothes placed second on their thieving ladder. Find the stores with no cameras. Walk in wearing baggie pants and a jacket. Walk out with two extra pairs of jeans and a couple of shirts.

When his mom asked, in one of those rare moments when she noticed him at all, where he had gotten the new clothes, he would tell her that a friend had passed them down. Jack, of course, caught on and whooped his ass a couple of times, so out of defiance, when Eric set his sights on something bigger with higher potential penalties, Jeff jumped in.

Eric taught him how to break into houses. The smart thief doesn't waste time on the little guy but chooses wisely, homes rich with expensive jewelry, electronics, and precious heirlooms. All insurable, the electronics and jewelry mostly replaceable, the heirlooms, well at that time, he didn't give a damn.

He learned early on not to break the glass, pick at the lock, or kick the door in. Eric taught him simply to remove the door at the hinges. After prowling through the house, stealing everything of value, if time allowed, they would replace everything skewed. Eric told him repeatedly to slow down. Slow down, damnit. For Christ's sake, fucking slow down! Eric picked through things meticulously, showing Jeff the ropes. Where Eric learned his tricks, Jeff never really knew, but he had his suspicions.

Although they had had their hands slapped a few times, all went pretty well, until that August night of 1976.

—ɯ—

Jeff rolled the short sleeves of his black T-shirt up to rest on his shoulders. He tucked a pack of Lucky Strikes in the right curl and swiped away the sweat from his sparse brown whiskers. The summer night sat bloated with humidity as Jeff whipped through the lowlands where fog hovered over the desolate road, and the highland sat still as a cemetery. He headed for Denton, a nearby burg, in his Cherry Red GTO that he had bought with money earned from selling stolen goods and working part time at a racetrack.

Eric lived outside Denton with his father, a member of the Denton Devils Motorcycle Club, a notorious group of badasses who liked to party hard. Rick Thompson stood six feet and two-hundred-fifty pounds of pure ignorance, which worked in Jeff and Eric's favor, but led to the demise of other living things. He did not flinch when Eric blew birds out of the sky, caught someone's pets in live traps, and fought two stray dogs until death. Truthfully, Jeff felt afraid of Eric, but not enough to break the cycle of theft or the material goods the activity afforded.

He arrived at the Thompson home, a doublewide trailer, sitting back, way back into the woods. In the yard sat two rusted-out cars, one up on blocks, a broken down snowmobile, two piles of mechanical parts half buried in debris and fallen leaves, and one shining silver and blue Harley Davidson, so impeccably kept, one would think the bike just rolled out of a showroom. Parked next to the motorcycle sat a gold fleck '68 Camaro, Eric's toy of toys.

Rick sat on the porch in a green-and-white folding chair tinkering with a gas lamp, while his girlfriend, Carrie Joe, roamed around wearing pants tight as a second skin and a thin T-shirt covering heavy hanging titties. Jeff thought about sucking on those. In fact he did, a couple years before, behind the bleachers, as they dry humped until both came. This little fact Jeff and Carrie Joe did not dare re-visit in the present company. Neither would dream of it.

Jeff walked up to the porch and Rick looked up, as Carrie Joe rested her titties on the railing. She licked her lips, turned her head and called into the trailer, "Eric, your friend is here!"

Rick asked, "So what are you two up to this evening?" A smirk broke across his face. Apparently, he knew more than Jeff did.

Eric stepped out through the door, letting the screen door bang loudly behind him. He shrugged his shoulders and answered his father, "Ride around, pick up chicks, the usual, right?"

Rick said, "Well, don't do anything I wouldn't do."

Eric said, "Yeah, sure," as he and Jeff climbed into the Camaro and with a roar pulled away from the trailer and headed back down the long gravel driveway. Eric turned left onto the paved road, staring into the dusk. AC/DC screamed from the radio.

Jeff asked, "Where are we going?"

"I found a place. I've been watching it. They're gone on vacation or something. The house is loaded."

They rode through the growing dark, a bright white moon rising, shining down and illuminating the seven-foot-tall corn stalks on one side of the road and the rolling fields of soybeans on the other. Small farms and ranch-style homes dotted the landscape, as yard lights and interior lights began to blink on. They descended a hill into a wooded area where Eric slowed down and turned his headlights off. No one approached from the other direction, as Eric turned left between two red brick gateposts and eased the Camaro, dual exhaust now barely a purr, up the paved driveway toward a matching brick house, sitting back, nestled in the trees like a fortress. Eric backed the car into a dark corner of the driveway off to one side of the garage doors, as the beveled glass of the double front doors cast fractured prisms from the porch lights. Eric jumped out of the car, opening back doors and the trunk with a flourish. Jeff climbed out slowly, orienting himself to the surroundings, his heart beating like a drum and sweat running.

"You're sure nobody's here?" Jeff asked.

"Don't get all pussy on me, Tillman. We're going in on the side, come on!" For a big dude, Eric could move swiftly on his feet, a gift that once served him well in football, until his attitude ended that.

Jeff followed Eric down the sidewalk, fertile with bushes and flowering plants, the night heavy, almost too sweetly with the scents. In his hands, Eric carried a hammer and a flat blade. When they reached the door, Eric threw Jeff a pair of latex gloves and pulled his own on in two seconds flat. They went to work, knocking out the pins of the door and removing it at the hinges. In a few short minutes they stood in the garage, where a seven series BMW sat and an array of every tool, every piece of outside equipment a person could ever wish for sat organized like a hardware store display.

Eric growled, "Bedrooms first. Money and jewelry," as they approached the inner door.

Jeff asked, "We're taking this one off at the hinges, too?"

Eric laughed. "Stupid fuckers never lock this one!"

They entered the house, stepping into an expansive kitchen and dining area dimly lit by nightlights, perfect for what they needed to see. Out of nowhere a cat, white and yellow looking, ran towards them meowing. With a swift kick, Eric sent the feline halfway across the room, where the startled animal laid dazed.

Eric pointed down a hall to the left. "Let's see how you do alone this time."

In thirty minutes they collected fifteen hundred dollars in cash, a booze bottle-sized sack full of jewelry, some coins, a few other odds and ends that looked old, vintage as they say, worth something maybe. They left everything relatively neat except for a few scuffmarks across the floors, and Eric found a cigar and smoked it. He left that as the calling card, biting off the end wet with his spit. As they crossed the kitchen one last time, the cat picked itself up off the floor and quickly limped off to hide. They loaded the car, replaced the door back on the hinges and took their gloves off.

Jeff peered into every direction, still feeling the sweat running and his heart pounding. This just felt too easy. That queer mix of exhilaration and terror fought like mad dogs within him. They closed the trunk door, both side doors, and climbed in. They coasted down the long paved drive, no headlights, under a moon ripe to create illusion. He kept catching glimpses of something from the corner of his eye. Maybe a missed guard dog, though he would of barked. Perhaps a beast from his conscience. Hell, maybe police surveillance just waiting for them to pull on out. Down the drive they rolled, where the large square gateposts stood like guardians, and one last thrill awaited. The posts obscured traffic coming from either way. They had to inch up to detect any lights. They could not afford, in any way, to be seen. Eric cursed in growls, between the deep ragged breaths that matched Jeff's own. Jeff fought to slow his heart down through will. Slow down. Slow down. They inched forward and maybe just maybe the light brightened from the left. Did that light signal an approaching car?

Eric said, "Fuck, I can't tell. I'm just going." He stepped on it and swung out right, as the sound of squealing breaks rushed towards them from behind. The smell of burning rubber hit the warm summer air. "Fuck!" they screamed simultaneously.

The car swung around them on the left, and the driver turned and peered into the dim night light to see them. Jeff saw a man. Hard to tell, but yes, *it's him,* he thought.

Eric shouted, "Don't look over there!"
"Too late. He's already seen the car, and we know him."
"Who?"
"Coach Becker."
"Becker!? Not that son-of-a-bitch!"
Coach's car did not stop that night and neither did his mouth.
Jeff and Eric did substantial time for that one in Half Moon Lake for Boys, thanks to a tattletale.

—⚬—

Jeff wonders if anyone will remember him as anything but a thief, a juvenile delinquent, one of four brothers who stirred up the town. Will he see any girls he kissed or fucked? Any teachers that threw him out of class? Any of his old teammates? Friends that became enemies, when he started hanging out with Eric?

Will he see his old partner in crime? Reconciling his conscience had to do with Eric, as did his making of amends. Only this time, Jeff would be the tattletale.

3
Pearl Jam

They walk into the Willis Café on this unseasonably warm fall day. Early frosts a couple weeks earlier sparked the turn of leaves, but they look folded now, in need of rain. Dry cut corn stalks, and orange and white pumpkins sit near the door. Once inside, miniature gourds of greens, yellows and whites, in various sizes and textures decorate the tables. Flat cardboard ghosts, goblins, and arched-back black cats decorate the walls.

Heads turn as they walk in, which doesn't surprise Brenda. They once turned because of the scandal eleven years before. In a small town everyone knew everyone, or thought they did. More often than not they knew little to nothing, but nonetheless stories were relayed. The heads turn now because Lily Rose looks like a model: tall, thin, with honey-brown hair, blue eyes, and a face someone from another world would describe as quintessentially American. That world does indeed exist. The town of Willis had its share of people who lived there. People who refused to climb down from their high horses and acknowledge that things were different now. A rainbow of people lived within the shores and borders of this land, and all Americans.

Lily leads the way to their favorite booth, one Brenda and Billy chose years ago. They slide into seats across from each other. Brenda looks at her tan, freckle-nosed sixteen-year-old and asks, "Whose party is it?"

"Justin Linz. It's his birthday, I guess."

Brenda shakes her head. "I've never heard you mention his name before."

"He's a senior."

"A senior!"

"That's only two years older! Mom, please!"

"I'll think about it, Lily."

Her daughter leans in towards her. "I'm sixteen, Mom! Practically a woman!"

"JUST sixteen."

"Everyone will be there!"

"No, I will not be. Your dad will not be. I know many people who will not be!"

"You know what I mean!"

"Lily, let it go now."

Lily slides out of the booth and stands.

"Where are you going?" Brenda asks.

Lily answers, exasperated, "To the bathroom."

Brenda reaches down into her purse sitting beside her and pulls out a small blue velveteen bag. Inside coils the restrung pearls just picked up at the jewelry store. She loosens the top of the bag and reaches in to touch them briefly, with the tips of her thumb and index finger. She stares. After a few moments, she pulls her fingers out and tightly re-draws the string. Tenderly, she clasps the treasure in both her hands, then turns to gaze out the window. So much to think about today. So much to feel.

A voice startles her. "Hi, what can I get ya?"

Brenda looks up to see a young red-haired server, with a ponytail and pale skin, ready to write on a pad with pen. "A cup of tea and a small strawberry shake."

"You got it." The redhead turns and heads toward a table nearby, where a family of six celebrates a birthday; pink and white balloons bob against the ceiling, and a chocolate flat cake sits on a neighboring table.

Brenda turns back to the window. A sadness creeps up and chokes her. She swallows hard several times and breathes in and out with shallow little gasps. She looks out at the blue sky, the high, thin Sirius clouds, the yellow, reds, and oranges of the turned leaves. Her mother loved October.

The shallow breaths become deeper, as the lava rises. This emotion dwarfs the first; this one she had shoved down deeply and locked up for years. Up until recent months, Brenda had accepted that they would never find her mother's killer. But, no more.

Six months ago her brother Peter died, after a long illness. He lived in New York, and they spoke occasionally on the phone, though seldom saw each other through the years. He had found a new family, one that embraced him entirely. Before he died, during their last conversation, he confessed to her that he had been afraid all these years that the person who killed their mother would kill him, too. Someone mad at the family. Someone who would stalk him down and take him out. He said that the world wasn't safe anymore. That he had not felt safe since the murder. He said that she, Lily, Christopher, and Billy were not safe either. Brenda remembers feeling the same way, as if an attack could occur at any time, but she conquered that emotion out of a need to survive, or had she just shoved it down and locked it in with the other?

A few days after that last phone call, she rustled through the top right drawer of her dresser, reaching into the back past the panties and the bras. There they were, nestled down inside the blue bag, mostly loose, but occasionally a pair or a triplet strung together with frayed gray thread. The gold clasp nestled there too. In 1991, she found the pearls buried shallow on the killing ground of her mother. She carried them home and hid them in the back of the drawer, under a green and white cotton scarf, back, way back, where the ghost of her mother would be safe and protected. She had to; she wasn't there to save her.

On that day, after the last phone call with Peter, she grabbed the blue bag from the drawer and gently shook the beads out to roll freely on the bed, her brother's face haunting her in the ether. The sun's early rays cut in through the window, shining down upon those pearls, now luminescent in the light, alive with spirit. This spirit sparked the lava, awakened all that she had shoved down, packed down, stomped on because the pain became unbearable.

Now she wants the animal, the monster, two legged at that, who snatched away her mother's life to suffer; if he still lives, he must pay. He's been lucky, whoever he is, but the time has come for that luck to run out.

Lily plops down in the seat across from her. Brenda turns and looks at her "practically a woman" daughter, and thinks, yes, she cannot deny it.

"Mom, are you okay?"

"Pretty much." Brenda swallows hard and breathes deeply.

"I'm sorry, Mom, to be bugging you on this day. I know it's really hard for you, but... I really want to go to this party."

"I know you do."

"I promise to be careful."

"I'm not worried about you, Lily Rose. I'm worried about all the other people that will be there, of all ages, who will be drinking and doing drugs..."

"I'm not into that!"

"Even if I say yes, your father may say no."

"This could be the last party before winter."

Brenda looks intently at her daughter. "Please, let it go now."

At that moment, the server walks up with a tray. "I'm thinking you have the tea," placing a teapot and cup in front of Brenda, then placing the shake in front of Lily. Brenda and Lily say, "Thank you!" Brenda notes that they spoke at the same time in the exact same tone.

Lily rips the paper off her straw and begins drinking her shake, while Brenda steeps a teabag in the pot.

Lily looks up. "Could I see them, Mom?"

"The pearls?"

Lily nods.

"Sure." Brenda pulls the blue velveteen bag open, turns it over and shakes the strand of pearls into her hand, then offers them to Lily Rose, her mother's one granddaughter whom she will never meet or watch transform into this lovely young woman. Brenda turns to the window and blinks back tears. Again, thankfully succeeding, she turns back.

Her daughter holds the pearls in both hands, examining them closely. She looks up teary eyed. "I didn't know that pearls were so beautiful."

"Your grandma wore them every day."

"Will you wear them?"

"Maybe."

"Will you let me wear them sometime? Now that I'm practically a woman?"

Brenda laughs. "We'll see."

Brenda looks at her daughter, about the same age as she was on that fateful day. For a moment, she remembers what it felt like, the yearning to be adult, to possess some freedom of her own. "As far as I'm concerned, you can go to the party. But you still have to ask your dad."

Lily jumps up and slides in next to her mother on the other side of the booth, throws her arms around her neck and hugs her. "Thank you!" Then the long, thin girl slides back out and practically squeals with excitement, "I'm going to go tell Kristen. I'll be home for dinner!"

"Wait! I thought we were spending some time together."

"We can hang out this evening! Watch a movie or something!" She grabs her shake. "I'll tell the server to put my shake in a cup."

"How will you get home?"

"Kristen's dad just bought her a car!"

That last news does nothing to make Brenda feel better about Lily going to the party, but the joy she sees in Lily's long strides lighten her emotions for a moment. But only a moment. She slips the pearls back into their soft, safe bed.

—⁂—

Technically, *she* did not find the pearls. Jake found them, their Australian shepherd, masquerading as a bloodhound. The night had called her, a gnawing silent voice, and with dog in tow, she headed for the field. Billy had just arrived home from the Persian Gulf, and the scandal that involved his best friend, James, swirled and twirled in full tilt. Her mother had died ten years before, and she felt petrified by the dark. Out of the dark, a murderer came, and he could come again. Her grandmother Martha had been coaching her on how to be stronger, pressing the importance upon her. Uncle Sammie had fallen ill, her father had become lost inside a bottle, and Martha must have sensed her own time clock slowing. What called her into the dark that night? She does not know, but she ventured forth through the fields, feeling her way, until she found herself on that killing ground, where they found her mother's body. Jake, crouching before a small shallow hole in the earth barked and wailed. When she inched her fingers into the hole with her pulse racing, she found the nest of pearls, their disintegrating string and the small gold clasp. This small hole in a field, once fertile now barren, had become a tomb of treasure.

The pearls were a gift from her father to her mother in a younger day, a wreath of prayer for the hopes of her marriage. Unfortunately, her father controlled and shamed, and her mother withered.

Brenda carried the pearls home in her pocket and placed them in the back of that drawer, out of sight, out of mind? Actually, she thought of them often and each time remembered the morning she and Peter woke up to find their mother gone.

Peter woke up first and, at ten years old, walked into Brenda's room. He gently shook her shoulder, and she awoke to see him rubbing the sleep from his eyes while his dark curls fell around them. She remembers his exact words. "She's not here."

She asked, "Who's not here?"

"Mom. She's not here."

Brenda sat up in bed. "She's probably outside working in the yard."

"She isn't! She isn't anywhere. I looked!" Peter began to hyperventilate, and panic widened his large blue eyes.

Brenda peeled the covers off and swung her legs around

to the floor. She threw on her favorite pink flowered robe and quickly headed out of her bedroom. She moved from room to room, scanning, even outside through the yard calling for her mother. Their father was on one of his many golf trips, and she did not know how to contact him, in fact, did not even know exactly where he had travelled. As Peter had stated, their mother was gone. She remembers her heart pounding, and she fought to keep a sense of panic at bay. As the older sibling, she needed to be stronger.

As if on automatic, she returned into the house from the backyard, walked into the kitchen and began to prepare breakfast, just as her mother would have been doing, had she been there. Because the car sat in the driveway, she decided that her mother must be off on a walk. She would surprise her by cooking breakfast. Her mother would feel proud of her. She calmed Peter as well as she could, insisting to him that Mom would return soon.

Peter asked, "Why was the door open? She would never leave the door open when it is so cold outside."

Brenda said, "She just forgot," while thinking her brother correct. That October morning the thermometer read forty-five degrees, and the panic really descended. She continued to make pancakes, Peter's favorite, and distract him as well as she could. When Grandma Martha's car pulled into the driveway, she felt the pounding of her heart stop. Grandma walked into the house, and Peter ran to her and wrapped his arms around her. Brenda saw the tears in her grandma's eyes, placed the spatula down that she held and ran out into the yard and the boundless space before her, emitting a sharp high cry.

They held the funeral seven days later after the autopsy, and for some reason, her father, Martin, decided that Mother needed an open casket. The funeral director had also encouraged this, though one glimpse of her mother's lifeless body, in the private family showing, sent her to the bathroom where she fell to her knees before the toilet and hurled out every remnant of food, every bit of bile, every emotion held so deeply, leaving her a rag.

She could see from the corner of her eye, as that glimpse sawed in, her mother's neck bare of pearls. No pearls. Not a one. There was not one. In that glimpse, she also saw her mother's hands crossed and the unnatural color of the skin, not the ivory of her mother's skin, but a revolting color she would never forget. No one came for a while as she hurled, spit and sobbed, feeling like she just might spend her days there in front of that ceramic bowl. There existed no end to the purge. Then, Grandma Martha walked in silently and sweetly and drew her up from her prone position on the floor, cradling her like a baby. She experienced no heartbeat in her own body, instead depending on the rhythm of the older woman's. Broken hearts cannot pump blood.

When she again walked into the room where visitation would begin, she averted her eyes from that satin lined box, instead gathering her young brother into her arms, sitting in a corner behind a curtain where no one would see them. She watched from around one edge of the dark brocade as her father stood like a soldier on guard, hands clasped before his groin, face cemented into something pale and hard, nodding to those who came, speaking only when necessary. He never broke; he never shed a tear that day, standing so resolute. Brenda felt so angry with him. She imagined running to him and pounding upon his chest with her fifteen-year-old hands, forcing his heart to feel. She would do it; she swore she would. How could she feel so much and he feel nothing?

That night back at home she awoke in the early hours, and on her way to the bathroom, glanced into her parent's room and there she saw him. He slumped on his knees beside the bed, on the side her mother slept, sobbing so hard that he hung half-fallen to the floor. She had never heard him cry before, in fact, had never heard any man cry before except maybe on TV or in a movie, and the sound seized her up inside. She knew then that regardless of his transgressions, he loved deeply, and the society that had encouraged his tough upper lip, a shaming that a man would bare his soul, had let humanity down.

She turns away from the window and transfers her attention into the teacup. Three little leafs move like crabs on the floor of the ocean. Floating really, but touching down to scuttle along the bottom of the cup from time to time. If only she could read those leaves.

Peter told her in that final call before he passed, "That monster is out there! I know he is!"

Brenda thought of the pearls. The one thing she had in her possession from the killing floor. Once a sign of her mother's hope now some kind of umbilical cord, a spirit of connection back to the woman who had birthed her. It had rained that night, rained very hard. No trace of anything led up to her body. No sign of how she even arrived to that place. Maybe dropped from the sky? No, that night only the rain fell from there. The storm that rumbled through had cleared away each and every clue but somehow had left the pearls in that hole, somehow eluding the expansive and thorough search that found nothing. How had the pearls laid intact for years, even after many separated from the string? No doubt covered with water. Covered with snow. Covered with dirt that cleared with the breath of the wind, only to return and blow away again. They waited there for her.

Peter said, "The world's not safe. Not for me. Not for you. I wanted to help find the killer, but I never had the strength. But you do, Brenda! You and Billy. Do it for me. Do it for Lily Rose and Christopher."

He said it so many times, and she believed him, ever more incensed by the repetition that became a chant. "The world's not safe. The world's not safe."

Now that Peter had died and she suffered the loss of another family member, she had the pearls restrung, though they reminded her of all that was gone. No mother for her. No maternal grandmother for her children. No friend, no community member, no human being who lit the world up with her presence. Now no brother for her. No uncle for her children.

No artistic, handsome, sparkling man to leave his mark.

She needed a plan. She felt resolved to do her part for all those left vulnerable in the world. But what is her part? Grandma Martha told her one time in one of those precious but infrequent moments, when the older woman would entrust her with a secret, a piece of wisdom really, something that she knew and became willing to share.

Grandmother Martha said, "When you want to know the answer to a question that is very important and you don't know where to turn, find a place. Go out onto the land and walk; let your need for an answer lead you. You will find the place, a place we call 'thin.'"

Could it be that easy? Brenda does not know, but she does have a question: How can the killer be found?

4
Spoon

Friday 5:45 p.m.

As Billy cuts a piece of oak for a set of drawers, he watches as Christopher tenderly sands the bow of the rocker. The tip of his small tongue rests in one corner of his mouth, and his eyes glue, rapt with attention. The dust of wood from his sanding rises and falls into tiny mounds and drifts, a fine golden-colored snow.

"You're doing a great job there, Buddy."

Without looking up, Christopher says, "Thanks, Daddy!"

Billy feels proud of his young son, who seems to enjoy helping him.

He and Brenda moved into the Becker family homestead four years ago, after Grandmother Martha passed. The matron begged many times that he, Brenda and the kids move in, when she was gone. Little remained of the farm, with barns torn down, corncribs fallen, and a shed sinking into the foundation, but the house, built in the early part of the twentieth century, stood strong. After Brenda finally put her ghosts to rest, she agreed to move in. Billy always loved the place nestled in hardwoods and firs, with fields of wild flowers and grasses stretching into the horizon, a creek – sometimes a trickle, other times a thin ribbon of a river moving –moisturizing, sparkling, beckoning. After the remnants were hauled away, they took the foundation of the garage and shed and rebuilt, turning the space into a two-car garage and extended workshop where Billy could build his furniture, a trade he learned from Brenda's Uncle Sam, gone too since 1993.

Billy had come back from Operation Desert Storm in 1991, with an inch of bone cut out of his right leg. He wore a lift in his

26

boot, and learned to live with this, but the injury kept him from climbing roofs and other jobs he engaged in before the war, working construction. The leg felt stiff in the ankle, the knee also hard to bend, but the injury did not hinder him from his new trade. He also suffered with PTSD that over the years had gotten better, thanks to drugs for a while, counseling, and group meetings. What had not improved were the string of mysterious ailments that plagued him.

He had a special relationship with Sam, Brenda's uncle, also a friend of Billy's father, both Marines who served multiple tours in Vietnam. His father had died in the jungle, and Sam came back sick himself, with cancers most likely caused by Agent Orange, but he never expressed any regret or fury he might have held. Sam made peace with his experience, saying that he would be wasting more time fussing. His guidance as a veteran, a man, and a carpenter of admirable skill proved invaluable to Billy

A deep sharp pain hits Billy in the belly, and his face contorts. After years of denial, they finally gave it a name: Gulf War Syndrome, a variety of ailments that hit the veterans, some said from immunizations given in haste, others said depleted radium, which covered the American artillery, or maybe the pollution that rose from burning oil wells, or any number of gases the enemy used. Some argued that the effects were normal for warfare, same as they had always been from WWI and on. Regardless of the reason, the soldiers and Marines were suffering, a couple hundred thousand or so at last count. At least he was not alone.

Christopher looks up to see Billy's face, and concern crosses the lightly tanned face of the boy. He quickly looks back down and continues his sanding. Billy's chronic pain stresses the boy; he knows this. Billy tries to hide the sudden waves of pain as well as he can.

His leg and his ailments were not the only challenges he had to face when he came back. His wife, Brenda, had taken up with his best friend, James, while he, Billy, lived out in a 120-degree desert, where sand spiders as big as his head kept him company at night. After his injury, they discharged him, and although a battle between he and James broke out, it was an accident three days after Billy's return that killed the best friend that betrayed him. Although Billy still loved Brenda, it took five years before he forgave her. They both dated other people and shared in the care of their daughter, Lily Rose. Although Billy's mom prayed over them ferociously, and his sister, Kate, also worked to get the two back together, it was Sam, the man who taught him how to work with wood who played the biggest role in Brenda and Billy's eventual reunion.

The same year Billy returned from the war, doctors gave Sam six months to live; his cancer had spread. He stopped the chemo and turned to natural therapies, including a few visits to a Native American shaman, and herbal formulas like cannabis oil. Whether his stubborn and positive outlook helped, the alternative medicine or both, he ended up living two more years, mentoring Billy, generally spreading good cheer, and playing matchmaker.

—⟋⟍—

The thought of Brenda being with James in that way ate away at Billy. Even though the three had shared moments that bordered on something dangerous. There was the time, once he thought about it, more than one time, when in the dead of winter the three lied intertwined in a snow shelter, seeking warmth and reprieve from a blinding blizzard. Out on cross-country skis, out on snowmobiles, out into the winter white regardless of weather forecasts, advisories or warnings. They were all friends after all. What did it matter that his leg crossed the leg of James' or one of his best friend's hands rested on his shoulder. There snuggled Brenda in between, always facing Billy, her attention not divided, though the warmth of James' body apparent.

In the summer, the bodies were almost bare, glistening wet from a dip in the lake, golden brown from the hikes, the volleyball, the dirt bike rides across the fields. James had his girls; he just couldn't make a commitment. One summer day, however, a turning point occurred, recognized and marked, and even then, if someone had said look out, your best friend will do you wrong, Billy would not have believed it. On that day, the three had drunk homemade cherry wine and headed for the favorite cove, tucked into the end of a road shaded by willows and river birch, the water warm as a bath. That day for the first time, Billy saw James' glances on Brenda's breasts, little sneers caught from the corner of his eye, James' nude body leaned back exposing what he had. His best friend made a play.

So maybe Billy was not completely surprised when he opened the Dear John letter in the vast and endless sea of sand in the Arabian Desert. The anger that he felt and acted out on that might have contributed to Glover's death, his brother in arms, sprang out of the certainty the letter stated. Suspicions confirmed, fears manifested, and betrayal doubtless.

He arrived back on homeland fueled and ravenous for revenge, justice really, and nothing would stop him. He set out to kill James and nearly did, but destiny finished his best friend off. He could not kill the mother of his daughter, not in a physical sense, but he hardened his heart into stone. Every time some sense of affection arose for Brenda, he walled it up; even the tiniest ray of light could not break through.

Brenda's Uncle Sam determined to break the wall down.

It took five years. Five long years.

Brenda tried to pull him in. They shared the care for Lily Rose, and Brenda seemed to find excuses for them to meet up. He could not even look her in the eyes. In her eyes, he saw her heart. He could not bear it. Sometimes she would touch his arm or his hand and he drew away as if burned. She tried for a year. After the year ended, she began to date the veterinarian she worked for, an older man who had been after her from the start. Billy didn't know if they ever slept together, the doctor and Brenda, but he believed they did because what man wants a woman without it. Billy started dating a girl they graduated with, a girl willing to oblige him in any way. He enjoyed the sex, but as difficult as it was for him to admit, only one woman possessed his heart, damnit, no matter how hard he tried, but she had betrayed him. How could he ever trust her again? Brenda finally gave up and filed for divorce.

Billy had experienced pain before from more injuries than he could count. He lived recklessly as a kid, a teenager, and a young man. He motocrossed professionally, jumped out of airplanes, bungee jumped from places no one else dared, but there was something different, deeper and more acute about the pain in his heart. He felt so weak for experiencing the deep emotion, and certainly never told anyone that he did. That pain of remembering what he and Brenda shared, a connection that he never experienced before or after, seemed impossible to forget. Not a fairy tale or an illusion. Losing that connection but remembering felt unbearable. The longing for what could have been, a long life spent with someone that he deeply loved. Gone. Never to be recovered.

While he apprenticed with Sam, a day barely passed that the old warrior did not mention her.

"Saw Brenda the other day. Did she cut her hair?"

"I couldn't tell you."

"She must be working out, man. I've never seen her in such good shape."

"I didn't notice."

Sam would toss his long gray ponytail over his shoulder, take another hit from his joint and say, "I hear she's volunteering time in that women's shelter and thinking about going back to school to study counseling. I don't know where she finds the time and energy."

Without looking up, without pausing for a moment, Billy said, "I guess that explains why I have Sweet Pea so often."

"You enjoy your daughter."

"You bet I do."

When that tactic did not work, Sam tried another. "Saw

Brenda and that doctor friend of hers."

"Yeah? What about it?"

"That dude really seems to be into her."

This time Billy did pause, and he did look up. "Why do you say that?"

"Cut a couple sides for these drawers, will ya?"

"Sure. What makes you think he's really into her?"

After taking a long drink of water, Sam continued, "Oh, you know, the way he looks at her, talks to her...touches her."

Billy remembers his face growing hot. "I don't know why she wants to be with an older guy like that."

"Cause he knows what he wants."

Ouch! That hurt.

"How's it going with that little gal you're seeing?" the matchmaker asked.

"Okay. But she wants a commitment."

"You don't?"

"What? To just get stabbed in the back again?"

When what he had been trying didn't work, Sam found excuses to bring Brenda over to the shop. "She's going to help us clean. Oh, she is bringing us some lunch over. Oh, she picked up some parts for me."

Billy would glance at her from the corner of his eye. His heart would beat faster. He would want to take her in his arms, but he didn't.

In 1993, Sam passed. That sad event almost brought them together. They did clasp each other's hands standing at the gravesite. Lily Rose jumped up and down with joy, and Grandma Martha smiled away.

Still it took two more years and a close call before he allowed his heart to open.

Lily Rose, ten and a tomboy, fast and agile as a gazelle, was playing soccer. Both Brenda and Billy were there to watch, one on each side of the field. Lily had the ball, moving towards the goal, when a player on the other team flew out of nowhere and collided with their girl, sending her head first into the goal post. When Brenda and Billy reached her, running in from opposite directions, Lily Rose laid unconscious. Medics ran out, the ambulance arrived, and they carefully lifted the still-unconscious girl up onto a stretcher. Brenda rode with Lily Rose, as Billy drove his truck to meet them at the hospital. After an MRI, CT, and other tests, she had not regained consciousness, and everyone began to worry. Both Brenda and Billy were beside themselves, Billy even forgetting not to look in Brenda's eyes, not flinching when she grabbed his arm, his hand, and at one point falling against his chest; he wrapped his arms around her without a thought. Neither left the hospital the twelve hours it took for Lily Rose to gain consciousness. They kept her at the hospital for another day or two, Billy and Brenda swapping out time a bit but mostly there the whole time together. Doctors finally released her. Without asking, Brenda assumed Billy would take them home, and he did. After Lily settled into her bed to rest, Brenda headed for her own. Billy followed. They fell into the cool, fresh sheets, rolling into a spoon, and just like that, as if nothing wrong had ever passed between them, Billy and Brenda became man and wife again. They remarried nine months later, and Christopher Samuel Bagwell entered the world three months after that.

Billy glances out of the side window of the shop and watches Brenda as she approaches the door, walking in that way that looks perfectly centered between earth and sky. She walks into the shop and Christopher's face lights up, "Hi, Mommy! Look at what I've done!"

She walks over to her son, brushes his bangs back and kisses him on the forehead, "Wow! That looks great!" She leans over and pecks Billy on the lips. "Hi, honey, how's it going?"

"Great. We've almost finished this rocker. I couldn't have done it without my buddy here."

Brenda says, "I'm proud of you, Christopher."

"Thanks, Mommy."

She looks up at Billy, "I've got some chicken simmering on the stove. The potatoes are cooked, and I made a salad. Grace called from the shelter. Do you remember me telling you about that woman that came in a couple of months ago beaten so badly?"

"I think so. Named after an Eric Clapton song?"

"See, your memory is getting better."

"Maybe. I hope so."

"Well, she's back. She wants to talk with me. We made a connection when she came in the last time. I'm going to run over there. I won't be long."

"We'll manage. Is Sweet Pea home?"

"Yes. Look, she wants to go to a party tomorrow night. I think we should let her go."

"I'll talk to her about it. You be careful. You never know what those beaters are going to do."

5
A Pair

Friday 6:35 p.m.

Jack hears the car pull into the driveway and walks over to open the front door. He watches as his brother steps out of a newer Lexus and strides towards the front porch smiling broadly. He barely believes what he sees. Jeff's hair trimmed and neatly styled. His button-up shirt tucked in, and his handsome face, which looks pretty much the same, cleanly shaved.

Could this be the longhaired punk that raced around in his GTO, spent time in juvie, and hung out with all the bad girls?

He can see the family resemblance. He once thought that James and Jeff had the same father. The high cheekbones, the dark eyes. Unlike his dead brother, Jeff has wheat-colored hair, not black, taller too, but the hands. One mother, different fathers, yet three out of four brothers had those same hands: big, long.

What happened to the pierced ears and the perpetual five o'clock shadow? Oh, wait, maybe a little ink there peeking out from the collar.

When he reaches out his hand, Jeff meets him with his in a strong, firm shake, confident, and the once rather shy young man looks directly in his eyes. No more grease under those broad fingernails. Somehow, his brother has been transformed.

What happens next really surprises him. Jeff lets Jack's hand go and steps closer to embrace him. Jack freezes up but manages after a few seconds to give over what he can; after all, they are the surviving brothers out of four, but the embrace grows awkward. Jack breaks away and says, "Come in, come in!"

Jeff steps further into the foyer of the small house, and Jack watches him startle a bit as Debbie steps up to the two men. Jack suspects the age difference between Debbie and him surprises people, but maybe Jeff did not expect to see a woman at all, or at least not one this pretty. Debbie reaches out her hand and smiles in that beautiful way she has.

"Hi, I'm Debbie, Jack's wife."

Jeff shakes her hand. "Nice to meet you."

Debbie directs, "Why don't you guys sit a bit and have a beer. Dinner will be ready in about a half hour or so. I hope you like spaghetti?"

Jeff smiles. "Who doesn't like spaghetti?" All three break into brief laughter, which dissipates a bit of tension.

Jack runs his hand lightly over her shoulder, his fingers stiff. He is still learning. "Thanks, babe. You want a beer, Jeff?"

"I gave that up a while back."

"A coke, iced tea?"

"Iced tea would be great."

Jack watches Jeff gaze after Debbie as she walks through the living room split by a long counter with bar stools, from the white and yellow kitchen. She opens the one door of the double-door refrigerator and reaches in for the beverages. Jack feels happy, when Jeff averts his eyes, but he himself cannot help but continue to watch her, the curves of her ass and breasts, her shiny hair. He thanks god every day for his fortune. He spent many years wondering, while incarcerated, whether he would ever get out alive at any rate. When he did get out, would anyone give him a chance? Somewhere in his life, he must have done something good because Debbie agreed to marry him, and his old boss, years older at that point but still a business owner had not lost trust in him. He heads for his easy chair, and motions for Jeff to follow him and take a seat on the overstuffed couch. His brother effectively sinks his six-foot frame.

Jack states, "I looked up your area code. You been living in California?"

Jeff answers, as he readjusts his seating. "Most of the time. I moved around some. Idaho for a while. The Northwest. Been working for a company the last few years in Southern Cal."

Debbie walks back into the living area carrying the beverages, handing them to the two men. As she turns, Jimmy runs into the room, Gameboy in his left hand. The eleven-year-old looks at Jack and then over at Jeff. Pushing his long dark bangs out of his eyes, just as his daddy did, he asks, "So you're my uncle?"

Jeff sits forward on the couch, with face more animated, and extends his hand to the boy. "Yes, I guess I am." Looking over at Jack, he states, "I didn't know you had a kid."

Jimmy, looking a bit uncomfortable, just stares at him.

Debbie prods him, "Take his hand, Jimmy!" The boy takes Jeff's hand and they shake.

Jeff looks at Jack. "So you named him after our brother. I like that."

"Actually, Debbie named him after his father." Jack notes a bit of shock and confusion wash over Jeff's face.

"Wait...what?"

Jack sits up straighter in his chair. "Jimmy is your brother James' son, and Debbie is his mother." Jack swears he sees a jet of mist hit his brother's eyes, something else he did not expect.

After a few moments, Jeff finds some words. "I am honored to meet you, James."

The boy corrects, "You can call me Jimmy. That's what everyone calls me. They never called my real dad Jimmy, right?"

Jeff says, "That's right, but we did call your daddy Jambo, when he was young. You remember that, Jack?"

Jack laughs lightly. "Oh, yeah, that's right."

Jimmy asks Jeff, "How come I haven't met you before?"

Jeff settles back into his seat. "I've been gone for a long time."

Jimmy perches down tentatively on the seat of the couch. "Jack told me you used to race cars."

"That was a long time ago, too."

Debbie speaks up, "Jimmy, why don't we let Jack and your uncle catch up."

"Okay, but, wasn't the car that my mom and dad crashed in yours? The GTO?"

Jack watches the pain reflex over Debbie's face. He has seen it many times before at the mention of the crash. She turns, as her shoulders drop, like a weight behind her, the skull at the Sundance pulling hard against the pierced flesh. Jack has read about such things. The weight rips at the flesh, but Debbie never allows the break through. Jack watches Jeff flicker his eyes from Jimmy to Debbie and then back again. He hesitates. As Debbie walks back towards the kitchen, her steps stiffer now, a leftover from the crash, and the smile all but faded, she throws over her shoulder, "I said, let them be, Jimmy."

"But..." Curiosity holds the kid there.

Jack speaks up, "Jimmy, you heard your mom. Jeff will be around for a while, right, man?"

"Ah, yeah, I'll be around for a while. We will get to know each other, Jimmy. I promise!"

Jimmy breaks out into a grin and drags his heels as he leaves, head down, anxious to buck up against rules and parameters, just like all of the Tillman brothers, except maybe for Jordan.

Jack laughs a little, "I bet you're wondering 'what the fuck' now?"

Jeff scoots back up on the edge of the couch seat. "Looks like I've got some catching up to do."

"You've got your long story, I'm sure, and I've got mine." Jack tips his beer back for an extended gulp.

—⁂—

In 1995, they finally released Jack from prison. He served twenty years out of an eighteen-year sentence. By rights, through good behavior, he should have gotten out on his ERD (earliest release date), but an incident occurred. His anger had cost him again, the issue that landed him in prison in the first place. He also had the misfortune of gaining two COs (correctional officers), who did not like him. The officers, dicks to begin with, had no recourse, or so it appeared, to prey upon the man so many others admired. Jack was not bragging here. He led by nature, and his size didn't hurt. At six feet, two inches of bulky muscle, bench pressing 330 and lifting 520, he presented a formidable force, and he went in that way. He always enjoyed bodybuilding, starting as a young teen.

He doesn't know where he picked up the temper but guesses from his father, a man he met once in between his own prison stays. At nineteen, Jack beat the piss out of his mother's boyfriend, Sisko, a decent enough guy when sober but a devious piece of shit when drunk. Jack suspected something, observing his youngest brother, James, whenever Sisko visited. James, a rather shy kid anyway, seemed to avoid all eye contact and made himself scarce. His youngest brother, always a good-looking kid, grew up to be an even better looking man. Ask any female in town. Many of them for better or worse had known him, as they say, carnally. One summer night, when James was the same age as his son Jimmy now, Jack caught Sisko patting his brother's ass, and the shit hit the fan.

When Jack walked out of those prison doors, he could not wait to see Jimmy, his only nephew that he learned about through letters from his mom. She never did visit him much, always too caught up with her latest no-good boyfriend and her cheap sweet wine. His brothers Jordan and James were both dead, Jeff gone and no one knew where, only his mother and Jimmy remained as family. His mother, dead now for two years, succumbing to cirrhosis was always hard to love. She had been an alcoholic most of his life, leaving him to mind his three brothers. He couldn't wait to see Jimmy, four years old at the time of his release.

He tracked down Debbie, living in a small apartment in Willis with her son. She was still recovering since the accident, which left her in a comma for two weeks, the little embryo, whom would be his nephew, barely seeded inside her. He knocked on the door and felt a bit shocked, though he shouldn't have been, knowing his brother James, to see a young petite and curvaceous strawberry blonde. She wore tight blue jeans, hanging on her hips, and a long-sleeved white shirt that plunged in the neckline to reveal about half her tits. The girl had a pair.

Keep in mind now that Jack had not touched a woman in years. Beating off was his primary release. Of course, he could have had some action with his fellow inmates, but avoided that road as much as possible. In fact, the incident that occurred behind the razor wire, which cost him an early parole, involved a few inmates who jumped him in the shower. That did not work out so good for them either.

So there he stood, in front of the girl who could have been a centerfold, and he instantly hardened. She smiled up at him, swept her eyes over his body from head to toe, and he swears she spent an extra beat measuring him in her mind, and asked, "Can I help you?"

If he had been drinking something, he would have choked and sprayed. Jack imagined that in this girl, James had met his match.

He answered, "I'm Jack Tillman, James' older brother."

"Oh, my god," she said. "I...I...forgot that he had a brother living around here. You were in prison, right?"

"Just got out."

She opened the door wider. "Well, come in. Come in. I bet that you want to see Jimmy."

"If you wouldn't mind. I know that it's a little late, but..."

She stepped aside, so he could walk in. "Not at all. I think that he's still awake."

Jack never left that night.

The apartment looked small and messy. Not dirty exactly, but if everything has its place, the things in this apartment were lost. She quickly moved through the living area grabbing items like articles of clothing, pop bottles, and toys, carting them off to other rooms. He did avert his eyes when she bent over, ass in the air or tits dangling, though he sensed that, if anything, she meant to display herself. Not that they looked anything alike, but the girl reminded him of Doris Rentchler, a local gal that the boys loved. As far as he knows, the boys still do. She broke Jack in when he was sixteen. Watching this young woman, and knowing what he does now, he feels sure that her dance of movement amounted to a seduction.

As she walked back into the space, she had his young nephew by the hand, rubbing his eyes of sleep, light brown hair mussed up, and what amounted to a scowl on his face. She led him up to Jack, squatted down next to him, in the jeans that threatened to rip and said, "Honey, this is your father's brother, making him your uncle."

The good-looking boy looked up at him. "You're tall. And big!"

Jack laughed, as the four-year-old trotted back out of the room, and the woman reached out to stop him. Jack said, "Let him go. It's late. I shouldn't have come. But I would like to get to know him."

She stood up, struggling a bit with one hip, coming up to chest high on him. "That's fine with me. I want him to know his family."

Jack turned towards the door. "I'll come back…"

She grabbed his arm, glancing at the muscle, and quickly released it. "Would you like a beer or something harder?"

Jack thought about his own hardness, hoping it didn't show. "Ah, sure. A beer would be great."

Pointing to a chair, she said, "Have a seat!" He watched as she sashayed, literally, out of the room to return with two beers. By the time she did, he had sat down and adjusted himself for a little more comfort. She handed him a beer and sat down opposite, legs spread rather than together like a so-called lady might sit.

After a long drink from her bottle, she asked, "You said you just got out?"

Jack nodded. "Served twenty years."

"Wow! That's a long time. You don't look that old."

Jack laughed. "Well, that's good."

"What were you in for?"

"Assault."

She nodded her head. "You don't look much like James. Much taller and bigger muscles. Different coloring, too," she said, as her legs fanned in and out.

"We had different dads."

"I remember James telling me he had three brothers, but I don't think he told me much else."

"Jordan died when he was seventeen, and Jeff left after they released him from Half Moon. We haven't heard from him in years."

She glanced off and hesitated, then turned back brightened. "I was crazy about James, even though we were only together for a short time. I knew about him; I saw him around. I wanted him more than anything."

"Well, he was a good-looking guy." Their heads bobbed in agreement, then Jack leaned forward, forearms resting on his leg tops. "Would you tell me about the night he died?"

She gazed off again, squirmed a bit in her seat. She turned back, her eyes flooded. "I still can't talk about it." She began to chew on the end of one thumb.

"I'm sorry. I shouldn't have asked."

She jumped up. "You ready for another beer?" He still had half a can. He shook his head no, and she walked out and back in with another beer for herself. They talked for quite a while, went through probably three beers each. She was easy to talk to, seemed interested in who he was, told him about Jimmy whom she described as smart, imaginative, and somewhat shy. At one point, she checked on the boy, and as time passed, she returned to a sensuous posturing, fanning her legs, rubbing the top of her chest, smiling and laughing coyly. Jack felt surprised he hadn't come in his pants. At last, she made a move, and although he did not know if he should or he shouldn't, he could not, at that point resist.

She licked her sweet plump-looking lips. "So, Jack, have you gotten laid yet, since your release," the last word stretched out with a little hiss.

He hesitated, then answered, "No."

She stood up, fell to her knees and crawled over to him, looking him straight in the eyes. She ran her hands slowly up the inside of his thighs and began to knead him. He heard her breath catch.

He said, "Look..."

She looked up. "Don't look me." She unzipped his pants, pulled him out, and pleasured him in a way he had not been in two decades. In seconds he exploded, his back arching, a loud moan escaping.

He said, "I'm sorry..."

"For what?" she said wiping her mouth with the back of one hand. "I know you won't take long to get hard again."

They fucked three times that night. She and Jimmy moved in with him a month later, into a house he rented, and they married six months after that, the ex-convict and the sex addict. Quite a pair.

—⚹—

As they sit eating spaghetti, Jack keeps an eye on Jeff, wondering where he has been and what he has been doing, why his answers to most questions are vague at best. Although he has his own collection of tattoos, he sees snatches of Jeff's peeking out from his collar and his sleeves, and reads what he thinks are the letters WAR above his right wrist. Not a veteran, not an anti-war protester, as far as he knows. He also notices a shaking in his brother's right hand, as he lifts a glass, holds his fork, wipes away food from his mouth, the last a sign that old manners hadn't died, replaced by this conservative front.

Debbie flirts, as she does with almost every man, not seeming ever, even if she tries, to not. His brother seems unaffected; instead, his attention shines on Jimmy, drinking in the only family member, at this point, to promise legacy, a carrying on of the Tillman line. Regardless, Jack keeps digging. "So what you doing for this company out in Southern Cal?"

"Keeping books. Believe it or not, I went back to school and studied accounting."

"Oh, yeah? What about a wife, kids?"

Jeff takes a long drink of his tea, the ice cubes tinkling in his glass. "Nah. Not the marrying kind I guess."

They finish the meal, then sit around the table for a bit longer. Jeff clears his throat. "Do you remember Eric Thompson?"

"That punk you got into trouble with?"

"Yep. You ever hear anything about him?"

6

Headband

Friday 8:16 p.m.

Lily sings into the phone, "I've loved you forever in lifetimes before. And I promise you never will you hurt anymore..."

"I love that song! When Joey sings, I could go crazy!" her friend Kristen exclaims, on the other end of the line.

"Oh, no! Justin is the cutest!"

"No way!"

"Yeah, way!" Lily throws herself back down on her bed, telephone in hand. Dressed in lavender sweats, she crosses her yellow-socked feet and dramatically exhales. As her heart beats wildly, she crosses the fingers on her free hand and asks, "So is Lucas going to go with us tomorrow night, or not?

"Mark said when Lucas found out you were going, he was definitely in!"

"Wow! That's exciting! And scary." Her eyes travel the journey of her walls, over the posters that dominate: Mia Hamm in action out on the soccer field, a head shot of Justin Timberlake, and a poster for *Lord of the Rings*, featuring a blond Orlando Bloom as Legolas. Her eyes rest on Orlando and her heart beats even faster. Lucas looks a bit like him, but darker skin. "Does he understand that it's a...double date?"

"Yeah, I think so."

Lily again sings along with the song in the background, "When the visions around you bring tears to your eyes, and all that surrounds you are secrets and lies..."

"Stop singing in my ear, would ya!? You know, Mark says that Lucas isn't the friendliest guy."

Lily uncrosses and then re-crosses her ankles the other way, feeling a little frustrated. "Well, he's the new kid at school. Maybe he doesn't feel comfortable yet. Where will we meet them?"

"Mark said I could park my car in back of Big Boy. He doesn't think anyone will see the car back there. He wants us to meet them at eight fifteen, so I'll pick you up at eight."

Lily scoots herself up into a seating position. "You sure you want to leave your new car there?"

"It will be fine."

"Yeah, I guess." Lily grabs a chocolate chip cookie off a plate sitting on a small wooden side table beside her bed and takes a bite. While chewing, she asks, "What are you going to wear?"

"I think I'm going to wear a dress and tights with a sweater."

"It's going to be chilly! I'm not wearing a dress."

"What are you eating? You're crunching in my ear!"

Lily shoves the rest of the cookie in her mouth, chewing quickly, holding the receiver away from her mouth. "Oh, sorry!" She swallows. "If I wear a dress, I feel like Lucas is going to think I'm looking for action."

"You aren't looking for action? You know that Mark and I will be making out."

"I'm more comfortable in pants."

"You are such a tomboy sometimes."

"Yeah, what's wrong with that?"

"Boys like girls to look like girls."

Her dad's voice interrupts through the door. "Peanut, are you still on the phone?"

Lily breathes out loudly, shakes her head and yells, "Just a few more minutes, Daddy!" To Kristen, she says, "I'm hoping he wants to talk with me about going to the party."

"You haven't even asked him yet?"

"Usually, when my mom says yes, he says yes." She stands up and stretches her legs.

"How late do you think he will let you stay out?"

"I'm hoping I can stay out until at least midnight. Are you sure we can count on the guys to bring us back on time?"

"I wish you could stay out later!"

"How late can you stay out?"

"I'm supposed to be back by twelve-thirty."

"That's only another half an hour."

"Every half an hour counts!"

"Can we rely on the guys giving us a ride back, or not?"

"I don't know which of them will drive. I know we can count on Mark, but I don't know about Lucas. I think that you should wear a dress."

"I'm wearing jeans, my purple flowered shirt, and my headband."

"Of course, your headband."

"Not just my headband, my lucky headband." She continues to sing, "I will take you in my arms, right where you belong..."

"Oh, you might get lucky, alright." Her friend pauses for a moment. "I don't know if I should tell you this, but Sue Klein told me that Lucas put some fast moves on her."

Lily plops down on the corner of her bed. "When?"

"At a game a couple of weeks ago."

"She lies, you know. She knows that I like him and she's just trying to make trouble."

"Maybe. We all know that she lies."

Lily stands and walks over to her vanity, sits down in front of the mirror and looks at herself. "I hope it's not true." She begins to brush her hair with her free hand.

"You know he's going to try, Lil, and first base isn't kissing anymore."

"You don't know what he's going to do, and why are you talking to me like I'm a child?"

"Well, I know that you aren't very experienced."

"Oh, like you're the big whore around town!"

"I have a boyfriend and a lot more experience than you."

"People talk about it like it's a contest! It's not a contest!"

Again, her dad yells through the door, "Lily, I'd like to talk with you!"

"Okay!" Lily puts down the brush. "I've got to go!" she says to Kristen.

"We're going to have fun, Lil."

"I know. See you tomorrow at eight. Unless my dad says no."

—⚏—

When Lily was five, her dad served over in the Persian Gulf as a Marine sniper. She had always been Daddy's Girl, and she missed him terribly. Her mother also missed him, missed him so much that she became friendlier with Uncle James, not a real uncle, but a close friend of her parents. Lily liked James because he made her feel pretty, but he began to spend more and more time at their house. She would go to bed and he would still be there, and even if she never saw them touch, as a child, she somehow knew that something was going on. She did not like it.

One night she climbed out of bed to go to the bathroom and her parent's bedroom door stood ajar. She peeked in and felt at first surprised, then scared, and finally she became glued to the spot. Her mother laid on her stomach on the bed and Uncle James lay over her, his bare butt moving up and down, his long bangs covering half of his face. Her mother moaned increasingly louder as James pumped, the muscles in his butt flexed and his eyes closed. At one point, he stopped, pulled away and Lily saw a man's genitals for the first time. He pulled her mother up onto her knees and began to pump again. Now both groaned louder, her mother even emitting little cries that made Lily wonder if she should scream or run over to pull James off, but she could not move. A little more time passed, and her mother screamed out one last loud wail, as James groaned deeper; a final thrust of his hips ended the movement. She watched then as the two collapsed onto the bed, side-by-side, fighting to regain their breath. Her mother rolled over to be closer to James, but he threw his legs over the edge of the bed to stand. When he saw Lily, his eyes widened; she ran quickly back down the hall to her room.

She laid there holding her breath, so afraid he would march down the hall to yell at her, not that he ever had, but because she had witnessed something she should not have. He did not, and he never acknowledged that he saw her, but a few days later, her favorite stuffed animal, Growlie, disappeared. A day before her father returned from the war, their dog, Jake, found the toy buried in the backyard. Three days later Uncle James died in a terrible car crash, and to be honest, Lily did not feel very sad about it.

—⁓—

Lily feels confused about sex, confused about all the messages that say don't do it and the stirrings inside her that scream the opposite. Abstain, her school taught them. Abstain. Sex should not occur before marriage. She slides her hand slowly down into her sweat pants and touches herself. She thinks of Justin, Lucas and Orlando, a composite of lovely male faces that lean in to kiss her, run their hands down her back, push her hips into theirs. The face of Lucas wins out, and she sees his chest muscles and the ripple over his abdomen, his small hard butt. Yes, yes, she will wear a dress, and she will stop being afraid that Lucas will not be kind and gentle, and when she says no, if she does, he will listen. Wearing her lucky headband will help protect her.

A knock on the door startles her. She pulls her hand out of her sweat pants and turns. Finally, her dad has returned to talk to her. "Yes?"

"Peanut, are you off the phone now?" her dad asks.

"Yes, Daddy, come in!" She jumps up and turns her stereo down.

Her dad limps into the room because of his war wound, dressed in jeans and a tee shirt, moccasins on his feet. She has always thought that her dad was the most handsome man, so lean, so strong, and someone she can always trust to be there for her. "I'm sorry if the music was too loud, Daddy."

"Well, it's a little loud, but that's not what I want to talk with you about. Your mom tells me that you want to go to a party tomorrow night."

"Yes! I do! I promise that I will be home when you tell me to. I'll be careful! I promise!"

"Who you going with?"

"Kristen."

"I want you home at midnight. I mean it!"

Lily runs over to hug her dad, and he wraps his arms around her tightly, tighter than usual. "Thank you, thank you!"

He releases her and looks her squarely in the eyes. "I'm counting on you to make good decisions."

Lily smiles up at him, and for one minute, wishes she wasn't almost a woman but a little girl again.

"Don't forget to take care of those dirty dishes." He turns and walks out of the room, as the phone begins to ring. She watches as he breaks into an uneven trot and throws over his shoulder, "I'll get it!"

She walks over, grabs the plate and cup sitting on her bed stand and walks out of the room towards the kitchen. She hears her dad say, "Who?" A couple of beats pass. "Jeff? I forgot there was another brother. Wait! Wasn't he on the football team? I remember seeing him as a kid." Then a pause. "What time?" A pause. "Let me run it past the wife. I'll get back to ya."

Lily quietly rinses off her dishes and places them in the dishwasher. She sees Christopher playing a video game in the living room and hears the water running in the shower. Her mother must be cleaning up for the day. She walks quietly back to her room, excitement and fear competing inside her. She cannot wait until the party tomorrow night, even though her stomach begins to fill with fluttering butterflies mixed with something else, something scary, she cannot quite put her finger on. Then she steps into her room and hears Justin singing sweetly. She may be too old for fairy tales, but she is not too old for a fairy tale ending.

7

Face Off

Friday 10:30 p.m.

Eric throws the shot of vodka back and slams the small glass down on the bar. The bartender turns, and Eric can see that the fucker has marked him. This new bartender has an attitude, acts more like a cop than a lowly beverage pourer. Eric, wanting to punch him in the face, clenches his fist out of habit and flinches. Looking down at his right knuckles, he sees split flesh from his earlier beating on Lola. Fucking bitch. She should not have...what was it that she did? Jesus...well... He lifts his hand and licks the blood away, mostly coagulated now, quickly glances around from the corners of his eyes, then drops the hand back down out of sight.

Only Lola knows he loses it sometimes. Everyone else considers him an upstanding citizen. Okay, he has a record. He has a past. Shit...he has a past. Very few know about that now, his thieving and carousing. And that other thing, so long ago that he barely remembers himself, only one other person might suspect something about that, and he's been gone for years and years. Could be dead for all he knows. He hopes he's dead.

"Another beer here," he growls.

The bartender fills up a short one and places it before him. "That's it!"

Eric wants to take the bartender by the throat and thrash his ass, but he smiles broadly and says, "You're probably right." Keep up the face.

Keep up the face at all costs. His father taught him that.

They think him charming.

No one could convince them otherwise.

He slipped a few minutes before. Shouldn't have banged the glass down. Any of the other bartenders know that he gets a little dramatic from time to time, but that doesn't mean he passed his limit, whatever that might be.

He has done everything he can to walk the line, not slip, not make any mistakes to give them cause to scrutinize him. When the tension builds, he wallops a bit on Lola. He can't help it. She asks for it. She gets in his face. Harps on him about cleaning up, giving her money, taking the garbage out, fixing the hole in the roof. A man can only take so much. Besides, he doesn't really hurt her. He knows when to stop, how to control the force. Hurt her enough to shut her mouth, but not so much she needs medical attention. Of course, last time she ran off to some women's place. He went after her when she called him and said she wanted to come home. She kept her mouth shut for a while. Until this afternoon.

The dumb bitch.

She ran off, probably to that place again, only this time he has yet to hear from her. He came to the bar to drink and think about what he will do if she presses charges against him. He will be under scrutiny, and scrutiny is not good.

He had not been a saint, but the last time he served time spanned from seventeen to nineteen, after he and Jeff Tillman robbed the fortress out on Dell Rd. By some fucking freak accident, Coach Becker caught them pulling out and he squawked like a Blue jay, but Eric paid him back big time. You know what they say: karma is a bitch. Oh, did he get him good. His size, his charisma, his do not fuck with me attitude had kept everyone at bay, except for fucking Martin Becker. Coach kicked him off the football team even though he was a star linebacker, who mowed them down like pins in an alley. Coach said he had a bad attitude, did not follow direction, and some of the other players were afraid of him. Said he needed players willing to work together in a team, not some "rogue element." At the time, Eric did not even know what fucking rogue meant. Coach said he did not want a one-man demolition crew. Said all this shit in his face while the other players were standing around in the locker room. Eric stood there in a towel, half his ass hanging out. The other players averted their eyes, attending to their business, but he knows each one of them had their ears tuned in for every sentence, every word, every syllable uttered. Probably smirking to themselves. He did not see that though, too busy fighting the urge to smash Coach's face against the tile floor, so hungry for the bastard's blood he could taste it. Instead, he clenched his fists, planted his feet, and almost broke a tooth or two grinding.

But he paid him back.

He paid him back good.

His actions must have been supported by heaven that opened up, dropping water in buckets, blowing rain across the earth in waves, wiping away footprints, drag marks, broken branches, and smashed down islands of spiky grass.

The next morning he laid real low feeling remorse...no...just kidding. He felt triumphant.

—⁂—

He gazes past himself in the mirror behind the bar, into the room at large to see a dude he knows from the old days back in Willis. Shit! He picked this bar out in the sticks, so as not to run into anyone. Eric seldom goes into Willis for anything anymore; he lives outside of a neighboring town. How the fuck did that dude end up here? He slips his eyes past him to see a couple young chicks dancing around the jukebox. Sleeveless tee shirts, tight-fitting jeans, heels on their shoes. They are looking for it. In this place, they will find it. Two small crowds gather loosely around pool tables, at this hour a bit more boisterous, the girls reaching out from time to time to lightly touch the arms of the boys, the boys cracking the balls, sending a few into pockets like little rockets. Those that do not find a hole glance off wildly, disturbing order. Chaos reigns on the table now. Ha, ha, ha, they laugh. Ha, ha, ha, sips from bottles and glasses. Sips of beer and wine. The occasional shot of something heavier, helping to turn the world into a blur.

Eric swings his eyes back to the dude he knows. Shit! The dude spots him and starts to walk over to where Eric sits at the bar.

"Long time no see, Thompson." He slides onto the stool next to him.

"Yep."

"Looks like you have an empty glass there. Can I buy you a beer?"

"Bartender cut me off."

"That dude is super paranoid about over serving."

Eric turns to him with the face. "You can buy me a shot. He doesn't have to know it's for me."

"Sure. You still drink Stoli?"

Eric nods, thinking *this old "friend" has a memory like an elephant.*

The dude calls the bartender over. "I'll take a lite draft and a shot of Stoli."

The bartender brings over the beer and shot, places it in front of the dude, grabs his twenty and says, "Do not give that shot to him," indicating Eric with a nod.

Keep up the face. Be charming.

Keep up the face at all costs.

The dude looks at Eric after the bartender turns and steps away. He picks up his mug of beer as Eric grabs the shot glass and throws back the liquid fire. As he begins to place the glass back down, the bartender turns. Swiftly, he moves back to where the two men sit at the bar. He throws the dude's change down and leans in towards them. "Get the fuck out," he hisses just above a whisper.

The dude says, "You can't..."

"I'm in charge here at this moment, and I'm saying get the

fuck out. I told you not to give him the shot."

Eric stands up, fist clenched, teeth grinding, but he says to the dude, "Let's get out of here."

"Yeah, but..."

Eric grabs his arm, noting the bartender's glance on his torn up knuckles, "Plenty of bars around."

The dude and Eric head for the door. The man from his past spits out, "That's bullshit."

"Yeah, well..." Eric takes a last glance at the young ones dancing around the jukebox. They are ripe, he thinks. Ripe as peaches.

"Hey," the dude says. "I remember now what I was going to tell ya..."

"What's that?"

"Guess who I saw riding through Willis today?"

"Hell, I don't know."

"Jeff Tillman."

Eric stops in his tracks and turns to look at him. "You shitting me?"

8
Torment
Friday 11:03 p.m.

Martin sits in the kitchen, staring at the rock glass containing three fingers of Canadian whiskey. He licks his lips repeatedly, while revering the warm amber color of the booze lit from the overhead light; Mary, his wife, walks into the room. She states emphatically, "If you take that drink, I walk out that door forever."

He remains quiet.

She continues, "I know it's the anniversary of her death."

"Murder."

"Okay, the anniversary of her murder, but you don't want to start the trip down that long dark road again. I know you don't."

He stands up and with a sweep of his hand knocks the glass of booze off the table. The glass shatters into pieces; the brown liquid splashes across the floor. He stomps through it on the way to the back door, grabs his jacket off a hook and leaves. He climbs into his champagne colored Buick, starts the car, puts the shifter into drive and heads down the road, into the night and torment.

Self-pity washes over him. Why shouldn't it? A murdered wife. A dead son. How did his life turn out like this? Somewhere a murderer may still be running free, reliving a moment-by-moment recount of the havoc he wrought and laughing, while day after day his family suffers. His only son burned to ashes, the urn buried in another state or maybe sitting on a stone fireplace mantel in the home of his boyfriend. Yes, Petey made his bed; he chose a lifestyle that killed him. Some say, if officials had taken the epidemic more seriously from the beginning, many less would be sick and dying. The erupting diseases hit the gay population especially hard and some saw them as dispensable. Martin gets it.

A wife. A son. It's not fair!

Just one clue, one stinking clue. Was he, is he such a terrible human being that he deserved all this? Just one clue! One eyewitness! Something to help track down the person who killed her. The police said he had to be a drifter, but Martin doesn't feel sure about that now. Bill and Brenda had planted doubt. He lived as an ignorant man for many years, lost inside a bottle and his own arrogance, and he did indeed rub some the wrong way. He could have made an enemy or two, just as he made an enemy of his own son.

Petey stuck out his thumb that stormy June day, ten years after Jeanine died. The night before, he, Bill, and his brother Sammie found Petey down on his knees in the back of a bar. They tried to save him from himself. They tried! Martin still feels sick about how that piece of shit pornographer seduced his son. Hell, maybe he picked Petey up from the side of that road, prowling around waiting for the boy to start hitchhiking, sensing the itch that the fucker preyed upon.

Nobody heard from Petey for six months, everybody wondering and worrying.

Finally, Petey called his sister, Brenda, just to say that he was alive and making some money, over all okay. Then another six months passed with no word. Martin hated the fact that his son claimed to be gay. Martin had been an athlete, a coach, a man for Christ's sake! Petey never was. Not in that sense. Martin felt disappointed and something even harder to admit, disgusted, but he loved his son, and he began to feel desperate, so he took the only action he could think of. He decided to go to a video store and look for a picture of his son on the boxes. Maybe there would be a city listed, a place of distribution. He would have to travel to Three Rivers, where at least one video store had a gay section. To take even one step inside that door, he would have to disguise himself. He sure as shit didn't want the word to get out back in Willis that he was some closeted homo. He rustled through the box of Halloween costumes down in the basement and found a mustache, sideburns, and a straw hat like some ass-hole in a Hawaiian shirt might wear. He asked his brother, Sammie, to go with.

"I found some crap down in the basement to disguise myself with."

"What for?" Sammie asked.

"I don't want anybody to see me looking at faggot porno!"

"Jesus, Martin, can't you just call it gay porno?"

"Are you going with me or what?"

"Sure! Pick me up on the way."

"You want me to find you some stuff to wear?"

"No, Martin. I'll just go as myself."

Martin jumped into his Buick, picked up Sammie, and away they flew down the back roads past the farms with barns and silos, new subdivisions with ponds and decks, old cemeteries with gray and falling tombstones, clumps of woods parted by shallow wetlands, and fields upon fields of corn and soybeans. His brother smoked jays, or joints, whatever they call them, and the two men tussled over what music to play. His brother looked gaunt, thin, a color that bordered gray. They did not talk too much; they never had, but the blood bond binds anyway.

Sammie knew the location of everything no matter what. He directed Martin to the video store, not far from the two bars they searched for Petey a year before. The piece of shit, Eddie the pornographer, whose genitals were hanging out for all to see, in the back of that bar, Peter in front of him on his knees, had sold out and disappeared.

They pulled up to the store, Family Video, a name that irritated the shit out of Martin, knowing that they rented "gay porno," but as Sammie kept telling him, it's 1992, time to "accept the things that you cannot change." His brother, the philosopher. Martin stuck on the sideburns, the mustache and the hat, looking in the mirror to see just how stupid he looked, and Sammie laughed. They climbed out of the car and walked inside.

Sammie walked in first, his tie-dye shirt bursting with color, his gray ponytail hanging to his waist, and Martin in tow, looking like a lost soul from a Jimmy Buffet song. They moseyed around until they found the curtain that separated the porn from the "family" video and slipped inside. Only one other person shopped in there, a tall, thin dude dressed in leather pants and vest, even though summer had arrived and the thermometer read seventy-seven degrees. He glanced at them, but Martin's return glare quickly shut him down. He and Sammie began to scan every outside box looking for Petey. For a small Midwest town, they had a hell of a selection. Martin's stomach tied into knots, as he looked at the video covers one by one. He kept cursing under his breath, until Sammie told him to cool it.

"Jesus, Martin. Cool it on the editorializing."

"What's that mean?"

"Really?"

"What?"

"Keep your comments to yourself." A couple of beats went by. "You know, I just thought of something. If that Eddie guy uses underage boys, we aren't going to find his videos here."

"He seemed to be interested in Petey. He was twenty. Must be he sometimes uses older boys."

"Young men. That's a good point. I'll keep looking."

One by one, tape by tape. Half-clad men. Some in leather looking violent. Some sweeties looking like girls. Whips and chains. Horse sized dildos. Mustaches and muscles, tight pants and tattoos, you name it.

One by one, tape by tape, and the more furious Martin became.

Time went by. Minutes grew into an hour.

They found one, and Martin winced, his stomach dropped and he grew nauseous. He stared at the photo to see his twenty-year-old son, and two boys that definitely looked younger, much younger. All three were shirtless, wearing tight jeans and smiling into the camera sweet as angels. Martin cursed aloud before he could catch himself, and Sammie snatched the box from his hands. Martin grabbed the dog-eared box back again. He noted as much of the info on the back that he could, including the fact that he did not see his son's name listed. There was however a Pedro Beck. Could his son have changed his name? Martin's anxiety skyrocketed; his skin turned red, and his gestures became agitated. Sammie drew him out from behind the curtain, out the front door and back to the car.

"It was distributed by a company in New York City," Martin remarked.

"So you're going to go to New York to look for him?"

"I can hire a snoop." He did just that, and the man, highly respected, found the company, but no one would talk, pretended they never heard of Pedro Beck, let alone Peter Becker.

The months went by and then unexpectedly, Petey contacted Brenda and asked if he and a friend could come for a visit. She enthusiastically said yes. Martin's nerves set on edge from that moment, wondering what "friend" meant. Would he have a boyfriend in tow? Could he be sick like many of them were? He felt happy that his kid was coming home, but he still didn't feel comfortable with his being gay.

—w—

The full moon lights up the landscape like a stage, as Martin cruises down the back roads, and although he had no destination consciously chosen, his unconscious must have had a plan. He finds himself approaching the field where the killer took Jeanine, and he hits the brakes, sliding a bit to make a turn onto a dirt pathway that takes him in, but only so far. Will he step out of the car and wander by foot? He doesn't know if he can remember the spot. He did visit that day, her body already removed, and the exact location marked with that yellow tape, and his friends, the cops, and he covered every inch of the ground again for miles in every direction. One of the cops, also his friend, Doug Holder, led the investigation. Just Martin's luck that an once-in-a-lifetime storm hit, dropping four inches of rain an hour and winds blew steadily at 75 to 80 miles per hour. Nothing. Not a clue. As if the son-of-a-bitch had colluded with a powerful force. If that was true, it must have been Lucifer himself.

How did he end up here? Why did he come? Did he come to talk with her? Pray to her, maybe? Doubtful. He never prays.

He opens the car door, climbs out and begins to walk deeper into the dark field. The details of the murder begin popping up one by one in his mind. She lay practically nude in a position no one alive could. A stick violently thrust up into her. Her hands tied tightly by a strip of cloth. Another gagged and stifled any sound. Scrapes, scratches, small punctures and bruises covered her. No signs of a fight were on her or around her. He lifts his hands, places them on either side of his head, falls to his knees and begins to wail. Mean words he said to his sweet wife and his children tumble from his memory now. To his wife: "You stink." "What have you been doing all day?" "This food tastes like crap." To his daughter: "You are acting like the town slut." "You aren't good enough for Bill." "Nobody is going to want you." To his son: "If I ever see you dressed up like a girl again, I will kill you." To them all now: "I'm sorry. I'm sorry. I'm so very sorry." He cries like a child, well, any kind of crying looks and sounds unmanly, but he cannot stop. He grieves deeper and harder than when he broke down beside the bed the first night of Jeanine's showing. "I'm sorry. God, I'm sorry." With arms wrapped around his head, he falls forward to the ground. He begs the earth to take his grief. *Please. Please take it. Please, please take it. I will never speak to anyone like that again. I swear.* Little by little, his sobs subside, leaving him still and exhausted. He falls back onto his ass and sits there staring into the dark; he sees nothing. Not even the slightest feeling that she might be here, and that seems like a good thing. She shouldn't be here. She should be safe somewhere, maybe looking down at him. What would she think? What would she say if she could speak? Would she feel proud that he stopped drinking? Accepted his son, in his own way. Lives now as a better man.

Martin slowly stands, walks slowly, too. Struggling with his stiff hips and knees, he makes his way back to the car, and once inside and on the road again, he begins to think about the last time he saw Petey.

—⟋⟍—

Brenda picked up Petey and his friend from the airport. Martin didn't know what to expect. They had not seen Petey in a year or more. Brenda decided to make his visit an occasion and threw a barbeque. The whole family showed up, including his mother, Martha, brother, Sammie, Sammie's girlfriend at the time, and Lily Rose of course. Everyone but Bill. He and Brenda remained estranged. Martin drank two drinks before going over, something his mother always referred to as "liquid courage."

He feared more than anything that Petey would show up with that little prick that gave Martin a race one night, driving Petey's Celica that the punk had stolen, eventually taking flight on Bethel Church Road, sliding to a crash into the side of a tree. Martin chased after him on foot before his age caught up with him, but they were destined to meet again in the back of that bar, where he and Bill found Petey down on his knees. That kid was trouble. Martin would have prayed, if he thought praying would help. The prayer would go something like this: *Please, do not let his friend be that little son-of-a-bitch.*

He walked into the backyard and looked around. The steaks were on the grill, smoke rising, fat sizzling, while potato salad and three bean salad, desserts and chips laid out on a table. Lily Rose played with another little girl on the swing set, while Sammie and his girlfriend sat closely together on a wooden bench built for two. Martin could see Brenda inside at the kitchen window, Martha beside her, but he did not see Petey.

Brenda met him at the sliding door.

"Got a drink for an old man?"

"You know where the stuff is, Dad." She bustled past him and back out into the yard, carrying a plate of hot dogs.

His mother looked up at him from her place in front of the sink. "How are you today, Son?"

"Not bad. Where is the kid? Don't tell me he didn't come."

"He's in the living room with Jack. They're catching their breath. Please be civilized."

"Civilized?

"You know what I mean."

Martin quickly fixed himself a drink, three fingers of brown with a splash of water, then moved towards the living room. Petey and "Jack" were lounging together on the couch holding hands. When the two young men saw Martin, Petey tossed Jack's hand to the side and they both sat up straighter. Jack jumped up and stuck out his hand to Martin.

"Hi, you must be Pedro's dad." The kid had a strong handshake and good eye contact. He did not look like a fag. Then "Pedro" stood up. Pedro, what the fuck? Pedro's dark curly hair cut short, curls all but gone, and a serious look cloaked his face.

What happened next surprised Martin. Without forethought, he found himself wrapping his arms around his son, and he held him closely. At first, Petey stood stiffly, but then something inside of him gave away because he wrapped his arms around his father, and for the first time in many years, they reclaimed each other. Martin remembered, as a series of images flashed, of his son as a baby, so much hair, so long, so...sweet; he was a miracle, a blessing, and then Jeanine smiling so broadly, holding their little son. Jeanine's face now, somehow reaching through the ether of the other side, hovering nearby, tears falling, so happy to see their son yielding, and Martin making a "break-through" he could never have foreseen.

The two young men never admitted to the dark world that Pet...Pedro or maybe both worked within, but they did talk excitedly about contacts they were making, Pet...Pedro a costume designer, Jack an actor. They felt optimistic about the future. Sure that their dreams would come true. The family rallied around them, and Martin's dreams of who his son might become finally diminished into dust, but something else wedged open.

—⁓—

Petey died six months ago from the disease that someone infected him with somewhere along the tough and uneven path of his chosen life. He never came back again to visit, but Brenda and Bill visited him in New York a couple times after he became sick. His death deeply affected everyone, but it spurned something in his daughter to take matters into the family's hands to find the killer of Jeanine. Martin has never stopped wanting to find the person who killed his wife, but he grew numb with alcohol, numb with time that reshapes, reframes, until all that he knew to be true became foggy. The scab though has been picked upon, the wound open and oozing. Someone meant to undo him on that cold October night, and maybe, just maybe, that person still lives somewhere nearby.

9
Hieroglyphs

Saturday 6:00 a.m.

Jeff awakens with beams of sunlight striking his eyes through the open slots of a shade. It takes a few minutes for him to orient, as the last glimpses of a dream that included Desiree, dissipate. Speeding away in a blue boat named No Regrets, he can just see her left behind in the spray, the bright sun half blinding him as he steers. She looks so sad, weakly waving goodbye with one hand. The other rests lightly on her baby bump. The further away he travels the more relief he feels.

He looks around at the small den, not taking time the night before to see a five-shelf walnut bookcase jammed with hardbacks and paperbacks, framed photos, and what his mom used to call "dust collectors." In fact, dust coats everything everywhere in the room. He shudders to think of the mites, the flecks of dead skin, and even pet dander because he remembers seeing a cat or two. All that miniscule substance, floating down, piling on everything stationary, which sits untouched, well, for a while. Stacks of papers, some an inch thick, several others cover the walnut desk where a Dell computer sits. A rocking chair from another decade crowds the corner, laundry, maybe clean maybe dirty, strewn the seat. The green-colored walls sooth him, but the carpet, a green color too, stretches across the room dotted with clumps of animal hair and a small but occasional stain. His need for order and cleanliness springs him off the couch that he's been sleeping on, suddenly anxious about what sort of debris and spills inhabit the dirt-colored tweed.

He reaches for the ceiling to stretch his cramped torso, notes the bugs lying dead at the bottom of the light globe, then stretches down to face the carpet, and holds his breath. Pulling on his khakis, he pauses as his intestines begin to churn.

—m—

Jeff woke up in the middle of the night, glanced at his watch to see 1:07 am. He had to take a leak. Jack's wife went to bed earlier than the two men, who crashed about midnight. He had only slept an hour, lucky to fall asleep at all after three glasses of iced tea.

He pulled on his pants, stumbling as his right leg caught and reached out through the dark for the door. He located the cold knob, pulled the door open, and looked both ways down a hall, straining to remember where the hell the bathroom sat. He made a guess and headed to the right where he saw a faint light. Quietly, he tiptoed down the hall, so as not awaken anyone; he reached that light and to his delight the bathroom. Walking in, he closed the door mostly shut, unzipped, and let it flow, and flow it did. With his head back and his mouth open in pleasure, he did not hear the door open, if even a sound occurred. The smell of a flowery perfume hit him first, then the sense that he was no longer the only breathing being in the room. He turned to see Jack's wife, long strawberry blond hair mussed up, and as his eyes dropped, he took in the little black lacey number she wore. He averted his eyes, stuck himself wet back into his khakis, cringing, and he zipped up.

She said in a husky, sleepy voice, "Oh, I'm sorry, I didn't know anyone was in here."

He thought to himself, *Yeah, right. That rush of piss fell like a waterfall.* He said, "Let me get out of your way." She did not move, so he had to shuffle past her sideways, noting the pink toenails, the tits falling out of the nightgown, and her hand reaching out to cup his groin. He sucked in a breath, looked her in the eyes and said, "Don't do that."

She smiled sweetly. "It's okay."

He reached down and removed her hand from his growing hardness. "No, it's not." He pushed past her, almost rudely, and felt embarrassed for his brother, his big brother, the only family he had left except for little Jimmy. Not that long ago, regardless of the situation, he would have pushed the bitch to her knees, someone he used to be, someone he spent years taming. Controlling. The fact that the woman was mother to his nephew riled him, frustrated him, and as he made his way back up the hall, his eyes more adjusted to the light, he saw framed photos, and he felt like punching something, maybe these cute little mementoes, no doubt of the happy family, but he wouldn't. He, too, had a mother like that, a woman who loved her sweet Gallo wine, the party and fun that followed, generally ending with the grunts and groans of one-night stands.

He ended up tossing and turning on the narrow couch, eventually falling into a light and desperate sleep. He dreamed about her. Not Jack's wife, but the brown-skinned woman he fell for two years ago. The one that told him two weeks ago that she was pregnant. The one that he left in the sparkling spray, as he sped away in the boat.

—⁜—

He glances at the clock, half buried in paper on the desk, 6:10 a.m. Again, he has to take a leak and wants desperately to shower. He opens the door, sticks his head out and sees Jack, standing down the hall dressed for the day. Jeff already decided he would not mention what happened with the wife, but his heart beats hard anyways. After all, she could have told her husband and embellished upon the truth.

Jack, spotting Jeff's head in the doorway, walks down the hall towards him. Jeff sprints back into the room and throws on a shirt, then races through the buttoning of the bottom three.

In the doorway now, Jack asks, "Did you sleep okay?"

"Oh, yeah," Jeff answers, as he buttons the second from the top.

"I'm heading for the gym. Want to go?"

Jeff shakes his head. "No, I've got a few things I need to do."

"Well, you're welcome to stay, if you don't mind sleeping on that couch."

"I'll get out of your way. Stay at a motel."

"I don't blame you. I thought maybe we could all go out to eat tonight."

"Sure, that sounds good."

"I invited Billy Bagwell and his wife to come along, too."

"Do I know them?"

"He was James' best friend. She's Coach Becker's daughter."

Jeff startles for a moment. "You said...Becker's daughter? Boy, that's a name I haven't heard in a while..."

"Billy's a good guy; you'll like him. Marine sniper from the first Gulf War."

"Yeah?"

"He laid his dog tags in your brother's casket. I think that pretty much says it all. The wife's very nice too. Look, make yourself at home. Take a shower, grab some breakfast."

"Are...are they up yet?"

"No. Probably not for a while. See you later."

Jeff tiptoes towards the bathroom. With any luck, he can shower and leave the house before she wakes up. He wouldn't mind seeing Jimmy though. The bathroom, although not dirty per say, looks as cluttered as the rest of the house. A bamboo clothes hamper overflows, towels hang over bars, from hooks, and a variety of toiletries clutter the small counter around the sink. Jeff closes the door, disappointed not to see a lock, quickly strips, grabs a clean towel off a shelf in a small closet and steps into the shower. Although the hot water feels great running over his stiff body, he soaps up and rinses quickly, determined not to see her. He turns the water off, steps out and dries himself, wraps the towel around his waist, grabs his clothes and opens the door. To his surprise, Jimmy stands in the hall. The young boy's mouth falls open. "I thought you were Jack."

"No, he went to the gym."

Jimmy's eyes grow wide as he takes in Jeff's tattooed torso.

The kid's eyes, brown like his dad's, squint, widen, and eventually grow alarmed. You have to love kids for their uncensored, honest response. A ten-year-old stringing together a personal history of violence and social unrest, though he doubts the kid knows what it all means. Mixed in with the ink, looking like extensions or enhancements, some kind of added dimension were scars, some nasty, some pinker and new, most ghostly white with age. The kid blurts out, "Isn't that a swastika?"

At this point, Jeff begins to feel self-conscious and grabs a towel, dirty or not, which he cloaks around his shoulders, to hide the hieroglyphs of his journey. "Yeah. Yes. That's from a long time ago."

"You have more tattoos than Jack. Were…were you a Nazi?"

Jeff grabs his clothes and turns back to the boy. "Come on; let's walk back to the den. I don't want to wake your mother." He walks behind the boy down the hall and into the room. "What do you know about Nazis?"

Jimmy sits down on the rocker, strewn clothes and all. "Jack reads a lot of history and he tells me about things, and I've seen some movies about WWII. They were the bad guys. Really bad guys."

Jeff pulls a clean pair of underwear out of his suitcase and pulls them on under the towel. He reaches back in for a clean pair of black pants and pulls them on too. Finally, he grabs a clean light blue button-up, but before he can pull it on, Jimmy speaks up again. "Can I see your back?"

Jeff slowly turns and stands staring at a wall where some more fucking family photos hang. He sees Jimmy as a baby and a small boy, the wife as a young teen mom, a wedding photo of her and Jack, and in one corner near the bottom, a snapshot of James, a glass of booze in one hand, a cigarette in the other, staring into the lens with all the distrust Jeff remembers in his brother's eyes as a boy. Shit. A mist hits his own.

Jimmy blurts out question number two, "Were you shot?"

Jeff turns slowly back towards the boy. "Stabbed and cut up."

"Why? Were you in a fight?"

"More than one, kid. More than one." Jeff pulls the clean shirt on and begins to button, bottom to top. It feels like *Groundhog Day*.

"So, you didn't answer my question."

"You mean, was I a Nazi?"

The kid gazes down at the floor and then lifts his eyes to meet his own again.

"I was not a Nazi, but for a period of my life, I believed some of the same things. Some people called us Neo-Nazis."

"What kind of things did you believe?"

"Like white people were superior to all others. Especially white Christians. That the Jews were running and destroying America. That no one but whites should live in our country or those of color should live in designated areas. I was angry and hateful."

"Why do you have the word WAR tattooed on your wrist?"

"That's an acronym. Do you know what that is?"

"Um...the letters stand for something?"

"You are a real smart kid, aren't ya?"

"That's not what they tell me at school, but I like to read things and know things. Jack says that knowledge is power."

"He's right. He's absolutely right." He remembers he wants to avoid *her,* so he quickly folds his dirty clothes, sticks them into a plastic bag, and neatly packs them into one corner of his suitcase.

"So what does it mean?"

Jeff stands and turns again to the boy. "It means White Aryan Rebels, the name of a group I was once affiliated with."

"So you don't believe those things anymore?"

"No, I absolutely don't."

"Since 9/11, everybody seems to hate people from the...the Middle...East?"

"That's right. The Middle East. Well, kid, unfortunately, people always seem to have to hate someone."

"I don't hate anyone."

Jeff walks up to Jimmy, takes him by the shoulders, looks him in the eyes and says, "That's great. You try as hard as you can, to keep it that way. I've got to get going."

"Are you coming back?"

"Not to stay here, but I'll be around for a while."

Jeff bends over to click his suitcase shut, grabs it by the handle and wheels it towards the door, the kid walking out in front of him.

"So, what are you going to do today, kid?"

"Jack's taking me to see the hobbit movie!"

"It's a good one. We saw it last week. I'll see you later."

The boy stands aside and lets him by. Jeff strides because the kid watches, but he does so quietly down the hall and towards the front door of the house. As he reaches for the door handle, a voice startles him.

"I already told him what happened, so you don't have to."

He turns to see the wife sitting on the couch in her little nightgown thing and a flimsy robe falling off her shoulders. "I just hope you told it exactly as it happened." He turns and walks out of the door, down the porch steps, opens the trunk of his car, places the suitcase in, slams the door down, climbs in behind the wheel, and heads down the road.

The sun shines brightly down on one of those amazing fall days, illuminating all of the colors left on the trees and strewn over the land. A breeze rolls and scatters the fallen leaves across the road and fields, as Jeff heads back into Willis. A silhouette of the full moon sits ghostly in the sky, translucent, reminding him of some sci-fi film he saw. He loves the rows of dry corn stalks interspersed with fields of pumpkins and gourds lying on the ground, waiting to be picked from the fields, and posted on porches, by lampposts, and under trees. In a couple of weeks, Halloween arrives, a time of the year that he loved as a kid. Trick or treating, mostly tricking, exploding firecrackers in mailboxes, coiling toilet paper through the trees, soaping words on windows, and for those special cases, scooping dog shit into a paper bag, placing the stinky stuff on the front porch and setting it aflame. A long time ago. Seems like so damn long ago.

Now, for the matter at hand.

—⁂—

After they released him from Half Moon, at the age of eighteen, he worked construction for some months, and then he joined a stock car circuit as a mechanic. He had to get the hell out of town. After a year in juvie, he felt crazy. He did not use his time wisely while incarcerated, instead fretting and worrying he'd never live free again. He could have studied, could have taken classes; instead, he worked out, became tatted up, and acted as ignorant as most of the others. A locked up animal, with guess who? Eric pissed and moaned about the food, the COs, their fellow inmates, you name it, and he always ended with one final note. Coach Becker, the fucker who took him down, would pay and pay dearly. Blah, blah, blah. If it hadn't been for Coach, he would be a free man and a football legend. Blah, blah, blah. Jeff stayed away from him as much as he could. Of course, Eric had everyone bamboozled with his ability to bullshit, but Jeff knew he would eventually hurt someone, or buck up too hard against the wrong authority. Eric eventually did catch another bit, dealing weed inside Half Moon. They road him out to one of the big houses.

Travelling through the country with the circuit, Jeff rarely if ever thought about Eric, but one night, holed up in a little hotel down in Florida, a night off racing, he caught the news. Someone murdered Becker's wife, and the police were asking for help. Still caught in a cycle of his own destruction and nowhere close to making amends, he ignored that call.

10

Glue

The bruises and split flesh on Lola's face haunt Brenda, as she awakens. How can a person abuse a child or someone he or she claims to love? As hard as she tries she cannot find forgiveness for the actions, even though she knows that the perpetrator often has his or her story too, often suffering abuse themselves as children. She does not know if her father's abuse and the murder of her mother singly propelled her towards this work, counseling battered women, but they certainly played a huge role in the process. When she expressed to her maternal grandmother that she would like to pursue the field, Martha supported her completely, even helping to finance her schooling and assist with the care of Lily Rose. During those years, Billy also helped take care of their daughter, and although still too angry to support her openly, she could tell that he respected her efforts. She completed her early classes at a local community college and finished her degree at the university, carrying a 3.8 GPA. The many hours of fieldwork, without pay, left her exhausted in one sense and excited as hell in another. Her work would make an impact, and this mattered to her. When Lola came in the first time, bloodied and bruised, she stepped up with all her will, and when this woman came in the second time, last night, she knew she would need to approach the case differently. Lola just wasn't getting it. This man could kill her.

—⚬⚬⚬—

The black haired woman, petite and small boned trembled, and nothing Brenda could do at first brought that shaking to rest.

Lola's teeth chattered, her brown eyes looked wide and wild, and she held her arms firmly crossed against her chest. They often cover their hearts this way, the battered, perhaps to say that he may crush and fracture the bones, leave red and tender welts, pool the blood within the flesh, but he will not touch this tender beating organ; or do they cover their heart because the cave of emotion sits empty now? Not a feeling left there alive.

She protected what sat hollow now. This Lola.

What would happen if she did not go home?

He would be hot upon her trail.

Brenda knew this, so she had to hide her.

As the battered woman curled herself deeper into the sofa, a blanket tightly wrapped around her, the blood mostly coagulated from a deeply split lip, she began to calm.

"Lola," Brenda addressed her, sitting in a chair close to the couch, leaning in toward her. "Why have you stayed? You came here six months ago in a similar condition, but this time he hurt you more."

Lola hung her head and emitted exhausted quiet sobs. "I love him."

"What do you love about him?"

"He puts up with my shit."

"What do you mean by shit?"

"You know."

"No, I don't know."

Lola looked up at Brenda. "He hardly ever hits me, you know. Most of the time he's good to me. Maybe I...maybe I asked for it."

"You did not ask for it." Brenda gently placed her hand upon Lola's lower leg. The woman with bones like a sparrow winced and she clenched her left arm more tightly against her rib cage, casting her eyes down.

"I'm sorry," Brenda said, removing her hand. "I didn't mean to hurt you."

"No. You didn't. I...I just can't be touched right now."

"Of course. Lola, you did not ask for it. Look at me!"

Lola met Brenda's eyes with her own red and swollen, then darted them away. "I don't know."

"I know. Nothing you did or said gave him the right to do this to you. Not ever. Lola, look at me!"

Again, yet still reluctantly, Lola met her eyes.

"Not ever, Lola. Not ever!"

"When he's good, he's so good. He...he takes care of me."

"How does he take care of you?"

"Better than anybody. Money. We have a house. He buys me things. And he makes love to me. That's...the *pegamento*...the glue. The glue that keeps me with him. Él hace el amor conmigo. He makes love with me."

"You mean *la lujuria,* lust, don't you, Lola?"

"Lust? I don't know. It's...so good. It makes it all better again."

"Well..."

"And...he needs me."

"So is the... love...good enough to look and feel like you do right now? What if he kills you the next time?"

"He's not going to kill me!"

"How do you know?"

"He has control. He knows when to stop."

"That sounds like something he would say. This is way past stop, Lola. You need to go to the hospital. We need to know if you have anything broken or injured inside of you."

"No. No, I can't!"

"Then I will take you somewhere safe."

"Where? Where will you take me? I don't know if that..."

"You want to go back there? You want to live like this?"

"I'm scared, so scared to be on my own..."

"We'll help you. No woman has to put up with what you've been through. We have a place you can stay tonight, and you can think about it. Do that for yourself."

And Lola did.

—⁕—

Christopher runs into the bedroom, throws himself against Brenda and places his head on her right shoulder, holding her tightly.

He asks, "Are you sleeping in, Mommy?"

"Not now I'm not! Did you have breakfast?"

"Daddy scrambled eggs."

"Oh, good."

"He's going to work for a while, and then he's taking me to the batting cage."

"I know! That sounds fun. Is your sister up yet?"

"Nope."

"Why don't you go and watch some cartoons. I'm going to be up in just a few minutes."

"Okay." Off her young son runs.

She wants to ponder Lola's words. Think about that force that keeps people together even when they shouldn't be, or wouldn't be, if they could separate themselves from the pleasure. If she or he could just be objective, separate sense from sensibility. She knows. She spent six months drowning in sense, a lust-driven sensuality that damaged her marriage and threatened other relationships, too. She could look back at her relationship with James, now that eleven years had passed, and separate the force that drove them together from the feelings she had for him in her heart. She remembers the lust, but she also remembers a good-looking, sexy man, who escaped his wounded heart and psyche through pleasure. In quiet moments, she had witnessed his tender underbelly, a precious little boy. Isn't that what really coheres two people together? Even more than the pleasure, the precious little boy or girl captures the heart. At this moment though, the lust, the glue screams out of memory.

—⁂—

She honestly did try to fight her desire for James. She did not invite him over that first time. He showed up. Billy asked him to watch over her and Lily Rose, while he served his deployment in the Gulf. To begin with, Billy had never asked her how she felt about him enlisting. He just did it. Was she pissed? Hell, yes! She felt like he should place his child and his wife above his country. She grew lonely, very lonely, as her husband baked away in the Arabian Desert. At that time, eleven years ago, she felt terrified of being alone. Billy, her protector, her knight could not help her.

So there he stood, James, in her living room, so handsome in his tight black jeans, and she had just come out of the shower. She had never decided, oh, I'm going to cheat on Billy. The force moved over her, against her will. She wanted James to fuck her, the man who had already bedded who knew how many women and girls in town. His comfort with his sexuality, the confidence he possessed drove her over to the sink, and before she knew it, she was reaching up, in complete awareness that her ass showed, hanging out of the bottom of her short cotton robe. One breast too, dangled out of the open front. She could feel herself getting wet, and at that point, she knew she would not be able to turn back. Sex with Billy had always been good, but James turned the act into something animal. No nibbles on the neck or even kissing. He walked up from behind, reached out for her breasts, and from that moment, she could not turn back. After they came, sweating and out of breath, she swore never again, never!

That lasted three days.

Then she went looking for him.

She found him in his shop, working on a black pickup truck, bending over the engine under a hood. He did not hear her drive up, but turned when he heard her steps walking across the cement floor. She stood staring into his eyes, reached down and unbuttoned the first three buttons of her shirt. She pulled the sides of her shirt open enough to reveal the top half of her breasts. James walked over to the sink in slow motion, washed his hands thoroughly and wiped them on a towel, all the time looking at her, taking her in, licking his lips, and she could see him growing inside his green work pants.

Finally, he walked over towards her, grabbed her hand and

pulled her into a backroom, where a small desk and a chair on rollers took up most of the space. He pulled her into him with a snap, and she could feel his hardness up against her lower abdomen. Placing his hands on her cheeks, he bent to kiss her, his tongue inside her mouth, his full lips gnawing on her own. He backed up and sat into the chair, and breaking away for a moment, unzipped his pants and pulled her towards him. Slipping his hand under her skirt, he moaned to find her without underwear and pulled her on top of him. When her muscles fluttered with the deep orgasm, he came too, uttering his own cries of pleasure. Then he kissed her again and she pulled away from him, the shame already blooming. She pulled down her skirt, buttoned her shirt, and turned to go. As she walked away, he stated, "You can't stay away now, and you know it."

As she walked out of the shop, she saw her brother, Peter, driving by. Somehow, he knew; she could tell when she saw him next, and he asked her why she was there. She answered that she was visiting, but the blush in her cheeks gave her away. Soon others in town knew, though she and James tried to keep their liaison hidden. A couple of months down the line, James moved in with her and Lily, and the Dear John letter to Billy went out. She could say that passion blinded her, and that would be true, but revenge also played a part. Shamefully, she had pitted two best friends against each other. She had a chance, over years, to make things right with Billy, but James dying the very night the two men fought, robbed her of doing the same with him. She deeply grieved over the loss of her friend, her teacher, who taught her so much about herself, but perhaps mostly for the precious little boy whom so many, even her, deeply hurt. Yes, it takes two, and James would never have forced himself upon her. Her consent sprung the union into motion. Did she love him? Yes, but not as a wife loves a husband. She loved him as a human being. She loved only one man like a husband, and the five years it took for Billy to forgive her felt unbearable.

Brenda thinks about the people who have given so much of themselves, even died for lust or love. The people who knew so little about themselves, lacking the self-love to understand what they deserved. Like her mother. She thinks about all the words her father said to her mother that held her down and shamed her. Her mother never spoke up, so Brenda defended her at times, only to become the target herself. Then someone took her, on that night, while she and Peter slept, someone who might still be alive, even living next door to them, who knows? How could such a horrible thing happen? How?

Brenda sits up, suddenly feeling nauseous, throws her legs over the edge and stands up. She heads towards the bathroom to shower and imagines her mom alone in that field, on that killing floor, and her heart screams. Do not go there! Do not imagine what happened to that woman who lived like a rose bud, never to bloom. Do not go there! Her desire not to cannot hold back the images that torment her now. There were deep cuts, scrapes and bruises upon her mother's body, indicating that the killer had dragged her. Clumps of hair were missing from her head. Only a few shreds of her favorite nightgown covered her. Did she cry out? She could not have. No one ever heard her. Did she fight and flail? The police told them there were no signs of that. The monster shoved a branch up inside of her that tore her, punctured organs, bled her out if not already dead. Why didn't her cries fill the field, spill out into the land, and ring across the vast expanse and alarm someone? Why? Because there were none.

Brenda steps into the steaming stream of water and lets the flow hit upon her face and wash away the tears that spill. The sobs, which once visited every day, had been set to rest, shoved down, locked inside a safe of forgetting, no, ignoring, no, surviving. They move up now; she can feel them, tunneling their way up from the dark within, and moving quickly now, tumbling out and wrenching her body. She cannot stop them. Her body convulses as her howls rise and release. This release goes on, and on.

In the distance, or so it seems, she hears knocking, a frantic firm pounding that breaks the moment and slows the cries. She seems to come back to her senses, find herself in the shower, as the soothing, hot water purifies the angst and grief. She hears the door open and the steps of her husband, as he quickly pushes the shower curtain to the side, pulls her out of the shower and holds her to him. He wraps his strong arms around her and utters again and again in her ear, "Shhhhhh. Shhhhhh. Shhhhhh." She clings to Billy as the sobs continue to move up out of her, until little by little, they subside. She hears her young son ask, "Mommy, are you okay, Mommy?" Glancing up from Billy's shoulder, she sees Christopher, his little brow clenched in concern and her daughter too, worry on her face. Lily holds out a towel in her right hand, and Billy grabs it and wraps the thick warm cloth around Brenda, still holding her, still soothing her.

As she calms, an even deeper conviction rises. Today she will allow the words of her brother to lead her. "The world's not safe." She will help find the person who killed her mother. She will do so for her brother, herself, her family, and for every woman harmed at the hands of a monster.

II
Something Sick
Saturday 9:26 a.m.

Billy looks up from his sawing to glance at the clock. Nine eleven. He feels his stomach drop. The numbers conjure up images of the catastrophe that occurred just one year before. How the hell could something like that happen? Where were the military jets when those planes veered towards the towers? Something just wasn't right. Under any other circumstance, those jets would be up in the sky protecting and defending.

Something else preys upon his mind today, as well. The anniversary of the murder of Jeanine. Hearing Brenda sobbing in the shower this morning, watching her body heave and roll through the translucent curtain as he walked in brought the tragedy all back.

He walks over to the open garage door and lights a cigarette. Yeah, he's smoking again. Unrest and discomfort haunts the air. He can feel it. Smoking helps.

He likes October and wishes he could enjoy the colors, the decorations. Colorful signs for the corn mazes and the haunted houses hang around, and scarecrows perch at every turn, battered now, their days of duty diminishing as the fields grow bare. The pumpkins and the gourds stand out from the withering vines, and the dry corn stalks shred as the wind, the rain, the small and large living things brush through. Now, the memory of a woman found in one of those fields. He cannot bear to think about what she went through.

A country attacked and not defended. A woman murdered and the killer never found. He shakes his head in disgust.

Fucking defies reason.

80

Billy only knew Jeanine for a short time before she died. Brenda and he had just begun dating. He remembers a pretty woman, pretty like Brenda and sweet. Wavy brown hair, a bit lighter than his wife's. He remembers her cooking in the kitchen or working in the yard. She cooked things he loved like macaroni and cheese, stews, and even his own mother could not beat her pot roast. Jeanine kept the house very clean, and she endured more than any woman should have to. In truth, Martin, his father-in-law, acted like a tyrant to the whole family. Hell, Martin acted like a tyrant to just about everyone around him. However, he must admit, since Martin stopped drinking, his tyranny had abated.

Billy flicks his cigarette butt into a trashcan and begins to put together the pieces of sawed wood to form a drawer. He smiles to himself to see the corners meet perfectly. The grains of the oak match, too. Reverend Elliot's wife will be happy with this chest. Although he has met the Reverend on an occasion or two, this job came through like most of his others: recommendation. When he began his apprenticeship with Sam, he thought it impossible to earn a living building furniture, but time proved him wrong. Inheriting Sam's clients certainly helped, but Billy gained his own through word of mouth. Martin did not show support in the early days, maintaining that a man must have a nine-to-five job with benefits to support a family, but Brenda urged Billy to pursue his dream. Martin once conceded that he has been successful, but the job still lacks the fundamental needs. Good 'ol Martin. Always right. Always in control.

Billy has never been crazy about Martin, his father-in-law. Sure, sure, men from that generation followed in the footsteps of those before, acting as the heads of family and sometimes ruling with an iron fist, although his own father did not follow the pattern. Just a small boy when his father died in Vietnam, he remembers playing catch and riding on his father's shoulders. On his few leaves from the far off jungle, Billy remembers him smoking and gazing off, saying very little, the young boy sitting on his lap, playing with his dog tags, the two rocking in a chair.

He still treasures those tags tucked in the top drawer of his dresser.

Why would Martin abuse his family? Billy knew Martha, Martin's mother, but he never knew Samuel, his father. Could the father have been abusive? No one has ever said. Maybe people are born that way, dragging in garbage from another life or destined to learn valuable lessons set up by a higher power. If a higher power exists. Billy feels uncertain about any of that, especially since his deployment to the Arabian Desert.

After the murder though, Billy saw a glimpse of something he had not seen in Martin before: emotion. First, he held everything behind a wall. The stoic head of the household. Then the cracks in the wall began to appear. While sharing a beer with Martin around a summer bonfire, he witnessed the man gaze off on more than one occasion, and a sadness descended on his face in a way that choked Billy up. Martin did not shed tears, but the emotion dragged upon the flesh and dulled any sparkle in his eyes. If Billy had to describe in one word the emotion he witnessed, he would call it desolation. He saw this same emotion on the faces of the Middle Eastern fathers as they gazed upon the charred remains of their children, their wives, their friends. Desolation. A terrible emotion to witness and certainly no better to feel. He too has felt desolation, when his brother in arms, Glover, died beneath the starry night, after carrying him through the desert over his shoulder for...a long time. And too, when he thinks about what he took part in overseas, not a mission to be proud of, maybe a cover-up of lies and deception. Finally again, when he knew that Brenda had taken up with James, as he read her words on a dog-eared letter.

He steps outside the garage door again into the warm fall day, and glancing around, he notes something strange: a murder of crows gathering in the morning instead of dusk, flying overhead, circling, and cawing. Why the hell are they doing that? He lights another cigarette. He quit before, and knows he can again. For now, he inhales deeply.

Billy knows desolation, and not that long ago, he saw it on Martin's face again, in the early spring six months ago.

—⁓—

Billy, Brenda, and the kids had stopped by Martin and Mary's to celebrate Martin's birthday. They were all sitting in the backyard on an unusually warm spring day, with the threat of thunderstorms looming, dark clouds marching in from the west and the air still. Since Martin stopped drinking, they were all sipping on iced tea or soda and Mary, being the gracious hostess, carried out snacks. The conversation had been light, no dramas, no heavy talk, Christopher zooming around kicking a soccer ball, and Lily Rose listening to music through headphones.

Brenda cleared her throat and the peaceful day fell to pieces, as they say. Although everyone in the family knew that Peter was terminally ill, no one had heard from him in a few months. He had come home for one visit just a year after he first disappeared. Brenda and Billy had visited him a couple times in New York City, but communication had fallen off. Phone calls not returned. Letters returned unopened. Everyone in the family knew that Peter was HIV positive, which had now developed into AIDS. He had been taking drugs they called cocktails, and for a long time he held his own. Why Brenda decided to share the news on that day, the day her father turned fifty-five, he did not know, but as wonderful and forgiving as his wife could be, Brenda carried a chip on her shoulder in regards to her father. As important as this news was, Billy wished she had waited at least until the following day.

She blurted out, "Jack called this morning. Peter is dying." Billy remembers her voice wavering, and in fact, she did not say anything else; she couldn't. She stood up from her chair and moved quickly towards the house, her shoulders heaving as she began to sob, the flesh and bones rocking as he had witnessed that very morning in the shower.

Billy jumped out of his chair and stood at the end of the patio, crossing his arms across his chest. He looked over at Martin and saw the desolation, a sadness older than time, deeper than lava, more powerful than any words conjured to relieve it. Mary, standing next to Martin, reached down to take his hand, and although Billy half expected the crusty old coach to toss her hand away, he clung to it in his own.

Lily Rose, who had pulled her headphones off, looked down with wet eyes, and then quickly escaped back into her music. Billy walked back over the red patio bricks and slid the headphones off her head saying, "This is important family business."

The teenage girl looked up at him. "I'm sorry, Daddy."

Only young Christopher remained exempt, allowed to continue kicking away at his ball.

Before long, Brenda slid the screen door open and stepped back down onto the patio, Kleenex in hand, composure recovered. The questions began.

"How long does he have?" Martin asked.

Billy walked over and wrapped his arm tightly around Brenda's shoulders. She answered, "Hospice is there. A day or two. They aren't sure."

"Why the hell haven't they been in communication?" Martin asked, exasperated.

"Jack said the care has been non-stop. He said it's unbelievable what the disease does to a person. He apologized over, and over."

Billy asked, "Did you talk to Peter?"

She nodded her head. "He sounded so weak." She began crying again. Billy pulled her into his chest.

"What did he say? What did my son say?" Martin asked.

"He told me to tell you that he forgave you. He wished that you had forgiven him." She looked up at Billy. "I want to go, but Peter said no. He said he was okay, had what he needed. We'll go to the funeral though. Okay?" Billy nodded.

Mary added, "We should go too, Martin."

Shaking his head, Martin muttered, "I can't go there and see all that. I just can't!"

"Dad's afraid that the faggots will kill him," Brenda said, and Billy shushed in her ear.

Martin insisted, "He should be buried here. His family is here."

Brenda looked up from Billy's shoulder. "He found another family there, Dad. One that accepted him for everything that he is. I don't blame him for not coming back. I don't blame him at all." Brenda broke from Billy and fairly stomped her way back into the house, and when she came back out a few moments later, she held a glass with a couple fingers of whiskey in one hand and the bottle in the other. She tipped the glass up and drank half in one gulp. Billy watched Martin eye the bottle, licking his lips.

Brenda said after tossing back the other half of her whiskey, "I've had it. I've fucking had it!"

Christopher stopped his ball playing and looked at his mother. "You're not supposed to say that word, Mommy."

"You're right. You are absolutely right, but sometimes it slips out, honey. I'm sorry." She continues, "Peter also mentioned something else. He said we should work to get Mom's case opened again. He said the person is still out there, that he can feel it. I think he's right."

Martin jumped up out of his chair. "For crying out loud! They tried! This might not be some flashy big town with big time law enforcement, but I know that they tried. Certainly, State helped. There wasn't anything there! You went out, Bill. We didn't see anything. Nobody saw anything. You don't think I'd like to see the killer behind bars? I could kill him myself. Living behind bars for the rest of my life would be worth it. But it has been twenty years. The killer could be dead..."

Billy interrupted, "Yeah, and he could be actively killing or sitting back in some nice easy chair relishing the moments that he was evil." He released Brenda and walked over towards Martin. "Between you and me, I have never bought that the killer was some drifter passing through. He stalked and chose." He turned to Martin. "I think he knew you."

"Me? Why me? What are you saying?"

Brenda nodded her head and said, "Listen, Dad."

Billy continued, "I think that he's still in this area."

"You're some fucking psychic now, Bill?" Martin asked.

"Martin, with all due respect, you have been a tyrant your whole life. Is it so hard for you to believe that someone just might have hated you enough to murder your wife?"

Martin sat or rather fell back down in his chair. "Jesus! I can't believe you are saying that."

"Well, Martin, give it some thought."

Brenda sat down in her chair and said softly, "I agree with Billy. I think that someone hurt Mom to get back at you, Dad. Are you going to help us or not?"

—⁂—

At one time, Billy wanted to investigate the murder himself, and in some ways he has, asking questions, never forgetting how deeply affected, deeply traumatized, Brenda, Peter, and Martin were – his wife and father-in-law still are. He brought the subject up to Brenda numerous times over the years, but she refused to talk. He has always felt like the killer, or killers, lived or lives in the area and acted out of revenge.

Billy understands revenge. He almost killed a man himself once. Outside war. In war, he picked a few off like flies on the ass of a horse. That did not come from revenge. He acted out of duty as prescribed by the Marines, the duty to shoot particular men for particular reasons, and he did not ask why. He also did not think about their wives, children, or anyone else of value to them. They were a fly on the ass of a horse, and nothing more. Back on the soil of the good ol' USA, he almost killed James, his best friend, and truthfully, he almost died himself that night. Both delivered potentially killing blows, blind with fury. For him, the betrayal by a brother constituted the greatest offense. Yes, Brenda betrayed him also, but he could not kill the mother of his child. In his mind, he has always believed that James seduced her. To this day, he has never asked. Over the years, he gained greater insight, and because he chose not to suffer, he found a way to survive. He chose to forgive his wife. If James had not died on that hot June night, would he have found a way to forgive him, too? Maybe. But the murder of an innocent woman snagged from her home? No forgiveness for that under any circumstance.

Jeanine's murder smacked of revenge.

No one should be able to get away with such a brutal act. Dragging her, violating her. Because there were no clues left anywhere, and no eyewitness who stepped forward, only one solution remained: Confession. Then the person, hardly a person, an animal, no, not even that, a monster, a fallen angel, something sick. Haul that aberration downtown in the square for everyone to see and kill him.

Satiate the hunger.

Heal the wounds.

Everyone lives in peace.

Billy tacks the parts of the drawer together now, until he suddenly feels dizzy and the stab in his belly returns. He half sits, half falls into a chair near the workbench and begins to breathe easy in, easy out, easy in, easy out. God, he feels tired of this. He considers himself lucky because some Marines and soldiers seeded children born with debilitating health conditions. So far, Christopher seems fine, but the possibility haunts him. He's a happy man, married to a good, strong woman that he loves dearly, a wonderful home to live in, family and friends, and a profession that he enjoys. But like Peter told Brenda, and there's no better way to say it, the world's not safe. He worries what will become of his kids. A world where leaders are so drunk with power that they will do anything to maintain it, even wage war for reasons less than honorable. Where killers kill and somehow escape penalty. Perhaps the world has always been this way. Throughout history, atrocities pepper the years. Since all time, for all time. Is there any hope of that changing? The religious will say that the world as we know it must end. He does not want to see that. They will say that the time has come upon us. When children are killing children, and the world spins in chaos, the time appears nigh.

Billy looks out into the day, so full of sun, a few clouds, wispy and white, slide across the blue. The green of the grass contrasts with the brown of the earth. The colors of the autumn, almost blinding in their warm brilliance. He hears the high chirp of the chickadee, the deep rhythmic moan of the mourning dove, and the trill of the red-winged blackbird. Then a caw, and another caw, as he notes a large crow standing on one roof corner of the garage. The black iridescent feathers glisten in the sun. Another caw. Loud. Louder than all the other birds. Holding the pain in his gut, he lives present in this moment but does not concede his will to find the killer of Jeanine. In the afternoon, he will meet with the detective who led the search.

Virgin

Saturday 10:11 a.m.

Boy, what Lily would give for a normal family. No murdered grandmother. No dead uncle. No sick father suffering the aftermath of war. Lily struggles, not wanting to think about her mom crying so hard in the shower. The sounds rose up like something heard in another world, a primitive place where snakes swallow people whole, and bright-colored birds with big yellow beaks cry out from behind umbrella leaves. She wants to ignore the pain that periodically volcanoes out, not her pain but that of those around her, so difficult to watch and hear.

She would rather think about tonight.

The butterflies in her stomach swarm, an icky, unpleasant cross between excitement and dread. On one hand, she cannot wait to see Lucas. On the other, she feels afraid that what Kristen told her about Sue and Lucas might be true. Lily wants to keep the interaction simple and romantic. Hold hands. Exchange a hug or two. Maybe a brief kiss, but no tongue. As horny as she feels, she still wants to take things slowly.

She has seen him looking at her, taking her in, as she walks with Kristen and other friends down the school's bustling and boisterous echoing halls. He has said hello on more than one occasion. Making fast moves on Sue Klein, one of the class "easy" girls, doesn't mean he will on her or does it?

She sits down at her desk, and taking a pencil in hand begins to ponder and write the beginning of a poem:

I am not a baby in a cradle anymore.
I am a young woman taking the world by storm.
Will you treat me like a precious jewel?

Or just another silly girl from school?
Let's take it slow now, take it slow.
Treat me as someone you really want to know.

Lily stands up from her desk and walks over to her full-length mirror, oval shaped, encircled in oak, made by her daddy. She steps closer and scrutinizes her face. She sees his full lips and his bright blue eyes, her mom's chiseled nose and her cheeks sprinkled with constellations of freckles. Her eyelashes are not long, rather on the short side, and even mascara doesn't do all that much. Her hair not golden and wavy like her daddy's, also not brunette like her mom's, but some in between shade they sometimes call wheat. She picks up a brush and begins to run the soft bristles through the long strands, willing her heart to slow down. Why does she feel so nervous? Is it normal to feel this way? She feels terrified to think that her teeth might chatter, her hands shake, her face grow red, and he will know. Lucas will know she's still a baby in a cradle. When he finds that out, he may not want her.

She draws the brush more roughly through her hair. Her class voted her Homecoming Queen! She's a popular girl! So why does she feel so scared? So afraid he won't want her. So afraid that he will.

She puts the brush down and turns her body to the side. Though she has a bit of a butt, she has no breasts. Okay, not flat chested, but why couldn't she have gotten a bit more? They say that girl athletes lose some of their chest because of the hormone shifts; that might account for some of it. But all of the female celebrities have breasts. If they don't have them, they buy them. They wouldn't have them, if they weren't desirable. She has nice legs. Strong and long. Maybe she should wear a skirt, but she doesn't really like being looked at. Not like that. She has noticed men undressing her with their eyes. Isn't that what they say? Is that all they want? She's smart. Doesn't that count? She's kind. Shouldn't that matter? She thrusts her chest out and pulls her hips back. She begins to practice walking in front of the mirror, then pirouettes, stumbling a bit as she comes to a stop. Graceful? Not really.

She walks over to her closet, opens the door and begins to shuffle through the hanging garments. Her skirts, her shirts, her pants, her dresses. What should she wear? A knocking on the door interrupts.

"Lily, can I come in?" her mom asks.

"Sure!"

Mom walks in wearing a hippie shirt and jeans, looking as beautiful as any girl at school does. "What you doing?"

"Trying to figure out what I'm going to wear tonight."

Mom walks over and sits on the edge of the bed. "Well, it's going to be chilly."

Lily turns to her mom. "I want to wear jeans and boots. Kristen wants me to wear a dress."

"You can wear whatever you want, Lily. Don't let other people dictate what you do."

Lily throws her long hair over her shoulders. "That's how I feel! She can wear what she wants, and I will wear what I want. And I'm going to wear jeans, a shirt, jacket, and my lucky headband."

Her mom clasps something in her hand. That small blue bag that holds the pearls. "Maybe with a string of pearls?"

Lily claps her hands together and jumps up once. She says, "Really? They'll look really great with my headband!"

Her mom reaches slowly into the bag and pulls out the ivory colored beads. They look lovely, as Lily walks over and her mom hands them to her, but they feel heavy, heavier than they did this afternoon, defying that fragile almost ethereal look.

Lily runs over to the mirror, as her mother follows. Carefully, she wraps the pearls around her neck. Her mom steps up behind her to help with the clasp. They look beautiful and fit perfectly. "I will take care of them, Mom. I promise!" She throws her arms around her mom and they hold each other.

Lily softly says, "It makes me so sad when you cry like you

did this morning. I could stay home if you want me to." She pulls from the embrace but does not let go. "I mean it!"

"No! But thank you. Actually, your dad, Christopher, and I are meeting the Tillman's for dinner. There's some leftovers ready for you to heat up." They drop their arms but continue facing each other.

"I can't eat, Mom! I'm too nervous."

"I remember feeling that way."

"That guy that I like is going...well, I mean he might be there." She caught herself, but lied to her mother, which only adds to her agitation.

"Oh, the Lucas guy."

"Yeah, him."

"Just be yourself. If it clicks, it clicks. If it doesn't, it doesn't."

"Yeah, I guess so."

"Don't let anyone pressure you into doing something that you don't want. Promise me that, too."

"I promise."

Her mom turns to leave. "I'm going to run an errand or two and then meet your dad. I probably won't see you until tonight, if I'm still up. I want you to have a good time, but I want you to be careful."

"I will."

"Be home on time!"

"I promise!" Her mom gives her a kiss on her cheek and leaves. The butterflies swarm with that excitement and dread, as Lily throws herself back down on her bed; she fluffs up her pillows behind her head, grabs another and shortly presses the downy softness upon her face, then tosses it to the side. Much to her surprise, a dreamy fatigue drifts up and she surrenders.

—⁂—

She walks down the hall in school. Boys turn from opened lockers to watch as she moves by, purse hanging over her right arm, two books cradled in her left. Some only stare, some sneer. The girls huddle in threes and fours and whisper about her behind their books. She wears a brown skirt, which flows over her taut belly and her hips, but flares to swirl above her knees. Today she wears heels, but her stride defies the girlie presentation, a tomboy after all.

Teachers, male and female, coming back and forth from their classrooms scowl at her. How has she acquired so many enemies? How did Homecoming Queen acquire so much disaffection? Sue Klein says everybody's out to get her. Little Lily Bagwell. Too cute for her own good. Just too damn cute.

She teeters on her heels now knocked off kilter by the stares, the glares, the whispers that ricochet as her heels click and clack across the hallway tiles.

She looks for Sue Klein. She will tell the troublemaker off at last.

Sue, with her long dark hair, big boobs, and an ass a boy in class told her, every boy wants to ride.

Out of all of the boys she could have, Sue wants Lucas.

Still the boys turn from their lockers, their eyes cruise her body. The leg boys start at her ankles and glide their way up. The boob boys stare directly like a bull's eye, the eye a homing pigeon, the eye peeling away the clothes that hide the nipples; yes, it's the nipples they want. The guys too shy to look directly as she passes steal a glance from the corner of their eyes. Lily smiles at them. They are harmless and kind, when they find the courage to spit out a word or two.

Where is she? Sue Klein.

Where could she be?

The teachers turn with one last glare as they ready to pull their classroom doors closed.

"Lily Rose!" they call. "Get yourself to class!" they snarl.

The doors all closed and nobody left to stare, she begins to look through the windows of the classrooms. She feels panicked now.

They have left her behind, looking for Sue Klein.

But where?

Students sitting in the classrooms point at her and laugh. How did she make all of these enemies?

Classroom to classroom she peers in click, clack, click, clack, her heels tap rhythms on the hallway tiles.

When she finds Sue...

Suddenly the windows of the classrooms become portholes on a ship, which allow her to see inside small and white cramped rooms. King-sized beds dominate. Someway, somehow, walking nude now, she moves through the halls, gazes through the portholes, and watches classmates inside engaged in various sexual acts. They resemble those she once saw, her and Kristen, in a book called The Kama Sutra, *a big book with lots of pictures that Kristen's parents stuck on the back of a bookshelf in the basement. It is dark there. Legs and arms, torsos and butts, boobs and penises folding and forming origami designs in the whites, yellows, blacks, and browns of human flesh.*

Suddenly, men and women crowd the halls of the ship dressed in the latest fashion, not the kick-back clothes of the average American, but those of flash and taste, style and design, the apparel of the rich, like those she sees in Vogue, *a magazine she never buys but flips through, when she goes with her mom to shop. Who are these people? Are they real?*

"Why not model, Lily?"

"You would make a perfect model!"

Friends have said. Friends of her parents have said. But never Nana, Mom, or Dad.

Oh, yeah, she would make a great model, especially walking in heels.

They, those dressed in the highest fashion, take her in from head to toe, making notes on pads with pens. She flattens herself against a wall, covering her boobs with her right forearm and hand, and her bush with the other.

Sue Klein. Where is she? Where could that bitch be?

Lily runs down a hall away from the parade of fashion, and begins to peer once more into the portholes. She will recognize Sue's boobs and the rounded ass, she swears she will, but whom will she be with?

As she approaches another porthole, one larger than the others, she hears Sue's giggle, a sound she has heard so many times, as she flirts with boys. She peers in, and there they are. All elbows and knees like some abstract primitive insect, Sue Klein and yes...Lucas's grunt and giggle, sigh and moan, scream and snarl; they are wild animals engaging in the human ritual of sex.

Perhaps they sense her. Perhaps her own sudden sucking in of breath tips them off.

They turn as one to look at her, their eyes wild, lips red as cherries, skin glistening with their sweat. They smile deviously. They know what the sight of them does to her. The girl too cute for her own good. Smart, athletic, and the trait most despised: sweet. This little gal, beloved of her parents, envy of the plain girls, object of desire to so many boys, even those who will never have the courage to say hi; this gal remains a virgin.

—⚶—

Lily awakes with a start, the sights and sounds of her dream haunting her, floating in the ether between that world and this. The butterflies, present before her nap, flutter wildly inside of her now. She rolls onto her right side to see the clock: 11:05 a.m. Nine hours until the rendezvous with Kristen and the boys. Can she look Lucas in the eyes? Now? The image of him and Sue having sex looms largely. Sue will be at the party. She will make a play for Lucas as soon as Lily turns her back.

Okay, she will wear a skirt. She will wear a shirt that makes her small boobs look bigger. She will show off her long, strong legs, and let her clean, shiny hair hang free. She will look desirable and face the consequences. The virgin.

However, she will not, under any circumstance, give up her headband, her lucky and lovely gift from Nana, her grandma. Cornflower blue velvet with tiny pearls sewn into little floral swirls. Nana bought the decades-old headband in an antique store, and gave the treasure to Lily the year she died. She wrapped the gift in another cloth she had tucked away for years, something so worn and soft, it felt almost weightless. Lily once saw the piece of cloth in one of Nana's drawers, along with the piece of ribbon, ivory-colored satin, a remnant of her wedding dress that tied the gift together. The little card stuck under the ribbon read: Lucky today and every day of your life. Nana had a gift of recognizing when an object held luck. Lily knows. A lucky rock she found as a little girl and gave to her daddy helped to heal him, when he first came back from the war.

Lily feels the butterflies in her belly stop. She has nothing to worry about. She has the headband to protect her, and the pearls to help her feel all grown up.

Eric woke up and rolled over hoping to have a little morning sex with Lola, only to see her side of the bed empty and in disarray. Eric had tossed and turned all night, leaving the sheets and blanket crumpled. His anger rose like a rocket, and he determined to find her, uttering and spitting every piece of profanity he knew, and then some. The dumb bitch! That last time he beat her she called the same night, asking him to come pick her up, and there she stood, looking like he hoped, a wide-eyed puppy dog with her tail between her legs. Not this time.

Truthfully, he did not like to see the bruises pooling beneath her soft brown skin, his skin after all. He did not like to see the cuts either, the raw pink oozing red, looking like little mouths or cunts, gasping with a hungry need for air, but cruelty has come easy to Eric for a long, long time.

She should feel grateful that he saved her from the fields. Up here with her family to pick the strawberries, asparagus, the apples, and the cherries, too. She doesn't look Mexican. Not much Indian in her. A bit more compliant than the white girls he'd known. Compliant. He likes that word. Learned it in a crossword puzzle, when he was serving his bit. He did, he saved her from those orchards, farms, and fields.

He had to find her. She could cause him big problems.

He rolled out of bed, showered, and went down to the gym, the small one sitting out on the edge of town in a strip mall. One few frequent. Some big dude all pumped up that looked vaguely familiar pushed his buttons. The dude bench-pressed 300 and lifted 500 without so much as a grunt, perfectly measuring his inhales and his exhales, reminding Eric of a bionic man, maybe Robocop, Jesus, not even a grimace, a tightened jaw, a furrowed brow, and needless to say, not a bead of sweat.

He must have served time, too.

He had lots of practice.

—⁂—

Fresh from a shower at the gym, after his workout, if you can call it that, Eric pulls into a Burger King, pulling his cap down low, cruising to the drive-thru. He orders a Whopper and a tall soda. After he pays and places the bag of food and the drink to the side, he pulls into a space to eat and think. How can he approach this place for women and either leave with her or coerce someone for her whereabouts?

Put on the face. Might not be enough. Good thing he prepped in a number of ways. Wore his tightest jeans. Lola told him once or maybe more than once that he was "crotchy." A beaner knowing that word surprised him. They all want it. They really do.

After inhaling the Whopper in eight bites, he pulls out of the BK parking lot, listening to and appreciating the dual exhaust on his Chevy Silverado. He gave up sports cars years ago, turning to trucks to beef up his image and to cart shit around. A good portion of his time he spends on the road as a semi-truck driver, another reason he works to keep Lola in line. He has no idea how she spends all of her time when he's away, but he suspects she doesn't sit at home twiddling her thumbs.

As he enters Willis, he begins to think about and keep an eye out for Jeff Tillman, his old buddy who, along with Lola, could stir up some shit. He pulls his cap down lower, shrinks his large frame into itself, and hopes his driving a truck, unlike the days of old, will help hide him.

As he moves closer to the joint for women, he begins to sweat, even though cold air blows directly on him from the air conditioner, and the fresh October air flows through the windows. He knows he will have to be his most charming self, when he walks in there.

The joint stands single-story brick with wilted and dying flowers hanging in cutesy plastic pots around the front door and sticking out of large clay urns. Metal black cats, ghosts, and pumpkins soldered onto thin rods, with silly painted faces, arched eyebrows, bulging eyes, and smiles looking more like smirks share the urns with the dying flowers. He pulls into the drive and heads towards the rear. If he has to carry her out, better be out of view. Looking into the rearview mirror of the truck, he practices "the face," three times, reaches down and pulls his package up behind the zipper of his jeans. Two other cars are parked in the lot, neither he recognizes, though not surprising; a person would have to be stupid to spend time in a place where one wrong move could potentially cost him everything.

He will find her, and when he does, he will want to pull her out by her hair. Saw that in a porno movie many years ago, and he used the move a time or two already, including that night when he got Becker back. He pulled that bitch for a long ways.

He must convince them that his Latina is hysterical, making up stories; hell no, he did not touch her. The bruises? She goes wild, throwing herself up against walls and down onto the floor. The cuts, those gaping cunts? The hungry mouths? Self-inflicted. Isn't that what they do these days? Or maybe he can blame it on her father.

Eric gathers his momentum, steps out of the truck, closes the door and walks around to the front of the Grace Shelter, the name engraved into wood and painted, the sign hanging over the door. He clears his throat, throws out his chest and enters.

The place inside looks exactly as he expects. Overstuffed sofas and chairs fill the room, the upholstery all girlie colors, a couple of pieces flowered. Framed pictures hang covered with words he does not even begin to read, but imagines that they are words of "encouragement," or "how to stay strong," crap like that. A bell on the oak door jingles as he opens and closes it. No one sits at the front desk, but as he hears footsteps approaching from down the hallway, he puts on the face.

A good-looking older woman walks into the room, wearing, yeah, you guessed it, a flowered skirt and a bright pink shirt. She asks, "Can I help you?"

"I think so. I'm here for my wife. Her name is Lola Ramirez. She called me to pick her up." Eric watches as her face changes, rather abruptly from friendly and open to squinted eyebrows and a sudden distrust, but she catches herself, motivated now by something different. Reading people comes easy to him. A smile returns on her face but far from authentic. She reaches towards him with her hand, as he puts on his most pathetic look.

"I'm Grace Hopkins, the director of the shelter, and you are?"

He does not take her hand, already feeling like he could shove her wrinkled ass against the wall. "Eric. Name's Eric." He hooks his thumbs into the belt loops on his jeans, as a sort of punctuation. He likes that word. Punctuation. Sounds just like what it is.

"Well, Eric, Lola Ramirez isn't here. And even if she was, we're not required by law to tell you…"

"I'm her husband."

The bitch backs up a couple of steps and walks around behind the old oak desk, no doubt for protection, though he certainly hasn't acted menacing. He likes that word, too.

"That's curious, Eric, because Lola told us she was not married."

"So she was here."

"She was here, but she is not now."

Eric steps towards the hall, cups his mouth with his hands and calls, "Lola! Lola!"

Gladys, or whatever her name is, steps out from behind the desk and blocks him. "Please don't do that." Is she nuts? He could push her against the wall with two fingers.

"She's my wife," he growls, then catches himself. He puts a whine into this one, "Did she come in here all banged up again?"

"You need to leave. She's not here."

"Her father has been abusing her since she was a little girl. How bad does she look?" He calls down the hall again, "Lola! Lola!"

A door bursts open and a good-looking brunette, thirty or so, big tits, wearing jeans, strides up towards the older broad and him. She asks with concern, "Is everything okay here?"

Gloria, or whatever her name is, turns to her, ""This...ah... gentleman..." Eric notes the disdain around her mouth. His face drops, but as he looks at the sexy chick, he props the mask back up. He'll work this one. Gloria continues, "He's looking for Lola." The two lock eyes for a couple of counts, hatching some kind of plan. They turn back to him.

The young one says, "Lola's not here."

"Yeah, I got that. So who are you?"

She stretches out her hand to him. He figures he better take this one. Her hand feels firm and dry, not soft and sweaty like his own. He tempers his shake. She introduces herself, "I'm Brenda Becker Bagwell."

First thought, now that's a tongue twister. Second thought, holy shit, and the name slips out of him, "Becker?"

"Yes. Do you know the Beckers? Maybe Martin, my father? He's County Supervisor."

He lets her hand go and the face drops. His mind races. Who the fuck could she be? He snaps himself back to the present. "Look...I'm worried about her." Clearly, not safe here, he needs to find Lola. "Do you know where she is?"

"I'm sorry, no," the brunette answers, but she doesn't look sorry.

"We're prohibited by law," the old one says.

The law! The law! The fucking law! One part of him, the part that landed him in trouble all those years ago, wants to slam these two bitches, but he feels hot and his hands are sweating more. Anxiety, yes, he feels anxiety not fear. He blurts out, "Look, I know what you're thinking. Like I told her," pointing to the old one, "Lola's dad has been beating on her since she was a kid. She went to visit him yesterday..."

"Mr....what did you say your name was?" the good-looking one asks.

The older one fills in, "Eric. His name is Eric."

The Becker broad needles him, "Eric what?"

"Well, it ain't Ramirez." Shit! He fucked up again.

Surprisingly, the Becker connection steps up closer to him. Both these bitches have balls. Did Coach have a daughter? "Lola's not here and there are plenty of laws protecting us from telling you where she is."

"Brenda...," the older one pulls her back and declares to him, "You need to leave now, or we'll call the police."

He raises his hands in surrender, and even though his heart races, he manages not to strike out. "I love her. I'm just trying to find her."

Brenda, and he likes that name, steps up to him again. "I think that Lola will call you when she's ready."

"She did call me."

"Why would she tell you to pick her up here when she's clearly not?"

He drops his hands, feeling his face turn redder. "You bit... you, yes, you're right. I must have misunderstood where she was."

"Yes, that's probably it," the older one condescends.

Eric, unable to maintain the face a moment longer, caught between kicking the two bitches' faces in or turning and fleeing says, "Thank you. Thank you for your...help, ladies." He turns and as his boots pound hollow across the rug, also flowered, also girlie colors, and another prick in his skin, he heads for the front door.

Back in his truck now, Eric raises his hands from his lap and watches them tremble. What the fuck! He's not a pansy! Why is he shaking? Jesus! He cannot believe women could affect him so. And this Becker chick? She could be his daughter. He's pretty sure Coach had one. What's the chances of that? Of course, she could be a niece or who knows what, maybe not related at all.

Where is the bitch? Lola. Why hasn't she called? Will she press charges? This could be trouble.

The beginning of the end. If she opens her mouth about that other matter… If Tillman opens his…

Without evidence, they have nothing. The car is gone, the earth where he wrought his revenge scrubbed clean by rain, by snow, by wind, by the paws of critters making their daily and nightly tracks. They have nothing. They never had anything. On that night in October so long ago heaven smiled down upon him, worked in concert with him, to help even the score.

—⁂—

The night after he did it, he hiked back to his car, pulling the woolen mask and the gloves off, disposing them into a plastic bag. He drove out slowly, down a path cut long ago, not a tire mark anywhere along the 35 feet; but when he hit the road, he began to blast AC/DC "Big Balls," and a sense of triumph exhilarated him. He headed for a local bar, and pounded shots and beers. He stuck to himself, didn't invite the company of anyone he knew, just sat there swaying back and forth on the black vinyl of the barroom stool, tapping out beats blasting from the jukebox with finger tips and palms. When he began to see the world in a blur, he headed home.

She didn't plead for herself one time. That thought made him laugh. How could she with her mouth stuffed? And her face…revealed nothing. Maybe the cold had numbed her.

Or maybe she wanted it.

He remembered her fair skin in that full moon light, yes, he remembered that moon, how ghostly she appeared, that white skin covered, barely covered, in the shreds of a nightgown, those scrapes long and red, with the thinnest threads of blood, and the cuts, those angry mouths, those angry cunts open and oozing.

Still living with his father at that time, he arrived back to the trailer. More a pigpen than a home. His father's live-in. Carrie Joe, a pill popper, unconscious half the time, cranked out of her mind the other, sat up that night watching the tube.

She looked up as he stumbled in. "Well, looks as if you've had your share." He plopped down on the couch, brown suede shiny in spots with wear, and dipped his hand down between her legs.

She thrust his hand away. "Are you fucking crazy? If he walked in here…"

Eric leaned over and sloppily kissed her neck. She jumped up. "Go to fucking bed and leave me alone!"

"I gotta hard one," he slurred.

"Yeah, maybe, but probably not."

Pushing himself up into a stand, he backhanded her in the face, and as she covered the sting with one hand, he stumbled to his room.

A night of triumph that ended badly.

—m—

His shaking under control now, Eric heads out on the road considering his options. He knows he needs to get the hell out of the area, out of the state. He needs to head south, and he will, but before he leaves, why not one last hurrah? Yes, why not one more excursion into cruelty? After all, he's so damn good at it. Why let a gift go to waste?

14
Belly Up

Saturday 1:21 p.m.

The morning started out a little on the strange side. At the gym a beefy dude walked up to lift next to him, ricocheting his eyes all through Jack's routine and growing perceptually agitated by the minute. Jack just kept his mouth shut, and fortunately, he did too. Jack was naturally strong, and always had been; his muscles developed quickly. In the end, the dude's jealousy threw him off his own game; losing concentration can do that. Jack walked away while the dude drenched his gym towel, mopping sweat off his face and body.

That same envy contributed to the incident in prison, when three inmates jumped him in the shower, costing him his ERD (early release date). Shit! He didn't like thinking about it, so he punched the play button on his tape player and listened to Herbie Hancock to soothe himself.

He headed for the car wash where he drove his SUV through and then stopped to have a cup of coffee at the diner and talk with a few old timers about the state of the world, war in Iraq, and the frenzy to keep tabs on every American. After all, there could be a terrorist among us. Jack wondered why the U.S. was over in Iraq when the terrorists, who hijacked the planes all came from Saudi Arabia, but the old timers didn't question anything, exhibiting an unwavering patriotism. Our leaders are educated men, wise about the world. They would never lead us astray. These same men believed in the red, white, and blue, of opportunity – every one equal and all that. One learns very quickly when incarcerated that equality in the good 'ol USA is a crock of shit. He spent twenty years behind bars with many men who lacked opportunity, well, they did have offers, if they wanted to follow in the footsteps of uncles, brothers, sometimes even mothers and aunts, because the fathers were seldom in the picture. Uncle Tyrone gives his nephew a shiny blue Olds 98 for a graduation gift and asks how he affords it. Uncle T drapes his arm around the kid's shoulders and says, "Well, Son, funny you should ask." Grandma runs a gambling ring out of the dining room, and both sisters work the gang members to buy designer clothes. One dude he served time with watched two assassins pump seven rounds into the chest of his drug-dealing daddy. One of his brothers caught a bit for Murder I, and the other for Murder II, and he himself was serving time for manslaughter. There were many stories like that. Men striving to work out of poverty with a knife, a gun, a line of bullshit, so long it could reach Mars.

Jack himself grew up without a father, as did all his brothers. Mom lived in the bottom of a gallon jug of Gallo, out most nights, rarely cooked or cleaned, rarely talked to them, let alone touch them. She worked in a bottling plant, and who knows where the money went. Jeff and he made their way okay, except of course his younger brother's thievery. Jordan, the second youngest hid away, occupying himself with books and drawing, disappearing out into nature whenever he could. Ironically, this sensitive one, the creative one was shot in the chest by a hunter's bullet, or so authorities assumed. Jack was incarcerated, at the time, and Jeff had hit the road, working the cars. James told him about it, just twelve, when Jordan succumbed to his wound. He and his friend Billy went out to the spot where Jordan died. Afterwards, they asked the police questions. It just didn't add up. James said he remembers seeing Jordan that morning dressed in a red shirt. There ain't nothing red on a white tailed deer. Anyway, they know that the hunter stumbled upon what he thought would be his "kill." His footprints trampled into the sand of the forest leading up to and then away from his young brother's body, so the chicken shit coward, whoever the son of a bitch was, left the boy to bleed to death. Jack imagines his young brother his back against the tree, sketch pad on his lap, that red shirt saturated with the blood of his body, eyes losing focus with the loss of vital fluid, mouth hanging open, so weak, so close to death. Did he even have the strength to utter the words, "Help me." The piece of shit ran, allowing that boy to die alone.

James, the youngest and by far the best looking, resembled a handsome Indian brave. James did have Indian blood. His brother, painfully shy, could not even look a person in the eyes, but he worked miracles with his hands. Could take just about anything apart and put it back together without a manual. Jack had nine years on him, and when he started bringing cars home, James, even as a little kid stood under the hood with him. The kid could not keep his gifted hands off something else. Jack caught him masturbating so many times it became laughable. Jack figures in an empty house, where needs were seldom met, James took his pleasure where he could. Didn't take long before the women in town caught on. Jack knows for a fact that Doris Rentchler got her hands on James. Pulled that boy into the back of her car when he was fourteen and fucked him hard. Told James that he had the biggest and most beautiful dick she had ever seen. James told him that, and knowing Doris that was quite an admission.

Around that same time, James and Billy Bagwell hung out like brothers. Did everything together. They were hell on wheels. The two boys engaged in every sport and outside activity imagined. Absolute daredevils. James often told him stories when he visited Jack in the correctional facility about winning trophies from sports events, jumping out of planes, plunging off viaducts on bungee cords, zooming over the hills on dirt bikes. Jack can't remember how many times James came to visit with Jeff before he left, or with Billy, and very occasionally Mom, sporting a patch, a sling, or a cast.

Then came the day that Jack foresaw trouble when James started talking about Brenda. Jack sensed something there that shouldn't be for the wife of a best friend. He didn't feel surprised when he heard that James had moved in with Brenda while Billy served over in the Gulf. Jack feared it would not end well. Not well at all. Why should it? James and Brenda were wrong in hooking up, but Jack knows how strong the forces of nature can be. After all, he let his anger incarcerate him for twenty years. He could have killed the man, shit, not a man, a fucking pedophile that molested James. Sometimes he wishes he had killed him. What happened to the son of a bitch anyway? But if he had killed him, he wouldn't be where he lives now with Debbie and helping to raise James' boy. Things turned out well for Jack. He's a lucky man and he knows it, because if he had killed Sisko or any one of the three fuckers that tried to rape him in prison, he would have spent the rest of his life incarcerated.

After his powwow with the old timers, Jack swung back by the house to pick up Jimmy. He promised to take him to the show. Jimmy loved media, video games, and films with lots of special effects. The kid wanted to see *Two Towers*. Jack looked forward to seeing the film too.

Jack walked into the house, and Jimmy came running out of his room.

Before they could leave, Debbie walked out of the kitchen, approached him and laid one beautiful hand with pink painted nails upon his arm. She looked up into his eyes and said, "I have to talk to you." This sounded ominous. Without saying anything to him, Jimmy walked back to his room.

"What's up, Babe?" he asked.

"I did it again," she stated.

She didn't have to tell him what. "Okay, with who?"

Her eyes pled for understanding. She avoided the question, never a good sign. She must be afraid to tell him because he will be especially unhappy.

"I hope you're not talking about Jeff?"

She grabbed his arm with both hands. "I never planned it, I swear..."

He turned from her, heading for the door. He yelled over his shoulder, "Let's go, Jimmy!"

"I'm sorry, Jack. I'm very sorry," she called after him.

"Go to a meeting, Debbie."

Jimmy ran down the hall and together he and Jack left.

—∽—

Jimmy and Jack stand in line at the theatre, waiting to get in. Jack watches the boy with his Gameboy in hand glance at the pre-teen girls milling around on the indoor-outdoor carpet, covered with ugly purple and green geometrics. He watches the girls glance over at Jimmy as well. Not expecting the theatre to be this crowded, Jack begins to fidget, rocking his weight from one foot to the other, crossing and re-crossing his muscled arms, a bit sore now from the morning's workout. He just wants to sit his ass down into the seat and escape, give his brain a rest, and especially not think about Debbie and her addiction. No wonder Jeff seemed a bit flustered this morning. He doesn't want to imagine where or how she confronted his only living brother. Jeff probably looks at him as a schmuck.

As he stares off into space, two young men and a girl wander up and just sort of position themselves in line, in front of Jack and Jimmy, cutting in as if no one would notice.

Jack's anger still rises like a fire in the hole, and he wanted to take the two male smart asses by the collars of their jackets and escort them, no, fling their asses down the stairs of the theatre entrance, but he's worked hard, very hard, to check his behavior. After all, he took anger management classes in and outside of prison. Instead, he steps up closer to the one longhaired little prick and whispers in his ear, "Unless you feel like going to the hospital today with a few broken bones, I'd turn and take your two friends with you to the back of the line."

The prick turns, curling his hands into fists, ready to take some action, but his eyes widen as he takes in Jack's girth and height, and steps back. He mutters, "Sure, buddy, sure."

Jack doesn't hear what he says to his two friends, but they scatter out quickly.

Jimmy turns and looks up at Jack. "I thought they were cutting in. I felt like pushing them out of the line."

"You can still make your point without getting physical." He places his hand on Jimmy's shoulder, and the gesture actually feels okay. The boy smiles up at him. "Take it from me, who learned the hard way. Words and presence can say everything, and save pain and hardship."

"Even someone my size?"

"You'll be a man before you know it."

With that, the line starts filing into the theatre.

They sit down, snuggling back into the comfortable chairs, not the straight back monstrosities of the older days, but more like a lounger, with even a bit of leg space for a big man like Jack.

As soon as the film begins, Jimmy's eyes grow big as donuts, the Gameboy dangling out of his hand. Jack too becomes lost into Jackson's world of incredible detail, beauty and special effects, but he remains haunted, feeling like today he wades in his shit. Maybe because of Jeff's visit, and the past that inevitably rolls out, the memories of their childhood, his role more or less of father for his three brothers, and ultimately the poor example he gave them, letting his anger, which once unleashed became impossible to corral, cause him to lose twenty years of his life. He had been close, so close to his ERD, but the shower incident changed all that.

—❦—

Razor wire mounted like a halo on the fencing surrounded the prison. Nothing abnormal about that. A couple towers with armed guards rose above to give a bird's-eye view of the mice in the maze, or more accurately, the sharks in a tank.

Shake them up. Keep them agitated.

Inside the fences topped with what surely would slice and dice were the administrative building, the school, the chow hall, and ten housing units. Each unit housed one hundred and sixty men, in quarters so tight, the sharks could not help but be rattled. Cubicles bedded eight men on bunks with a wafer-thin mattress, pillow, blanket, and a locker for belongings. The stench of bad breath, dirty feet, farts, and armpits floated above like a strange and repugnant perfume. The walls surrounding the cubicles were four-feet high, eliminating any semblance of privacy. In addition, the unit held three small shower rooms, replete with corner fungus, mildew, cum, and small pools of stale water. The inmates fought amongst themselves for three telephones, creating lines of men so hungry for contact with the outside world that fights often erupted. Desperate men flung caution to the wind and brandished shivs to cut, poke and penetrate. A simple desire to make a call could result in a trickle to a river of warm and sticky red.

While incarcerated, Jack spent time working out, something he saw as a lifesaving measure, and did save his life on the fateful day in the shower. They also assigned him work duty, paid him pennies for it, but he managed to climb his way up a ladder to eventually be assigned yard maintenance, which meant mowing lawns, attending to gardens, and regularly breathing in fresh air. Studying also occupied his time. He spent countless hours studying the Native Americans, and everyone knew it. He spent so many years filling his mind with their customs, beliefs, and general culture that the other sharks began calling him "chief." For many years, no one bothered him. His size and attitude, a humble authority that offended few, kept him in a place of respect, and earned him admiration from some. But not everyone.

Three of his fellow inmates had banned together early in their bit. All three involved with the Gangster Disciples, had run drugs and killed or so the tattooed teardrops indicated under the outside corners of their eyes. They were serving long sentences under the federal Maximum Minimum Law. The fact that they were men of color meant nothing to Jack, but the fact that this pumped-up honky held so much power in Unit Three meant a lot to them.

They were going to nail his ass.

Literally.

Jack could feel their resentment. Well, any dumb shit could see their seething vehemence for him, but feeling fear or showing fear was uncharacteristic for Jack, a code he lived by as a "warrior." He figured they would work to defeat him, but he just carried on. What didn't help at all were two COs that sometimes worked together who also resented the hell out of the "chief." The fact that he was looked up to, respected, and in some aspects admired, irked the hell out of those boys too. They were the authority. They wanted what he had.

Jack stood in the shower that night, and he remembers being lost in his head on detail, beauty and, yes, the special effects of an Apache war dance. He could see the ceremony in his mind's eye; he could hear the chants invoking bravery, clarity, and the blessing of the Great Spirit. Smoke rose in trails off the fires, evoking the assistance of the ancestors.

His eyes closed, he felt the space around him shift. He opened his eyes to see the shower room empty except for the two gang members standing behind him and another one at the door. He swore he also saw just the briefest glimpse of a CO uniform pass quickly.

The man behind him grabbed his arms and pulled them together behind his back as the other began to punch him repeatedly in the guts. Now these men worked out, too, and although not as tall or bulky, they were far from pushovers.

Jack began fighting with all his might to pull his arms free as the man behind began to kick his leg out to knock Jack off of his feet and onto the floor face down. If he succeeded, Jack would be theirs. The man in front began punching him in the face now, as the third gang member rushed in. Three against one. This one began to throw fists into his head. The goal to make him dizzy, even unconscious, to do whatever it takes to bring him down onto his belly. He swore he saw, from one corner of a sore and swollen eye, both COs hovering in the doorway, sanctioning the act, cheering them on in silence.

But as they say, hell hath no fury like a man fighting for his life. Now maybe the Native chants he heard in his head served him that day, calling forth the assistance he needed, the smoke rising like a prayer, for he felt a surge of energy rise like a wave before the break, and suddenly he was a giant, his muscles doubled in size. Maybe his ultimate benevolence in character and humble ways bought him, or earned him, the help of special powers. Just as he began to fall, his arms broke free and with the strength of Hercules, he grabbed one man throwing him against the wall, the sound of bones breaking like wet timber. With his right elbow, he struck another in the throat, forcing a cloud of breath out into the hot, humid air. With his right foot he kicked the third in the balls, forcing him to double over, his face contorted with pain like no other. Before the three had a chance to recover, Jack went to town, punching and kicking in a hurricane of adrenalin, pumping, pumping, watching as blood drops flew through the air, to land, dilute, and dissolve down the wet shower walls. Every crunch of cartilage fed his fire, every cracking bone a spark, every moan and groan, squeal and scream a song that soothed his ears.

When he finished, when his adrenalin ebbed, the three "bad asses" laid crumpled on the floor, their limbs jutting out in unnatural angles, two out of three unconscious, the floor littered with hair, and teeth, and blood. The two COs rushed in, slipping and sliding on the strange soup and tazored him; the painful volts of electricity rendered him helpless but did not knock him down. They then forced him into a belly chain with cuffs and hustled him away as the crowd of inmates pulled into the ruckus through the magnet of curiosity parted like the Red Sea.

—⚛—

As the credits for the film roll, Jimmy bubbles with excitement, "Aragorn was such a great warrior, wasn't he? And the faeries, weren't they cool? I want to learn to shoot an arrow, Jack! It was so great when…"

"They were cool! Come on, Son, let's go."

Jack feels claustrophobic, as they slowly walk out into the swarm. As they reach the doors, Jack and Jimmy pick up speed, and the unseasonably warm October wind hits their faces. Warm or not, the air still feels like freedom.

Jimmy looks up at Jack as they quickly walk towards the SUV. "Mom said we were going out for dinner."

"That's right."

"Will Uncle Jeff be there?"

"I believe so."

"Jack, have you ever seen his tattoos?"

"No. Why?"

"One is a swastika."

"A what?"

"A swastika."

"That's what I thought you said."

"Is he a good guy or a bad guy?"

"He's a good guy, Jimmy. I'm sure," but Jack wonders.

As they climb into the vehicle, Jack thinks about how lucky he has been. Free of prison, working a good-paying job, a beautiful wife, a boy to raise, but he cannot ignore the agitation chawing at his insides. Yes, the issue with Debbie's addiction serves as part of it, but something else lurks. Jeff came back to visit, but returned for another reason too. A reason that Jack thinks involves the past and dirty deeds.

15
Twirl

Saturday 4:30 p.m.

Now that another day had dawned, Jeff could catch a closer look at the town. His first sweep, the evening before, reflected those impacts of national phenomena like outsourcing, and the expanding gap between top and bottom classes through diminishing wages. On this second look, he could see the microcosmic changes in this place he once called home: small factories and businesses closed, strip malls looming on the edges of town, and smack in the middle of what once was a huge field where strawberries grew, a sprawling, industrial-looking Walmart. Oh, yes, one-stop shopping at the fingertips, and the unfortunate reason so many family owned shops had closed. A few remained: Joe's Barber, Willis Flowers and, of course, the Willis Café.

On the other hand, Willis Park looked expanded with more swings, bars, slides, and a field or two of baseball diamonds. A couple of new schools replaced old ones, including the old brick middle school built in the early twentieth century. Of course, banks and churches flourished. They always do. In hard times, people often turn to religion for solace, and loans to help them through. These changes to his former home spread out before him, as he searched for a man, probably a murderer, who has lived under the radar for too long.

Once his life slowly turned around and he recovered a sense of integrity, he imagined two scenarios: contacting the local police and tipping them off, or better yet, tracking down Eric and confronting him. What would happen if he brought the murder up to Eric? Would his old "friend" admit what he had done? He just might kill Jeff to keep his mouth shut. Eric must remember how many times he pissed and moaned about Coach Becker, while incarcerated. He vowed he would get Becker back good. As for Jeff? He held no animosity for Coach. If he were to witness the same thing now, unlike the days of old, he would feel morally obliged. The problem was that even if Eric confessed to him, it wouldn't help much. Only a confession to a police officer or concrete evidence could convict him. Jeff's task would be to seek out and find Eric's Achilles heel, bring him to his knees, appeal to his better self, and convince him to surrender to police.

First, he has to find the man who could well have left years ago or even be dead. He had scoured public records, including those of prisons, state and federal, and found nothing.

He had to make up for lost time.

He started at what this small town passed as a gym. Some chain joint sitting on the outskirts of town in a strip mall. Eric had prided himself on staying ripped, and he used his size and bulk as a form of intimidation. Jeff thought he might catch Jack there, too, but didn't find either. Jeff stopped at the front desk and asked if Eric Thompson came today, and the young blonde girl working there stated she did not know him.

Then Jeff headed for the café, riding there in his Lexus with windows rolled down. He figured he could sit over a cup of coffee and strike up a chat with the town's folks. He spoke briefly with the server, the cafe owner, and a few of the old timers who all spoke highly of his brother Jack and professed no knowledge of an Eric Thompson. He even ran into a girl he had gone to school with, and she seemed happy to see him, even flirtatious. She asked him if he would like to meet sometime for lunch or dinner. He took her number, but doubted he would be around long enough to call her. Besides, his heart belonged to someone else, though he tried like hell to forget her. In his mind's eye, her smile would flash, and then he would remember her long strong legs, and her skin that felt so soft, the color of cocoa. He could hear her voice, too, sometimes whispering in his ears, and he wondered if, although he felt foolish to think it, he conjured her in spirit form. He wanted desperately to harden his heart, but considering it took thirty some years to reopen it, he felt dumbfounded on how to shut the organ down again. Up until Desiree, he spent so many years beating off to porno and negotiating hand jobs, blowjobs, or a quick fuck, he considered himself an adolescent in the world of relationship. During the height of addiction, he jacked off a half dozen times a day, mostly to small girls and big dicks. Desiree introduced him to a completely new world, one in which people of all colors and religions dwelled. Much to his surprise, though the transition didn't happen overnight, he felt comfortable there.

Once his thoughts began on Desiree, coupled with an avalanche of memories from being back in Willis, Jeff found himself feeling itchy, a feeling that even chain smoking could not touch. After a while, he fought and succeeded bringing his attention back on Eric, but as he headed for the local watering holes to find answers, an old challenge loomed.

The first bar, Harvey's, another of the few holdouts from former times, held only a handful of afternoon drinkers. Like a good boy, he ordered a Coke, and switched between watching a golf game on an overhead tube and exchanging words with the bartender, a man as old as the bar itself. He didn't start asking about Eric, but worked his way up, not wanting the bartender to think he was a cop or something. When he finally did, the old man, Mike by name, said he remembered Eric, but hadn't seen him in years. He described Eric as a smart ass, a loose cannon, someone he never felt happy to see walk in.

Bar two was a newer joint with tall tables and hanging plants, a place where he figured the yuppies, if there were any in Willis, hung out. Another Coke, another chat with the bartender, this time a woman who never heard of Eric, but she wasn't good at remembering names, she said.

Now he sits in tavern number three, and this one named The Brown Bear, situated between towns, held quite a crowd.

Four large-screen TVs perch above the three pool tables, three dartboards decorate the walls, and a scattering of tables and chairs fill the room. A long black-topped bar horseshoes one end. Jeff, on a stool, sits roughly in the middle, his body stiff with stress. The barrage of hometown memories and thoughts of a pregnant Desiree continue to hammer down on him; a feeling creeps up that he fights like mad to hold down, a desire for alcohol. The memory of fruit flies lighting around his mother on a hot summer day, her wine-soaked body drawing them in does not stop his urge. The memory of Jack beating Sisko to a pulp, also on a hot summer day, when his big brother realized that the drunk had been molesting James, does nothing to quiet him. Nor does the memories of his own drunken days, when aggression and revenge were his driving forces, leaving innocent people lying still in their own blood. Oh boy, does he fight to keep the barrage at bay. Just one.

Just one shot of bourbon.

One little shot.

That's all.

He's stable enough now not to let one roll into a dozen. He's stable enough.

Yeah, right. Can't take another drink ever again.

That's what the friends of Bill say.

As he nurses his third Coke, the sugar and caffeine already causing his palsied hands to shake harder, someone slips up to sit on the stool to his right. He turns to take a glimpse, and to his surprise, there sits an old friend of his from high school, Chad Malcom. Chad looks about twenty-five pounds heavier, and grey streaks his hair.

Jeff says, "Jesus, Chad, what a sight for sore eyes!"

Chad responds, "How the hell are you? Haven't seen you in what, twenty-odd years or some, I'd guess."

"That's about right. What ya been doing?"

"Working in a bank as a loan officer. Got a wife, a couple of kids. Believe it or not, even a grandkid."

"Whoa! Now that's scary!" They laugh. Jeff remembers his laugh, a distant jackhammer on a summer day.

The bartender strolls over to them, his steps squishing along on the rubber floor mat, and asks, "Are you ready for another?"

Chad answers, "Sure. What about you, Jeff? What you drinking there?"

"Coke. I'm fine right now."

The bartender turns and squishes away; Jeff imagines the filth and germs lurking beneath that mat.

Chad asks, "You don't drink?"

"Oh, yeah, just drank too much last night."

"I don't know what I'd do if I couldn't drink. Twenty years married. Kids. A job sitting at a desk all day. What can I tell you? I'm grateful for everything I've got, but sometimes I need a little break. Are you back here now?"

"No, no. Just visiting." The bartender sets a fresh drink in front of Chad. Jeff hands him a ten.

Chad says, "You don't have to get that."

"Of course."

"Well, thank you! Where are you living, Jeff?"

"Southern California. Keeping books for a company. No wife, no kids."

"Still playing the field, huh?"

"Something like that." He watches Chad assess him from the corner of his eye. Probably wondering if he's gay. So what. He will not be staying in Willis long enough to make any of that matter. Besides, at this point in his life, he doesn't give a damn.

Chad grabs at something to fill the silence. "We sure had good times out on that football field. You know, they use that as a middle school now. Built a new high school."

"I saw that while riding around today. Yeah, we had some good times. Is Coach Becker still around?"

"Oh, yeah, but he doesn't coach anymore. He's County Supervisor. Has been for quite a while." Chad hesitates and looks at Jeff solemnly. "You heard his wife was murdered, right?"

"Oh, yeah. Heard it on the news."

"They never did find the killer. Probably one of those psychos you hear about sometimes. Just passing through."

"Yeah, probably."

"Coach had a drinking problem for a long time. Everybody knew it. I think he finally sobered up, though." Chad hesitates, but only for a moment. "Hey, whatever happened to Thompson? You were friends with him for a while."

Jeff startles. Now why would Chad ask about Eric a beat after Becker? Sure, they all played ball together, but did Chad suspect Eric, too? "Funny you should ask that. I was just about to ask you the same question."

"I saw him around some after he got out of prison, then not for a long time. A couple years back I saw him riding through town in a pickup. He looked the other way. Then Andy Dibble, do you remember him? He told me he thought he saw Thompson driving a semi out Denton way a few months back."

Finally, some good news. He's probably still in the area. "I'd like to find him."

"I don't know where he lives, or who he drives for, but he is around. He got you in some trouble back in the day, didn't he?"

"Yeah, well, nothing I didn't do willingly. Young and stupid, you know. But like I was saying, I would like to find him."

"I wish I could help."

"Well, let me give you my number, and if you hear anything..."

"Sure."

After giving Chad his number, his old friend leaves, and Jeff eyeballs the row of Bourbon, licking his lips.

—⁂—

Chad insinuated that Eric somehow manipulated Jeff into the delinquency they shared. Au contraire, Jeff very willingly collaborated the crimes. He felt pissed off at the world as a teenager. He didn't like growing up in a fatherless home. He didn't like that his mother drank herself silly and rarely mothered any of the four boys. He didn't like how, although she made pretty good money, the boys saw little to none of it. Damn right, he had a chip on his shoulder. A chip the size of Mars. Add into that the minorities rising and the poor white boy falling, and you have a recipe for one pissed-off teen.

That frustration snowballed over the years following his release from Half Moon Lake for Boys. He kept a tamper on it while incarcerated, but once out in the world on his own, he developed bit by bit into a dangerous person. Though he was never prosecuted for his crimes, he damn well should have been. If he had been, it would have slowed him down. Although not a murderer ever, he came close to it; his reconciliation of conscience had to do with apologizing to the people his ignorance had affected, and making sure Eric paid for his crime. In this way, he could complete the Eighth Step, making amends for his own transgressions. He actively worked the steps over the last couple of years, a system that worked for him, though he never felt crazy about the Christian element, for he knew well the centuries-old dirty work of the church.

Working on the stock car circuit took him into the South on many occasions. In the bars, in the cafes, places the circuit folks hung, the red necks flared. He even met some members of the Ku Klux Klan. No shit! They roared. They spent every minute on a podium. They took pride in their robes and hoods. They took pride in the crosses they erected and set on fire. Their words were on fire, too, as they teetered on those podiums, spreading messages of hate; they were young, old, whiskers on their jaws, their eyes alight, with that dark force of prejudice that served as kindling.

Jeff understood their disdain against particular populations. He shared that disdain. He did not like the injustice, the inequity; he flat out didn't like it. In those taverns and cafes, he listened as they identified the culprits: the Jews sitting in the seats of power, the people of color, whatever color, who stole their jobs, and especially the blacks for the audacity of thinking themselves equal.

Jeff listened, but he did not join.

He continued working in the circuit, moving from town to town. Somewhere along the line, he met a member of The System. Now these were some badass dudes. To them, donning hoods and robes and burning crosses looked like dress up and playtime. Although in years gone by, the KKK had certainly committed horrendous acts, The System had a long-term plan. Stockpile weapons of terror, including cyanide, and drop the deadly chemical into the water systems of metropolitan regions, rob armored trucks, cut down enemies who spouted "out-right lies" in front of microphones. No child's play here.

Jeff listened, but he did not join.

In Southern California, in a place densely populated with people from around the world, the separatist white boys still managed to find him. Jeff still wonders how. Did he have a sign on his back, something stamped upon his forehead? A band of brothers, and a few sisters, too, intent on wreaking havoc. Skinheads, Nazi tattoos, hard-core music, and the dream of another kind of country – one where only white men ruled, and always would.

Jeff listened, and he joined.

At the mosh pits with his newfound brothers and a few sisters too, he found an outlet for his rage. He often came home bloody, a mixture of his and theirs, and covered with bruises, bumps and cuts. They were lords of the mosh pits, and though most of those who attended these concerts were of like mind, the brutes preyed on the weak to toughen them and themselves.

Jeff worked his way up. Sometimes, emboldened after a show, they would stalk the streets looking for a person of color to harass and beat. Jeff never felt fond of these attacks, but now one with the White Aryan Rebels, he had to prove his manhood and allegiance to remain a member. He shaved his head, sported eight-inch Doc Marten's with steel toes, and began inking on his body the philosophy he lived by.

Then he met Tom Washke.

Nothing stood out about Washke, except his self-importance. Middle aged of average height, average weight, he fathered three boys, one a skinhead, the others not, and kept a dog, a Rottweiler at his side. The father of the Rebels, he ran a repair shop, and lived in the rural suburbs of Southern Cal. He collected Nazi paraphernalia, which he displayed in one room, and two swastikas hung out openly in two other areas of his home. The Rebels had their very own newsletter, which depicted people of color in despicable terms, and every editorial spot lighted the Jews as the people who ran the banks, established the rules, and wielded the power. Because the middle class continued to disappear into the elite and the poor, the Jews were in need of a good round up and sent forward into designated states, if not murdered outright, as they had been once before.

The Rebels worked to speak out, vociferously, and act out, even if that meant arrest. In the height of their mania, these actions included the murder of a man up in the North. Jeff, though not a part of it, knew well the young men who were.

By that time, in the 1980s, Washke had realized that their small-time actions accomplished nothing really, and that the change he wanted, although wished for in a rebellion, as pictured in *The Turner Diaries*, would have to be accomplished differently. When the former leader of the KKK, David Duke, won a senatorial seat, Washke realized substantial change would come through working from within, embedded however peripherally around the seats of power, small and large.

Washke guided Jeff through an education and helped find him a job in a company large enough that covertly espoused similar philosophies. Jeff grew his hair out, covered his tattoos and spoke when necessary. His temper cooled and he enjoyed the conservative business attire, and through much of the nineties the former Rebels watched as conservatives, especially those on the extreme right, took seat after seat, higher position after higher position. Jeff bought a house, hired call girls, or spent evenings alone beating off to small girls, big dicks.

Even then, through those years, he took little pleasure acting out violently, but when rage releases, sometimes like a tornado, fed by chants and stats and images of inequality and jobs stolen and the rich getting richer and the poor getting poorer, the calm feeling after, a depletion, an emptiness became the ultimate goal.

When he heard that Becker's wife had been murdered and suspected who the culprit might be, he just looked the other way, already a man cut off from humanity. He had set aside emotion and burnished up his steel. He never felt the bumps, the cuts, the bruises, not even the stabs, especially not them. With a sharp knife, the flesh cuts like butter. The tornado of discontent and his emotional neutrality kept him captured in its twirl, and not until Desiree did he begin to manage his integrity.

—ɷ—

Unhappy to feel vulnerable again, capable of pain, his resistance wears thin, so he asks the bartender for a shot, just one, just to sandpaper the edges, just to dull the acute nature of the heart. After all, he cannot confront Eric as a wounded man. He orders the liquid fire. He throws the bourbon back, and it tastes good.

16

Thin Place

Saturday 4:45 p.m.

Driving out into the country surrounding Willis, Brenda begins slowly and deeply to breathe in and out, and in and out, hoping for calm. She heads for the woods, a woman on a mission. Maybe once she enters the woods and watches as the trees sway, listens to the birds tweet and trill, shriek and coo, maybe then. She will walk across the earth covered with moss and needles, dried grass and weeds, and through the branches and the brambles, maybe then, nature will work in concert to absorb the heaviness from her heart. She will see more clearly. The small lakes and ponds will reflect the sky, erase separation, connect her to both heaven and earth, and hold her in the middle.

Just stay present and breathe.

Breathe. Just breathe, damnit!

Let the past go, embrace the present and breathe.

Yes, yes, there, the beauty of these country roads, so lovely, they are even marked with small blue and white signs that designate them as scenic. The hilly, finely planed roads wind through hardwood forests, evergreen stands, wetlands, grassy fields, and sparkling ponds.

The palette of colors look so bright and vivid before her eyes, brought to brilliance in the sunlight. The red of the maples, the yellow of the poplars, the crinkled brown leaves of the oaks that will not fall until spring. The leaves that have fallen scuttle across the road in the wind, in one moment just a whisper and in the next a gust. Large cottony clouds dot an otherwise clear blue sky, floating across to shutter the sun, casting shadows, dark spots upon the ground. The moon will be full, and if the clouds do not thicken, the rays will illuminate all that moves and all that stands still. No rain predicted. No storms on the horizon, but a cold dry night ahead with a temperamental wind that rattles the dry cornstalks, rustles through the dying grass, whirls and swirls around the trees, the old wooden barns and silos.

The road continues down into clearings, out of the forests and the stands, where the land opens into the fields left wild or those planted and reaped, resting now, soon to be covered by snow. This full-moon night her daughter will venture out and because "the world's not safe," she will worry. She will keep her eyes peeled for angels, though she doubts they exist, as the sun goes down, and the moon rises, large and yellow in this harvest time. She will glance out of windows, looking for the moon rays upon a wing of white. There has been no premonition, no painting fallen from the walls or any other sign that would alert one to danger or predict potential death; though this seemed to happen once before, during those days when Billy returned from the Gulf, and he and James fought to right her wrong. She could have missed the angels that others saw, including Peter and Grandma Martha, and she did feel what could have been the draft of a passing wing, a feathery softness across her back in the garden. So much more to life than what meets the eyes, or so Grandma Martha said, though Brenda still feels doubt. This day she looks for calm and maybe, though not religious, she will pray. *Help us. Help us find a killer.*

Maybe she will stumble upon a place, a "thin place" that Grandmother Martha told her about. After all, she feels desperate now.

At the edge of one forest, before the landscape opens once again, Brenda spots a trail, one she has never taken, but this one, on this day, calls to her. Enter me it seems to say. Walk me, if you dare. She pulls her car over to a small narrow area set aside for parking. Stepping out of her car and pulling a sweatshirt on, she readies and commits herself to finding calm.

The light of the day already grows longer. The shade in the woods diffuses the light even more. Brenda heads down the trail trenched in places by the repetition of running rain. Pebbles, stones, and even rocks lay tumbled down the path too. Tuffs of spiky grass, small weeds now dry also decorate this path, which opens and offers leeway through the one-hundred-foot white pine stand. The fallen needles dust all of the surfaces, the rocks, the trenches, the grass, some needles still green from a recent falling, some brown now, long dead, and ground into pieces under heels or disintegrated through time.

On the side of the trails and stretching into the stand are baby pines, ferns and brush, life capable of living in the filtered light pools of shade and in dense areas almost dark. In these variances, fallen trees lie, limbs and trunks wildly and strangely protruding, creating known shapes and abstracts of anyone's guess.

The tall pines dance with the light wind in subtle whooshes reaching Brenda's ears. Another person alone in the stand might feel alone, but here Brenda feels safe, and that calm she has been seeking begins to descend.

She continues walking along the trail that climbs now, ribboning into a break of light. When she reaches the top, almost breathless, she looks out upon two ponds, one a small lake really, surrounded by red brambles and yellow poplars, battered snake grass and disintegrating cattails. The sparse and fluffy clouds in the otherwise clear sky reflects in the blues and greens of the water, creating that illusion that connects and disorients, earth and sky indistinguishable from the other.

The path splits, one trailing back down into the woods, skirting the pond, the other heading towards the lake, where a wooden planked bridge traverses the wetland to the side that leads into yet another white pine stand. Detecting movement from the corner of her eye, maybe an animal or something else alive, she heads there.

The path down, so steep, the incline forces her to trot. In one spot, where gravel has collected, her right foot slides and she plunges head first, but catches her balance before she falls. Close, so close! Suddenly she begins to clomp, clomp, clomp upon the wooden planked bridge. She searches for the movement, scanning the tall grass, cattails, snake plants, skeletons of trees, and notes a pair of geese, swimming in the distance and a blue heron, his or her stick legs measuring the lake's depth as his or her eyes concentrate intently in the water for the flash of fish. Overhead, six more geese fly in formation, honking.

Although lighter because Brenda walks through open space, already, the shadows grow very long, alerting her to impending dusk. She knows twilight can invite a crack between the worlds to open, or so Grandma Martha told her, and "magic" to appear, but Brenda wants to be in her car driving by the time dark descends.

Although she no longer fears the dark as she once did, a phobia brought upon her by her mother's murder, she would not want to be in the woods alone when the night falls. Not a place she does not know. Not because she fears bear, boars or coyotes, but because the dark can disorient and she could easily become lost. She strikes a pact with herself. She will wander as far as the second white pine stand, stretching from the edge of the wetlands and the lake, and no further.

Suddenly, as the sun disappears behind a cloud, Brenda senses a change in the air. Everything around her has grown quiet.

At the end of the planked bridge, as the white pines stand ahead, a grassy clearing appears to the left. Surrounded by the pines, firs, and an occasional red maple, Brenda watches as the sunlight coming out from behind the cloud illuminates the space. The tall, dry grass dotted with dying wildflowers calls to her. She walks slowly into the center, and here she drops into a sit, legs crossed, ears alert, eyes peeled, for what she does not know, but she waits.

Brenda watches the leaves of the hardwoods descend to the ground in graceful swirls. Besides the occasional bird sound and the rattle of dry leaves when a small critter crashes through, this late afternoon stands quiet. Now she turns her gaze out onto the edge of the wetland bordering the lake, approximating the place where she saw movement as she approached the area. There they stand. Three young bucks, their growing horns still covered in velvet, turn as one to look at her. They lower their heads, again as one, and raise them, repeating this action several times. The one that stands in the middle raises and drops his right leg, then hooves at the ground. Brenda does not move, so the three move toward her, so close together one might think them attached. Twenty feet from her now, she remembers what Grandma Martha once told her; the deer are the keepers of "magic," one foot in both worlds. Has she stumbled upon something? Could this be a "thin place?" Maybe one doesn't have to believe it to be true. Maybe this would be a good time to pray. She clears her throat as the bucks' tawny color so sweet in this light, their black noses and eyes draw her in. If she speaks aloud, will they run? She decides to take that chance.

Clearing her throat, she speaks. *I don't know where to begin. I'm not even sure what to ask for. I only know that my family suffers, not unlike others whom have lost someone to tragedy.* Brenda feels amazed that the three bucks, their ears twisting and turning to hear her words, or probably the sound that her voice makes, continue to stand near her. No snort of alarm, no turning to flee, no fear displayed in any way. She continues. *I'm not saying that the police were hasty or incompetent. I did not see the crime scene, nor did I want to, and everyone who did said that the earth appeared scoured, cleaned of any trace of the horror that occurred there. I do not, nor will I ever believe that a higher power orchestrated the act. If anything, the person just got lucky. But it's wrong that this person may still be walking on this earth, perhaps harming others. I am asking for assistance in finding this person, if he still lives. We are committed now in finding him. Now that my brother has also passed, I ask for this, so that he can dwell with you, whomever, whatever you are, knowing that at least in concern of this killer, the earth will be safer. I don't want to be angry, but I am. I am very angry. We have suffered so much, and I only ask this of you. Help us find this monster. Please. I beg of you!*

Tears run freely down Brenda's cheeks, and it seems to her, imagination or not, that the bucks look at her with kind compassion. When she lifts her hand to wipe those tears away, the spell breaks, and the three bucks turn as one and begin to leap away, their white tails so tall, their grace unworldly. Suddenly, as she watches them disappear into the white pine stand, she hears words. Frantically, she begins to look in all directions, pushing her torso towards the ground to hide. Where did they come from? Is there someone here with her? Fear does rise; she can't pretend it doesn't. She continues searching in all directions, and then she hears the exact words a second time. "The pearls will find him." What? She waits for more. She waits for a minute, two minutes, five minutes, continuing to look desperately around, and then one word travels up and out of her without any thought of her own, "How?" Again, one minute, two minutes, five minutes, but no more words come. As she digests the words, a panic rises. Firstly, the sun has begun to sink into the horizon that she glimpses through the trees. Secondly, she remembers that she gave the pearls to Lily Rose to wear. Has she put her daughter into danger? Oh, my god. Oh, my god!

Quickly she stands, and she begins to walk towards the path, noting how the surroundings look different now. She came one way down this path. She has only to retrace her steps. She begins to run. Her feet skitter through the fallen leaves, crunching them, pulverizing some, kicking up a little sand, while needles scatter. She begins to feel the panic she once felt every time she walked out into the dark alone. A fear that she had put to rest, which rises its ugly head now, as Peter's words that became a chant circle in her head, "The world's not safe. The world's not safe. The world's not safe." She begins to see flashes of black moving through the indigo light, from the corner of her eyes, which begin to play tricks on her. Fallen trees begin to look like prehistoric monsters, and because Halloween time comes soon, and the Day of the Dead, a ghost seems to appear here and a wicked witch there, and soon the flying monkeys from *The Wizard of Oz* approach. She begins to run, and her flapping sweatshirt snags on brambles, and occasionally she stumbles and teeters off center when her feet hit low spots or protruding rocks. Now she becomes again that little girl that escaped from the back seat of the car when she feared her father would strike her mom. She ran through the corn stalks and the wheat, towards some safe house that she had seen in dreams, only to stumble and fall, lose consciousness, too. The silent woods grow loud with the last call and song of birds amplified and mixed with something else, wild sounds, and unearthly. She swears she hears the sound of footsteps running from a distance behind but gaining. She throws a glance around her shoulder, and though sees nothing, really, she feels something, truly, and runs faster, past the wetlands, into the first white pine stand; nature sits silent now as her fear blocks everything out.

Suddenly, she reaches the head of the trail. Her car sits waiting; she can see the wagon in the dusky light. She unlocks the door and jumps inside, and though she can see that no one or nothing runs behind her, she locks the door, completely out of breath, sweating, shaking, heart beating, no, pounding on her chest wall. Before she even calms, key sparking the ignition, she heads home. One thought drives her forward: Lily Rose out in the full moon night wearing the pearls that the voice told her would help them find a killer. Real or not, the panic seizes her.

17

Closed Case

Saturday 6:08 p.m.

When Martin called Billy an hour ago, he could barely believe what he heard. Brenda and he had been waiting for months to hear Martin utter the words, "Let's do it." Martin did not use those exact words, yet Billy had reason to feel optimistic. Martin held important influence because he and Doug Holder were good friends. Holder led the state investigation of Jeanine's murder. "Bill."

"Yeah, Martin. What's up?"

"Didn't you say you had a meeting with Holder today?"

"Yeah, we're meeting at Harvey's."

"Well, that's a hell of a place."

"He chose. I didn't. Why?"

"I want to be there, too."

Billy let out a deep breath. "I'm really glad to hear that."

—∿—

Billy pulls into Martin's driveway and honks once. Christopher jumps out and runs into the house to hang out with Mary, who always manages to keep the boy busy. A few seconds later Martin walks out the back door and limps a bit as he approaches the car. His father-in-law's days as an athlete have caught up to him. He opens the passenger door and, with a groan, climbs into the car.

"Jesus," Martin states. "Barometric pressure must be changing."

"You're just an old man, Martin, admit it." Billy smashes a cigarette out in the ashtray.

"You're smoking again?"

"Just for the time being."

"Well, I don't need your secondhand smoke." Martin settles into the seat, closes the door, then opens the window. "Brenda know?"

"Not yet."

Billy backs out of the driveway and heads towards the bar, the shadows stretching long across the road, creating a barred effect like crossing a bridge made of logs or a railway trestle perched above a river.

"What made you change your mind, Martin?" Billy glances at him from the corner of his eye and in a glimpse notes the sag of Martin's face, the deep wrinkles, and the darkness around his eyes.

"I ended up out there last night."

"Where?"

"Where she was murdered."

"Oh." Billy feels his stomach drop and thinks of the TV show *Lost in Space* and the robot waving its arms screaming, "Warning! Warning!" Oh, shit! Already feeling overwhelmed with Brenda's morning breakdown, he lets out another deep sigh. What can he do now? He's trapped in a car with the man, not that he doesn't feel sorry for him. "So, was it useful to go there?"

"Useful? I guess you could say it was useful. Your car smells like cigarettes."

"Okay, I won't smoke in the car anymore. Even though it's mine."

"You have kids..."

"Yes, you're right. I get it. When was the last time you saw Holder?"

"Maybe two or three years. I was still drinking at the time. Did he seem eager to meet with us?"

"I just told him that we had a few concerns about the case. To answer your question, no, he did not seem eager."

Martin adjusts himself in the seat. "That figures. I have to tell you, though. Once when he was drunk, he expressed that not finding Jeanine's killer was the disappointment of his career."

"Well, maybe that will work in our favor."

Billy pulls into the parking lot of Harvey's. The two men climb out and limp into the building. For a moment, Billy remembers another time when the two walked into a bar together, the night they found Peter, on his knees servicing the piece of shit out in Three Rivers. Billy had just returned from the Gulf. That had been a gay bar; this one is far from that.

They built this hole in the wall in the 1950s, and the old wooden table and chairs, nicked, scratched, and carved upon tell the history, as does the old wooden bar. The metal stools with black vinyl seats are battered and tattered too, and the old dust-covered bottles behind the bar scream old school. No messing around. Only a few modern beers on tap bring this establishment into the present.

Martin heads for a back table so Billy follows. There sits a tall, gaunt, mustached sixty-or-so year-old man with four fingers of something brown in a rock glass that sits before him. He has large eyes and thin lips. A blunt thick cigar burns in his right hand. Martin turns around to Billy and shakes his head. More smoke. What a world, the glance seems to say.

Martin thrusts out his hand for a shake. "Good to see you, Doug."

Holder shakes his hand. "I sure as shit didn't expect to see you here."

"Well, that's a hell of a way to open a conversation."

"It's good to see you anyway."

"That's more like it."

Martin introduces Billy to Holder, and the cop says, "The sniper."

"I'd prefer Marine."

"Of course."

He and Billy shake, and Billy and Martin pull out chairs, which scrape sharply against the worn and cracking tan and white linoleum.

Holder gets right to it. "What is it that you want to know about the case?"

Billy follows suit. "We want to know what held up the case from being solved."

"That sounds like an accusation."

Billy opens his mouth to speak, but Martin jumps in, "No. That's not it. But we were wondering if maybe everything could be looked back over, to make sure nothing was missed."

Holder shakes his head and throws back one of the four fingers. "Do you have any idea how many cold murder cases there are in the state right now since Jeanine's murder?" He does not wait for either of the men to answer. "Over three thousand."

Holder waits for the fact to sink in, Billy guesses, but the pause goes on too long, so he speaks up again, "I know you want to make a point about how overworked the state is. But to me, that statistic says more about the inadequacies of the people involved..."

Martin jumps in, "Bill, hold it a minute." Although the interjection pisses him off, Billy realizes he has lost his composure, which will not be helpful. Everyone seems to be out of sorts today, including himself. Under any other circumstance, Billy would be thinking before speaking. Martin states, "It was the anniversary of the murder yesterday. My daughter, her husband," he indicates Billy with a sideways nod, "they, WE, want to see the case open again."

"Why after all this time?"

The owner of the bar, Mike, strolls over slowly and asks Billy and Martin, "What can I get ya?"

Billy says, "Jack and coke."

Martin says, "Black coffee."

Holder says, "Put it on my tab." He directs his words back to Billy and Martin. "Did some new evidence come to your attention? A witness come forward? Because without one or both of those things, there's not a chance in hell the case will re-open."

Billy shakes out a cigarette and lights it with the lighter Brenda gave him when they were teenagers, a silver lighter with a heart etched on the side that reads, "My heart is yours." He knows that he should have told Brenda about this meeting, but he didn't want to get her hopes up. He sucks in a deep one and exhales, hesitating to see if Martin jumps in on that. Not the exhale. He blew that over in the other direction, but Holder's words. When he does not, Billy states, "We're afraid there's a killer out there, in our community."

Holder exclaims, "For Christ's sake! It was a drifter! That we know. Someone passing through."

"How did you come to that conclusion, Doug?" Martin asks.

"Nobody saw anything. Nobody. We interviewed half the town..."

Billy cuts in, "Then someone in that other half knows something or saw something."

"You're insinuating that the killer was someone from this community."

Billy leans his torso in towards the table, holding the arm with the cigarette out. "We think..." He watches his words this time, "We know that your workload was overwhelming, but maybe now that time has passed, something new could be discovered."

"You have no idea how few the leads were," Holder states with more force.

"So there were *some* leads," Billy confirms.

"That led *nowhere*. We followed every one of them. Nobody even reported a relative or friend, even neighbor or colleague acting strangely."

Billy asks, "No one?"

"Okay, well there might have been a few, but again, we followed every lead." He throws back another finger, shakes his head again, gazing down at the table. He looks back up. "No one has killed since. If they kill once and get away with it, they usually kill again."

Billy asks, "How do we know he hasn't killed again? If the case has been cold, nobody is cross checking..."

Now Holder leans in. "You may find this hard to believe, but I always keep Jeanine's murder in the back of my mind. If something came along that seemed similar, I would have followed it, I assure you. In fact, oh, about five years ago, a woman was killed upstate, and I did talk to the lead in the case, but it didn't pan out."

"That's good to hear, but just because a killer hasn't killed again yet, doesn't mean he won't. He just might have a particular agenda."

Holder adds, "The person could well be dead by now, or incarcerated for another crime, whoever the fuck it was. It's been twenty-one years."

"He could be," Billy concedes.

"Look," Holder says low and firm. "I knew Jeanine. No one wanted to find the killer more than me, except of course you and the other family members. I felt that we worked very hard on the case. We just could not find the killer. I'm sorry!"

Harvey brings over the cocktail and coffee, sitting it down in front of Billy and Martin. They say their thanks.

Billy did not really expect this. He thought the cop might take offense, fight them. This solemn confessional though, as sincere as it seems, does not mean that he'd help them either. In fact, this approach meant to console, calm them, in effect, get them off his back. He leans in towards Holder again. "I have my own theory..."

"Bill," Martin warns.

Billy glances at Martin, but continues barely missing a beat, "I think that Martin pissed somebody off along the way. Real bad."

Holder leans in and exclaims, "Martin?"

"Don't tell me you never thought about that!" Billy continues, gesturing towards Martin, "This isn't Mr. Congeniality here. The murder stinks of revenge!"

Holder wrinkles up his nose. "Yes! Yes! Of course, we thought of that. Anyone in politics runs the risk of pissing people off."

Martin speaks up, "I don't recall a problem so serious that someone would want to do that to…"

Billy looks squarely at Martin, "Not when you were sober."

Martin shakes his head exasperated.

Billy continues, "Someone came up to the door…"

Holder continues, "There were no tire tracks up to the house. Of course there were numerous tracks out on the road. That's why we felt it was a drifter, someone on foot. We thought we had a boot print up by the house, but it was so minimal and matched to a brand everybody and his or her brother wore. Of course, the storm that hit that night didn't help. The kids said the door was wide open when they woke up in the morning…"

Billy questions, "You think a drifter knocks on a door?"

"We don't know if he knocked or not. We do know there was no break and entry."

"Why would Jeanine open the door to a stranger?" Billy asks. "She might have known him."

"Now…what are you insinuating?" Martin says, as he slides his chair back and stands.

"Sit back down, Martin. You have a wife, right, Doug? How would you feel if your wife was murdered and the killer never found?"

"Do you have something concrete, or not?"

"Not yet. You interviewed all of his cronies?"

"Of course!"

"How about his students, his athletes?"

"They all spoke well of him."

"So, you're not going to help us, are you?"

"They're not going to open the case, Bill. Not without a witness stepping forward or hard evidence. They're just not."

Martin says, "Let's go, Bill."

"Yeah. Let's go." Billy slides his chair back and stands up, reaches down and slurps up his Jack and coke in seconds flat.

Martin drinks half of his coffee and stands, too.

"Look, I know how hard it is, especially when the anniversary comes around, but there's a process, and if nothing has changed, the case stays closed," Holder says.

Billy finishes, "I understand your position. I really do. I just hope you understand ours."

—⁂—

Billy and Martin climb back into Billy's truck and they head down the road. The shadows stretch longer now almost flat, and the trees, most leafless, create stencils stretching across the road and into the fields. A flat forest of skeleton trees. Almost dark now, yard lights and house lights begin to blink on. The two men sit silent and Billy watches Martin slump down further into the seat; once a tyrant, now sober, and much mellower, any sense of false bravado that he once utilized to prop himself up has disappeared.

He asks, "How you doing, Martin?"

Martin turns to Billy, looking through him. "I knew those sons-a-bitches wouldn't open up the case."

"It's okay. We'll handle it."

"How the fuck are we supposed to handle it?"

"Keep our eyes and ears open. Talk to people. I have a feeling about this."

"Yeah, well, I wish I did."

"I asked you before to think back through the years. Is there anyone, anyone at all that you really pissed off? Someone combustible. Will you do that for me?"

"Of course!"

"Someone around the time that Jeanine died."

"I have been thinking. It's a long time ago, and you know that I was under the influence quite a bit of the time."

"Just think about it."

They arrive to Martin's, and he climbs out without a word and heads for his back door. He looks like a shadow of his former self now, shoulders hunched, gait slow, and a bit unsteady. Christopher runs out with a couple of papers in his hand, which turn out to be some coloring he did. From the side window, Mary waves to Billy, and he waves back. He pulls out of the driveway and decides to ride around with Christopher, looking at Halloween decorations, until they meet up with the friends for dinner. He looks forward to seeing Jack, whom he can question about the criminal mind. Not that he sees Jack as a criminal, but he lived surrounded by them for a good chunk of time. Sometimes it feels a little odd to be friends with James' older brother, but when Jack contacted him five years ago to meet with him, out of curiosity Billy gave him a shot. Jack thanked him for being such a good friend to his brother through the years, and stated that he felt indebted. He offered to help Billy in any way he could, if ever needed.

Billy heads for the restaurant now with his agenda intact. He will ask Jack to help.

His phone rings, startling him. "Hello!"

Martin says, "I thought of someone."

"No shit. Who?"

"He played football for me. I saw him and another player, pulling out of a driveway of a house. Damn near hit them. Turns out, they robbed the place. My statement put them away for a while. Before that, I cut him from the team. A one-man demolition derby. All my players felt anxious about him. He didn't take it well. Not well, at all."

"What was his name?"

"Thompson. Derek or Eric, something like that."

18

Bad

Saturday 7:18 p.m.

Sometimes Jimmy walks down the hall to the den and sits down on the floor to look at photos of his father. Two hang on the wall, and three sit on a shelf. Grandma Tillman didn't take many photos. Mr. Bagwell gave them a few taken over the years, when he and his father were friends. He wants to know who his father was; he stares at the handful of photos and thinks about the stories he's heard, but no matter how hard he tries, he can't figure it out. What did he sound like when he talked? When he laughed? How did he smell? Would he like me? Knowing these things feels important, like something he has to know, if he wants to know himself.

And he does want to know himself.

One person called his dad a badass with the fastest car around. Another person said he screwed all the girls in town. He guesses screwed means fucked, which is a word he's not supposed to say. So he was a badass that got all the girls?

He stands up, walks out of the den and down the hall to the bathroom. He stops to look at himself in the bathroom mirror, smiles, and feels like a jerk. Does he look like the man in the photos? Will he be a badass who gets all the girls? Is that who he wants to be? He lets out a big sigh and pulls the door open to head towards the living room.

Damn, his mom walks towards him. "Jimmy, comb that hair! Don't let it dry like that."

He likes his hair ruffled up.

As he walks by her, she grabs his shoulder and kisses him on top of his head. He can smell her. She always smells good.

141

"Did you enjoy the movie?"

"It was awesome!"

"What were you doing in the den?"

"Just hanging out."

Mom asks, "You were looking at his photos again, weren't you?" She nods, looks down and begins to walk away.

He calls after her, "Is it okay if I play a video game?"

"Sure, but remember that we're leaving around 7:45. Be dressed and ready."

"I'm dressed and ready."

"Except for that hair."

He reaches up with both hands and quickly combs through his hair with his fingers. Doesn't feel like it's going to lay down. He slumps towards the living room couch, falls back into the brown cushions, and sprawls. His mom seems sad sometimes, and he hates to see her limp in cold or rainy weather, or watch her struggle to stand up from sitting. Nearly everyone has told him that his father did not cause the accident. So he can't feel mad at him for that, though his Grandpa and Grandma Jacobs still refuse to say his name.

Jimmy feels mad at god. His mom would have a fit if she knew that, even though they don't go to church anymore, not after that one time, but god seems very important to his mom. She wants him to pray, but he just feels silly. Nobody in video games prays or even in the movies, so why should he? Why pray when you can practice magic, like Gandalf or Harry Potter? He snuggles further into the couch but can't seem to keep his mind on the game.

—⁂—

He was maybe six when he and his mom pulled up to the orange brick church with a tall white thing poking up on top, which he now knows is a spire. He remembers the colored windows, which seemed to tell a story in bright blue, red, green, and yellow. He feels sure about those colors. He counted them later, when he needed something to do. When they arrived, a friendly short, skinny man met them at the front double doors, at the top of the stairs they climbed. Jimmy remembers the man shaking his hand; the man's hand felt soft and wet. Icky.

A small group of people, including him and his mom, stood around the man; she started fidgeting, tapping her fingers on one arm and exhaling little puffs of air out of her nose. Finally, she pulled him in through the doors. Inside, the colored windows looked even cooler; that's when he started counting. He also noted that most of the long wooden benches of the church were full of people. He remembers that people turned to look at them as they walked down the aisle, but he figured they liked his mom's dress or maybe her hair.

Mom pulled him into a row of benches and there sat Grandpa and Grandma Jacobs. They looked happy to see him and Mom. He doesn't remember the exact words of the conversation, but it went something like this. Grandma asked his mom, "What's wrong with you?" His mom answered, "They are all staring at us." Grandpa said, "Of course they are. You are a beautiful woman, and Jimmy is a handsome boy." Mom said, "Nice try, Dad." He remembered exactly what Grandma said next, something he had never heard her say before or since, "Fuck them, Debra."

Now the friendly man at the door stood at the front of the church and talked for a long time, so long that Jimmy remembers holding the edge of the seat afraid that he would run out. He occupied himself by counting the colors on the windows again, then crosses, people wearing white shirts, kids, and whatever else he could think of. When they left, Jimmy didn't look at anyone; he didn't want to see them watching him and his mom. At one point, he heard someone say the word "bastard." He had never heard the word, so he asked his mom what it meant. She sucked in a breath and held his hand tighter, pulling him back out through the brown wooden doors and down the stairs, her pulling so hard on his arm he thought she might pull it out. He remembers seeing tears roll down her cheeks, and he felt mad, very mad.

They hadn't gone back since. Jimmy didn't care. It was boring.

—ɷ—

Jimmy hears Jack walk in through the back door. He has been out raking leaves. Usually he asks Jimmy to help, but not this time. He hears his mom say, "Jimmy and I are finished cleaning up. The bathroom's all yours."

Jack answers, "Ok," and walks by the living room, heading towards the hall. "What ya doing, Jim?"

"*Lord of the Rings*. Legolas and I are kicking booty!"

Jimmy loves his uncle Jack, but sometimes he wonders if Jack loves him. Today at the theatre Jack touched him, something he has done only a few times in Jimmy's whole life. Not that he wants to be touched a lot, but he likes to feel wanted. Sometimes he feels lost as if he doesn't belong anywhere. Of course, his mom touches him, but moms always touch their kids. Maybe if he could live in another world, maybe the *Lord of the Rings* world or *Harry Potter,* he wouldn't feel so lost.

Jack spends time with him, but he doesn't talk a lot. He knows that Jack spent a long time in prison. Could be men don't talk a lot when they're behind bars. Maybe Jack became so used to not talking much he forgot how.

What kind of family was he born into anyway?

On his mom's side, Grandpa and Grandma Jacobs seem normal. No one in prison or jail. No one with tattoos. They look like the good guys on TV and in the movies. But his father's side look kind of like the bad guys.

His mom walks into the room at this point and sits down next to him. She throws her arms around him in a big hug, and he breaks free. Sometimes she goes overboard. "Mom! I'm playing!"

"Didn't look like you were playing to me!" She tucks one leg up under her and her bad leg she stretches out and rests on the coffee table in front of them. She keeps one arm loose on the back of the couch behind him.

"Yeah, you're right. I was thinking."

"What were you thinking about?"

"Did my father have tattoos?"

"He had a few."

"Of what?"

"I remember one. A heart with a name in it."

"Your name?"

"No, not my name."

That sad look moves over her face again, so he doesn't push it. "You can't remember any of the other ones?"

"Not really."

"Was my father ever in jail?"

His mom throws a couple long strands of hair over her shoulder. "I don't think so, but I didn't know him that long before he died." She looks off to the side of the room; maybe she's looking for Jack outside the window or watching the leaves fall, so he changes the subject.

"Was Uncle Jeff in jail?"

"I don't know."

"He has lots of tattoos and scars. He was even stabbed!"

"Really? Did he show you?"

"Yeah, this morning."

"So what are you thinking?"

"I'm wondering if my father's family are bad guys."

"Bad guys. Do you think that Jack is a bad guy?"

"No. He seems like a good guy. So does Uncle Jeff."

"Jimmy. Just because a person has been in jail or has tattoos doesn't mean he or she is bad. Sometimes people make mistakes, and as for the tattoos? They're art!"

His mom slowly and stiffly moves off of the couch, and she walks down the hallway where she will no doubt sit in front of the mirror in the bedroom and comb her hair and paint her face, ready herself for the dinner.

Jimmy switches over to his Gameboy now, prepping the console for *Super Mario Sunshine,* a game he can play during dinner when all of the adults talk about things that don't matter to him. He begins the game while waiting, anticipating the cue to leave. Jack walks into the living room cleaned up, his goatee and mustache neatly trimmed and smelling like the after-shave he wears.

"You ready to go, Jim?"

"Yep."

"Put your shoes on." Jack calls, "Debbie, you ready?"

She doesn't answer. Jack walks back down the hall and Jimmy can hear them talking in low voices, but he can't understand the words. It sounds like Jack trying to get his mother to do something. Jimmy jumps up and runs over to the back door, plops down and pulls on his athletic shoes, ties them, pulls on a jacket and runs outside with Gameboy in hand. He sits down on the back porch steps and wonders if he will have to play with the little kid, Christopher, tonight.

Another ten minutes or so passes and finally Jack and Mom walk out the back door, and the three walk out towards Jack's SUV. Jimmy sees that his mom's eyes are a bit red. Outside the car window, Jimmy sees the full moon half way up in the sky, shining brightly, looking yellow. The glow lights up the ground so that it looks more like when the sun goes down than night. They live on the outskirts of town, and Jimmy notes the pumpkins, corn stalks, and bales of hay that people are using to decorate their houses. One even has orange lights around a large front window. He looks forward to Halloween, not only to collect goodies but because last year he and two friends, Mark and Tony, soaped a few windows and even TP'd the front yard of a classmate who pissed them off a few weeks earlier. Jimmy really enjoyed doing those things, which makes him wonder if he takes after his father's family.

He hears Jack quietly ask his mother if she's feeling better. She answers equally quietly, "I'm okay."

Jack says, "They like you, Deb."

Jimmy watches her turn and stare at Jack. "She stares at him."

"What are you talking about?"

Jimmy busies himself looking out of the window, knowing that Jack can glance in the rearview mirror to see him and he doesn't like him to be part of these conversations.

"Brenda. She stares at him."

"I've never noticed that."

"She does. She wishes he were her boy."

Jimmy doesn't know what the heck that means.

In town now, he sees more decorations, including ghosts, zombies and lots of witches. Since he first watched *The Wizard of Oz*, he has felt scared of witches and flying monkeys, too. They say that these things do not exist, but Jimmy wonders.

Jack says, "He's a good-looking kid. People look at him. You should have seen the girls in the theatre."

Jimmy feels his face grow hot. Good looking, Jimmy thinks, but also disabled. That's how they described him at school. They said it has something to do with his mom being in a comma for so long. He hates when they describe him like that. Sometimes they give him special treatment, and he doesn't like that either.

"It's more than that."

"Debbie, you can only account for yourself. I learned that the hard way, my first year serving my bit. Let's just have a good time, okay, Babe?" Jimmy watches in the gap between the front seats as Jack reaches over and places his hand on the top of his mom's leg. This surprises him. Rarely has he seen them touch. His mom takes both of her hands and covers Jack's. She turns to Jack. "Okay."

He watches as his mom pulls Jack's hand between her legs. Jack questions her, "Is that what you did with him?"

Even in this light, he sees his mom stiffen and pull Jack's hand back out. Jimmy quickly looks away, turns and focuses outside the window again, as a pickup pulls up alongside them at the light. The driver turns to look at him. He has a stocking cap pulled down low, very low on his head, and he's slunk down in his cab as if he doesn't want anyone to see him. Jimmy feels the hair stand up on the back of his neck. That's a weird feeling. He's not a good guy. Jimmy feels like he can tell about this one, and he feels relieved as Jack pulls away when the light turns green. The night somehow doesn't feel safe, like suddenly all of the ghosts, zombies and especially the witches are going to come alive and start roaming through the town, through the countryside, killing everything in their path. He feels glad that he's with Jack, because no one would mess with his stepdad, though his imagination begins to roll.

—⁂—

The sky looks peppered with all of the witches flying around on their brooms. Beneath their pointy hats, their hair flows out behind them and their voices, shrill as a saw, cut the air with their wicked laughter. From the corners of his eyes, the ghosts appear and disappear only to appear again somewhere else. They float above the ground, and he can see through them like a foggy window. The zombies scare him the most, looking dead but moving anyway on stiff legs, arms dangling to their sides, eyes glazed over like road kill.

One zombie becomes many, and Jimmy begins to imagine himself a warrior like Legolas, with bow in hand and arrows tucked neatly into a leather bag he carries on his back. He's not a faerie, hobbit or dwarf, or any of those magical creatures, but more like Aragorn, a man, an expert shot with his weapon, and he begins to pick off the zombies one by one. They fall to pieces on the ground and a liquid, though not blood, darker in color and thicker too flows out into sticky pools and in them, the pink sky reflects.

He moves through the flurry of zombies, picking them off one by one, light on his feet, the witches swooping down just above his head, their cackle harsh upon his ears. The magical creatures peek out from around trees, bushes and large gray rocks, watching as he makes a name for himself. He reaches around, pulls another arrow from the bag and sets it into the bow for flight.

From every direction, the zombies move towards him, and their numbers grow and his fear rises. He begins to worry they may overcome him, and death by their hands, more accurately their teeth that would chew him alive, his fluids spilling, and red blood spurting out.

He becomes terribly out-numbered; as fearless, as courageous he feels, he cannot keep up, so he turns in a swift circle in search of an opening, however narrow, where he can run. The witches are so happy now, gleeful that from their various perches, not swooping and sweeping, they can witness his demise.

He turns and moves toward the sun, a light blue in this land where a narrow passage cuts between the zombies as they reach out to grab on to him anyway they can. On the lightest of feet he runs, as a form moves toward him, accompanied by the thunder of hooves. Friend or enemy he doesn't know, but this time more than any other he wishes he had magical powers.

The horse gallops toward him. The rhythm of the hooves hit the ground in a very loud roar.

The zombies, dead to most of the world, turn because the sound forces them to do so.

As the horse approaches swiftly, on top of him now, one muscled arm swoops him up, the witches shrieking in protest, the zombies still captured by the sound, his body thrown in front of the rider, and he knows, he's sure of it.

On this stallion rides his father.

—∞—

Jimmy turns back into the front seat and hears Jack say, "I'm sorry. I shouldn't have said that."

"No, no, you have been so patient with me. I thought I was getting better, and I was, but not as good as I had hoped. And for the record? It was all me. Your brother had nothing to do with it."

Jack pulls into the driveway of the restaurant, stops the car, and turns to look at his mom. "It's okay. Let's forget it for now. Have a good time. Okay?"

His mom nods.

The three of them climb out of the large vehicle, and Christopher runs over to Jimmy. He says, "Jimmy! Did you bring your Gameboy?"

Jimmy rolls his eyes. He had a long night ahead of him. He doesn't feel thrilled about having to hang out with a little kid, but then he spots Uncle Jeff.

Pow Wow

Saturday 8:00 p.m.

As Jack introduces Billy and Brenda to Jeff, Debbie discreetly checks the other woman out from head to toe. Again. She feels envious of Brenda's long dark hair, but especially her height. Of course, many people have told Debbie that she has beautiful hair, but she stands short, even in heels, though they do help. She wore her favorite pair, the pink stilettos, fortifying her confidence in every way she could. Now Debbie has good-sized breasts, but Brenda has her beat, wearing a canary yellow lace shirt under a brown leather jacket. She also has a small round ass that men seem to like. Debbie understands why James loved her; she's a desirable woman, and although Debbie wishes she could say that Brenda acts bitchy, she can't. The other woman always seems nice.

Ah, proof now of Brenda's good looks. When Debbie steals a glance at Jeff, he sweeps his eyes over Brenda's body too. He will not even look at Debbie, not after what she did last night. Sometimes she behaves badly, though it happens less often now. Meetings help.

Everyone takes a seat around the restaurant table, dark, heavy wood with matching chairs. The forest green tablecloth and napkins look homey, and the steam rises from the hot bread tucked down into linen-lined baskets. Jack sits to Debbie's left, Jeff left of Jack, then Billy with Brenda beside him, and Christopher beside her, and finally Jimmy to Debbie's right. One happy gathering. *Yeah, maybe,* Debbie thinks, and a few minutes click by before conversation opens. Although she occasionally catches Brenda throwing a look Jimmy's way, she must admit that this other woman neither stares nor mopes, but seems only to enjoy that the boy has joined them. The two couples don't always hang out with their children in tow. Christopher, joining them this evening, reminds her that Brenda has an adorable son of her own.

—⁓—

Billy can see some family resemblance between Jeff and Jack, but honestly, the man looks more like James. Although he sees a little ink, Jeff looks conservative with his button-up shirt and khaki pants. He tries to imagine this man racing around in the cherry red GTO, the one that rolled across the field with Debbie and James inside.

"What kind of work do you do, Jeff?" Billy asks.

"I keep books for a large import business out West."

"Importing what?"

"Hmm...you name it, but mostly vehicle accessories. I hear you make furniture."

"Yep."

Now that the conversation has opened, Billy sits back and tries to relax in the not so comfortable chair. Not a fan of small talk, he feels restless, adjusting and re-adjusting his sitting position, and hungering for tobacco.

An older server, thin with wrinkly skin walks up to the table. "Would you all like to start off with a beer, glass of wine, or maybe a soda?"

Jimmy speaks up right away. "I want a Coke!"

Of course, Christopher seconds that, "Me, too!"

Brenda points her thumb at their son. "Make his small!"

Debbie nods at her son. "His too!"

Brenda leans in towards Debbie, and Billy hears her say, "You'd think it was rocket fuel instead of carbonated sugar." Debbie nods in agreement, rolling her eyes.

Jesus, the small talk. Why does he even agree to these dinners?

All the adults order alcohol, including Billy, who orders a single Jack and Coke but really wants a double. His leg throbs and a low-grade pain gnaws on his insides. Opening up a dialogue with Jack sits foremost in his mind. Out of respect for Brenda, he waits to time the exchange just right. He can always pull Jack to the side later.

—♒︎—

When she first saw Jeff, Brenda's heart skipped a beat or two. His resemblance to James, more so in some of his mannerisms than his appearance, throws her a bit. She tells herself she's not mooning over James, but reminiscing about the years she and Billy shared with him. She does not want to feel guilty; she cannot bear one more moment of that. It's just that...just... something about this brother stirs a longing inside of her she has not felt in awhile. A longing for what? Something more.

This feeling disappears in a snap, as she remembers the words "heard" in the woods. They echo in her head; nausea rises. Jesus! Should she say something to Billy? He'll think she has lost her mind for sure. This "thin place" crap. The voice sure didn't come out of the sky. How could it? She probably imagined the experience through her own fear and paranoia. By the time she arrived home, Lily had already left for the party, so she isn't sure she even wore the pearls. She didn't see them laying around anywhere in her daughter's room. So what if she did wear them? Doesn't matter how they glowed in the sunlight, as if lit from inside. Pearls cannot find a killer.

The server drops off the drinks, and Brenda grabs her pint of beer and drinks down a third.

Billy chuckles. "Thirsty tonight, honey?"

She looks at him and nods rapidly reminding herself of one of those toys you stick to the dashboard, and the head bounces up and down, and up and down, this way and that way on a small flimsy spring.

He leans in toward her. "Are you okay?"

She blurts, "I'm fine! Just fine!"

He looks at her, his eyes squinting.

"I'm fine, Billy."

"Okay, if you say so."

She continues to guzzle her beer.

—⁓—

Debbie notes Brenda acting a bit weird, fidgeting in her chair, scratching on her neck, tossing her hair over her shoulders, and gulping her beer like there's no tomorrow. Billy leans in toward her; she bets Brenda feels his warm breath on her neck. He's a good-looking man. Tall and lean, not body-builder strong, but certainly well built. She doesn't usually like blond men, but his wavy hair, blue eyes, and tan skin look attractive. His lips are one of his best features, full almost plump. Fun to kiss she guesses.

When she musters the courage to look over at Jeff, she catches him throwing back a shot and wiping his mouth off with the back of his hand. Their eyes meet, but they both quickly look away. Wait. He said last night that he had given up drinking. Uh oh! He even mentioned the friends of Bill, so obviously he attends meetings. Jeff fell or maybe jumped off the wagon, just since last night. She wonders what happened. Guilt washes over her; shit! She hopes she didn't play a part.

Jack breaks her thoughts, "What ya going to eat, Deb?"

Eat? She didn't want anything, but she picks up the menu and opens it. "Oh, a salad, I guess. What about you?"

"I'm thinking about a steak."

She picks up her wine glass and takes a swig, sweeps her eyes around the table and begins to feel an itch herself.

—⁓—

Waiting for the food to arrive, Jeff throws back his second shot, and feels his stiffened limbs begin to soften. God, he likes this feeling. How will he stop this time? On the bright side, drinking again gives him a great excuse why he can't go back to *her*. She will walk away pregnant or not, if he comes back using. Great, he fixed that; even though a pesky and unwanted envy crawls over him as he watches the two couples interact. He grew used to a body in his bed, someone there when he came home after a long day, the arms that reached out to him when he finally stopped running. He began to expect those comforts; he became dependent upon them even. Well, he fixed that.

Now how could he fix the problem with Eric? He laughs cynically to himself and glances quickly around the table again, to see if anyone heard him. Nope, everyone seems preoccupied. He just downed two bourbons without a wince. Off the wagon for sure and ready to right a wrong. If Eric killed, he needs to pay. He looks over at Becker's daughter and thinks about how it must have been, losing her mom like that. A strain seems to pull upon her face. He thinks about bringing the subject up, but hesitates, not wanting to add to her pain. He hears his name and turns towards Jack.

His brother asks, "What year was Jordan shot?"

"Nineteen Seventy-Eight. The year I left. They released me just a few weeks after he died."

Billy adds, "James and I went out to the spot." He shakes his head. "I never seen James that mad. I remember the cops saying a stray bullet killed him, and that was probably true."

"Yes, but weren't there footprints all over where the body was found? I remember James telling me that they told him the prints were there before authorities arrived," Jack growls.

Billy agrees, "I remember that, too..."

"That means that the hunter came to check on his kill, and if he wasn't already dead, he let Jordan fucking bleed to death..."

Brenda looks up, "We have tender ears here..."

Jimmy corrects, "I don't have tender ears!"

Christopher looks up from his Gameboy, "What?"

"Of course, sorry," Jack apologizes, and then confirms to Billy, "In my book that's murder."

Billy pulls a pack of cigarettes out of his pocket and pulls one out. "Hell yes, that's murder."

Brenda watches her husband with her mouth hanging open. "What are you doing?"

"It's just temporary, Bren."

His wife shakes her head, clearly frustrated.

Jeff softly mutters, "That was a hell of a way for Jordan to go." He shoots his right hand into the air and looks at Brenda. "I'm sorry! I just hate the fact that people get away with murder." He takes a deep breath and plunges forward, hoping even as he speaks the words that he won't regret them, "Like your mom. Her killer was never found either, right?"

—⁓—

Debbie watches everyone react around the table. Brenda winces. Billy stretches his arm around her shoulders. Jack picks up his pint of beer and guzzles. Jeff lets out a deep sigh and says, "I never have had the best of timing." Only the two boys act oblivious, busy playing their Gameboys.

All eyes are on Brenda who says, "I'm very sorry about what happened to your brother. That must have been very hard for you boys and your mom. As for my mom…"

Jeff holds up his hand again. "No! I shouldn't have brought it up. I apologize…"

"It's okay! And no, they never found the killer, or killers. We've been talking about it a lot lately. In fact, yesterday was the twenty-first anniversary." She looks at her husband. "We're working to get the case reopened."

Billy states, "Actually, Martin and I met with the lead detective today."

"What?" Brenda asks, "Why didn't you tell me?"

"I was going to, but I didn't want you to get your hopes up."

"So what did he say?" Her voice sounds like she's about to cry. Debbie feels sorry for her.

Jeff jumps in again sounding very excited, "Are they going to reopen the case?"

Billy questions, "Why are you so interested in the case, Jeff?"

Debbie watches Jeff scan everyone's face around the table, including her own, and then lets out another deep sigh.

At that moment, the server, too old and too thin for the job, carries out one of those huge round food trays. After she places plates and bowls in front of everyone, Jeff and Billy order another drink. Those boys are on a roll. The server leaves and everyone remains quiet, looking expectantly at Jeff.

—⁓—

Now we're getting to it, Jack thinks. Last night Jeff tells him he gave up drinking and tonight he downs Bourbon like water. There goes number three, his hand shaking so hard, the brown liquor splashes out over the edge. He came back for more than a family visit, and Jack has a hunch now that it has something to do with the Becker murder. He looks at Jeff and prompts, "So?"

Jeff licks his lips, then begins, "I knew Coach. I played football for him. Then I screwed up and spent some time in Half Moon." He looks down at the table and then back up at Brenda. "Your dad witnessed me and…another dude pull out of a driveway after robbing a house."

Jack says, "I didn't know that Martin Becker nailed you guys."

Billy lifts a hand and points a finger at Jeff. "Wait." He hesitates a beat or two. "Was the other guy named Derek or Eric Thompson?"

Jeff emphatically nods his head. "Yes. Do you know him?"

"No, but today Martin remembered him as someone he could have pissed off enough to want to do him harm. I never have believed that Jeanine's killer was a drifter like the police claimed. I think the murder was a revenge killing. Do you think this guy's capable of murder?"

"Yes, I do."

All the adults around the table stare at Jeff; the silence marks their held breath. Jack stares down at his medium-rare steak, wanting to tear into it, but the look on Billy and Brenda's faces hold him back. Jack doesn't know where this startling admission will lead to, but he senses it won't be conversation suitable for the two boys. He looks at the women and says, "Maybe the two boys could go play some darts over there." He gestures his head to the left. Brenda and Debbie nod their consent and the two boys take off like rockets.

—⁓—

Brenda swears she can hear her own heart banging in her chest and a knot of something rising into her throat. Could this Thompson guy really be the killer of her mother? She looks at Jeff and fights to keep her composure. I won't cry, damnit. I won't! But there's something she has to know. She glances at Billy, whose eyes are wide, and she notes that subtle beat of jawbone as he clenches. He looks about to speak, so she shakes her head. This one is for her. "Did you suspect him at the time?"

Jeff scoots his chair away from the table, lights a cigarette and nods his head up and down just like one of those fucking little toys, one of those obnoxious little toys that you stick to the dashboard. "Yeah, I did!"

Billy drops the fork he had clenched in his hand and pounds loudly on the table one time. The fire she sees in his eyes scares her, but who can blame him? She feels the same. When she opens her mouth to speak, her husband lifts his hand to stop her. He turns his attention to this man, brother of his once best friend, someone whom Brenda wanted to like but hates at this moment. Hates in a way that frightens her.

Billy spits the words, "You suspected that he killed Jeanine Becker, and you never came forward..." He slides his chair back, stands up and strides towards Jeff, but Jack jumps up out of his chair and quickly steps between Billy standing and Jeff sitting, the later taking a deep drag off a cigarette.

Jack pleads, "Can we hear him out?"

Billy freezes and Jack lifts his right hand, motioning for him to step back, step back, keep it cool, keep it cool, please, the gesture seems to say. Billy returns to his chair, casting his eyes down, so Brenda can't see what's in them. She blinks rapidly to keep her tears back. She will not cry, damnit!

Jeff exhales his cigarette smoke and looks around at the other four adults sitting at the table. Brenda looks around too, to see Jack seated again, his full attention on his brother. Debbie darts alarmed eyes from one of them to the other, probably completely ignorant to the past that has led to this moment. Jeff finally speaks, "I was in the south at the time. I heard it on the TV. I remembered how many times Eric had mentioned while we were in juvie that he was going to get Coach back, not only because he fingered us but because he also kicked Eric off the team." He takes another deep drag. "I'm not going to lie. I was not a nice man. I did some bad things over the years. At that time, I just didn't care about anybody or anything. Two years ago, I sobered up. I became involved with...a woman...and she helped me. I know that's hard to believe watching me drink tonight. I just fell off the wagon today. Obviously, I am not a strong man, but I am trying to be better and make things right. I am deeply sorry for not coming forward all those years ago, and I'm hoping that someday you can forgive me. I came back to make amends and see my family, or what's left of it. I intend to find Eric and make this right. I swear I will. I will make it right."

Brenda succeeds in holding back her tears because that other emotion sneaks back up, the one that feels like lava. She doesn't care about his weakness, and his apology leaves her cold. "You knew all these years..."

"I had no evidence, and I certainly wasn't a witness!" He turns to Billy. "You never answered the question. Are they going to reopen the case?"

Billy answers, "No! Because there's no new evidence, and no one has come forward."

"We can find him. I saw an old friend today that said he seen Eric in a pickup, and another guy saw him driving a semi over Denton way. The last dude saw him just a couple of months ago..."

"He should be in the book then..." Billy clarifies.

"He's not. I looked into every public record I could get my hands on, off line and online. He could have changed his name or living off the grid like some people do. Look, I'll help you find him."

"And then what?" Billy asks.

Brenda thinks about all the years of torment, wondering about the killer, whether he would ever strike again, and this son-of-a-bitch knew or had a suspicion. She jumps up from her seat, leaning over the table and screams into his face, "You knew and you let us suffer all these years? You fucker! You fucker!"

Billy pulls her down into her seat by the back edge of her jacket. "That's not going to help."

Jeff apologizes once again, "I'm very sorry, but we can find him now."

Billy reiterates, "And then what?"

"We find his Achilles heel. We bring him down."

—∞—

Billy feels divided. On one hand, he wants to beat the shit out of this asshole, but on the other, he feels excited because they have a collaboration on the name. They might not have evidence, or a witness, but they have a place to start. Maybe Jeff is a badass like Jack, as James could be, and maybe if Billy could set aside this will to punish him and instead use him to help, it could be a win/win.

Jack questions, "You started looking for him today, didn't you, Jeff?"

"Yeah. I looked all over town and visited all the local watering holes, asked questions; that's how I ran into that old friend."

Jack continues, "I have some sources that might be able to help find an address, telephone number and other info, whether he's on the grid or not. I made some connections when I was serving my bit. We might have to use the backdoor."

Billy jumps in, "You don't have to get involved with this, Jack…"

"I owe you, Bill. I told you years ago. Looks like I need to help my brother, too. I'll do what I can."

Billy feels a sense of relief that he didn't have to ask for help, something that has never come easy to him.

Jeff stands up and puts his cigarette out in the ashtray. "I'm ready to continue looking. There's no time to waste. If he finds out I'm in town, he could run. He made a solid vow to me that he would get Coach back."

"You can't just go after him," Brenda states.

Billy turns to her. "Why not?"

"The police need to be involved…"

"They had their chance."

"Billy…"

Billy nods to Jeff. "Let's do it!"

Jack adds, "I'll go home and contact my sources. Consider me the backup, more muscle if needed, but I have to tread lightly. Once a felon, always a felon."

Billy nods at Jack. "We'll keep you out of it as much as we can." He turns to Brenda and speaks quietly, "We're just going to lay the groundwork for police."

"How do you know that you can trust him?"

"I don't, but I can take care of myself."

"Look, I'm happy we have a lead but…"

"We can't stop now." Billy looks over at Jeff, who stands ready to go. "Jeff, I'll give it a couple of hours tonight. If we don't find him, we can start out early in the morning."

Jeff nods, with a little smile. "We can take the Lexus. He'll never recognize me in that."

———ɯɯ———

Debbie feels completely lost, not knowing about any of this. Shit, she was probably just a kid when it all happened. She feels happy that Jack isn't going with them, but concerned that they are looking for a man who might have murdered.   S h e looks at Brenda and feels in even greater awe. How can this woman be so nice, when she has suffered so?

She watches Christopher run back over to Brenda from his dart game with Jimmy, as Jeff and Billy head for the door. "Where's Daddy going?"

"To take care of some business." Brenda, standing now, grabs her son and backs him tightly up against her legs.

Jimmy speaks up next, "They're going after him, aren't they?"

"Him, who Jim?" Jack asks.

"The bad guy in the truck."

"What bad guy?"

"He pulled up next to us at the light, coming here."

"What makes you think he was a bad guy?"

"The way he was sitting in his truck. The way he looked at me."

Jack puts his arm around Jimmy's shoulders and leads him towards the door. "I think maybe you need a break from the video games."

But Debbie wonders, as they climb into the SUV. Kids know. They have an untarnished sense about things.

Part 2
Caws Echo

American Midwest – October 2002

20
Facts of Life

Saturday 8:09 p.m.

The boys pull into the Big Boy parking lot with windows down and big smiles on their handsome faces. Lucas opts to drive his Mustang, a stick shift, so Lily doesn't have to worry about sitting next to him. Kristen crawls into the backseat with Mark, and Lily doesn't have to turn around to know they are sitting closely together; she hears them whisper, giggle, and make little lip smacking sounds that make her feel jealous on the one hand, and uncomfortable on the other.

Five minutes outside town, Lucas pulls a joint out of his shirt pocket, sticks it between his lips, and lights one end with a red Bic. He offers the stinky stuff to Lily, but she shakes her head. Lucas sucks in a huge inhale, and then passes the joint back to Mark. Lily hears the lovebirds sucking hard, too, followed by one prolonged coughing spell.

Mark remarks, "That's some good shit. Kristen, you okay?" She answers inaudibly, maybe nodding or shaking her head.

Mark passes the joint back to Lucas, who taps the ash off on the edge of his open window. The three start giggling and laughing, everything funny, no matter what. Fortunately, they ride out on dirt roads, which are mostly desolate of other cars, because at times the Mustang veers to the right or left, as the two boys pass the burning weed. After a couple of passes, Lucas again offers Lily the joint, but she says, "No, thanks."

"You don't smoke at all?" Lucas asks.

She shakes her head then watches as Lucas looks up into his rearview mirror to make eye contact with Mark.

Kristen pipes up, "She doesn't party."

The words hurt Lily. "I party. I just don't smoke or drink."

Lucas turns to look at Lily with his pretty eyes. "Nothing? Never?"

She shakes her head again.

"Oh, I get it. You're a "good" girl."

Kristen giggles. "Try it, Lil. You might like it." The three of them laugh heartily.

When they quiet down again,   Lucas adds, "One toke isn't going to hurt you," his pretty eyes glassy now, his lips curled up in a smile, almost a sneer.

She hesitates, feeling uncomfortable about being the odd person out, then gingerly reaches out and takes the joint more than half-burned down now, and sucks gently on the end. She blows the smoke out quickly and begins to hand it back to her "date."

He corrects her, "No, no. Take another toke and hold it for a while, then blow it out."

If only half as cute, she would refuse, but she does as directed, takes another toke, then fumbles with the burning paper, as she hands the joint back to him. After two more tokes the joint burns down too small to pass, and her world begins to look differently. The passing of time slows down, and her visual and aural perceptions become more acute. The music blasting from the CD player moves her more deeply, and although she doesn't find everything hilarious as the others, she does find herself laughing at things that would sound stupid at any other time.

Next she hears a can tab pulled, and Mark hands Lucas a beer, followed by two more pulls, and Lucas asks, "How about a beer, Lily? Try it. You might like it." The three of them laugh like mad.

"No, thank you." She's tempted though, feeling a little bit more at ease now, as they continue to laugh and sing along with the music. When Lucas begins to drive faster, Lily feels paranoid of crashing, paranoid the police will stop them, but she keeps quiet because one part of her also feels exhilarated. She looks over at Lucas, his strong body molded into tight jeans and a pullover shirt that skins his muscles. She sits back, plants her feet into the floor of the car, and determines to enjoy the night air flowing through her hair.

A half hour passes. Two beers down each for the boys, probably one for Kristen. When she glances over at Lucas, he glances back, dropping his eyes to her chest, then her legs covered with tights beneath her skirt. She pulls down on the hem of her skirt as her heart skips a beat.

They turn down another road; vehicles line up on either side, and as they pass an old farmhouse, cars, trucks, SUVs scatter like tossed pickup sticks in the yard of the party location. Live music pounds, a voice lifts loudly, and guitars hammer rhythms; she feels excited, but that subtle paranoia continues to descend. The confidence she felt going into the evening begins to brittle, but the accompanying party of three, loose, laughing, and practically screaming with delight pull her along.

Once out of the car, the two boys walk ahead, leaving Kristen and her trailing a distance behind. Kristen calls to them, "Hey, wait up!" The two boys turn and wait, Mark wrapping his arm around Kristen's shoulders. Lucas grabs Lily's hand and pulls her behind him, as he heads quickly for the most populated part of the crowd.

Lily feels free of the car now and less paranoid, but being dragged along behind instead of walking beside Lucas feels humiliating. She has never seen her dad walk in front of her mom, or pull her behind like a caboose. Not once. Ever.

Moving along in Lucas' wake, she takes in her surroundings. The moon shines like a huge spotlight down on this scene. The old brick farmhouse looms darkly in the front, but the moonlight shines on the rear like a movie set. A large barn stands to the right and behind the house, also lit up in this eerie way. A wagon, flat bedded with side rails also sits to the side full of dried corn stalks, orange pumpkins, a variety of gourds, and stacked bales of straw. Obviously, the family sells this harvest at Halloween time. She gazes, as Lucas pulls her along, out into the fields that surround the house. She notes the moon rays lighting the rear of the foliage, casting shadows that in her present state take on animal form, or maybe the bones of dinosaurs, or better yet, rocks that create an abstract sculpture garden. She must admit that this part of being "loaded" feels fun, as the high frees her imagination.

The temperature has already dropped, creating an October chill to hover over the ground, where kids on the outer edges of the party hang in groups, three to four in number, passing joints, pints of alcohol, and in some cases jars of what Lily figures are homemade brews. Many of the boys wear shorts, short-sleeved shirts, even flip-flops, proving their manliness, and the girls cloaked in light jackets or sweaters over dresses more appropriate for a summer day reveal skin and cleavage. Their legs bare or covered in tights, they hop their weight from one leg to the other, hoping movement kindles warmth, as their arms hug around themselves in desperation.

The four move deeper into the heart of the crowd, Lucas letting go of her hand and integrating into the herd. Kids nod at them, some call out a hello, some stare, watch them pass and say nothing. Lily notices that the crowd includes more than juniors and seniors from high school. People older, in their twenties, are also present, and some looking even older than that. Already she figures a hundred people are present and the night has just begun.

After stopping a moment to speak to another friend of hers, Donna, she turns to find Lucas gone now, out of sight. She doesn't feel sure of what she expected from him, but abandoning her was not one of the scenarios. Okay. That's not true. Actually, she feared his abandonment the most. She reaches up to adjust her headband, touch the pearls draped around her neck, and tip up her chin in defiance. If he wanted it this way, she would adjust and look for people she knows. She can always go back to hang out with Donna, or looking around, find Kristen and Mark, although being the extra person hanging out with a couple only makes her feel lonelier. Besides, she feels ticked at Kristen, who instead of supporting her for her choice not to get high, encouraged her and even embarrassed her in front of the guys. Looking around, she does catch sight of the "happy couple," standing in front of the band, Kristen's back rested up against Mark's chest, looking content to be together, their heads bobbing and toes tapping. She doesn't feel like disturbing them, so she wanders through the crowd searching for familiar faces.

Suddenly, she feels her arm pulled from behind, and there stands a classmate named Kevin, a cute boy she knows likes her, but his approach has always been too aggressive. What makes him think he can just grab her like this? He would try to own her. She has seen that with her grandpa Martin and his wife, Mary, but she puts up a fight, one of the reasons Lily likes her stepgrandma.

"Hey, Lily. What are you doing here alone?"

"I'm not alone," she says, pulling her arm away and continuing to walk. She stumbles into a stranger, feeling a bit dizzy, disoriented even. Fortunately, the boy laughs. This doesn't feel fun to Lily, as she regains balance and her sense of depth. She parks herself on the perimeter of the band, her back up against the wall of a small stone building, maybe an old milk house. Lily watches some kids already dancing, reserved now but sure to grow less inhibited, as the evening wears on. The paranoia that began to dissipate clutches her now, as she looks around and begins to feel like a leper. When she catches view of Lucas talking with Sue Klein and her best friend, Monica, she feels sick in her belly, and wonders why the hell she ever decided to come to the party, especially with that boy. She notices that he holds two beverages, one in each hand, and as if tuned into her in some strange way, he looks up and meets her eyes. After speaking a few more words to the two girls, Sue at one point leaning over to whisper in his ear, he heads towards Lily. She turns away from his advance, though a part of her, her needy side she supposes, feels happy that he hasn't forgotten her, but an anger rises towards that wicked girl, Sue.

He hands her the plastic cup in his right hand, flashing her his great smile. "Do you like Pepsi?"

"Sure. Thank you!" She takes a sip and her nose crinkles. "This tastes weird."

"Tastes fine to me," he says, as he throws back a good third of his beverage and loosely wraps his arm around her waist.

He likes her! He wouldn't be standing with her now like this, if he didn't. She tips her cup and drinks, her mouth feeling dry; she doesn't enjoy the funny tasting Pepsi, but after another sip or two she no longer notices.

By the time she empties the cup, Lucas pulls her out into the small crowd to dance, and although she feels slightly dizzy, she finds herself moving easily to the pounding rhythms of the rock band. Someway, somehow, her confidence level has boosted, and she no longer feels self-conscious but more sensuously alive, and Lucas notices. He pulls her to him with a snap, and they begin to dance together and she thinks, although not sure, that she feels his groin area up against her own, and a hardness she experienced only one time before. This time she does not feel alarmed but affected in the opposite way. She feels turned on. Really turned on.

⸎

Her mom told her the facts of life, and in junior high, the health classes showed a video and answered questions, boys in one room, girls the other. She understood the way in which the body works, the precautions needed, but the school seriously encouraged abstinence, presenting sexual activity as something only adults should do, when trying to make a baby. So when she began to feel stirrings of desire, which every kid feels, or so she assumes, she began to feel sinful. When she reached down to touch herself because the urge felt so great, she questioned whether she was a good girl, or bad.

As a freshman, she stood taller than most girls and quite a few of the boys, as well. Her height made her stoop a bit, and even though people told her many times that she was pretty, she felt like an ugly duckling.

Only she, Kristen, and a couple of other friends know that when they were freshman, a handsome tall senior named Brandon Love cast his eye on her and for two months tried every which way to gain her attention. A typical school day looked like this: all or most of the kids in school walked the halls in the morning before classes began with books in hand, while others stood with backs against walls or metal lockers watching. Lily walked with her friends, and in the early weeks of the school year, Brandon walked by and smiled, then he started saying hi, and after about two months, grabbed her hand one day very lightly as he passed. As she feels now with Lucas, she felt then with Brandon, like an electric current shot through her. She didn't know this person. He could have been the meanest boy in school, yet she reacted and guilt set in.

At lunch, she and her friends, mostly girls but a couple boys too, sat together, talked and laughed, and from the table they sat at every day, she saw Brandon watch her and sometimes his friends would glance over too. They knew he had his eye on her.

One day, Kristen said, "Brandon Love wants you bad."

Lily answered, "He's just kidding around." Great, thanks to her friend, Kristen, now all her friends knew, but only Lily would ever know what happened between her and this older boy, unless of course, he told his friends.

One day after a meeting with her soccer coach, following her last class, she set out to walk home. Her dad had offered in the morning to pick her up, but she told him she would walk and enjoy the warm bright October day. Fortunately, she wore flat shoes most days, already towering over others. That day she also wore her favorite black jeans and a purple shirt Nana had given her for her birthday, once too big, now after years, just right.

Three blocks from the school, a blue sports car pulled slowly up to the curb, with convertible top down and Brandon sitting at the wheel. He brought the car to a slow roll, calling her name. She ignored him at first, but when minutes passed and he still rolled beside her, she walked over to the car, adjusting her heavy backpack.

"Where ya going?" he asked. His hair shone in the sun, light colored like her daddy's. He wore fashionable shades, and she noticed the golden tan of his arms.

"Just walking home."

"She speaks! I've waited a long time to hear that voice. Want a ride?"

"No. I like walking," her mouth said, while her body told her something else; she wondered, however, how he knew that she would be walking. Was he following her or just lucky to be going by?

"It's just a ride, Lily."

True, she thought. Just a ride.

"Okay." She pulled the straps down on her backpack, slipping the pink and purple canvas off, and placed it in the back seat. She opened the passenger side door and slid in.

The car took off with a roar, and Lily immediately felt exhilarated. Up to that point, three different boys had kissed her, and what may be shameful to say because she liked it, too, one girl, all at house parties or school dances, and besides that she remained virgin.

"Aren't you going to ask me where I live?"

He glanced over with a little smile. "I know where you live."

Then why was he heading in a different direction? Brandon took a turn down a back road to Willis Park.

"Where are we going?"

"I thought we could just sit for a bit and talk. Is that okay?"

By this time, her heart raced, and sweat rolled down from her underarms.

Brandon pulled the car under a tree in the shade, looking over the Willis River. The leaves were turning, she remembers, and falling, but the grass still looked green and the water warm, although it probably wasn't.

Out of nowhere, he grabbed her and began kissing her, not in a gentle way, but shoving his tongue into her mouth, literally stealing her breath. At first, she resisted, even tried to pull away, but found herself falling into the embrace, the passion. Then his right hand dropped down roughly cupping her breast; though the gesture sparked desire, she began to feel overwhelmed. His next move not only surprised her but outright frightened her. He grabbed her right hand and placed it on his hardness. She pulled her hand away as if touching fire, but he forced her hand again.

"No! No! I don't want this!" she cried, but he continued to kiss her and hold her in what felt like a trap.

As an athlete, she had physical strength. She jerked herself away and threw herself against the car door, as tears began to run.

"Don't do that," he pleaded.

She reached desperately for the door handle and threw the door open.

"Okay! I'll take you home. I thought you wanted this. Really, I'll take you home."

She did not even look at him; she couldn't, caught between anger and humiliation. Slamming the door, she walked away, adding at least two extra miles to her journey because of Brandon's side trip. When she walked into the family home, she tried to scurry down the hall, before her dad saw her. He stood in the kitchen prepping dinner because her mom worked late. He heard her come in, stuck his head around the corner of the room, and his face lit up. Luckily, he didn't notice her shoes were dusty, her shirt wet with sweat, and her lips red from stolen kisses, but he noticed something else. He said, "Hi, Sweet Pea. Are you okay?"

"Hi Daddy. Why?"

"Your eyes look red."

That day she lied to her dad for the first time. She said, "Hay fever."

—〜—

Lily and Lucas continue dancing, his hands moving down over her bottom, pressing his hips harder into hers. The beats of the drums and grinds of the guitars drive her. Then she separates from him and begins to dance in circles, eyes closed, somehow staying erect, not stumbling, feeling like a bird soaring; when she opens her eyes, she sees that Lucas has disappeared again, and Kristen now dances with her equally abandoned. When the band stops for a short break, Lily's bird lands and she asks,

"Where's the guys?"

"Smoking a joint," Kristen answers.

Beads of sweat roll down from Lily's forehead and she feels them also descending her back. A chill creeps up, but she feels determined not to let anything compromise her elation.

"Here they come," Kristen says, a relief in her voice, her head swiveled to the left.

Lily looks over into the crowd to see the boy every girl wants to be with walking towards them, two more drinks in his hands. She doesn't hesitate to reach out for one, but Lucas holds the cup over to the side and approaches, swooping down into her just like a bird himself. He plants a kiss gently on her lips. From the corner of her eye, in the same direction he came from she sees Sue Klein watching. The wicked girl leans over and whispers something to Monica, and Lily feels a growl rising.

Lucas wraps his arm around her waist.

"Are you cold?"

"Just a little," though that's far from the truth. She shivers as her warm sweat cools in the autumn air and pulls her sweater to close in the front.

"Drink up. That will warm you."

"Pepsi again?"

"Well, it's actually more like a punch. A Pepsi punch."

Why should she care what's in the Pepsi? She stands here with Lucas, Mark, and Kristen, and at this moment she fits in, she feels great, though at times a bit woozy, and nothing can break the spell. She tips up the plastic cup and drinks deeply. When she comes up for air, the other three tap her cup with theirs and another gulp goes down.

The crowd thickens as the two boys leave the girls alone again, going over to shoot a shot, or so they say. The girls begin to dance, and Lily warms back up and begins to feel lighter than a feather, confident, and even more sensually alive. As she dances, she begins to run her own hands over her body, and she and Kristen giggle, twirl, wiggle, and prance as time fades away.

When she resurfaces for a glance around the crowd, she

notes the dancers becoming more frantic, those on the sidelines laughing, smiling even yelling, but everything seen and heard through a tunnel and somehow distorted. She stops dancing though Kristen continues with abandon, and Lily begins to weave on her feet from side to side. When she lifts her hand to reach up and steady her head, Kristen stops, and Lily suddenly feels the strange concoction of Pepsi mixed with something, what she does not know, rise up into her throat. She dashes over to the outside of the crowd, under a pine, away from others, but not too far, falls to her knees and vomits as the dry needles from the tree dig into her tender knees and palms. Kristen appears at her side, kneeling also.

"Lily, are you okay?"

Lily lifts her head, wipes her mouth with the back of her hand and looks up at her friend, the one that encouraged her to "party" and taunted her along with the two boys. Were the three all working together to undermine her? At this moment, she doesn't feel sure that this girl is her friend. A friend wouldn't do that. "Just go away. I don't want you here."

"Don't say that."

"You wanted me to party. Are you happy?" Her voice sounds strange inside her head.

"I know. I'm sorry, Lily. Lucas must have really loaded yours. I didn't know he was going to do that. I swear!"

"I just looked at my watch, and it's 11:30."

"Oh, shit!"

Lily pushes her weak body up erect with her hands, her knees stinging, and the palms of her hands sore now too, as the sharp dry yellow-brown pine needles stick into her flesh. Kristen helps her stand up. Two boys they don't know walk by and one says, "Uh oh! Drunk already." Their laughter fades as they move away.

Lily's face grows hot; her stomach churns. "We've got to find the guys! I have to be home or my parents will be furious! Do they think this is funny?"

"I'm sorry, Lily. I didn't mean for this to happen. Can you walk?"

"I think so." Her words feel so heavy on her tongue,

but throwing up cleared her head a bit, and anger replaces embarrassment, driven by a need to get home, even if she has to hide her condition. She will not disappoint Mom and Dad, not for anyone, especially a boy that not only abandoned her but intentionally worked to get her even more "loaded."

"I'm mad, too, you know," Kristen states. "Mark should be with me, not fucking around with Lucas."

"Let's find them, Kristen." Catching a second wind, Lily continues, "Let's go find those assholes."

She trembles now, not only with the chill as her sweaty body cools, but also because the heaving of the poison Lucas gave her. Her euphoric state crumbles, leaving her to feel frustrated, angry, and sad, perhaps disappointed more than anything.

The two girls walk through the crowd, the moon high now, casting a circle of light upon the madness. Lily knows she must look disheveled, probably reeking of puke as well, but at this moment, she does not care. The emotions, bouncing inside of her drive her forward.

Lily sees the two boys before Kristen does, standing over by a table behind the old house. Kids surround them, some Lily recognizes, some not, but two she knows well, Sue Klein and Monica. Kristen walks up to Mark and punches him in the arm. He turns just as he was about to throw a shot back of something golden in color and he freezes. "Hey!" Kristen yells.

"Hey, what?" he asks, weaving on his feet, too.

"We need to get back to the car!" People standing around all stop and turn to watch. Drama. Sucks them in every time.

Lucas, up to this point, preoccupied talking to the guy standing next to him turns also and when he sees Lily, he quickly grabs her two hands, pulls her to him with that snap she so recently found adorable, now irritated as hell by, and then on top of everything else, he twirls her.

"Don't! She just threw up!" Kristen shouts.

Great! Now everybody knows. Lily stumbles to catch her center and snarls, "Don't you ever touch me again."

Sue Klein and Monica giggle, as do others within earshot,

but only Sue speaks, "Is little Lily a little drunk?"

Lily, centered now, looks Sue straight in the eyes, and steps towards the bitch, as Lucas tries to pull her away by one arm. She aggressively yanks her arm away and stepping up further, into Sue's face asks, "What did you say?"

"I said, is little Lily a little drunk?"

"That's what I thought you said." Lily pulls back her arm, curls her fingers into a fist and hits Sue squarely in the middle of her nose. Her enemy flies back and falls on her ass, a look of complete and total shock on her face, a trickle of dark liquid dripping already from one nostril.

The group of people erupt into laughter, which drives Sue back onto her feet, and she rushes towards Lily and grabs her hair. Lily lifts her arm and jabs Sue hard in the chest with her elbow, tumbling the bitch into the table, spilling open bottles of liquor and full shot glasses that tinkle together as they fall.

Kristen yells, "Lily, stop!" as Mark grabs Sue and Lucas grabs Lily, pulling the girls away from each other.

Lily yanks her arm free yet again from Lucas and screams, "I told you to keep your hands off me!"

Kristen pleads, "Lucas, just take us back to my car. We have to be home."

"You two crazy bitches can find your own way home," his words sharp but slurred, as he turns to walk away.

"Please take us home," Lily pleads.

Sue imitates what she said in a snotty voice. Lily moves toward her, but Kristen pulls her back now. "Lily, don't." She turns to Mark and pleads, "Tell him. He needs to get us back to my car."

"I can't tell him what to do."

"You promised."

"Find someone else to give you a ride. Someone will be going that way." He turns and jogs to catch up with Lucas.

"You fucker!" Kristen screams after him.

Lily looks at her watch and feels like Cinderella, waiting for the hands to strike twelve, though her prince turned out to be a scoundrel.

21

Pant

Saturday 11:33 p.m.

WHAT Eric noticed first were the pearls, reflecting in the firelight. The little blondie girl danced, her long hair swinging, her face exhibiting a kind of bliss; her body language grew less inhibited by the minute. Sweet.

He could barely keep his eyes off her. Was she the one? Maybe. He would have to make his move tonight; the police came by the house in the afternoon to talk to him about Lola. He of course put the blame on her father, but what happens next would be up to her. On top of that, Tillman was back in town, and he more than any other person knew Eric's intent to seek revenge against Becker. Eric had little time for his last hurrah.

The chick she danced with didn't look bad either, but there probably were few men alive that didn't like those tall, thin all-American blondie girls. The other chick had dark hair, maybe brown; she stood shorter and had bigger tits, but he was more of a leg and ass man.

The first sight of the pearls stabbed him in the gut, but he didn't know why. Did his mother or grandmother wear them? Maybe one of the girls he hung out with once upon a time? Lola never wore pearls. She liked turquoise and wore the stone in her ears, on her fingers, and around her neck, looking like an Aztec princess waiting for the sacrifice.

The firelight played on those pearls in a way that appeared ghostly.

He watched as some young dude, lean but muscly brought her drinks, danced fiercely with her, but mostly kept running off. Eric felt sure little blondie didn't know where he went and what he did. Oh, sure, he shot some shots, smoked some weed, but mostly he kept checking in with another snatch, a medium-height girl with a few extra pounds, and from his vantage point, sitting on a bale of straw, he could see her eyeing the crowd like a bird of prey. He watched at one point, as the slut grabbed Blondie dude's package, drew him into some trees and fell to her knees. The dude possessed no stamina. He blew his wad in moments. Maybe she sucked that good. Made Eric feel like he should get in line.

He watched, too, as blondie started touching herself, as she danced, clearly drunk now, thanks to the dude. He felt like beating the kid's ass, until he realized that the punk's actions might benefit Eric in the end. At first, he didn't know exactly how he would get close to this girl, but after watching the dude abandon her time after time, he began to see his opening.

The sight of the pearls though kept affecting him, dancing around her neck as she and her friend gyrated, yeah, gyrated; he learned that word, too, while he sat behind the wire. The chicks pranced and twirled, butted hips, and laughed, and laughed. He could see the beads of sweat, glistening in the firelight, rolling from blondie's forehead down her cheeks and neck, her long lily-white neck, where those pearls draped around.

Why did those pearls make his gut twist? Why, damnit? He felt like a worm on a hook. Fuck!

He was on his sixth beer, which he brought in with him in a cooler, when he watched blondie trot unsteadily over into the trees, pines they were, only ten feet from where he sat, fall to her knees and puke. Now what good would a drunk girl do for the dude, unless he liked his girls out, unconscious, and open to whatever devious pleasure he had in mind. Eric went through that phase himself, until he discovered how fun it was when they fight.

That was the problem with Becker's wife. She didn't fight at all. She went willingly to the slaughter. Dumb bitch.

Wait.

No.

Wait.

Was she wearing pearls?

Fuck!

After all these years, he hadn't remembered those pearls one time, and how they looked like teeth, bouncing around her neck one moment and gone the next.

Not since that night, had he wondered what happened to them. He supposes the string broke and the pearls scattered, left to look like a handful of pebbles thrown. Maybe a gift to the god, who looked down upon him that night and rewarded him for his kill. He doesn't know why, but the storm that blew through became his partner in crime.

So he watched as the chick, with the help of her friend, stood back up equally unsteady and headed over to where the dumb shit – dumb because he didn't seem to know what he had – and his friend were pounding shots and acting like assholes.

He never expected in a hundred years blondie and the slut getting into it. He climbed down from his bales of straw, well, more like slid down in one place, and as he stalked toward them he heard himself begin to pant.

Blondie pulled back and punched the fat one, sending her flying to the ground. Who knew that under the little girlie sweater toned muscles rippled. Of course, the legs should have given this away. Little all-American was an athlete.

Eric easily integrated into the circle of mostly drunken teens surrounding the catfight. The flute player sat back up a bit dazed, but the little grin she carried as a badge broke shortly, when she reached up to wipe her nose with a finger. The sight of blood snapped her onto her feet, incited now as a taunted bull. She rushed forward, digging her fingers into blondie's hair and yanking. Blondie's next move convinced him that she had taken martial arts or at least taught to fight. She managed swiftly and precisely to jab the fat one in the upper chest with an elbow, and the slut exhaled a stream of air in a pop. By this time, friends of the two, including the "faithful" boyfriend of the one pulled them apart, uttering words to deescalate the violence. Eric figured every man standing around watching had a hard on. In fact, he felt ready to explode.

He lit a cigarette and felt let down, hoping to see the two rolling around on the ground, maybe a flash of little panties or, better yet, ass floss, as the skirts wiggled their way up. But, no, the boys talked the girls down, and he watched and listened. He had slid up closer now, and blondie and her brunette friend begged the boys for a ride. The slut slunk off wiping her blood away, while furious emotion raged in her eyes. One dude, the punk that brought drinks to blondie, walked away too, which didn't surprise him. He wouldn't be getting any of that tonight, not after blondie puking and fighting. The dude with the brunette left, too. The punks left the two drunken girls to fend for themselves. Eric recognized that as his opening. Now that he knew Lola meant to do him harm, and Tillman was sniffing his trail, he figured he had just a few more hours before he'd disappear from this Midwest hellhole forever. He would leave a final mark before he left. He had to do something with this buildup.

—⟁—

He had worried all afternoon. Why the fuck hadn't Lola called? Did he beat her too hard? Did his blows cut, crack, or bruise her more than he thought? He had to admit, the knuckles on his right hand looked more battered.

One worry that nagged him like a mad dog nipping at his heels was of course that she would press charges, but another more profound worry that he had conveniently stuffed into a deeper darker recess of his mind also surfaced this day.

Months before Lola went running to the women's place for the first time, she and he had engaged in another altercation. People always assume the man at fault when it comes to domestic fights, but they don't ever see what led up to the knock-down drag-out. Both he and Lola had been drinking, and unfortunately, when the twit drank too much, she became more confident even bitchy, and an attitude like that guarantees trouble.

"I thought you were taking me out to dinner," she taunted, sprawled on the large blue sectional, in front of the TV.

"I changed my mind," he snarled with the remote control in one hand and a rock glass full of vodka in the other. "I'm not moving my ass off this sofa." He settled further back into the cushions of that sectional on the other end.

"You never take me anywhere, Eric," she sassed.

"Gee, I wonder why that is. I don't want to be seen with you."

She sat up from her recline, and he swears her eyes caught on fire. "What did you say?"

He looked over at her. "You heard me."

"You *pinche Puerco!*"

He didn't speak Spanish, but knew cuss words when he heard them, so he snapped. Maybe he had a long week on the road, driving, popping pills, pushing past safe limits. He threw the glass of vodka against the wall beside the TV where it shattered, and pinned her down against the sofa with his right forearm up against her windpipe. He watched the fire fade from her eyes. "What did you say?"

"*Pinche Puto Puerco!*" she spit in his face.

He forced his arm down harder on those little bitty bones in the front of the neck. "You hear me, and you hear me good you fucking bitch! You keep your mouth shut or I will shut it forever. I've done it before, and I can do it again."

He remembers her eyes round as saucers, brown, deeply dark, with eyelashes that he envies. He also remembers that he had confessed to something he had never before or since. Lola had something on him that he could well regret.

Could that day be today?

Now she drank a lot that day also, more than usual, and probably doesn't remember what he said. She has never mentioned it, and he sure as shit didn't ask.

He released her and sat back up. "Go fix me another drink, and clean up this mess!"

She did both, not looking him in the eyes, not saying a word, just doing what he demanded. Afterwards, she sat back down on the sectional farther over to one end. To ensure later she met his needs, he compromised, "We can order food. Pizza. Meat lovers."

She did what he asked because living with him, even if he did work her over from time to time, would always trump going back to the fields and orchards to pick fresh food. He had her by the short hairs, as they say. The fact that they fucked good together didn't hurt.

Months later, she opened her mouth again, he worked her over, and she ran away to the women's place, only to come back home after a half day.

This time she hadn't called. She could well hold his future in those strong worn hands of hers. Day, months, and years of picking that fruit, lifting those baskets, living in a shed of a home, receiving very little pay. She could easily blow the whistle with that loud mouth, and she did, but they only asked him about roughing her up, nothing else.

After the cops left, he grabbed a few things he couldn't live without. He wanted to take a bit of time to trash a few of her prize possessions, like crosses and skulls, brightly colored shirts, shoes made of canvas and more crosses, but he had to move fast. He didn't want them to discover anything that would arouse suspicion of old deeds done. At the last minute, he ran to the garage and shuffled through boxes to find journals kept during his bit. He tore out pages, where he recounted moments of the murder and burnt them quickly in his back rubbish pile. He would disappear. They would never see him again.

As the hours passed, he began to feel nervous, paranoid even. He never liked being locked up, not for a minute. He would do anything to make sure that didn't happen again, but the nervousness spread into a hunger to kick back against everything and everyone who had ever done him wrong. It wasn't just Becker.

Oh, no. A line of fuckers had crossed and crisscrossed his path along the way. He would leave the area and more havoc behind him.

—◊—

He weaves his way through the crowd keeping his head low. His black stocking cap, jacket, and dark jeans keeps him from sticking out. He does make himself useful, by helping a couple dudes right the turned table, not that he wants to be of service, but because the two chicks stand near there talking in quiet voices. He stoops to grab a bottle of vodka laying on the ground over turned but fortunately capped, tips it up and guzzles, straining to hear what the two chicks are saying.

The brunette says something like, "We...through the crowd... give us a ride..."

Blondie, sounding a breath away from hysteria adds, "...now!

Like deciphering some strange language.

The brunette says, "If we wait...already late..."

Then blondie, "...embarrassed! Look...!

"Call them, Lily, and..."

"Wake them up? I...gotta get out of here!"

At one point, blondie looks around and her eyes rest on him for a moment. He might be older, but he has never had a problem attracting women, and he's always been very good at choosing the most vulnerable. Maybe he will use his age to work this one. He can play the caring adult. He breaks into a giggle, turns away and watches now as a young dude walks up to the girls, joint in hand, big grin on his mug.

He speaks loudly. "Lily Bagwell! How ya doing, girl? I heard you just whooped some ass!"

Bagwell. Where did he hear that name before? In the bar today? The gears in his head spin round and round.

Blondie says something that he can't hear, and the dude continues, "Oh, man, I can't. I'm a roady for the band tonight, and they would be pissed, if I left. Sorry. Hey, want a hit?"

The two girls shake their heads.

Bagwell. Becker Bagwell. Yes! The chick at the women's place. Coach's daughter, niece, or some shit. Jesus! Could he hit the jackpot a second time? Could this girl be related to her? She had dark hair and big tits. This string bean doesn't look a bit like her, but she might take after Daddy.

"You two be careful out there." The stoner strides away with a smile covering his face.

Blondie says, "...where the cars are...will give us a ride..."

The two chicks turn now, walking with some urgency though the maze of cars parked all over the yard, towards the road where vehicles line either side into the dark of both directions.

The girls will find a ride.

Tucked into the cab of his big shiny truck.

22
Tipped
Sunday 12:00 a.m.

J eff and Billy drove through Willis again and the neighboring towns, including Denton, stopping in every bar along the way. They didn't find Thompson anywhere. Holding himself back, Jeff only pounded two shots, and the earlier feeling of euphoria shifts now into a quiet despair. He wants to see his mission through, but begins to realize the magnitude of the situation; finding Eric Thompson amounted to a search for a needle in a haystack, but just before midnight, his phone rings.

"Jeff, I've got an address for you and also a vehicle description. Couldn't get a license number because it's from another state, but at least you have something to work with. Last known vehicle is a 2000 Chevy Silverado, black. Last known address, 5417 Dell Road."

"I can't thank you enough."

"If you need something else, don't hesitate to call."

Jeff doesn't know how Jack did it, and he didn't ask. He's just happy that the needle just grew larger.

Jeff slips the phone back into his shirt pocket, and they drive out to the address Jack gave him. Once there, they see the ranch house, sitting back from the road behind a line of hundred-foot spruces. The house looks dark as pitch inside, and not a vehicle in sight except for a semi-cab parked on the side of the dirty light-colored aluminum-sided garage. They take a chance, turn into the driveway, and cautiously drive in over the cracked and broken asphalt. Alongside the cab, the car headlights reveal a red canoe half covered by a tarp, a rusted wheelbarrow, and a heap of metal parts. One bright outside light perches high up on a pole, illuminating a fair share of the property and the house. They see a large dog, probably pit bull mix, straining to free himself from a long thick chain in the backyard. He barks and howls, spittle spraying out of his mouth in all directions. A ratty looking striped cat sits on the small cement slab of a back porch. As they open their car doors, the feline takes off on three legs, the fourth swollen and held up like a clutched bag.

Billy jumps out of the Lexus, after grabbing a flashlight out of the glovebox and knocks on the backdoor, but no one comes. Yes, risky business considering Eric, a ruthless bully type, could easily show up at the door with a gun – hell, maybe just shoot off a couple rounds and ask questions later. As Jeff steps out of the car, his phone rings again; he pulls it out and checks the number before answering. He thinks maybe Jack forgot to tell him something else, but no, it's a call from Desiree. His heart pounds as he slips the phone unanswered back into his pocket. Not yet. He's not ready.

He grabs another flashlight from under the driver's seat and moves quickly over to join Billy; they take the liberty, ignoring the chained beast, though the barking could alert a neighbor, and take quick peeks through the windows of the house, the garage, and the semi-cab.

The kitchen looks neat and clean from what they can see, a woman's touch most likely. The dark cloaks some areas of the rooms while the full moonlight brightens up others, so what they can see appears hit or miss. Two of the bedrooms have a look of disarray with open drawers, bits of clothes dangling out, some fallen to the floor, while hangers lie on the floor in closets, as if items had been hastily pulled away. Did someone tip Eric off, or did something else send him packing? Or could it be her, the female in the house?

Jeff says, "Looks like someone's on the run."

"Yeah. You think he's running from you?"

Jeff shrugs his shoulders.

They move on to the garage, glancing closer at the pile of

metal, canoe and barrow, and without even a say so, Billy lifts his right leg and kicks in the side door.

Jeff states dryly, "We could have taken the door off at the hinges."

"Now you tell me."

"I'm not interested in spending more time behind bars."

"I've waited long enough to find the fucker that murdered her mother. Besides, we're not taking anything and we can fix up the door. If he's on the run, it won't matter anyway."

"That's true."

Holding the flashlights, hesitating to turn on lights anywhere, they sweep into the garage, looking for who knows what, just hoping he guesses to find something, anything that could incriminate Eric. Jeff throws periodic glances out the windows, looking for headlights or house lights blinking on, even though the nearest neighbors sit a good quarter mile away. Otherwise, Billy's ruthless intent pulls him along.

They flash their lights over tools and lawn equipment, bags of grass seed, fertilizer, and boxes of paper. Rifling through the boxes they find a couple journals of sorts filled with word definitions and rants about time spent behind bars and the "pieces of shit" Eric shared time with. Some of the pages have been carelessly torn out of short sections of the journal and nowhere in sight, but they become excited when they find the word Coach on one page and how Eric planned to revenge Becker's "dirty deed." Not that the desire to act revenge constitutes an action, but isn't intent nine-tenths of the law? They sure as shit can't show this to the police, but at least they know it's here. Surely, because the journals lay askew near the top of an opened box, when everything else in the garage sits neat as a pin, Eric has run, tipped off somehow, and now they really need to scramble, or he could be gone forever.

In the middle of the garage, something stands covered by a heavy plastic tarp. They pull up the edges to see a perfectly polished Harley Davidson Sportster, and at that moment, Jeff thinks of Eric's father again, how he always owned a Harley, and how he felt like everything Eric knew he probably had learned from Rick Thompson.

Billy says, "That's a hell of a bike."

"I bet it's his father's. Eric never rode bikes, in the time I knew him. Wouldn't do anything that resembled his father. Funny too, they lived in a shit hole, but his father always had a top-of-the-line bike."

"So Eric wouldn't have gone to hide out with him or say a last good bye?"

"Shit, I don't know."

"Well, if they weren't tight..."

"The father was an abusive son-of-a-bitch, and he looked the other way no matter what Eric did, and Eric did some fucked-up things."

"Why were you friends with him?"

Jeff looks away as a collage of past dirty deeds flashes through his mind: blood running, bruises spreading, bodies lying prone. He looks back to meet Billy's eyes. "Well, Bill, as I stated earlier, I was not a good man either."

Jeff wonders what thoughts move through Billy's head, as he stares at him. Sizing him up probably. Wondering if he wants to associate with him at all. Finally, Billy asks, "Do you remember where the father lived?"

"I can probably find it. The old man might have died or sold the place, but I'm willing to give it a shot."

They close the garage side door, and smooth out the hinges and the lock pulled away from Billy's kick. They can't hide the fact that the door has been kicked in, but there shouldn't be any evidence of who did it left behind. They climb back into Jeff's car, and as they back out, Billy asks, "Would he leave a dog behind?"

"Oh, hell yes. He wouldn't think twice about letting it starve to death."

The night feels still and cold, as Jeff winds their way through the country roads. The hard woods look skeletal against the landscapes lit up by the moon, the evergreens stately and tall. The fields lay in waves of furrowed ground, ready for the spring's planting, many months away. At one point they come upon lines of cars bordering the road and pass a farmhouse where crowds of people gather in groups, dance around a raging bonfire; loud rock music jars the air.

Billy states, "Shit. That could be where my daughter is." He looks at his watch. "Well, she should be home by now."

"How old is she?"

"Sixteen. Quite a challenge."

"A little wild?"

"No. She's a good kid. Just growing up in a wild world."

"You can say that again."

Both men pull out cigarettes and light them, blowing the exhales out of the open windows. The crisp night air circles through the Lexus.

"No kids?" Billy asks.

"Not that I know of."

"Not married either?"

"Well, there's been a gal for the last couple of years, but I don't know if I'm cut out for it. Told me she was pregnant just before I left. I'm shitting."

"Oh, boy."

Silence fills the car for a few moments, while both men smoke.

"Billy, what happened the night James died?"

"Jack didn't tell you?"

Jeff shakes his head.

"James and I got into a hell of a fight. We almost killed each other."

"Why?"

"While I was away, he and my wife got...involved."

"Whoa!"

"I came back and they were living together in my house. Two days after I arrived back, we got into it at a barbecue. He wouldn't go to the hospital, took off with Debbie, and they were cruising down the road; an old farmer, Carl Dixon, pulled out in front of them. He must have been half-blind. He's dead now, but I know he regretted that with every ounce of his soul. Jesus, that car was a mess. I'm surprised she made it."

"I'm sorry to hear he did you wrong."

"For a long time James was like a brother to me. You know, he saved my life once."

"No. How?"

"After a game one night. Some fans from the other town wanted me dead, and if it hadn't been for your brother, I might well have been. Your brother just flew into a rage, pulled some kind of adrenalin out of the air and laid them out."

"Why the hell did they want you dead?"

"Drunk and stupid, I guess. We played against their team and skunked them. I was the quarterback. They wanted to get even. James fought four of them and then drove me to a hospital. He was fucked up himself. That's one thing you can say about the Tillmans; they are badasses when they need to be."

"Not Jordan, but yeah, I guess Jack, James, and I all learned how to hold our own and then some."

"He saved my life. He took my wife. What can I say? It all balances out?" Billy shakes his head and draws deeply on his cigarette. "Nah, I can't say that, but life goes on."

"You're a bigger man than I."

"It's about survival. Who wants to live dragging around that old shit? Not me."

"I wonder what he would be doing now, if he was still alive."

"I'd like to think that he would be settled down, but I don't know. He'd have little Jimmy, and that might have encouraged him to button up his fly. Debbie is a nice girl. I think it's great that Jack and she hooked up."

"Yeah," Jeff says, but considering she grabbed his nuts this morning, he wonders.

Just outside of Denton, on Dell Rd., Jeff starts looking for something he recognizes. He remembers driving in and out down a long dirt driveway. He just has to remember what the entry looked like, even though more than twenty years have passed.

Jeff slows now, straining for a landmark, and then he sees a 3x5 sign, white lettering on red, posted by a small pond that reads: No trespassing. Danger. Snakes. Not that the sign existed there years ago, but it feels right. Rick Thompson would post a sign like that.

Billy asks, "Is this it?"

"If there's a mobile home sitting back there about 1,000 feet, then this is it. One way in, and one way out."

"Maybe we should go in on foot."

"I don't know. I'm thinking we should go in nice and friendly."

"Just drive in and act like it's a visit? At midnight?"

"The joint served as party central in the day. Drugs and booze up the whazoo. Whether it's Thompson's place or not, we will probably get run off. Could get shot."

"We are taking that chance. Again."

"I can guarantee, if he still lives here, he'll be armed to the teeth."

"Well, I'm carrying."

"Good to know."

"Been carrying a pistol on me every day of my life since I returned from the Gulf."

"If I trusted myself with one, I would be carrying, too. I'm better with my fists and my feet than I am with a gun."

"That's also good to know."

They coast slowly down the long dirt driveway, the car rocking over and through holes of various sizes. The foliage runs up so close it creates a tunnel effect. In the distance, they can see a dilapidated mobile home with lights on inside. A curl of white smoke lifts out of the chimney and floats towards the stars. As they approach closer, through the large front window, Jeff can see an old man sitting in a chair, lift his head into their lights and begin to stand. Hard to tell, but it could be Rick Thompson.

Billy asks, "Look familiar?"

"The dump does, but I don't know if that's the old man or not."

There doesn't appear to be any dogs, or they would have already been barking. The only vehicles parked in the driveway are an old red Ford pickup and a battered white Saturn. Parts of machines, vehicles, appliances, cardboard boxes and newspapers, half-covered by leaves and branches surround the property, a cemetery of procrastination. Twenty years ago, the yard looked the same.

"His truck's not here," Jeff states.

"Doesn't mean he isn't. If he's on the run, he'd be hiding his truck."

"That's true."

"Hell, it could be parked in back of the place, or out in the woods somewhere."

"Yeah, but..."

Suddenly, two floodlights burst to life, and as Jeff brings the car to a stop, a voice booms out, "Freeze! Or I'll fucking kill ya!"

Billy and Jeff look at each other briefly, and then turn towards the home, to see the large bearded man, yes, Rick Thompson, standing on the porch holding a long gun of some kind pointed right at them.

"Get out of the car and put your hands up!"

Jeff and Billy oblige him, as Jeff shouts, "Mr. Thompson, it's Jeff Tillman, an old friend of Eric's! Do you remember me?"

"I'm an old man. How the fuck do you think I can see you from here?"

A woman steps out onto the porch; the wooden screen door slaps shut behind her. "Who is it?" she asks loudly.

Thompson turns briefly. "Get the fuck back into the house, Carrie Jo!"

"But who is it?"

Jeff feels surprised to see Carrie Joe still living with Rick

Thompson. "Carrie Joe! It's Jeff Tillman. Eric's friend. Remember me?"

"Oh, yeah!"

"Get back in the house, I said!" growls Thompson.

"I know him! So do you!"

"What the fuck do you two want, coming here so late?"

"We're looking for Eric! I'm in town for a visit, and I wanted to say hi!"

"At fucking midnight?"

"Yeah, I apologize about that. We didn't realize it's so late."

"You think he still fucking lives at home?"

Billy speaks up, "We couldn't find him in the phone book."

"Yeah, and who the fuck are you?"

"A friend of Jeff's just along for the ride. He wanted me to meet his old friend."

"Well, Eric isn't here. So just get back into your car, and get the fuck out!"

"Sure! Sure! Sorry we disturbed you." Jeff apologizes.

"Just turn around and get the fuck out of here!"

"Okay! We're leaving now. Sorry about the intrusion." Jeff adds.

Thompson squeezes down into a metal patio chair laced with plastic straps but keeps his gun on them. "Yes, you fucking leave now, and I'll be watching to make sure you do. Keep in mind that I have no problem shooting a man in the back."

Jeff and Billy turn back to the car and climb in. Carrie Jo calls out, "Good seeing you, Jeff!"

Thompson yells out, "Get back in that house, or I'm gonna punch you!"

Jeff backs up the Lexus, makes a sharp T, and heads back down the dark, long driveway. "Now what?" he asks.

Billy looks at his watch and says, "Twelve thirty. We still have some time before the bars close. Maybe we should make a second round and head out further."

"I guess," Jeff says feeling defeated again.

A few miles down the road, Billy's phone rings.

"Hello?" A couple of beats. "Hey, Babe. What's up?" A couple more beats. "She's not?" Billy starts rubbing his forehead. "I think I know where the party is. We can stop by and see if she's still there." A couple of beats. "You're right. It's not like her. I'll let you know. Don't go worrying yet." He closes the phone with a snap and shoves it back into his jacket pocket.

"Your daughter?"

"Yep. Do you mind heading over to that party?"

"Not at all."

The two men remain quiet as the tires crackle over the gravel road, stones occasionally firing out. When the right rear tire pops, both men jump, obviously more anxious than either of them would admit.

"Shit!" Billy exclaims.

"No fucking way!" Jeff pulls the car over to the side of the road. "Drove all the way across country without a hitch, and now it decides to blow?"

"You've got a spare?"

"Yeah, but it's just one of those miniature things."

"It shouldn't take too long to change it."

"I'm getting the feeling this might be a long night."

"You and me both."

The two men chuckle that little laugh where exasperation meets cynicism.

23

Trenches

Brenda stands at the north window, holding her breath each time headlights approach the farmhouse. This will be Lily. This will be the girls. But no. She steps back into the center of the room, and from here she can see the window in the next room facing south. She has control now. She can watch as the pairs of lights approach from either side. The next one will be Lily. She feels sure of it. Only five pairs of headlights have passed by in an hour, and no one drove up from the west – once a pathway from the back property, now a public dirt road that intersects the paved road. A beam of moonlight cuts in through the window to illuminate a square of carpet. In that small field of light, the toenails on her left foot painted red pulsate. She takes a deep breath to relax her trenched brow. She pivots her head to the right; she pivots her head to the left. Watching for those snakes of light. She wraps her forearms down across her agitated belly. Already three visits to the bathroom.

Kids can be kids; Lily Rose lost track of time. Maybe.

When the phone rings, she runs over to the oak bookshelf and grabs it so hastily, the slippery plastic falls through her hand. She bends and scoops it back up, hoping upon hope that Lily has called. "Hello?"

"It's me," Billy says.

"Did you find her?"

"Not yet."

"Did you go to the party?"

"Not yet," and he sounds exasperated. "If you can believe it, a tire blew out on Jeff's car, and the lug nuts are giving us a hell of a fight. As soon as we get it changed, we'll head over there. Are you okay?"

"No. I'm not, but I'll hang in there. Just be careful."

"I will."

She sighs.

Through the half-open window, she hears an occasional gust of wind, singing through the pine boughs, and crackling the dried leaves of the oaks. The fallen leaves continue to roll and tumble in waves with each new blast.

"Mommy?" She startles and turns to see her son rubbing sleep from his eyes. His hair looks rumpled and his pajamas askew.

"Did I wake you?" She grabs him, lifts him, and plants a kiss on his cheek. He smiles but his little feet flail for the floor.

"Why are you up? Where's Daddy?"

"He should be home soon. Are you hungry? Maybe a bowl of cereal?"

He shakes his little head. "Where's Lily?"

"She's going to be home soon, too. Everything's okay. Why don't you go back to bed?"

He turns and drags back to the stairs, leading to his and Lily's bedrooms and grudgingly begins to climb. She follows, and after he crawls back under his red, white, and blue baseball quilt, she pulls the covers up to his chin and gives him another kiss on his forehead. His eyes close, and in as little as three counts, his breath marks slumber. Quietly, she heads for Lily's purple and white bedroom, walls covered with posters of celebrities and female athletes. Although clothes tumble a bit out of half-closed drawers, and several discarded outfits lie on the bed, the room looks neat. A contrast of items reveals her daughter's hover between child and adult. Stuffed animals, including a purple and white kitty line up near her pillow, but on her vanity sits a variety of lipsticks, eye shadow, powders and creams, perfume bottles and hair clips. Lily Rose rarely wears makeup but the topless containers and disarray tells Brenda that her daughter painted herself up this evening. She considers riffling through Lily's drawers, to look for her mother's pearls, but doesn't. Everyone deserves a bit of privacy. Her brow furrows once again.

Maybe Billy and Jeff will track down this Thompson guy tonight. He will fall to his knees and surrender. He will beg them to take him in, where he will confess and pull out of whatever dusty chest he keeps the evidence to convict him. The pearls? What pearls he would say? Never saw them draped around her neck. Never saw them as they broke and fell upon the earth, rolling into a hole only Jake and she would find. Her daughter? At a party? Never saw her. Would never guess that she was hers, pearls or no pearls, placard on her back, announcing she's a Becker, or at least carries Becker blood. The men will hunt him down tonight, and if they don't find him, they will go out tomorrow and start again, for she knows Billy, and he will not rest until this man is found, convicted, and locked away forever. It will be over soon. These extended days and nights of suffering. Brenda's coils inside her churn, driving her to the bathroom once again.

She sits and her intestines dump. Walking away after flushing with right palm rubbing lightly on her belly, she walks back downstairs and resumes her position of window guard. Head pivots to the right. Head pivots to the left. She begins to feel dizzy, places her hands on either side of her head, to hold the globe steady; she will not lose her equilibrium. She half sits, half falls back into Grandma Martha's green vinyl rocker, and with closed eyes fights to quiet her thumping heart.

There have been so signs. No one has seen an angel. No one's going to die.

The words she heard did not come from the sky; they came from inside herself where fear and paranoia dwell.

Lily Rose has always made good decisions. She will be home soon. Maybe Kristen's car broke down, too. That cell phone Lily has been asking for? Brenda will buy it tomorrow.

She rocks her agitated belly, so weary from the bathroom

trips. The pearls, the pearls, he did not see them. Even if he did that night so long ago, the details will all be faded. He will remember snapshots only, flashes of the highs and lows. Her lack of fight, his frustration. Her last breath, the most satisfying. Nature assisting him with his crime, his triumph.

She worries for nothing.

Except that Lily's still not home.

Why should she feel guilty, that crushing emotion she knows too well, from blaming herself for wreaking her marriage, to the death of James, and the one that tortured her for the longest while, the death of her mother.

—⁂—

She had beaten herself up for not awakening when the murderer came to the door. At least the police thought he had done that. Knocked, asking for help. They estimated he arrived around 2:00 a.m. No tire tracks, no footprints, how the hell do they know? The storm that blew through didn't just scrub the killing field clean, but everything in a fifty-mile radius. Both she and Peter had slept the night through. Why didn't she hear the knocking? Why didn't Peter? Didn't Mom turn on the porch light? Peek from the window? Did he pull her out of the house, then take her by gunpoint? Force the door open from her grasp and grab her? Why didn't she scream? Cry for help? He covered her mouth that quickly? Why didn't she fight? If only Brenda had heard a scuffle, a man's voice, her mother's pleas, something, anything that would have woken her. She would have fought for her mother; she would have given it all she had.

They buried her mother, and Brenda packed all the emotion down, down further, down so far that she sometimes forgot the murder ever happened. She pretended to herself that Mom went away on vacation. Headed for an island to find some quiet and some calm. When that didn't work, she pretended that she never even had a mom. She remembers the day the denial broke.

At the rehearsal dinner, the night before she and Billy

married, she had kept all her feelings about her mother at bay, but when she arrived home with her father and her brother, she stepped into the kitchen and saw her mother's red and white checked apron that she loved; her recipe book lay open on the clean counter, marking a peach cobbler she planned to bake that morning, a list of groceries chalked on a board hanging on the wall. Daddy's museum to Mommy: leave everything as it is. She fell to her knees, and the sobs came up from that deep dark place where she had shoved everything down. She rolled onto her side and curled into a comma, rocking, praying for the pain to end. Peter ran to his room, still fragile; her dad reached down into a cabinet for the bottle of whiskey.

He took a big swig while she sobbed; she heard him swallow. Then the glass bottom clinked against the counter and he feel to his knees beside her. The tenderest moment she can remember sharing with her father followed; he touched her shoulder gently with one hand, one large, warm hand. "Don't do this. Please. Please, don't do this." The feeling of guilt that she had pushed down, pretended that she didn't feel came to choke her now; in the middle of her sobs, she began to cough, and she couldn't stop coughing and crying, and her dad had fallen now on his ass beside her, with tears in his eyes, his hand on her shoulder, rubbing softly. She remembers rolling over and reaching out for his leg, "Daddy, Daddy, help me, please, help me!" She clung to his leg, and he placed the palm of his hand on top her head and left it there. "Stop. Brenda, stop!" He had never known how to comfort, though he gave it a shot, but after a few more counts, he stood up and walked over to the cabinet to make himself another drink.

The sobs subsided, and she slowly picked herself up off the floor, stood up, and moved through the living room like a ghost, noting her father now slumped in his favorite chair, a green La-Z-Boy, worn on the headpiece and arms, staring through the TV. Silently, she continued to her room and sat down in front of her mirror. As she stared at herself, brushing her long dark hair, half empty now of all those feelings exorcised from the dark, except for the lingering guilt, which haunted until six months ago when, with the prodding of Peter, she determined to find their mother's killer.

—m—

She doesn't want to feel afraid of the dark again, afraid that the killer could be alive and stalking her family. After all, she is older and wiser, but what if, as Billy suspects, the murderer killed her mother out of revenge? What if he kept tabs on the family? What if he plotted and waited until just the right time, and that time is now.

When another car approaches, slowly, she pleads to a god she barely believes in that it turn into the half-moon of the driveway. She jumps up out of her chair, runs to the window with anticipation, but the car continues past. She turns and glances into the oval mirror hanging on the wall and sees, she swears, the faintest image of an angel standing in back of her, the face so gentle looking, the eyes full of concern. No! No way! Her mind is playing tricks with her again. She quickly blinks her eyes several times, feeling the terror rise. When she focuses her eyes once more, the image has gone, but Brenda finds herself breathless, heart banging on that bony cage; she slumps to the floor, and leans back against the wall to steady herself.

24

Three Bucks

12:40 a.m.

For thirty minutes, Lily and Kristen wandered around the parked cars, waiting for someone they knew, to ask for a ride. They even ruffled through their purses looking for cash, so that they could offer someone they didn't know some gas money. The air smelled thick with marijuana and cigarette smoke, and behind the steamed car windows couples engaged; clear patches of the glass revealed half-clad humans, rolling and twisting, limbs entangling. They heard moans, cries, and even screams as at least one couple fought. Lily gave little attention to the sights and sounds, focused instead on finding a ride, but also half-afraid that she might see someone she knows, worst of all, Lucas with Sue.

Although, she doesn't want him anymore, not after he deliberately gave her drinks spiked heavily with alcohol, and shamed her because she first refused to party, she still doesn't want to see the two together. Even after punching Sue Klein in the face, whether alcohol driven or not, she honestly could beat on her some more. Were these the actions of a mean drunk? She heard her mom refer to her grandfather in that way. Did she inherit the trait? Something has taken her over. She feels like kicking the sides of cars or pounding on the windows just to be wicked.

He put his hands all over her. How dare he?

She wanted a little romance, a little tenderness, a bit of affection.

The evening sure didn't turn out as planned.

Now over an hour late, her parents would be worrying,

maybe even out looking for her. She has to find a way home, as soon as possible. They would be furious to find her and Kristen stranded.

"Let's walk," Lily finally says.

Kristen turns to her. "Walk?"

"Yes, it won't kill us."

"But I'm cold."

"Walking will warm us up."

"It could be miles."

"Yes, miles for sure, but I can't stand around like this doing nothing. If we start walking, someone will eventually come along and give us a ride."

"Well, I'm sure not going back into that party. Which way do we go?"

The two girls stand in the middle of the dirt road, looking one way and then the next, their sweaters now buttoned up to their chins, hopping back and forth from one leg to the next, as Lily saw other girls doing earlier.

"I don't know. We smoked and I didn't pay any attention to how we got here."

"Me neither."

"From this night forward, when someone else drives, I vow to be more attentive."

"Me, too!"

"Maybe we can figure it out. The moon rises in the east…"

"And now it's overhead. How is that going to help?"

"Where's the north star?" Lily cranes her neck back to search into the starry night and almost falls over, still unsteady on her feet.

Kristen reaches out to catch her. "Are you sure you're okay?"

"I'm fine!" Lily spots a boy walking their way, smoking a cigarette and coughing. "Excuse me!" He hacks one last time into his hand then looks up. "Can you tell us which way to go to get to Willis?"

"North. To the left."

The two girls begin walking in long strides. The full moon lights their way, but the wind has also begun to blow in periodic gusts, causing Lily to shiver more, her teeth to chatter, but she pushes forward. She feels like she has to be strong for Kristen, whose arms wrap around herself to ward off the cold. They march forward quietly, not exchanging a word. Kristen's eyes look big as saucers, and Lily imagines her own look the same, as the two girls peer from side to side, into the dark, poised to run at the smallest sign of danger.

The road rises and falls over small hills; on the left side dry corn stalks rustle, and on the other, the last remaining leaves blow free of hardwoods. They float down upon the girls like confetti, or a strange snow, at times almost a blizzard, when the gust of winds are strong. Could this be a blessing, a sign that good luck comes their way?

This feeling dashes to bits in a heartbeat, when she reaches up to pull the right side of her hair back and discovers her hairband gone. "Oh my god!"

"What!?"

"My headband! I've lost my headband!"

"What!?"

Lily turns desperately to head back to the party. "We have to go back!"

Kristen grabs her arm and screams, "We're not going back!"

"It's my lucky headband! My grandma gave it to me!"

"Couldn't you come back tomorrow and look for it, when it's light?"

"I bet that bitch pulled it off of my head when we were fighting!"

"Yes, I think I remember now seeing it fall..."

"Why didn't you tell me?"

"I was too busy trying to calm you down! Please, Lily. I do not want to see Mark. I bet you don't want to see Lucas either. You can come back tomorrow. Please!"

Lily concedes, "I guess you're right."

The girls continue moving forward, though their strides shorten and their pace slow. Lily begins to feel more vulnerable, certainly not blessed, and her feet rapidly become sore, after so much dancing and now walking upon the packed down dirt of the road, but she doesn't complain. On another level, the walk through this night, pushing up against the dark, pushing up against the wind satisfies her need to battle.

Ten more minutes down the road, to the left, a distant rustle in the corn rapidly closes distance, and the sound becomes louder and louder, as if something stampedes towards them, not like a bull, or a horse, even light of foot, but the swift movement, the sliding through the silk and leaves, alarms Lily; her heart quickens, her body stiffens. She and Kristen turn as one and grab each other's arms, wide-eyed, mouths falling open, with anticipation of what will clear the cornfield. Suddenly, three young bucks leap across the road ten feet in front of them and fly into the trees on the opposite side, without as much as a glance their way.

Lily remembers her grandmother and her mom talking about signs: colors in the sunrises and the sunsets, knives, spoons, and forks falling, paintings sliding down walls, and of course, the appearance of particular animals. Spotting a deer means something and watching as three run across a path must mean something more. After what felt like a blessing of leaves, she wonders if the deer also mean something good lies ahead. Or could they...could they be a sign of danger?

And then, headlights approach from the top of the little rise of the road behind them, Lily still recovering from the shock of the deer, her breaths fast and shallow. Both she and Kristen turn, stepping off to the side of the dirt road, where the silt lies fine as flour, and they stand still, Lily anxious, but hopeful. Maybe at last someone will give them a ride. As the pickup truck pulls slowly beside them, an electric window moves down on the passenger side, and a man wearing a stocking cap pulled low on his head leans in towards the passenger side.

His voice is deep and kind." What are you two girls doing out here in the middle of the night? Do you need a ride?"

"Where are you going?" Kristen speaks first.

Lily grabs her arm and whispers, "Do you know him? Because I don't," though she might have seen him at the party. She faintly remembers a man wearing a stocking cap, standing on the sidelines, after she fought with Sue Klein.

"No. But I'm cold and tired," Kristen whispers back.

"We're fine," Lily speaks up to the man. "A friend of ours is coming along soon."

"Oh, okay. I just thought if you didn't have a ride." He points his right index finger at Lily. "I know you." They can see this by the light of the moon, slanting in through the rear window of the cab, revealing one side of his face. The other side remains in the dim light of the cab.

"Oh, yeah?" Lily says.

"You're Lily Bagwell."

"How do you know me?"

"I know your grandpa. And your...mom."

"You do?"

"Your grandpa used to be my coach. Your mom works in Willis at the place for women, right?"

Kristen and she exchange looks.

"It's late. Aren't you cold?" he asks.

Lily and Kristen nod their heads.

"Well, then get in. I'll take you home."

The lit side of his face breaks into a little smile, an arrow shooting. Her insides roll and toss. Never climb into a vehicle with a stranger. She's heard it so many times. He might know her family, but she doesn't know him. Yet she's desperate to get home.

"We need to go to the Big Boy in Willis," Kristen clarifies.

"Sure. Jump in." He leans over, unlatches the passenger door, and shoves it open.

Kristen turns to Lily as she climbs in, and Lily hangs back, a nausea rising, but she can't let Kristen go alone. She climbs in behind her friend, happy to be sitting by the door. She thinks about that little smile, that arrow flying, but it's too late now, the truck rolls forward. Besides, he knows her family, and why would anyone want to hurt them anyway?

Inside that truck now, Lily steals little glances at the driver from the corner of her eye. He wears all dark-colored clothing, from what she can see by the light of the dashboard, even the stocking cap on his head. A big man, he fills up the seat, and his head almost reaches the roof of the cab. Lily can't tell his age, barely able to see his face at all, as the headrest of the seat shutters the moonlight, but in her mind's eye she can still see that little smile, so hard to tell but maybe just a sneer. Happy, maybe, or something dangerous. Classic rock bangs out of the radio; she knows because her daddy listens to the same station. She notes a map laying on the dashboard, the neatly folded paper, but she can't read what state or country it represents. A small grinning skull hangs from the rearview mirror, jerking around on a chain as the truck drives over the rough gravel road. At their feet sits a shaving bag, a name her dad uses for the one he carries when they travel.

The man turns to them. "So, I know that's Lily. Who are you?" The one half of his face lights up again, and Lily searches the eye; there is no kindness there.

"I'm Kristen. What's your name?"

"Oh, it's...Tom. Tom Cruise."

"It is not."

He turns to Kristen again and shoots a look at Lily, as well. "Why?"

Kristen exclaims,   "He's a movie star! No one else has that name."

"Why can't someone else have that name?"

"Oh, okay, Tom."

Why doesn't he tell them his name? Lily glances down at the door handle and places her right hand on the cool metal, just in case. Now that Lucas has done her wrong, she doesn't trust anyone. Well maybe not anyone, but far fewer people than she has before.

"Oh, this is a great song!" He cranks up the radio volume. "You girls like Aerosmith?"

"Who?" Kristen asks.

"A little before your time, huh?"

The music batters at Lily. The night has been so long. She just wants to get home. *Please. I just want to get home.*

"Did you two have a good time at the party?"

Lily leans forward and turns her head to him. "You saw us there?"

"You were five miles out of town walking alone on a dirt road. Where else could you have been?"

"So you didn't see us there?" Kristen asks.

"Oh, I saw you."

"Did you have a good time?"

He clears his throat and sits up straighter, preparing for something, but what? "I had a good time watching your friend Lily there beating up on that slut."

Lily, in her own haze of alcohol and marijuana, although a bit lifted from the cold autumn air, would swear that he slurs his words. Just great. They catch a ride with someone probably higher than they are. Could he crash the truck? She does feel happy though that he called Sue Klein a slut.

He reaches up with his right hand and turns towards the back of the truck. Both girls startle. He laughs a little then reaches back behind the seat, Lily notices the skinned and broken knuckles as the hand reaches up in the moonlight and dips back down the other side so smoothly, as if he has done that a thousand times. He pulls his hand back up with a beer can in it.

"Want a beer, girls?"

He knows her family and offers her a beer? Maybe he doesn't know how old she is.

In unison, the girls say, "No, thank you."

"Yeah," he continues. "I watched that slut give your boyfriend a blow job."

Lily grabs the top of Kristen's leg with her left hand. Her friend jumps, which causes Lily to jump, too.

"She was probably blowing every dude at that party. Some chicks just can't get enough."

Did she imagine those last words? He did not say them. He couldn't have. A friend of the family's? A friend of the family would not talk to them like that. Yet, that thought takes second place to an emotion rising: anger. That jerk, Lucas! That bitch, Sue Klein! She should have known. She shouldn't feel surprised at all.

"Made me horny," he says. "I was hoping you could oblige me. You know, for the ride."

Lily and Kristen shoot each another look, as Kristen grabs Lily's hand squeezing her leg like a vice. A panic looms inside Lily, stealing breath and movement, but an all-consuming anger wins out. She leans forward and through clenched teeth states, "You can just stop this truck and let us out."

The man rolls his head back and starts laughing, pauses to take a swig from his beer and then continues, in a devious way.

"We can jump right out of here!" Lily says.

"Maybe. If you could open the door."

Lily pulls up the handle on the door, but nothing happens. She starts punching buttons with her fingers near the handle, hoping she hits one that will set them free, but although the window goes down and up and down and up, the door lock doesn't budge.

"Stop this truck!" she screams.

The man continues laughing and swigging on his beer.

"Please, just let us out," Kristen pleads

"You blow me, and I'll think about letting you out." His tone takes a serious turn, this one matching that eye, as he detours down a two-track lane, a farmer's side road into a field.

"We're not going to blow you!" Lily throws the words at him.

"Oh, no? Then, I'll kill ya."

He brings the truck to a stop, turns in the seat and leans up against the door. Quickly, he unfastens his belt, and then begins to unzip his pants. He rustles inside there and commands Kristen, "Since you're right here you can start."

Kristen and Lily slide away from him and up against the opposite door. He reaches over and hooking his large hand around Kristen's neck, pulls her face over towards his groin. She slaps out wildly at him as Lily begins to seethe.

With all the strength she can muster, Lily begins to throw punches at the man's face and head, landing a few, but he wards off most with his large hands and forearms. When he begins laughing again, she punches harder, and to her surprise, animal noises move up out of her in snarls and growls. He grabs Kristen by the hair, who has been bracing herself up against the dashboard, and secures Lily's right fist in his right hand, but that doesn't stop her. With her left hand, she reaches out, pulls the stocking cap off his head, and begins to pull his hair.

"You fucking little twit," he hisses through his teeth and slams Kristen's head back on the dashboard, but he's looking at Lily, his eyes jumping rapidly between her face and her neck, her face, and her neck. Kristen, unconscious now, slips into a heap onto the floor of the cab, as he pulls the keys out of the ignition. His eyes squint up into something mean as he opens his door, steps out with deliberation and slams it tight; he stomps around the truck towards the passenger side, as the lock on the driver's door clicks into place.

Lily pulls Kristen up, trying to reposition her on the seat, calling her name, touching her face, but her friend remains unconscious.

She turns facing the door, slides herself back on the seat and draws her legs up to kick, as he throws the door open. As he reaches in to grab her, she kicks out viciously with both feet, right left right left right left right left, landing a few on his lower abdomen, but none landing on her target, his half opened pants.

He grabs her left leg and pulls her out, her butt sliding across the seat, out the door towards the ground, the back of her head bumping against the stair, which hurts badly, very badly, leaving her jarred and dizzy. She gazes dizzily up into the sky now dotted with clouds, covering stars and one-half of the moon. As he reaches down for her, she rolls quickly away over, and over, and lifts her torso preparing to run. He grabs her right foot but gets only her shoe. Her eyes move rapidly in all directions looking for light, a safe place, and when she locates something in the distance, she begins to sprint. She's always been a fast runner, but without a shoe, her right foot in a short time begins to hurt, and the man, tall and rugged, and surprisingly light on his feet quickly catches up. She can feel him looming behind her, and smell his hot panting breath stale with beer. He grabs the back of her sweater and pushes her roughly towards the ground. She feels the hard dirt clumps dig into her knees and palms, as she lands, already tender from the dry spiky needles beneath the tree when she puked. Grabbing the back of her sweater again, he pulls her up and punches her soundly with his right fist on the left side of her face. She tumbles over into darkness.

She frantically runs in the complete darkness that surrounds her. She feels her feet upon the ground, as they carry her forward one by one, but even then, she feels terrified that the earth may open. She may fall through and into what she does not know. She thrusts her arms forward reaching out with her hands, grasping, guiding, even hunting for one object, not to collide with but to hold onto, to save her, to catch her if she falls. In the darkness, faint but growing louder, Kristen's cry for help rises, a pitiful cry, the cry of an animal wounded.

She stops, cocking her head, straining to determine, which direction Kristen's cries are coming from. Just as she turns to step into one direction, the sounds, twisting her insides, spring up behind her. She pivots on the ball of her right foot to face this new direction, but now hears her friend to her side, then the other side. Suddenly, her friend's whimper and whines surround her, moving out of the distance toward her and they grow loud, so very loud. Lily raises her hands to cover her ears for she begins to feel crazy. She shakes her head, breathing hard now, until out of desperation, one word begins a journey deep inside of her, moving up, and though some part of her knows she should hide her whereabouts, the word ascends swiftly and breaks the barrier of her lips, "No!"

The word echoes. Is she deep beneath the ground, in a cave maybe, where even the thinnest ray, smallest dot, the tiniest pinhole of light cannot shine through? She shivers and her teeth chatter, so she wraps her arms around herself, realizing Kristen's cries have stopped.

Where does she go? What does she do? So she begins moving again, hands leading, steps gingerly, her senses so aware, she feels brittle as a dry branch, as thin as angel hair, as light as a feather, terrified she may stumble down further or fall deeper within, disappear forever.

Out of nowhere, the sound of heavy footsteps encroaches upon her senses now. The sound comes from behind her, and the angry girl who punched Sue Klein and that man who picked them up, pivots again on her one shoed foot, to face what's coming; the steps grow louder and louder, closer, and closer. She has two choices: either stand still and allow whatever, whoever to reach her, or run for her life in a darkness that shields everything from sight.

She runs and so do the footsteps, approaching from behind at a fierce pace. Running in darkness takes more courage than she has ever known and any possible run into, stumble over, or fall within forgotten. One thought prevails: flee what chases her at all costs.

When she feels only one breath left, her legs half-numb from effort and cold, both feet screaming with pain, something or someone catches up and throws her over a shoulder. When she smells her daddy, she lets herself go, under, out, safe at last.

—✲—

She awakens, but only for a moment, to see the ground moving below her and large black boots stepping along with determination. They are not the boots of her daddy, and the pearls that would be hanging now banging on the cliff of her chin? Gone.

They had to put more time into loosening the lug nuts on one tire than it would take to change all four, but so the night unfolded. By the time they changed the tire, they were both drenched in sweat, and the profanity still echoed in the distance. The spare, one of those small mini tires now limited their speed and distance. When he called Brenda at 12:30 to let her know what happened, Lily was still not home; he threw out another few choice words. The flat and the tools closed inside the trunk now, they jump back into the car and head to the party, limping along on that spare.

Once they arrive, they drive slowly up and down the road, looking for a Ford Focus, the car that Kristen's father told Billy he bought for her. There must be a hundred or more cars along the road, parked in the yard of the farmhouse, and a few even scattered in a field of stubby corn stalks. After three trips past as many of the cars as they can see, they decide to park and stroll in.

"I really appreciate you taking the time to help me with this, Jeff," Billy says.

"No problem, man."

The party takes him back to his own youth; he drank, he smoked weed, he taunted fate more times than he cares to count, but this party, at his age, after Brenda's morning heartbreak, the fruitless meeting with Holder, the drive through town and country for a killer and, of course, the struggle to fix one metal piece that refused to give, all exert a toll. He grits his teeth to keep the gut pain at bay, and his leg, which rarely bothers him anymore, flares like a son-of-a-bitch tonight.

As he and Jeff head into the throng of drunken, high, and rowdy youth, he shakes a cigarette out of the pack, lights it and sucks in the smoke as if it's his last. He wonders why girls parade around half dressed, when breath clouds in the air, and the guys too, stumble around in shorts and even flip-flops. Of course, most feel little to nothing in their current states, but they will feel plenty in the morning, when their heads bang like bass drums, and their mouths feel dry as sawdust.

He searches for the girl that stole his heart from the first glance, and he whispers a silent prayer, though not a religious man, *please help me find my daughter.*

"What's she look like?" Jeff asks.

"Tall, thin, blonde-brown hair, but you're not going to see much of that in the dark."

"Any idea what she's wearing?"

"That I couldn't tell ya."

Billy likes Jeff. He seems good intentioned, though he suspects Jeff hasn't always been a clean-cut dude in a Lexus. Billy noticed a palsy in his right hand, and the rolled-up sleeves revealed ink-covered arms. Regardless, they are a team now, for better or worse.

What he sees spread before him disgusts him, riled further by the music, which the band plays so loudly, the sound distorts. Quite a group dances in front of them, again, in various stages of disarray. Boys' hands wander upon girls' body parts, which, okay, he did some of the same. Hell, his hands were all over Brenda when they were younger, but never as a spectacle in front of others. These girls are somebody's daughters, maybe even his precious girl.

Where is she?

Cans, cigarette butts, half pint booze bottles strewn around. Somebody owns this place. Where the hell are they?

Small circles of partiers pass joints, bottles, and cigarettes, as whooping and hollering ricochets around the dark. So far, they've walked by two skirmishes, and now approach a third and this one Billy intervenes, pulling a big kid off a smaller kid, whose red, swollen, and cut face appears visible now for moments as headlights flash from a departing car.

"Cool it, assholes!" Billy growls through a clenched jaw.

Heads turn, as he and Jeff stroll slowly through this riot of people, not all youths, as he first thought. A few girls smile, a few guys size them up, but none of that matters to Billy, a man on a mission, to find Lily Rose and, if not, someone he recognizes to ask, if he or she has seen her.

He wonders what happened to respect and honor, as he takes in the madness stretching out before him. You do not litter the earth. You do not act vulgar in public. You do not pick on dudes smaller than yourself or talk an innocent girl into giving herself to you, only to pretend she's a stranger the following day.

He doesn't see Lily or Kristen, and when the pain in his gut feels like a saber piercing, he covers and clenches the area with one hand.

"Are you okay?" Jeff asks.

Billy nods. Even if he falls to the ground, he'll crawl, if he has to, but one way or another he'll find her.

Then he spots what looks like Kristen's squirrely little boyfriend, whose name he can't remember. He stands under a tall, magnificent maple, almost nude of scarlet leaves, with a girl down on her knees, face into his groin.

Billy nods his head in the direction to Jeff, and the two walk up to where the kid stands, back against the tree, eyes rolled back into his head, muttering, "Oh, yeah, yeah, oh yeah..."

The kid pops his eyes open and panics, as he hurriedly shoves the girl's head away, then fumbles and packs his privates back into his pants. The girl falls onto her ass, looks up at him and Jeff, wipes her mouth off with the back of one hand and scrambles up and off at a trot.

"Mr. Bagwell..." he begins.

"Where's the girls?" Billy asks.

"They...they left I guess. I haven't seen them."

"When?"

"I don't know. Forty-five minutes maybe. An hour."

"They didn't come in Kristen's car, did they?"

"They came with me and Lucas."

"Lucas? Who the fuck is Lucas?

"A guy that Lily likes."

"You don't know who they left with?"

"No. I don't know."

Billy grabs him by the collar of his shirt and jams him up against the tree.

"I don't know!" the little prick cries. "They were looking for a ride."

"Why didn't you and the other dude give them a ride?"

"It was Lucas. He didn't want to leave."

"You left those girls alone? Your own girlfriend?"

"They wanted to leave! They probably got a ride."

"You punk," Billy says one inch from the kid's face, before he pushes him to the ground. "You better hope they're okay."

"I do! I do hope they're okay. You're right. We should have given them a ride."

Billy and Jeff start stalking around the grounds again, Billy holding that pain in with one hand. The girls couldn't be home yet. If they were, Brenda would have called.

"I don't think they're here," Billy concludes. "I just wish we could find someone who knows who they caught a ride with. Someone must have seen them."

As the music stops for a break, and the two men stand more or less in the center of things, Jeff lifts his right hand to his mouth, and with two fingers, emits one of the loudest and longest sustained whistles Billy has ever heard. A grin breaks on Billy's face, as he watches most of the partiers stop what they're doing, and turn to him and Jeff.

Jeff shouts, "We're looking for a couple of girls!" He bows and waves a hand through the air towards Billy.

Billy shouts, "We're looking for Lily Bagwell and Kristen Demming. Has anyone seen them here recently or leaving with someone?"

A few individuals shake their heads. Most turn away and resume what they were doing. One young man walks up to them in long strides. His eyes glisten in the firelight, as he holds a joint behind his back with two fingers.

"I saw them a while ago. They were starting off down the road." He breaks into a rattling cough.

"They left walking?"

"Yeah."

"Which way?"

"North. I didn't drive, so I couldn't help."

"Thanks. Let's go, Jeff. Maybe they're still walking."

Billy breaks into an uneven trot, his hand on his belly, leg screaming. Jeff runs ahead. They reach the Lexus, jump in, and with a spray of gravel, as much as one can with a baby spare on it, they drive off north. Maybe. Maybe they are still walking. Or does he hope that someone picked them up and gave them a ride? Why aren't they home already?

He and Jeff can't keep driving on the spare, and the longer it takes to find the girls, the greater opportunity for the killer to slip away forever. Jesus. What do they do? Billy pulls his cell phone out of his pocket in hopes that he missed a call from Brenda, but no. He drops it back into his pocket.

Billy keeps his eyes peeled, not just stretching in front, where the headlights brightly illuminate the road, but also searching the sides of the road, even off into the fields on one side and woods on the other. Although the headlights help enormously, he has to wait for the moonlight to break outside of a cloud to see into the dim distance. So far, he hasn't seen hide nor hair of anything alive, and only one dead skunk, flattened and stinking.

Jeff says, "Bill, I think we should call Jack and ask him to help."

"It's late."

"We need to get someone else out looking for Thompson, especially if he's on the run."

"I know. What a fucking predicament!" A few beats pass as his brain assesses the situation. "I know! If we don't find the girls up here, I'll call Martin. He lives close by. I can take his car and keep looking. Maybe Jack can come and pick you up, and you guys continue to look for Thompson. I'll hook back up with you when I can. "

"My concern…Billy, is that these two things might be related. What if Eric heard that I'm back in town, and he decided to strike again before he splits? I hope it's not true, and it probably isn't, but I know who we're dealing with here. At least I know him from twenty years ago. He has nothing to lose. Maybe he knows that Lily is Coach's granddaughter. I think that we need to be aware of that possibility."

"Fuck, Jeff. You're freaking me out here."

"I hope I'm completely off. Call Jack. Ask him to drive around and look for Eric and maybe go past his house again, too. I'm sticking with you until we find your daughter."

Billy nods, pulls out his phone and stabs the numbers. "Jack, it's Billy. Sorry if I woke you. Unfortunately, we need some more help. We have another situation. My daughter hasn't come home from a party. Jeff and I are looking for her and her friend. Would you drive around and look for that truck? Go past that address too, if you don't see anything. I'm not asking you to get involved with this, just be another set of eyes. Jeff and I can take care of it from there."

"You got it!"

"Thank you." Billy worries that they are asking too much. As Jack said before, once a felon always a felon. He doesn't want to cause any problems in his friend's life, but he feels desperate, hell, beyond desperate.

As Jeff continues driving along at a crawl, Billy searches every inch of everything he can see. So far, he hasn't spotted anything that looks like a track, paying special attention in the few areas where the sides of the road hold soft silt. Most of the road stretches out hard, packed down like cement. But wait. "Jeff, stop the car! Stop!"

The Lexus rolls to an uneven stop. Billy reaches for the door handle. "What'd you do with those flashlights?"

"I put one back in the glove-box."

"Back the car up a few feet, and angle the lights over here to the right."

Billy jumps out of the car and spreads the light, peering down into the dirt, the silt, and there they are, prints very lightly impressed, on the side of the road. The size looks correct for two girls, one's feet larger than the next, but too small to be a man's, too large to be a child's. They appear occasionally, as Jeff slowly follows him in the car, and at one point, where the silt sits especially deep, deer prints sit deeply embedded, too, as if two maybe three deer bounded across the road, the human prints crisscrossing them. They collect in one spot a bit further down, as if whoever was walking stopped, and from there do not continue. The road center does not reveal any car tracks, too packed to show anything. The owners of the prints either levitated or caught a ride, but with who? If the prints belong to the girls, the person or persons who picked them up either hasn't delivered them yet ,or the girls decided to go AWOL. Would his Peanut defy him and Brenda like that? He doesn't think so. Billy jumps back in the car as something crawls up and sticks in his throat. Jesus, he will not cry!

"You found something," Jeff half asking, half confirming.

Billy takes a couple of deep breaths, then answers, "Yes. Someone picked them up. Let's head to Martin's. Go up to the stop sign and turn right."

Billy's mind races now. What if Jeff's hunch is correct, and Thompson stalked his girl at the party? Or both girls? What if at this moment he...Jesus! Then another thought crosses his mind. He turns to glance at Jeff and he wonders what if. What if the dude he's sitting in a car with is part of it? He's not well intentioned as Billy believes but some predator working in concert with the other?

Jeff glances back at him. They meet eyes for a moment. Jeff states, "I've seen that look before. You're wrong. I am who I say I am. I swear!"

Billy nods, realizing that his thoughts have careened out of control. He's compensating for his torment. This must be the most helpless feeling in the world, and a parent's worst nightmare. Being a man who has always prided himself on fixing things, he feels like screaming or, better yet, striking out.

—m—

His mother told him one day after school she'd heard that Brenda's mom had been found dead that morning in a field. He wondered why Brenda hadn't been in school. Being fifteen at the time, he jumped on his bike and rode over to the Becker home, even though his mom told him that he would probably be in the way. He loved Brenda, and he would always take care of her.

Two police cars and an unmarked car parked in the driveway. They were inside with Martin. Billy could see Brenda slumping on a swing in the backyard, and Pete sitting on the bench of a picnic table. Their grandmother, Martha, sat beside Pete. He jumped off his bike, dropping it more or less on the ground and bounded over to them. Brenda jumped off her swing and ran into his arms. She began crying uncontrollably, as Martha and Pete looked on. Pete, too, began to cry, and Martha put her arm around him, holding him closely.

Billy didn't utter a word, not knowing what to say. He felt then the same way he feels now, helpless, but he vows to himself to find his daughter, and if she turns out hurt in any way, whoever touched her will have hell to pay.

—m—

"The house up here on the right. Just turn in the driveway," Billy instructs Jeff.

As Jeff turns in and the headlights glance across the picture window of the living room, Billy sees Martin stand up from his easy chair and look out. Before Billy can even open the car door and climb out, Martin has walked out of the house and onto the porch. As Billy closes the car door, Martin asks, "What's wrong?"

"Lily Rose and her friend are missing. I think someone picked them up a couple of miles that way, but that had to be a while ago. They still aren't home."

"Well for Christ's sake," Martin mumbles.

Jeff, too, has climbed out of the Lexus, and Billy introduces him to Martin, as the older man steps down the stairs and limps towards them. "This is Jeff Tillman, one of your athletes back in the day."

Martin points at Jeff with one finger, "Yes, and you're one of the guys who robbed that house, along with that smart-ass Thompson."

Jeff admits, "Yes, sir, that's correct."

"Well, it looks like you made something of yourself after all."

"I like to think so."

Billy interjects, "Come on! We need to find the girls. As you can see, Martin, we have a flat. We were hoping you would let us use your car. We could go back and pick up my truck or the wagon, but it would take too long."

"Of course," Martin says.

"We were out looking for Thompson, until Lily and her friend came up missing."

"So you think he..."

"Yes, Coach," Jeff says, "I think he killed your wife."

Martin rubs his lips with his fingers, slowly nodding his head. "Well, we better get moving..."

"Martin, you don't have to come..." Billy clarifies.

Martin directs, "Pull the Lexus up over there. We'll take the Buick. Let's go!"

26
Tangled

Sunday 1:45 a.m.

Jack startled twice, once when the phone rang, and once again when he found his flesh touching hers in a way he would describe as too close for comfort. Some people call it spooning, but this was more than that. Debbie glanced up from her pillow with sleepy eyes, as he finished speaking with Billy, and he whispered to her, "I'm going to go help Billy with something. Don't worry." She opened her mouth to speak, but before words were uttered, he coaxed, "Go back to sleep."

He swung his legs over the edge of the bed, feeling the cold air blowing through an open window. Is that why they were all entangled? He stood up and headed for the bathroom.

—✺—

Miles outside of town now, he's heading for a hole-in-the-wall bar, the Brown Bear, located halfway between Willis and the next town going east, Denton. He begins to think like a man on the run, one who decides to hit a watering hole, or two for the last time to say goodbye. Past deeds threaten today's freedom; he probably feels panicked. It takes a lot to say goodbye to everything a person has known. Jack knows. He did just that when they sentenced him to eighteen years. He thought about fleeing, too, if the judge allowed a bond, but he declared Jack a "flight risk." In the end, he received more time than the pedophile he beat. Funny how that works. But Jack knows better now. He's a kinder and gentler man; he must avoid violence at all costs, but if confronted with another situation like that one, could he walk away? He thinks he could, but he's not sure. He cringes at

220

the thought of serving more time, but his need for justice in a chaotic world could supersede his common sense or, better yet, self-preservation. Fortunately, he has others to think about; he has a wife and a boy, a...son. Yes, he is a father now.

He learned to think like a criminal while serving his bit surrounded by liars, shysters, rapists, and killers. He learned. Shit, did he learn! And he used it to save his ass on more than one occasion.

—m—

They did have a couple of drinks at the restaurant and a few more when they came home. Though he didn't black out, nothing near that, he can't remember making love with Debbie. Some way, somehow, he drifted over or did she? She tried so many times before. He always rolled away or gave her a minute or two, just to give her something. Not last night. There he lay flesh against flesh in a different way, apart from the old gnashing and pumping, grinding and coming, something sweet. Something scary.

—m—

He pulls into the parking lot of the Brown Bear, a pool hall and bar sitting in the middle of fields, like an oasis for anyone to slow down, pull in, throw a couple back. He drives slowly through, looking for that black Silverado, and there one sits, although he's not sure if it's a 2000. He doesn't even know what the man looks like, but he can do a little fishing.

He lumbers into the bar. In a situation like this, he uses his size to serve as a means of persuasion. He needs to be efficient. The clock ticks. He has driven through the parking lot of every bar, liquor store, restaurant, café in Willis, and kept his eyes peeled every minute for that truck.

A dozen and a half people populate the tavern, six or so sit at the bar itself and a few more at worn wooden tables. The bartender, a hefty looking female, looks up as he enters and watches him approach. He used to hang at this joint sometimes after his parole ended but doesn't remember her. He quickly sweeps the place, looking for anyone he knows and anyone he guesses might be the driver of the truck. The four pool tables spread out like emerald islands under long fluorescents, where the remainder of the occupants, bikers and other local yokels hit balls.

"I saw that good looking black Silverado out there and was hoping I could have a word with the owner."

"You a cop?"

"Do I look like a cop?"

"They come in all shapes and sizes."

"Yeah, but with this much ink? Oh, and a shot of Cuervo. Gold if you have it."

She turns, pours a good one and slides it in front of him.

"Thank you kindly." He throws it back.

"Why do you want to speak with the owner of the truck?"

"I'm thinking maybe you're the cop."

She laughs. "No, seriously, what's it to you?"

"My old man had a truck like that. Same year and everything. Recently smashed the fucker up. I'm looking for another one."

"Try a used car lot or Craig's List."

"I'd pay top dollar."

"The truck's not for sale."

"How do you know?"

"It's mine."

This time he laughs. "Oh, yeah?"

"Yeah."

"That takes care of that." He thanks her, pays her, and walks back out into the cold, mostly clear night.

No, it's not easy to say good-bye to everything one knows, even if a man's life felt hard as nails and at times equally unforgiving.

—⁓—

Jack's Mom never touched them. He never saw her touch her boyfriends either, but he knows she did. He heard the thrashing, the moans, groans, hell sometimes even squeals.

She never touched the dog. They did have a dog, a pit-bull, for a few years. Sweet as candy. No, not Mom.

The boys had no idea how to touch each other either, but at times they did, an awkward pat on the back, a hug, if a person could call it that, an arm around the neck, a canyon in between. Jordan, the neediest, although not the youngest, crawled into Jack's bed on many occasions. Sometimes James did, too. Jack pulled the blanket up to his young brothers' chins, then rolled away to fall asleep again.

They learned to touch themselves, not in the way that satisfies emotion, but certainly in a way that gives pleasure. Jack figures all the brothers became expert at that. Mom busied herself working the bottling line and partying until the sun came up. She barely acknowledged their birthdays. Those came and went most times without as much as a nod. Now Christmas, she loved that holiday and tried to make up for everything else, hanging green and red shit all over the house. She bought them gifts, one expensive thing each, her choice for each of the boys, usually something most of them didn't even want; sometimes they would trade, and a time or two they even sold one or two for cash. She didn't really notice.

—m—

Jack heads to the address he found for this Thompson dude. What will he do if finds him there? What's the plan? First, he'll call Jeff and Billy, then he'll work to stall him, keep him in one place, although Billy spoke adamantly about him not being involved. Just find the dude. We'll do the rest, but Jack can't help but assist; his need for justice prevails.

He has looked into the eyes of more than one man who murdered, and they're much like anyone else, but their fuse is short, their fire always brewing. One little provocation occurs, one little thing that jars their sense of righteousness, and they might strike like a cobra or brood, plan and sneak in on the sly.

Dare to step on the bad side; that's when murder happens.

You take someone's Ramen noodles. Yep, that's all it takes behind the razor wire. Someone serving a life bit has nothing to lose. Take his noodles, and a person better have his eyes on his back, his side, his abdomen, the hollows between ribs and organs where the weapons made from wire, a utensil, and any other bit of metal found or stolen can stab through. Bam, bam, bam! The sharp point enters and exits the flesh sometimes multiple times before the person even knows he's hit. They often see the blood first.

A mile or so from Thompson's house, Jack remembers how his right hand draped over Debbie's curvy side and cupped her breast. Her sleep breathing soothing as a purr, as peaceful as a mother shushing. He could smell the flowery scent of her hair and her perfume subtle on her neck. He feels a tug inside. It felt intimate. He knows the word. In a prison workshop or two when they prepared him for release, they talked about how to open up, how to let someone in again, how to bridge the gap that exists between a paroled felon and everyone else. Dang, another tug.

As he approaches the address, a ranch house 200 feet behind a row of tall raggedy pines, he notices a light on inside, and an older model Ford parked in the driveway with backseat doors open and the trunk popped. He pulls a pair of binoculars out of his glovebox and drives by slowly noting a woman inside, moving quickly, and sweeping up things in both hands. A large man sits on the couch in the living room. Could that be him? Jeff mentioned that the man they sought would be tall and muscled up, but not a word about him being obese like him sitting in the house.

He drives by and travels a mile up the road, turns around in a driveway, and heads back towards the house. As he passes this time, he watches the woman load things into the car in a quick and haphazard way. She glances over her shoulder as he passes and picks up her speed even more. Against his better judgement, he stops, backs up and pulls into the driveway up behind the car and the woman. She takes one sidelong look at him and jogs quickly up the porch stairs and into the house, the screen door propped open like a mouth. Inside, the big dude continues to sit.

Jack climbs out of his SUV and follows behind in her wake, as the fat man strains to stand, glaring at him through the front window. Jack walks at a crawl up to the open doorway as the man moves towards him in a heavy-footed shuffle across the wooden floor. They meet at the door, and the big man asks in a voice much higher than expected but not without power, "What do you want? Are you an *amigo* of the *puto*?"

Jack's eyes pop as he notes the pistol tucked into the front pants of the man, and his mind fights to remember what the word *puto* means. He thinks the word means cunt. If the word ends with an "a" it's feminine, with an "o" it's masculine, so he must be referring to Thompson. "No. Not a friend of the *puto*. An enemy. I'm looking for him." The woman, a good-looking girl with long black hair cowers in the doorway; bruised swellings and a cut lip paint her face.

"Are you the *policia*?" the man asks.

"No."

Suddenly, the woman steps forward speaking loudly and urgently, "We don't know where he is! We don't want to know!"

The man swings his large head toward her and yells, "*C`allate!*"

"He did this to me! Eric! I told the police!" she screams.

The bowling ball of a head pivots back, as the whale pulls out the pistol, yelling, "Get the fuck out of here!"

Defiantly, Jack articulates loudly and slowly, "We're on the same side. I'm just trying to find him." Is he nuts or what? He needs to leave, walk the fuck out of here before something happens.

The big man takes one step forward, and holding the gun sideways, aims the barrel at Jack's chest.

"Get out!"

"Okay, okay!" Jack backs up with his hands in the air, bowing down to the loose cannon. He steps off the porch and heads back to his vehicle. As he opens the door, the woman runs out onto the porch and yells, "Go to his father's house! Eric hates him, but he might go there! Go to Denton Road! You will see a red and white snake sign!"

The huge man roughly grabs her arm and pulls her into the house, bellowing now. A person didn't need to know the language to understand the threatening words.

—m—

He served his bit as a boy who had never been touched. Although sometimes a memory haunts him, of a distant and short-lived contact, a breaking smile, the sound of cooing in his ear.

His mother said his father was the one. Wild and wonderful. She said it more than once, usually three drinks over the line, when she dropped her guard and flashed her tender under belly; oh, it's scary to expose that last oasis of innocence; he watched as she covered it back up quickly.

He felt awkward with girls as a teen. They would reach for his hand, and he would stick it in a pocket. They would snuggle up after fucking, and he would reach for his clothes. The girl would ask if he loved her, and he would laugh.

Incarcerated, he could live in his own world, contract a blow job from time to time, but mostly take care of his own needs, not an easy task in the early days when he shared cells with one other inmate. It was even more difficult in the later years, when cells changed to cubicles – two men growing to eight in a space smaller than a two-car garage. Was that "intimacy?" He saw their dick, balls, ass, smelled their BO, farts, and rancid breath. They rolled and tossed, screamed and cried in the night, threw out punches at violent phantoms, kicked out at nightmare figures from their past, and tumbled out tussling with inner demons.

In the morning, all eyes averted, not a word said; a gentle touch, if ever exchanged behind the razor wire, the glass doors of the Bubble, the cubicles surrounded by four-foot walls, was rarely seen, unless you count one inmate working on another's hair out in the yard. If he went in as a tough but awkward young man with a quarter-inch fuse, he came out solid, impenetrable, cold to the touch, capable of rolling just about anything or anyone over.

Jack looks out onto the landscape; the fields stretch out below the moon, and the woods look dense and dark. He thinks about the lost souls out there, maybe the two girls, wondering if Jeff and Billy have found them, hoping they aren't scared to death or injured.

He turns onto Denton Road and begins to look for the sign, one he has seen a dozen times or more. Snakes. Not likely in that shallow pond, dark and weedy, or if something does live in that tepid pool, must be something small, something a man his size could handle like a noodle. Maybe the snakes live down the dirt driveway. Is the snake he's looking for saying his goodbyes or slipping below the border south, where dark-skinned girls with palm fronds cool his skin, boys in banana hammocks deliver him drinks on cork-lined trays, and smudge-faced children in filthy clothes pedal everything from chewing gum to statues of Mayan gods.

He pondered upon running south across the border, too, if that judge had only granted him a bond. Most people facing a long bit think about fleeing, but Jack decided, after long thought, bond or no bond, he'd serve as an example to his brothers instead.

Jack knows he's been lucky. Life has treated him well since his release. His old boss put him right to work and promoted him to supervisor after one year. Then somehow, someway he won over Debbie, yes, who wrestles with demons of her own. Molested by stepfathers in her early years and then abandoned by her mother, she too found luck; after living in the foster system for a few years, a good couple from Willis adopted her, bringing her a better life. But the trauma of those early years still haunted her.

There he laid, tangled up with her like a braid, so warm, so safe this morning. Could he willingly roll into that ball again? He swallows hard.

He slows down as he searches for the red and white sign. He does not want trouble, but he owes Billy and his brother, and he will help them, even though he dreads looking into the cold eyes of a man who has probably murdered. At this moment, he only wants to roll back into bed with her.

Just as his eyes spot the sign, his phone rings. "Yeah?"

Jeff, on the other end states, "We found the girls. Can you meet us at the Kohler farm, corner of Weber and Dell?

"Sure."

Jack disconnects before he can ask if they are alive or dead.

27
Constricted

Sunday 2:51 a.m.

When the phone rings, Bill fumbles in his jacket pocket and mutters something about Brenda. He says, "Hello?" Martin can hear the rumbling of a male voice, just barely, then he watches as his son-in-law sits up straighter in his seat. "Jesus, we'll be right there. No! Not until we get there."
From the corner of his eye, Martin watches Bill pull a cigarette out of a pack and place the filtered end between his teeth. Before he lights the thing, Martin demands, "Don't smoke in my fucking car." He notices Bill's hands trembling. "You going to tell us who that was or what?"

Bill opens his window, twisting the cigarette into pieces as the wind carries them away. "They're alive."

Martin puts the pedal to the metal, so they say, and they fly down the dirt road heading towards the Kohler farm. They are only three miles away. Martin could drive these back roads blindfolded, knowing every curve, dip and washboard section, even in the dark, pitch black dark, but he has a bright full moon to help light his way on this October morning. Bill rubs his forehead, obviously stressed.

Martin asks, "How the hell did the girls end up at the Kohler's?"

"Don't know."

"Are they injured?"

"He didn't say."

Martin almost passes the driveway leading up to the house, slams on the breaks and skids.

Bill exclaims, "We're in a hurry, Martin, but you don't have to kill us in the process!"

Martin throws the car in reverse and backs up, throwing gravel, turns into the driveway and shoots up to the side door.

All three men jump out of the car, and Bill bounds to reach the door first.

Randy Kohler meets them, opens the door for them to enter, explaining, "They were pounding on the door like mad, scared out of their minds."

Shoes and boots scatter through the entryway, cluttering on top of a large oval rag rug. Old black and white photos of people, probably ancestors, watch ghost-like as they head into the dining room. Lily, sitting on a couch in an adjacent living room jumps up and limps unevenly towards them. She runs into her daddy's arms and begins to sob. When she does catch her breath, she mumbles something that sounds like "sorry," over and over again. Bill murmurs soothing words and shushes in gentle rushes of breath. As Martin looks around the dining room, he notes old dishes sitting on shelves and inside a hutch; a light colored tablecloth covers the long oak table surrounded with heavy looking chairs. When he glances back into the living room, he spots Randy's wife, whose name he cannot remember at this moment, sitting on a plush comfy looking sofa, gently touching the hair of Lily's little friend, lying with her head in the woman's lap.

Bill pulls Lily away from him, but still within arm's length and looks her over. Tears continue to pour from her eyes. He assures her, "You're going to be okay," but his voice sounds shaky.

Martin looks away from her, swallowing hard because what he sees disturbs him. The left side of her face looks deeply bruised, including the eye swollen to a slit. Leaves and small twigs tangle in her hair; wet spots, probably from tears, mark her shirt and sweater. Her stockings look dirty and covered with holes, including her shoeless feet, where a few of her painted toes show through. She cradles her right arm, and scrunches up her face to continue crying.

Randy asks, "Do you want me to call the police or an ambulance, Billy?"

"No. How's Kristen?"

"Pretty much in the same shape. I called her parents, too. They should be here any minute."

Bill adds, "Let's wait until they're here, and we'll decide what to do."

Bill leads his daughter back into the living room, his arm wrapped tightly around her shoulders, and he and Jeff follow. Bill and Lily sit side by side on another sofa directly opposite the other, as Jeff sinks into a chair. Martin plunks down on the other side of Lily.

Bill says, "You know Martin, don't you folks? And this is Jeff Tillman, in town for a visit." Both Kohlers nod their heads. "Jeff, Randy and Carol Kohler."

All attention turns to Kristen, who continues to lie on the couch with Carol, wide-eyed, not crying, just lying still on her side. Carol gently brushes the girl's dark hair from her forehead.

Bill asks, "How ya doing, Kristen?" His voice sounds unlike anything Martin has heard before from the rough and tumble Marine; the words squeeze out of a constricted throat, soft, high, unnatural. His eyes look wild and his teeth gnash; Martin watches the jaw grow tighter and tighter, as if reeled on a spring.

The young girl doesn't answer, just stares at them, her hair mussed too, her bottom lip broken and bloodied, clothes torn on her upper body, her lower body covered with a blanket.

"Has she said anything?" Bill asks. Carol shakes her head. Lily begins to cry again and nestles her face into her daddy's shoulder.

Carol speaks up, "Just so you know, we haven't asked them anything."

Martin states, "I think we need to get the girls to the hospital, Bill."

Lily looks up and cries, "No, I don't want to go!"

"Peanut, you're going to have to go to the hospital," Bill assures her.

Jeff speaks up next, "Billy, you can go now, if you want. I'm sure these folks won't mind me waiting here for Jack."

"Not until Kristen's folks get here. Randy? Jeff's brother is going to pick him up here."

"Of course."

Lily lifts her head from her father's shoulder. "I'm sorry, Daddy. I'm sorry. We tried to get home. We tried..." Bill shushes her. "He offered us a ride..."

Suddenly, Kristen screams, "No!" Everyone in the room jumps.

"No!" she screams again.

Martin turns to Bill. "We need to get the police involved."

"No!" the girl screams at the top of her lungs.

A sharp loud knock on the door breaks the moment, and the girl begins to sob, causing Lily to cry harder. Lily mumbles through her tears, "Kristen..."

Randy jumps up and moves quickly for the door, as Martin hears Bill ask his daughter, in that voice, large words forced through a thread thin funnel, "Who? Who picked you up?"

Lily shakes her head.

"What was he driving?"

"A dark-colored pickup. A Chevy."

Martin watches Bill look over at Jeff, and in his son-in-law's eyes, he sees a ruthless coldness that he has only witnessed a few times before in his lifetime. Once, when a local farmer shot his dog in the head after attacking and killing a dozen sheep, and on the rare occasion or two when he watched a farmer slaughter animals. Lastly, when he identified Jeanine's body in the morgue, walked out and into a bathroom to look himself in the eyes. What he sees in Bill's eyes frightens him; that look always has. Martin asks, "You know someone who drives a truck like that?"

Bill turns those cold eyes to him, "The person you thought of."

Just like that, Martin's breath explodes out of him. "Jesus! He came after my granddaughter?"

Bill nods. No one else in the room moves or speaks. Martin senses a deep and violent stirring. The feelings that he closed behind a door all those years ago, which began to knock earlier in this day when they met with Holder, begins to strain against the hinges. He fears what he will feel, if that door opens, what he will want to do, because revenge can become ugly, even the desire for revenge is ugly, and he doesn't want to do anything that would compromise the life he has now.

Randy returns into the room with a man whom Martin assumes is Jeff's brother, and Jeff jumps up, walking over to him. Martin feels like he may have seen this large man around town.

The brother nods at the adults, glances   quickly over the two girls and exclaims softly, "What the heck happened?"

Jeff answers quietly, "I'll fill you in."

Bill asks Martin, "Can you take over here for a minute?" He untangles Lily and she tumbles into Martin's shoulder, then walks over to join Jeff and his brother. Martin hears Bill growl, "That fucker did this."

"What the hell happened?" the big guy asks.

"You didn't see that truck anywhere?"

"Only saw one, and it wasn't his. I went to his house."

"Yeah, and?"

"Some woman, his wife or girlfriend I guess, and a big dude were there. She was throwing her shit into a car..."

Jeff says, "Oh, boy. Now they're both on the run."

"Unless she's meeting him somewhere..." Bill adds.

"What the hell happened?" the brother insists.

Jeff states, "We don't know..."

Bill jumps in, "We know it's him. Lily said someone in a dark-colored truck picked them up. A Chevy. We have to find him! I don't care what it fucking takes. I'm driving my daughter to the hospital, but I'll catch up to you. Just as soon as possible."

Jeff reaches up and puts his hand on Billy's shoulder, "Take it easy, man; we will find him." A couple of beats go by. "We won't give up until we do."

The big guy nods his head in agreement.

Jeff says to Jack, "Let's get going."

Martin watches the two men stride towards the door; he feels uneasy about the three men taking the matter into their own hands, though he knows that time is crucial at this point.

The two men brush past a couple rushing into the living room, the woman falling to her knees beside the couch, pulling the girl into her arms. The man looks desperately around the room, fury or something moves his body parts in frantic little jerks. "What do we know?" Martin figures they must be the girl's parents.

Bill speaks, "We know who did this."

"Who?" the man screams, then catches himself, asking softer now, "Did you call the police?"

"They will call the police, when we get to the hospital. It's protocol."

"They need to know now."

Bill steps into the father's face and says softly; Martin can just hear him, "A couple of interested parties got a head start."

"What do you mean?"

"They're helping the police. It happened nearby. Who knows how long it will take for the cops to get out here."

The father takes a step back. Bill's tension probably forces him back. Martin can feel it from where he sits.

The man continues, "Okay. I get it, I think. Let's get these girls to the hospital!" In two long-legged steps, he reaches the couch and scoops up his daughter like a shovel; she's completely still again. He sweeps out of the room with wife in tow, their steps syncopated.

Bill says to Martin, "Call Brenda and tell her to meet us at the hospital."

Martin nods, stands up and walks back into the dining room, pulling out his phone. He speed dials the number, his head reeling; he licks his lips and thinks about Derek or Eric, or whatever the fuck his name was, Thompson. Fuck. He can only imagine what has happened to these girls. The sight of Jeanine's body in the morgue flashes through his mind. The stony look of her flesh, the unnatural set of her mouth, the wounds garish though dull in color. The knocking door strains even stronger on the hinges. Then his walk through the field where they found her. How it looked desolate, damp from the rain, footprints everywhere like the aftermath of a stampede. Still they found nothing. The face of Eric Thompson. His insolent, sneering face that defied him at every turn. Did he really kill Jeanine? Did he...hurt these girls?

"Hello?" Brenda's voice breaks his parade of torment.

"It's me."

"What's happened!?"

"The girls. We've found them."

"What do you mean found?" Her voice already rising, close to shrill.

"They're okay. I mean they're alive. Meet us at the hospital."

"What happened?"

"Just meet Bill and me there. We don't know much yet."

"But..."

"We don't know," he says firmly. A sob rises in Martin's throat and he feels ashamed, glad that he stepped out of the room, as some deep, strange, and unbearable tenderness sets in that he did not think possible.

—⁂—

Martin watches in the rearview mirror as Bill tenderly gazes down at his daughter; she sleeps with her head on her daddy's lap. They hurried out of the farmhouse, while profusely thanking the Kohlers, climbed into the car, and headed to the hospital not uttering a word. In a few short minutes, he could hear her gentle, little snores, not surprisingly, as the subtle smell of sweet liquor and vomit wafted lightly in the air around her. Did he, the sneering fuck, feed her that?

Even now, a few short miles from the hospital, Bill has yet to speak, but Martin can see the jaw bone dance, even in the diffused light, lips slightly parted, eyes wide, unblinking. Dare he say something? He knows that Bill wants a go at the fucker. He knows that Bill has hankered for years to find the person who killed Jeanine. If the same person has done this to Lily, God help him.

Forty-five minutes have passed since the three men walked into the farmhouse. Forty-five minutes the police could be working to track down the man...track down Eric, Derek, whatever the fuck his name is, Thompson who has created a nightmare for his family.

"Bill, let's call the police now."

"As soon as we walk into the hospital, triage will call the police."

"But..."

"Don't worry about it, Martin."

Martin quiets, knowing that nothing he says or does will change Bill's intent.

Martin hears Lily's voice, soft, almost a whisper, "No...no... stop it." He hears her begin to thrash around as Bill speaks softly in a whisper, then shushing. In moments, she settles back down, falling asleep once again, or so he hopes.

Bill spits, "God, I want a cigarette."

He catches Bill's eyes, "Do you think he..."

"Do I think what?"

"Do you think he ra..."

"I don't know, Martin. Don't ask me again."

"You're going to meet up with those two later, aren't you?"

"Yes. I am."

"Then I'm...I'm going, too."

"You think long and hard about that, Martin. No telling on how it's going to go."

"And when...when... we find him. Then what, Bill?"

"That depends on him."

28
Stick

3:35 a.m.

Eric glances down at his speedometer to see eighty-five. Oh, shit!

He backs off on the gas, shooting a quick look in his mirrors. Nobody around, but he maintains a slower speed. He will be there soon. Anyone even a little smarter would already be traveling the freeway south, but no, he convinced himself, after driving in circles out on the country roads, miles from the scene of his recent disaster, he had to do this one last thing.

If he had killed those two bitches, as he wanted to, he could be meandering his way. Yeah, another one of those words. Those two he would have buried, not left out for the whole world to see like the first one. He had a place already picked out. Instead, he has to rush now. He has to push to accomplish everything.

They will be looking for him. They will be hot on his ass. Between Lola opening her big mouth, and now those two little bitches...and then Jeff Tillman back in town. He could hope, or pray...okay, not the last. He has never prayed...that the girls didn't make it anywhere safely, but they were smart, especially that little Becker bitch, and tenacious, yes, another one of those words.

Not like the...grandmother. Yes, she would be the grandmother, whom went willingly to the slaughter.

Nevertheless, he can fantasize about the demise of those two little cunts.

They run across the field and fall into a hole, an old underground cave, or an unmarked well, perhaps the remnant of a gravel-pit, which swallows them up, their pink and tender flesh picked clean to the bones by those meat eaters that live in the dark. Oh, the flesh so young, so sweet, so delicious.

Now a mile or two from his father's, he plans to surprise the old man with a rundown of his crimes, then Eric will do one better. He will stick a blade into the belly of the beast.

Or maybe this...the two girls flee across the field and run into something wild. No, not human but something animal from this world or maybe from another. Two legs, four legs, he doesn't care. The predator sniffs their terror, signaling their approach across the fields; its fur bristles, and its mouth salivates, so happy what a wonderful surprise. Waiting for the two young things, the eyes peeled, nostrils flared, the taste buds roar with excitement. The evil being could rush out to meet them, but why not harness the energy for the feast? Delectable. Delectable indeed.

Now they know what he drives, what he looks like, how dangerous Eric Thompson can be.

The monster awaits, the nostrils flared into gaping holes, eyes red with fury and desire, radiating a heat that's palpable. He crouches behind a pile of wood, six feet tall by ten feet wide, thick enough to hide his furry hide, but thin enough in places to allow a little peek.

The girls approach with terror in their eyes, which feeds his hunger more, and mere feet from where he lies in wait they run into his lair. He grabs one in each of his paws, almost hands really, much more capable than the appendages of an animal, fur covered, black and curly, with claws long as forks and sharp as razors.

He doesn't waste time, biting off their heads, one by one. First blondie, then the brunette. The flesh and bone orbs pop like grapes. The red irony blood becomes the nectar of the feast. Their arms and legs chew tender as green snap beans, and when the torsos give way, the ribs crunch like stale noodles. At last, the organs, the oysters of the feast, the texture unbearably fine, full of juice surprises laced with intestinal angel hair.

He pulls into the long dirt driveway, marked by the red and white sign by the road: No trespassing. Danger. Snakes. This marks the beginning of the journey. Or is it the end?

Yes, a snake lives here. Has always lived here. A man. A father. He ejaculated the seed then determined who Eric would grow up to be. Eric knows he has done wrong. Somehow, someway he figured he could get away with it. After all, when he shot birds out of the sky, his father laughed and commented on his fine eye. When he caught beloved pets of neighbors in live traps and fought them to the death or tortured them until they screamed, his father looked the other way. No one told him he had done wrong. He moved through the world unpunished.

Then he met up with Coach Becker. When Eric badgered his teammates and ignored Coach's rules, the man dropped him from the team. Coach stepped up into his face and told him he showed no ability to be a team player. How dare he? Who did he think he was? Coach Becker paid. Oh, he paid. He paid again tonight. Blame the wrong on Eric's father.

He drives down the dirt driveway, a route he knows like the back of his hand, heading toward the den of the snake, the lair of the evil. The one who had a chance to form him into something good but chose not to.

As he approaches the rundown doublewide, lit up with one of the tall lights that circles the property, he sees the porch in partial collapse, roof covered in spots with tattered blue tarps. He spots Carrie Joe, bride of evil, though not bad herself, sweeping off the front steps. He doesn't feel surprised. They are the sort that sleep all day, stay up all night, fueled by amphetamines, brought back down with barbiturates. She turns as the truck approaches, smiles in her half-wit way and waves. He pulls the truck up and around the right side of the dwelling, off the dirt, onto the weeds, and carefully maneuvers his way through the minefield of debris, including old auto parts, used furniture, paint cans, oilcans, and anything else cast aside. He continues behind the dwelling and when completely out of sight, he parks, turns off the growl of the engine, a sound he loves and knows now he may never hear again. He walks around the rickety structure, back to the front, where Carrie Jo stands broom in one hand, the other on her hip.

She says, "Well, ain't you a sight for sore eyes."

"Where is he?" Eric asks.

"In watching some cow shit and dust on the tube. Where you been?"

"Here and there." Eric stomps up the stairs, pulls the screen-door open, and walks into the front room, where Papa, oh, he would love that, sits in his stained and worn easy chair, feet up, head back. He fills the chair, looking larger than he ever has, maybe a le...levia...leviathan, yes, one of those words; this one he thought he might never find the opportunity to use. A big fucking whale, yes, an old sea creature out of water.

His father's eyes widen, as if he somehow missed Eric's drive in. His father never misses a beat, ever aware of anyone or anything encroaching upon his domain. Maybe he expected Eric. Yes, that must be it. The big fish out of water slides himself up straighter in the chair and asks, "What took you so long?"

"What's that supposed to mean?" Eric continues standing. He wouldn't dream of sitting down, needing to maintain some semblance of advantage.

"They came looking for you. You wouldn't be hiding your truck, if you didn't know."

"Who?"

"Who!? Some dude claiming to be an old friend of yours and another in tow."

So Jeff came out here. Already. Fuck! He wonders who he had with him. "Not the cops?"

"No, not the cops! What the fuck have you done?"

"Now you want to know?"

The whale, the evil one places both hands on the arms of the ragged chair, kicks the foot stand down and pushes himself up to stand. His father carries more height and weight than Eric does, quite a bit so.

"Only because it might affect me. Looks like you're hiding here." He walks past Eric, so close in proximity, he can smell the older man's stale breath and pungent odor, a repulsive mix of fried food and sweet soda. Eric flexes his right calf to feel the leather sheaf where the shiny, sharp blade nestles.

"You might be surprised what I've done."

The father lumbers into the kitchen area, adjacent to this front room. "Oh, yeah? Shoot another bird out of the sky? Torture another useless mongrel?"

Carrie Joe enters the house, catching the door before it slams, so the deformed metal and screen closes lightly. "You boys catching up?"

Eric dismisses her, "Get out of here!"

"Hey..." she says.

"Get out!"

Carrie Joe, middle aged, but looking older scampers down the hall and into a bedroom.

The father turns to him. "Who the fuck do you think you are?"

Eric steps up boldly to his father. They stand two feet apart in the kitchen area, which looks neat on the counters, though the linoleum is worn and cracked, cabinets chipping of paint. Eric's fury and desire to make things right rises higher now, urging him on against odds. "I'm the dude that murdered a woman twenty years ago. Tonight I attacked two girls and came damn close to killing them, too."

His father begins to laugh, and although Eric wishes, shit, does he wish that this would feed his fury, the opposite occurs; he experiences a slight dissipation but pushes on. "Why are you laughing?"

"You murdered someone?"

"Yes, I murdered someone! Coach Becker's wife. Remember her? Found in a field. Case never solved. I did that! It was fucking me!"

"And you almost killed again tonight? Almost. That's the stand out word here..."

"You son-of-a-bitch..." Eric steps up quickly a foot closer and reaches down to push up his pant leg to pull out his blade, something he practiced at least a hundred times. Before he can, his father pulls a punch and blasts his fist into the side of Eric's head. He reels, dizzy on his feet.

"You're pathetic!" his father screams. "You have always been pathetic!"

Eric reaches again for his blade and the father, he sees from the corner of his eye, lifts both hands interlocked and bangs down on Eric's head, knocking him to the floor. Eric falls back onto his elbows and kicks out with his right foot, knocking his father against the counter. "Your fault! You are evil and encouraged me to be the same!"

His father begins to punch out and land a few blows in Eric's guts and ribs. "So they're on to you, is that it? Did you think that I'd save you, protect you?" He laughs again.

Even with the blows, agonizing as they are, Eric manages to reach down and pull out the blade, lifts up to stab the beast in the belly, but his father's right jab throws him off target, and the sharp blade jams deeply into the old man's thigh. The evil one yelps and then screams in pain pulling the blade out and dropping it onto the floor, where the metal weapon bounces and clangs a couple times before settling into the dust and dirt of a corner.

Carrie Joe appearing suddenly in the room screams, "Stop it! Stop it! There's a car driving up the driveway real slow like."

The old man screams, "Well, don't just stand there! Grab a gun! Both of you! While I try to stop this bleeding."

29

Branded

Sunday 4:03 a.m.

Brenda speed walks up to the emergency doors of the hospital, until something urges her to turn. There he is. Billy ambling in from the parking lot with Lily, her feet thick with socks, his arm so tightly wrapped around her she looks more like an appendage than a separate being. Yes. Yes, how she understands that need to hold the girl closely. She wants nothing more than her darling daughter back inside her womb.

Martin walks behind them; he looks very tired.

Lily looks up and breaks from Billy, but gently, pulling his arm, his wing really, away tenderly, and steps toward her, so gingerly, so tentative upon those feet socked but shoeless, her tights ragged, her other clothing also torn.

What she sees stabs her, so she pulls her eyes away for a couple of counts, takes a breath, then allows herself a more thorough once over; she walks ! Be happy for that. Billy does not carry his daughter in like Kristen's father, who arrived just before Brenda.

Her once over hesitates at Lily's neck. No necklace, no chain, no pearls.

She wraps her arms around her lovely daughter, her intelligent and strong-willed daughter, a little girl in some ways, but on that precipice, and in this case, falling. No not falling, fallen. She smells of alcohol, something acrid, maybe vomit, and something else she cannot quite identify.

Billy catches up to her and Lily, steps in between them, and wraps one arm around each of their shoulders. His arms are long like that. Her father continues to trail behind, but his head is lifted now.

The sick and the injured fill the emergency room on this full-moon night; at least two babies cry, possibly three, from opposite corners of the room. A scream pierces the wall from the other side, several people hack, blow, and sniffle, and somewhere, maybe over by the window, soft moans rise. The three break apart now, Billy staying behind while Lily and Brenda step up to the reception desk. She quietly states, "Our daughter was attacked."

"By a human being?"

At first, this strikes Brenda as odd, but truly, attacks come in many forms. Specificity matters. She throws a glance at Billy; his eyes close as he nods his head.

She stutters, "Yyyeyes."

The woman turns and speaks to a young man further behind the desk, and with a flurry now, two female nurses burst through the swinging doors, draw her lovely daughter away, and steer her into a room. Brenda and Billy follow. The room contains two doors, one front and one back, and all the usual equipment, including a table, cabinets, metal drawers, monitoring machines, wires, more wires, more metal drawers, more wires.

One of the nurses, gray hair pulled back into a ponytail, and small, wire-rimmed glasses shakes out and sails a sheet onto the floor of the room. She turns to Billy. "Maybe you can step back to the desk and provide the necessary information, while we process any evidence." Billy nods and turns toward the door, throwing a glance back at Lily and Brenda. She and he meet eyes for a moment, and Lily reaches out a hand towards him, softly saying, "Daddy..."

The nurse says, "It's okay, hon, we'll take good care of you. What's your name?"

Lily stands with her head down, shivering, in mini convulsions. She doesn't answer, so Brenda speaks up, "Her name is Lily Rose."

"What a beautiful name. My name is Nancy. Lily Rose, I need you to step away from your mom and onto the center of this sheet. Can you do that for me?"

Lily looks up tearfully at Brenda then does as directed.

The nurse continues, "We need to disrobe you piece by piece, shake each one out, and put it into a bag. We will cover you with a robe, as we do this. Sarah…" she says to the young blonde nurse wearing scrubs covered with little pink pigs, "…grab the box of gloves. We need to change gloves after handling each piece." Sarah grabs the box and places it within reach of her and Nancy.

Nancy gently pulls Lily's sweater off, shakes it out, and then places it into a bag that Sarah holds open for her. The older nurse pulls off the gloves, placing them also into the bag, reaches over for another fresh pair and pulls them on. And so it goes, piece of clothing by piece of clothing as her darling daughter stands arms wrapped around herself, the convulsions moving now into small violent jerks. At least twice, Brenda instinctively reaches out for her. The older nurse stares at her briefly in the eyes and gives one little shake of her head. No. No, she cannot touch Lily Rose. The girl winces from time to time, as Nancy removes the clothing and even cries out a time or two. The younger nurse keeps a tally of every item, marks and seals the bags, carries them out of the room, to return empty handed.

Tears roll down Brenda's cheeks now, matching those of Lily, as she views her daughter's body bit by bit and the injuries she's sustained. Scratches and scraps cover Lily's legs, some bleeding just a tad but mostly the blood coagulated, and her feet look torn and filthy. Her right arm appears swollen and bruised from the elbow up, and her torso also looks discolored in places. The entire left side of her face looks red and swollen, the eye closed except for a slit, and her hair tangled with leaves, small twigs and clods of dirt. Of course, although Brenda has many questions, the two that torment her the most: Who has done this? And did he or they rape her too?

Lily continues to look down, not even glancing at them for one moment, the one good eye glazed over, mouth hanging open just a tad, clearly exhausted, and something else. Ashamed. The emotion sits palpable in the room. Brenda counts the minutes until they finish this process, so she can hold her daughter in her arms.

Nancy directs, "Lily, you can sit on the bed now, as we take your vitals." Sarah folds up the sheet, places it to into a bag, marks it, seals it, and carries it away.

Lily gingerly sits down on the edge of the bed. Nancy takes her blood pressure, pulse, respirations, and other vitals. Brenda hears her state the numbers to the younger nurse, who marks them down: 130/82, 110, 24, 99%.

The older nurse asks, "Where do you hurt, Lily?"

Lily shakes her head slowly from side to side. "It mostly hurts when I move, but my head hurts a lot."

"Where on your head?"

Lily reaches up with her right hand, wincing, and motions towards her left face and the back of her head.

"If you had to rate the pain on a scale from one to ten, what would you say?"

Lily continues to shake her head.

"From one to ten, Lily."

Lily bites her bottom lip and finally mumbles, "Nine."

"You can lie down now under the blankets, while we wait for the doctor."

Lily crawls under the covers, with little moans escaping, as the younger nurse covers her up to her chin. Brenda immediately moves around to the left of the bed. Her sweet daughter immediately turns her head, to the left wall, wincing again. She reaches out her left hand to grab Brenda's.

A knock occurs on the front door of the room, and the nurses say okay. A tall, blonde-haired woman previously present at the front desk opens the door for a moment and nods. Through that momentary crack, Brenda notes two security women stepping into place on either side of the doorway. Before the door closes, Lily lifts her head and turns just slightly to glance that way.

Lily speaks out loudly, "I'm not ready!"

"You're not ready for what, sweetheart?" Brenda asks.

"To talk to them. I'm not ready!"

The younger nurse says brightly, "No. They're not the police. They're security officers to ensure your safety."

"Oh," Lily murmurs softly, drops her head and rolls it back left.

The older nurse adds, "We are expecting the doctor any moment."

"Thank you," Brenda says.

As the nurses quietly gather supplies in that efficient manner in which they have completed everything, in strolls the doctor, a small-framed woman, brown-skinned, perhaps Indian, who quietly confers with the two nurses.

The doctor nods, stretches out her hand to Brenda, who has stepped around the bed, closing the distance between herself and the person who can tell her more. She clutches the doctor's small, warm hand.

The doctor introduces herself, "Hello, I'm Dr. Lahiri. Hi Lily, how are you?"

Lily turns shortly to look at the doctor, shakes her head then shifts her head left again to the wall. Brenda follows her daughter's gaze to note a lovely painting of woods near a pond, the colors soft pastels, the brush strokes feathery, impressionistic. She imagines her daughter wishing she were there now, not in this room, in this hospital on a crisp fall night after...after what? Brenda can only imagine.

The doctor, hovering over Lily, begins to examine her face. "How are you feeling, Lily? Do you have a headache?"

Lily nods.

"Where does it hurt?"

Lily lifts her right hand, grimacing this time, and waves it over the upper left side of her face. "And the back of my head."

The doctor tenderly touches the painful area, Lily moaning and groaning from time to time and even yelping at one point, as she examines the bones above and below the eye, near the temple and the top of the cheek.

"I'm going to examine your body now, Lily."

Lily nods, her little forehead trenched. Brenda snorts a puff of air. Like mother, like daughter. That fucking trenched brow.

A subtle tremor awakens deep inside Brenda and begins to spread. She roots herself to the floor, to quell this mini earthquake, so her daughter, her girl, her angel does not see or feel her mother's weakness at this time. Did she wear the pearls? If she did, where are they? And her headband. She distinctly remembers Lily telling her she was going to wear that, too.

Her eyes take in every inch of Lily Rose's body again, this time more closely, as the doctor navigates her way, every fraction of an inch, and what she sees torments her as nothing ever has. The doctor uncovers each part of her body slowly and efficiently, and gently too. The bruise on the side of Lily's left face deepens, from red into violet and a deeper purple as she watches now, a shocking color, spreading from above her eyebrow, through the eye area, underneath and over the cheek ridge almost to the ear. The eye, the sky blue of Billy's eyes, less than a slit now. Another bruise encircles the top of her right arm, the large fingers of her attacker imprinted, as if his flesh seared hers, a brand more than a bruise. Perhaps a devil, not a man. Who else could do this to her sweet, lovely girl? A rising fury forces her out away from the bed; she heads towards the door, her own head down. She mumbles something like, "I'll be right back," and once on the other side of that door, she hyperventilates, suffering to take a deep breath, and bites her bottom lip. A sob that feels large as a boulder sits in her throat, threatening to choke her. Billy, speaking quietly with the two security officers, sees her and he squints his eyes with question. She spits out, "What happened?"

He walks over to her, grabs her two arms in his two hands and draws her away from the officers. He speaks in a whisper, "Someone picked them up…"

"Who? Who picked them up?" He doesn't answer her but stares teary eyed into her own.

She demands through clenched teeth, "Tell me!"

"Him," he pronounces.

She stares into his eyes, his hands constricting her arms as her body continues to shake. She glances up to see the security officers watching them, and one asks, "Is everything okay?"

Billy turns and answers, "Yes, fine." He wraps an arm around Brenda, draws her further away, and whispers in her ear, "We're going to handle it, Jeff, Jack, and I. We will find him. I promise. Go back in and be with her. Don't leave her alone."

Nodding, she turns on her heel and walks back into the room still trembling, but determined to steady, as her mind reels. Him? This Thompson person. He hurt her daughter? He killed her mother? Focus! Focus for your daughter! Inside the room the doctor speaks quietly with the two nurses, and upon seeing her, a look of relief lifts the face of her daughter.

The doctor steps towards Brenda. She states, her enunciation of English perfect, "We need information from your daughter. Could you please encourage her to answer a few questions?"

Brenda walks back over to Lily's left, grasps her hand and prays that her darling daughter not feel her tremble; a look of concern sits in Lily's eyes. For this reason alone, Brenda knows that she must keep herself as calm and centered as possible, and cage the silent screams inside her. She mustn't have Lily worrying about her at a time like this. She leans in and kisses her daughter on the forehead. "The doctor can't help you if you don't tell her what happened. Just answer a few questions."

Lily nods, although obviously reluctant.

Doctor Lahiri begins, "Did you at any time tonight become unconscious?"

"Yes."

"When?"

"When he punched me in the face."

Oh, my god.

"So there was only one man who hurt you?"

Lily nods.

Brenda bites her bottom lip, and plants her feet into the floor.

"Do you know how long you were unconscious?"

Lily shakes her head then asks, "How is Kristen? How's my... friend?"

"They are examining her now, just like you. When you were conscious, did he touch you, Lily, besides punching you in the face?"

"No. I mean, yes. When I tried to stop him from hurting us. He grabbed my hands...and...he grabbed my feet and pulled me out of the truck."

That boulder in Brenda's throat begins to shift and rise. Her eyes flood, as she swallows several times, and fights to hold herself steady. You can do it. Hold steady. You can do it.

"That's when you bumped your head?"

Lily shakes her head.

The doctor lifts Lily's head and turns it gently to view the underside. Lily yelps, when she touches the area in a particular spot. Dr. Lahiri guides her head back onto the pillow. "Lily, I must ask you a very difficult question. Did he ever touch you in a sexual way?"

Brenda holds her breath, every nerve fiber of her being standing in alert, her heart pounding like a kodo drum.

Lily shakes her head, tears running now, an effort visible upon her face, not to sob, not to lose control, not in front of strangers. Like her daddy.

The doctor clears her throat. "I would like to call in a SANE nurse to look at you anyway."

Lily looks frantic and asks, "What's that?"

Brenda answers, her voice shaky, "That's a Sexual Assault Nurse Examiner, sweetheart. I work with them all the time."

Lily slowly shakes her head and says, "No!"

"Sweetheart, we need to make sure that he didn't...he didn't..."

Lily cries out, "I was not raped! I'd know if I was, and I wasn't!" She loses that control now, and Brenda drops down and wraps her arms around her girl; her daughter can't help but lose control now, and for a moment Brenda can let go, too, though she whispers over and over in her daughter's ear, "You are so strong my darling, you are so strong..."

The doctor reaches out and places her hand on Lily's arm, a look of compassion on her brown face, a very welcome look. She states, "Lily, you are probably right, but if you were unconscious, we don't know what happened during that time. Please let a nurse from SANE look at you. We will do tests first, x-rays and a CT, and your mother and the SANE nurse will be here waiting for you."

The younger nurse reenters the room and speaks quietly to the doctor. This nurse so young looking, like a teenage girl herself, with her perky ponytail and scrubs covered in those little pink pigs.

Lily's crying slows, and she wipes away her tears with a tissue, blows her nose, and looks more composed now. That knack her daughter has for pulling herself together, Brenda wishes she herself had.

The doctor continues, "Lily, the police have arrived, and they would also like to ask you a few questions. The sooner you talk to them, the sooner they can catch the person who did this to you and your friend."

Lily nods and takes a deep breath.

The young nurse, Sarah, walks over to the door and opens it, allowing two police officers, both female, and Billy to enter the room. Billy quickly moves to Lily's right side opposite of where Brenda stands and grabs his daughter's hand. The doctor and two nurses exit the room.

Billy introduces the two police officers, "Lily, Brenda, this is officer Starling and Officer Reynolds. Sweet Pea, are you ready to answer a few questions?"

"I'm not going to tell everything! Only enough for you to find him."

"That's fine," says Reynolds, a woman that Brenda remembers from high school. She graduated in the class before, or maybe two years before Brenda.

Starling, a middle-aged woman with her hair up in a tight

little bun asks, "Lily, can you describe the man for us?"

"He was big. He filled the whole side of the truck behind the wheel. Not fat, but tall and muscular."

"You could see he was muscular?"

"He chased me and then he chased us. He was very strong."

"Was he young or old?"

"Maybe the same age as my mom and dad. Maybe a little older. I don't know for sure."

"What was he wearing?"

"Dark clothes. He had a stocking cap on. That was dark, too. At one point, I pulled it off his head."

"What kind of hair did he have?"

"Short. A little wavy, maybe."

A dark stocking cap. Dark clothes. A big man. Why does that sound so familiar? Brenda flips rapidly through her memories, feeling the tremors begin again.

"What was he driving?"

"A dark-colored Chevy truck. He acted real nice at first, and he said that he knew you, Mom." She looks up at Brenda. "He said that he knew Grandpa." She then looks up at Billy. "I'm sorry, Daddy. I'm so sorry. I tried to run but he locked the doors, and we couldn't get out. I tried..."

He shakes his head, "No, Sweet Pea..." Lily begins to cry again. Billy looks up at the two officers, and states, "She can give you a written statement tomorrow. That's all for now."

"Just one more question. Where did he assault you? I understand that you went to a party. Did he assault you there?"

"No. He picked us up on the road... and took us down a lane...the door was locked. I tried to open it..."

"That's it for now," Billy states between clenched teeth.

"Of course. Mrs. Bagwell, may I have a word with you about another matter?"

Brenda steps over to the two police officers, wondering what this could be about.

In a quiet voice, Starling says, "We took a statement yesterday from a..." The officer looks down at the pad. "Miss Lola Ramirez...

Brenda exclaims, "Oh my god, I'm so glad."

"Miss Ramirez told us that you assisted her at Grace after her attack. We located and questioned the man she identified. He matches the physical description that your daughter just gave us, and he drives a black Chevy truck. Did you ever meet..."

The blood rushes from Brenda's head, as she realizes that she may have been face to face earlier in the day with the man who murdered her mother and attacked her daughter. In fact, she feels herself falling and reaches out to the wall to catch herself.

Billy shouts, "Brenda!" He runs over, grabs her arms, and steadies her.

She recovers but feels flushed and weak, "Yes. I think so..."

"Momma, what..." Lily tearfully interjects.

"I think that he came into Grace yesterday looking for Lola."

"What?" Billy exclaims.

"Do you know this man, Eric Thompson?"

"No. But my father..." Billy looks at her wide eyed, and shakes his head one time.

"Yes, Mrs. Bagwell..." Starling begins.

Brenda scrambles to cover, "You would need to talk with him."

"Where is Mr. Becker? We met him when we came in."

Billy answers, "He went to check on our boy. I'll tell him that you want to talk with him."

"You talked to him yesterday? But you didn't arrest him?" Brenda asks incredulously.

"He denied the allegations, and although Miss Ramirez filed for a Restraining Order, she did not press charges."

Brenda exclaims, "So you left him out on the streets, and now you think he's the same man who attacked Lily and Kristen?"

Starling apologizes, "I'm sorry, but we're required by law to act with particular protocols. We'll issue an APB out on him, and we should be able to locate him quickly if he's still in the area."

"You let him go..."

Reynolds declares with renewed vigor, "We'll do everything

we can to locate him." They nod to Billy, Brenda, and Lily and leave the room.

The older nurse walks back into the room and states, "We need to get those tests going now."

"Can't I go with her?" Brenda questions.

"There's really no place for you down there. Security will be with us every minute, so you don't have to worry about her. When we get the tests done, you can join her again."

Lily cries, "No! I want my mom!"

The young nurse pops into the room. "Lily, I'm going to be with you every minute. We can talk about music, and movies, and stuff."

"Okay," Lily agrees but reluctantly.

"I'll be here when you get back, honey." Brenda kisses her on the forehead and lingers to take in the sweet scent she has known for sixteen years, a scent compromised by the foul smells from the evening.

"And Daddy, you'll be here?"

"If not right away. Not long after."

After they wheel Lily out of the room, Billy and Brenda meet, and he wraps his arms around her. She asks tearfully, "Why didn't you tell them?"

Billy pulls away to look at her, "What? That he's a killer too? They can arrest him for what he did tonight, but unless we find new evidence or he confesses to the police, he will get away with murder. Martin is coming back to pick me up. He should be here any minute, and as I told you, Jeff and Jack are out looking for him now. With any luck, we will find him before the police. I just need a shot at it. I know Jeff does too. Otherwise, he'll be back out on the street in no time."

At that moment, her father steps into the room. "Where is she?" he asks.

"Getting tests. How's Christopher?"

"He's sleeping now. He was upset earlier wondering what's going on."

"We need to go, Martin." Billy says.

"You're still determined, aren't you?"

"You bet!"

Martin stares at Billy for a moment or two. "I can't do it. I'm afraid that I'll kill him. I can't jeopardize all that I have now. I... can't. I'll stay here with Brenda."

"I understand, Martin. Brenda, I'll take your wagon."

"I don't know if this is a good idea. I don't know..." Brenda says.

"We're just going to talk with him."

"A man like that doesn't reason, Billy. I was face to face with him..."

"Trust me. We will get him."

"I do trust you. I don't trust him."

Brenda watches as Billy rushes out of the room. She cannot help but cry. The face of the man who attacked her daughter and probably killed her mother haunts her now, and she feels that tremor turn to a violent shake. Her dad walks up beside her and without a word puts an arm around her, and she cries into his shoulder, wondering if the monster raped Lily or touched her, and if the pearls could...could have played a part. It's impossible. They couldn't have. They couldn't have. Could they?

After a few minutes, that new emotion that has visited her and replaced the sorrow rises and dries her tears. That emotion that drove her to find the killer of her mother. That emotion that has sparked now into a fire. She hopes they find him, and some part of her wants to be there, wants to throw in a few blows of her own. Locking him up will separate him from the world, but without him feeling pain, there will be no justice. She imagines lashing out at him. Kicking him with all of her might as he lays on the ground, pounding his sneering, lying face with her fists. Calling him every derogatory term until she has nothing left to say.

She fervently hopes that they find him, but she also hopes that Billy, Jeff, and Jack make the best decisions possible.

Feels like *Groundhog Day* again, the movie, but this time Jack sits beside him, not Billy. They are inching their way back up that long, potholed driveway toward the dilapidated trailer brightly lit up inside. No black Silverado in sight, but Eric could still be hiding inside the dump or lurking out in the thick woods surrounding the structure. He would be hiding his vehicle by now.

The lights inside the "home" tell them that the occupant, or occupants, are still up. In fact, Jeff swears that he can hear shouting, as they reach the approximate halfway point up the drive. That could easily be Carrie Jo and the old man. No proof that Eric has taken shelter, an absurd thought really, considering Rick Thompson. Would the old man look the other way if he finds out Eric has probably murdered one woman and attacked two teenaged girls tonight? Most likely, yes. He'd probably slap his kid on the back and say, "You're not getting caught now are you?"

The thick foliage that borders the dirt drive creates that tunnel effect, which at this late hour seems to have closed in farther. Branches of large hardwoods, evergreens, and burning bushes with bright red leaves scrape along on the sides and the roof of the car. Jeff wishes they could walk in, sneak around a bit, see what's really here, but they decided to go in again up front and friendly. It could help put Eric at ease, if he indeed has stopped by to say good-bye to Daddy. Who knows how the second visit will affect the older Thompson; Jeff hopes he doesn't shoot first this time and ask questions later, if they have survived.

At one point, Jeff swears he sees a head creeping around the curtain or maybe a shade hanging in one of the back windows, the light inside the room throwing the human orb in shadow. Jeff figures that the outside lights should burst alive any minute. Eric or he and his father could have slipped out armed and be moving toward them as they drive in. When he hears what sounds like a dry branch snapping, Jeff holds his breath. When he hears what sounds like fallen, dry leaves ground beneath feet, his guts twist. When an owl hoots, he swallows hard. He hates to admit it, but a barrage of villains from every Halloween movie he has ever seen assaults him, including Michael Myers, Freddie Kruger, even Dracula at this moment. Yes, he wreaked havoc in the mosh pit, beat up men of color as a fun pastime, and fought until his adversaries were red and purple pulp, but he left all of that behind him. He feels weaker now. Desiree has tenderized him, or has she made his life a whole lot better? Confronting a man who he knew had no cap on cruelty, and a father that appeared just as black of heart, has created a potential nightmare scenario. His saving grace sits beside him, the badass dude that made it through twenty years of incarceration, including eight months in "the hole." Between the two of them, Jeff figures they can handle quite a bit, but only if he can conjure up the old him, the one that kicked with steel toes, punched with brass knuckles, and skulked around with iron balls. Where the hell is he? Billy will also be arriving soon, having checked in with him ten maybe fifteen minutes ago. Among the three of them, they should be able to handle most anything. Or so he hopes.

Jack turns to him. "How many seconds do you think before those lights flip on?"

"Two. Three."

"I see some fresh tire tracks, veering over to the right, and I kind of doubt anyone would be going out at this time."

"He's here. I can feel it."

They climb out of the car and walk slowly towards the trailer, close enough now that through the windows they see the old man, wrapping a large bandage around the top of his hairy leg, his sweatpants down around his ankles, his fat little sausage of a dick hanging pathetically amongst the hair.

Suddenly the lights blast on as a head pops up, which looks like Eric's, when the face turns towards the window. Jeff swears that the face looks red and swollen, hard to be certain from here, but he wonders if the old man already got a few licks in or maybe those two girls were a hell of a lot tougher than they look.

Jeff holds his breath as Desiree's face flashes through his mind, and the thoughts of a child coming, his child, maybe his only child, and never seeing him or her. He never did return her phone call or even listen to the message she left. Now he wishes he could have heard her voice one more time. There was just no way to know how this would turn out, but he had to do it. He owes Brenda and her family. He owes his brother too, for being here now, helping. "I know, Jack, it could be trouble for you, if the shit goes down."

"Yeah, well let's just make sure the shit doesn't go down."

Jeff nods.

"You said he was armed, right? When you were here earlier?" Jack asks.

"He's probably armed to the teeth, and we have nothing," Jeff answers.

"Yeah," but before Jack finishes his sentence, the front door flies open and Eric stands there with a long gun on bead with their heads. After a moment or two, he laughs and yells, "Is that you, Tillman?"

"Hey, Thompson! How the hell are ya?"

Eric drops the bead and the gun slips down to his side. "Who you got there with you?"

"My brother. Jack."

"Oh, yeah, the dude that was locked up." He motions for the two men to move forward with a sweeping arc of one hand.

They climb up the few stairs, Jack stumbling at one point over a jagged fragment of wood lifting its head from the whole.

But he catches himself, and they step into the doorway.

The old man, sweat pants pulled up now, stands in the kitchen leaning against the counter. He growls, "That's one of the assholes that was here before."

Eric asks, "You were here earlier with someone else, Tillman?"

"Yeah. But he had to go home to the wife."

Eric turns to look at his father.   "Shall I invite them in?"

"Looks like they're already in, shit bird. Search them!"

     "Sorry, Tillman, but it's his joint."

Both Jack and Jeff assume position, and Jeff says, "No problem." Eric props the gun up against the back of the couch behind him and pats them down doing a thorough job, one he learned well serving time. When he and Jack turn back, Jeff notes a couple of faint dried rivulets of blood striping Eric's face, matted spots of hair that seem red with blood, too, and his clothes are dusty, torn a bit, and he wonders how that all transpired.

"You look a little roughed up, Thompson. What happened?" Jeff asks.

"Hell of a bar fight. You should see the other guys." He looks at Jack. "When did you get out?"

"A few years back."

"How long was your bit?"

"Twenty fucking years."

"Wow," Eric says. "I only served one, but that was enough."

The old man shuffles out of the kitchen and stands behind an old easy chair. "Have a seat, and we'll have a little...conference."

Carrie Joe satellites the scene smiling a shy almost toothless smile, no doubt the effects of Meth or some other drug habit that stifles basic hygiene. Jeff remembers her before she became involved with Eric's father, and she was the cute chick with the big tits that every boy wanted to party with.

Rick Thompson moves around the easy chair, and Jeff can see a spot on the upper leg of his sweat pants growing redder by the minute. He watches as the old man falls down into that worn, battered chair and pulls the footrest up to, no doubt, elevate the wound. He feels curious about what happened before they arrived. Eric moves gingerly, as if he has bruises and wounds of his own; he sits on a chair facing the couch alongside the easy chair. He places his long gun down on the floor within easy reach. Jeff and Jack sit on the couch, a scary piece of olive green furniture covered with black stains, brown stains, yellow stains, oh shit, cigarette burns, and who knows what. His skin begins to crawl.

Eric speaks up, "So what the fuck have you been doing all this time, Tillman? What's it been, twenty years or something?"

"It's been a long time. Just working. Staying alive. What have you been doing?"

"The same. Staying out of trouble, too."

"Yeah?"

Then the old man asks, "Why the fuck did you come back?"

Eric says, "They wanted to see me."

His dad says in a whiny voice, "Oh, they wanted to see me. Why didn't they go by your house to visit you, shit bird?"

"Maybe they did. And stop calling me that!"

Jeff chimes in, "We couldn't find an address for Eric, remember? And you wouldn't tell us, so we thought maybe we'd stop by here again."

"Yeah," the old man says. "You had a real warm welcome last time. I'm going to ask one more time. Why are you here?"

Eric glares at his father, and Jeff's realizes that at any moment that gun laying there beside Eric's chair might just swing the old man's way. The sawed-off shotgun that sits beside the old man's easy chair tells Jeff that one hell of a battle could ensue. He and Jack better measure each word carefully, very carefully.

Eric's face registers a new thought. "Are you here for something else?"

The old man sits up in the chair and leans forward. "What the fuck do you want?"

Jeff speaks up, "I just wanted to talk about old times."

Eric starts to laugh. "We had some good ones, didn't we?"

His father says, "Shut the fuck up!"

Jeff throws a glance at Jack and then presses forward. "Yeah, we did. Picking up girls, drinking, stealing..."

Eric adds, "Sharing some time incarcerated." He enunciates the syllables of the last word like a second-grade teacher.

Jeff leans forward, "Yeah, and the old football days with Coach Becker."

"That old rat fuck," Eric adds.

Jeff asks, "Did you ever get him back? For kicking you off the team and ratting on us? You swore you would..."

"You have no idea," Eric says chuckling to himself.

Jeff's heart quickens. "You'll have to tell me about that sometime."

The old man says, "I think I'm getting this now."

Eric looks over at his dad. "What are you getting, fucking snake?"

Jeff's hair stands up on end.

"Keep your mouth shut, shit bird!" Rick Thompson and Eric lock eyes.

Eric looks back at Jeff and asks, "I see some ink above that collar and below the cuffs. You spend some more time behind bars?"

"I got into some trouble, but I ended up turning a corner and making amends."

"What the fuck does that mean?"

"Means I took responsibility for the things I did, and made things right."

Eric starts laughing almost hysterically. "Jesus, Tillman, you got all pussy on me. I always knew you would."

Jeff watches the old man look at Carrie Joe and hold up four fingers. She more or less skips into the kitchen, rustles around then walks back into the living room and hands the old man a tumbler of something brown, which he tips back in one gulp. "I get it. You are here to get him," pointing at Eric, "to confess to something he's done. That's it, right boys?"

"I'm not confessing to anything, and I sure as hell ain't making any...amends or whatever the fuck you called them!"

Jack speaks up for the first time, "Hold it! We just came here so that Jeff could catch up with an old friend. I don't buy into that amends shit either. The sex offender I beat just short of death deserved it. And the three fuckers they flopped me another two years for, they deserved it too."

"Now you're talking!" Eric says. "That bitch that I..."

"Shut up, Eric!" That was the first time Jeff ever heard the old man call his son by his name, and as tenuous as this scene was becoming could very well be the last.

Jack continues, "Oh, I don't mind if he calls women bitches."

"You should have seen these two little cunts tonight. They were begging me to fuck them."

That's when Jeff fucks up. He knows it even as he lunges towards Eric. Jesus! He shouldn't have done it, but he couldn't help it. Jack reaches up and grabs his arm to pull him back down, but it's already too late. Jeff feels the old him, the part of him he couldn't conjure a while back; that dude rears his head now. Eric grabs the gun on the side of his chair and the old man grabs the shotgun. In moments, Jeff and Jack are at gunpoint again.

"Sit back you assholes!" the old man sharply hisses. A couple of beats pass in silence. "Just what the fuck are we going to do with you two? The swamp is calling." He cups his ear and tips his head. "What do you think, shit bird? Is the swamp calling?"

"I thought you just came for a visit, and then you're lunging at me?" Eric asks.

Jeff confesses, "I overreacted. I just don't take kindly to girls being called..."

"My brother, I hate to say it, but he is a bit of a pussy," Jack scrambles to undo the damage. "Got a soft spot for protecting the innocent. We don't care what you've done. I had reasons for doing what I did, and I bet you did, too."

Eric stands up. "I don't need a fucking reason. I like it..."

"Raping girls? It's fun, isn't it?" Jack adds.

"Shut up! Fucking shut up!" Rick Thompson screams. "You two. Stand up, now!"

Jeff and Jack stand up with their hands in the air. Jeff says, "Okay, okay! We're leaving."

"Shit bird! You don't see what they're doing? I told you. They're trying to get you to confess to something. Are you two wired? You checked them for wire, right?"

Eric screams, "You son-of-a-bitch!" He lunges at Jeff, and Jack jumps up and throws his right shoulder into him before he can reach his brother. Eric stumbles back, but he doesn't fall.

Carrie Joe walks in the room and exclaims, "There's a dude sneaking up to the door!"

"Is he a cop?"

"Not unless he's undercover." Carrie Joe lifts another long gun and points it at the door.

The front door flies open with a violent kick and Billy stands there with his pistol in hand. Eric's rifle falls to the floor with a clang. As he bends to grab it, the old man levels his shotgun at Jeff and Jack's bellies.

The old man commands, "Keep your rifle on him, Carrie Joe!" He turns to Billy. "You're one of the assholes that was here earlier. Put the gun down on the floor. Slowly. I know she don't look smart, but she's one hell of a shot."

"That's right," Carrie Joes parrots. "I ain't smart, but I'm a hell of a shot."

Billy bends to place his pistol on the floor and lifts his arms up into the air, "You can kill me if you want to, but there's at least six people who know where I am right now. That know where all three of us are."

Rick Thompson laughs to himself. "I can shoot you and tell the police that shit bird did it." He nods over at Eric.

Eric looks at his dad and shouts, "Jesus!"

The old man says to Eric, "Go shake him down. See if blondie boy is packing anything else."

As Eric turns and bends to retrieve his gun again, which slid across the floor, Jack bends quickly to reach for it, a foot from where he sits.

The old man growls, "Touch that gun and you will have a hole in your belly. A hell of a hole. And shit bird, you don't need a gun to shake him down. Put your gun down by me and get your ass over there!"

Jeff turns to look at Billy, who moves his eyes from Jeff to the older Thompson and back again to Jeff. Billy means to do something, and Jeff interprets this subtle shift of eyes to indicate that the old man with the shotgun is Jeff's duty. His heart begins to race with the anticipation of action. Now that Billy has arrived they are at least an even number of three against three.

Eric swaggers over towards Billy, and Jeff wonders how the dude has the presence to look over-confident, when the father has been castrating him in front of them and probably has done so his whole life. As Jack and Jeff turn to watch the pat down, Jeff catches Jack's eyes, then glances over at the old man communicating intent. The tension in the room squeals.

One step from Billy now, Eric reaches out to pat him down, but Billy bends to swiftly scoop up his pistol, and in moments, has Eric's left arm twisted behind his back and the pistol pressed against his right temple. Jeff lunges for the old man, and before he can level the shotgun at him, Jack throws himself low onto the floor and under the footrest of the easy chair. Jeff knocks the shotgun up and it fires, blasting a good-sized hole in the roof. As Jeff grabs for the gun, Jack shoulders the footrest up and tips the chair over. Just then a shot fires, and Jack falls over onto the floor grabbing his right shoulder. As Jeff wrestles the shotgun from the old man, he hears Billy scream, "Hold it!" Jeff turns to see Carrie Joe with her rifle aimed at him, so he hits the floor with shotgun in hand. He looks up to see Billy pointing his gun at Carrie Joe, at the same time fighting to hold Eric with one hand. Eric squirms, tugs, and breaks free as Carrie Joe keeps her gun aimed at Jeff, and his old comrade in crime sprints, as much as he can for a large muscly dude, towards the back door.

Billy screams, "I'll fucking shoot!"

Carrie Joe aims at Billy now, and Jeff jumps up off the floor and aims the shotgun at her.

Jeff says, "Carrie, it ain't worth it. Don't die for these pieces of shit. If you shoot him, I'm going to shoot you."

The old man rolls himself out of the toppled old easy chair looking like a buffalo in sand, and Jeff takes the butt of the shotgun and hits him in the head. He falls back groaning, as Billy shoots at Carrie Joe's feet. She screams, jumps, and the rifle falls to the ground. She turns and runs like hell towards the back door but trips on a rag rug crumpled in the kitchen. Eric has stomped his way down the back stairs and into the night.

Jeff runs over to Jack, who sits up now, holding his arm, the blood running out of the wound. Jeff pulls his shirt off, exposing all of his tattoos and scars, and begins to tear it.

Billy asks Jeff, "Did you get what we wanted?" Jeff shakes his head. Billy adds, "Call an ambulance and the police, then help me find that son-of-a-bitch." Billy runs unevenly out of the back door and down the back stairs after Eric.

Jack says to Jeff, "Give me that shotgun, then go! I'll make the calls and keep my eye on these two."

Jeff races for the back door, adrenaline spiked by the violence, any semblance of a weaker him pushed to the side. The man he used to be rears.

31

Cower

Sunday 5:43 a.m.

She has no friends, only enemies. Even her mom perched on the edge of a chair by her bedside. Not a friend. Just someone else who wants to know what happened. She feels confused as a cascade of images, snippets to be sure, flash out of the dark to pummel her. They force her to remember what she fights to forget, so she keeps staring at the pretty painting of the woods and the pond on the wall. She will stop them. She can stop them, those quick cuts of what happened to her and Kristen. She reaches up to touch her lovely headband, to remind herself that there is still sweetness in the world. But it's gone. Instead, she feels dirt and crushed pieces of leaves. A leftover from the blessing? A souvenir of the warning? "My headband!" she exclaims, as she remembers now how Kristen told her she saw it fall during the fight with Sue Klein. Her sad heart becomes sadder.

"What happened to it?" her mother asks.

Lily shakes her head, as that cascade of images falls before her mind's eye. *Please! Please,* she prays, *find me a dark place where I can cower.*

"What happened to your headband? And the pearls. Did you wear them?" Her mother leans in closer. "Tell me."

Lily stares at the painting, falling into the cool blue water of the pond, not the darkness that almost swallowed her and Kristen whole. She mumbles just audibly, "They disappeared."

Lucas hands her a drink with that devious little sneer upon his lips. He runs his hands like water up and down her body as they dance, his hardness up against her.

Betraying her will at this moment, as she lies in this hospital bed, her desire rises once again. She knew she felt drunk, yet she took another drink from him because, honestly a part of her liked it. How can she tell her mother that?

Her mom brushes her bangs away and gazes into her eye; her mom's brown eyes look teary, but at this moment, she does not care. "Please don't touch me!" Lily rolls away from her over onto her right side, moaning, and pulls the covers up to her chin; the arm and shoulder, the one he grabbed her by, screams with the weight. She doesn't know what her face looks like, but she figures her modeling days are over. So much for marrying someone famous and living the fairy tale life.

She punches Sue in the face, and her enemy falls to the ground on her ass; Lily feels exhilarated, and honestly, she wants to kick her while she's down.

How does she tell her mother that?

When Lucas and Mark walk away from her and Kristen, she feels like beating on them, too. How dare they! She trusted them. Stupid girl!

The doctor walks back into the room and says to her mom, "May I speak to you?" Her mom walks out with her, leaving Lily alone. Why can't she hear what the doctor has to say? She rolls oh so slowly again over onto her left side, off the screaming arm, her bruised and battered face resting softly into the pillow.

The monster drives up in his pickup, the engine louder than the average truck. He looks friendly enough leaning over to talk to them out of the passenger side window. She doesn't want to climb in, but more importantly, she doesn't want to disappoint her daddy or her mom by coming home late. Before she and Kristen climb in, he tells her he knows her grandpa and mom, and she believes he's the answer to the prayers, the blessing of the falling leaves.

But the blizzard of leaves blew in as a warning.

She lifts her head and turns slightly to see two doctors, the original female, Dr. Lahiri, and now a male walk into the room, but not the dark one she prayed for to cower within. Mom and Grandpa follow behind. Dr. Lahiri says, "Lily, we want to talk to you." She feels like she might throw up. *Can I stay right here, please?* Right here on her side, her back to everyone and everything.

Dr. Lahiri continues her soft perfect English, but not American, and the way she pronounces every little syllable scratches on Lily's last nerve. "Lily, your arm is not broken or strained, and you did not suffer any concussion when you were punched and when you bumped your head on the stair. We are concerned about your face, so I asked Dr. Martin to confer with me on what action we should take. The punch you received deeply bruised the upper cheek and eye area. There is bleeding around the eye, and we may need to relieve the pressure. We want to keep you here overnight as we make a decision based on observations and tests, and watch for any other problems to arise."

The male doctor asks, "Lily, can you roll over onto your back for me, please? She obliges but she will not look at him. As she rolls over, the pain of the bruises, the cuts, the punches and the fatigue settle in. She feels so tired. He walks over to the left side of the bed and begins to look closely at the left side of Lily's face; as he reaches to touch her, she draws back instinctively. The word slips out, "No!"

The doctor draws back slowly. "I promise I will not hurt you."

She looks up at him briefly and his face looks kind, so she allows him to touch her gently with his fingertips, shining a light into her right eye and into the left, as well, though she sees little to nothing out of that one. "I'm very sorry this happened to you, young lady."

When he finishes, she rolls back over onto her left side and cowers. Lifting her right arm, groaning, she covers the right side of her head. She can shut it out. She will shut it out. She will.

When he turns down that lane that leads into a field, a panic starts in her belly then spreads into every corner of her being. And he turns down that lane again. And he turns down that lane again. And he turns. If she relives that moment enough times, one will come that he drives right by. But he does turn down that lane, and because she's smart and knows how to protect herself as Daddy taught her, she can jump out of the truck and run very fast. She can pull out Kristen as she makes her escape, and together they will run into the night and find a safe haven. But the door doesn't open.

She can shut it out. She will shut it out. She will!

The doctors leave to look at the tests again, and her mom says to Grandpa, "Why don't you go home? There's nothing you can do here. Please keep Christopher, until they release her."

She imagines her grandfather hugging her mom, when he says, "Are you sure you don't want me to stay?" She doesn't hear a reply, so she imagines that her mother shakes her head.

Her mother walks around to the left side of the bed and sits down to face her. Lily shuts her eye. Her grandpa gives her foot a little squeeze before he leaves the room, and she jumps with the pain.

He says, "Oops! I love you, honey."

Finally, she can lash out at something and she does. She punches out towards his scary face, and he transforms into a composite of Lucas and Mark, and every man who has ever mistreated a girl. She punches with every intent to break his bones, and when that doesn't work, and he walks around that big dark truck, she kicks out and aims for that tender spot that all men protect at all costs; she aims, musters up all of her might and kicks, and still the monster drags her out by her feet, and her head bumps upon the stair, leaving her dazed. Still, she thinks fast. Just like her daddy taught her. Get up on your feet and run as fast as the wind, not only for yourself but also for your friend you leave behind. She pushes, and she pushes, and she pushes harder, and still it's not enough. He grabs her arm and pulls her to a stop, turns her and punches her hard, and the light, the one light she sees off in the distance, so far away, like an angelic light in heaven goes out.

She remembers dreaming of being lost in the dark and frightened to the core. Until she was found. But Daddy did not carry her. He did. Over his shoulder like a sack of grain, and then he tumbled her to the ground. She thought it was her daddy carrying her to safety, that this story had a happy ending, like all good stories. But it didn't. Fairy tales do not come true.

She opens her eye and her mom continues to sit near her, and this time she can see tears rolling slowly down her cheeks. Her mom says, "Kristen's okay. She wasn't raped either."

Lily shuts her eye again, nodding slowly, remembering the SANE nurse asking her to part her legs. Scoot down. Scoot down further. The instrument so cold. So fucking cold!

She didn't think he'd gotten to Kristen yet, and she feels glad, so very glad. And she was always sure, whether conscious or not that he had not raped her.

Her mother begins to caress her uninjured cheek, and Lily reaches up to stop her, but her mom grabs hers instead. Her good eye pops open against her will.

Her mom says, "I know you're feeling a lot of things, but I'm on your side. I'm..."

"Please...don't touch me...like that."

"Look at me."

Lily closes her eye and rolls over onto her right side, her right upper arm screaming again.

She wakes up lying under the tree. He fumbles with his fly, hovering over her friend, lying in the truck on her belly. Lily's face hurts. Her arm hurts. Her feet feel raw, but she has two choices. Lie here like a victim or take action. She delivers the blows, with the heavy, fallen limb, as the frustration, the terror, the sheer will to live drives her. She will kill him. She will kill him. She will...

They run across the field, she and Kristen, heading for the light, the angelic light in heaven, and though the night feels cold, so cold, and their half-clad bodies shake and tremble with the shock, too, they keep running through the field and a small stand of hardwoods that snag at their sweaters and their skirts, their little feet stumbling over roots, losing balance in the holes, veering to the right and left, him a short distance behind them screaming, "You fucking little bitches! You little cunts! I'm going to get you!" Finally, they gain distance, somehow, someway, the light drawing them as if on a cable, an angelic thread, and finally, after what feels like a week or a month of running, so exhausted now, they collapse onto the porch of a house under that light that guided them, pulled them, and rescued them. Kristen falls to her knees sobbing and she does too, pounding on that door with both fists, screaming words, so terrified that he will find them and in moments will be there, scooping them up in his monster hands. The door opens. Lily thinks, oh, so the leaves were a blessing after all, floating down upon them like the feathers from an angel's wing.

Then suddenly a voice, "We're taking you up to your room now." She opens her eye to see a woman dressed in scrubs, who rolls her out of the ER and down a very long hall, the two security women and her mom walking behind.

The peach color of the room feels warm, and one window sits mid-wall with a blind shuttered down. A TV perches high in the corner, and the bathroom door stands wide open; the light hurts her eye. The woman adjusts her in the bed and smiles, but she doesn't smile back; she's forgotten how. "Do you feel comfortable?" she asks. Lily nods her head, yes. Here comes Mom again, dragging a chair over to the left side of the bed. Lily lifts her arms again to cover her head.

Her mom leans in closely. "I know that you're feeling overwhelmed right now, but I want to remind you of something. You got away. You survived. You are so strong. You and Kristen. So strong. It's a terrible thing that happened to you, but it could have been so much worse. So much. Think about that, darling."

Lily's bottom lip begins to tremble. Oh, no. Little puffs of air explode from her nostrils. She will not cry again.

Mom leans in closer now. Lily can feel her warm breath upon her cheek. Her voice sounds soft. Her words, "They're going to get him, and it will end this long nightmare. Daddy and the police are going to get him. He will never hurt anyone again. And you will feel better someday. I know that you will. I promise you that."

Lily breaks. She throws her arms around Mom's shoulders, and buries her head near the beating heart in her chest, a babe again. When her mom begins to rock her gently, she snuggles deeply into the human cradle.

32

Dire

The fucker runs faster than Billy thought he would. Because of his leg, former Marine or not, he's unable to catch up, so he uses his ears and his brain instead. Already the dark has absorbed this dangerous human, but no way can Thompson shroud the sound of his crashing through the brush and the brambles in the woods. Billy records his movements on a map in his mind. Between him and Jeff, who he hears approaching from behind, they will stop him. Billy doesn't know if his barging in was the best decision, but through the window he saw his two friends at gunpoint, and he chose to act. When he saw the fucker's face and clothes, Billy knew that he was already reaping what he sowed. He hopes like hell that Lily and Kristen got in a lick or two, but he suspects someone else gave the brunt of it. Maybe Jeff and Jack before he arrived? Unlikely. Probably the father, who also sported a wound, for Billy had noted the bloodstain on the top of the old man's leg.

Billy stops his uneven gait to allow Jeff to catch up. The Tillman brother, shirtless and out of breath, bends over with hands on knees, gulping in air. Billy says, "I can't catch him, but you can."

"Which way did he go?"

Billy points towards a stand of white pines just off to the right. "He went through there. I think he's heading for the road. He's stopped now, probably catching his breath too." Billy pulls his pistol out of the back of his pants. "You want this?"

Jeff answers, "No. Like I told you, I'm better with my fists and feet," and resumes his chase in the direction where the tromping through nature has begun again. He calls over his shoulder, "The cops and the ambulance should be here soon."

"Well, let's hope not too soon. I'll catch up. Hold him," Billy shouts.

Jeff sticks up his right thumb as he tears away.

Billy walks mostly, as his leg screams with pain in that one spot where the bits of shrapnel exploded into the femur, but he occasionally half trots, following behind Jeff until the dark swallows him as well. Before too long, Thompson will hit the road, and when he does, he can pick up both speed and distance before ducking into the thick brush and woods again.

They have to catch this man and hold him, or he could get away with everything: kidnapping and assaulting the girls, abusing a woman, and murdering Jeanine. If the woman doesn't press charges, what happened to the girls goes haywire, or he doesn't confess to the murder, he could be back out on the streets in no time.

Billy wants to be the person who catches him and makes sure he pays for everything he's done, but that's not going to happen. He could slide into self-pity about his wounds from the Gulf, but he refuses.

He pushes the boughs of the pines out of his way as he trots, keenly listening to how the chase has veered further to the right. The pine grove ends, and he enters hardwoods, where the underbrush, fallen limbs, and trees create an obstacle course. Brambles pull at his clothes, roots strive to trip his every other footfall, and an owl loudly hoots.

Time passes. How much, Billy isn't sure. The unfolding event reminds him of when he and his fellow Marine, Glover, climbed through the sand of the Arabian Desert, and the words of the Dear John letter Brenda wrote him drove him wild, into reckless behavior that contributed to the death of his brother in arms and almost his own, as well. He has to keep his senses about him. He can't catch up to this killer, pound out every bit of anger and revenge he feels. He and Jeff have to handle it just right.

The movement in the distance quiets, and Billy figures Jeff and Thompson are running on the road now. Yes, now he faintly hears the clomp, clomp, clomp of shoes on pavement. His ears strain again, this time for a siren, for Jack's sake, but concurrently he knows that he and Jeff need time. When the police arrive, they will spread out and move quickly. Thompson will hear the sirens and duck back into the thickness. He could have another vehicle stashed or someone to assist him with his run. He and Jeff have to reach him first.

He feels very grateful for the Tillman's today and wonders if James watches from above, as his brothers makes things right, not that they had to or that Billy ever expected they would; decent human beings step up.

Billy has picked up his pace as he bursts through the edge of the woods and there he stands on the road. Down to the right off shoulder he hears the brushing, breaking, and muted stomping that marks the pursuit, and mixed into those sounds, voices can be heard, not the words but the harsh tones, and he heads that way.

The night feels cold, and even though the moon and stars fill the sky, the woods, the thick brush obscure clear sight, but Billy learned when he was a Marine to find his way. Dark can be dense as pitch, but still the eyes can see assisted by some kind of navigation system directed from the gut.

The voices now rise in volume and pitch, and he begins to run regardless of the pain. He remembers when he ran like this before, years ago, when Lily Rose ran away from him in the park. When need arises, a need so dire, like that day when he ran behind his young daughter so terrified of him leaving again, that she bolted, he finds that nothing else matters; the pain moves into a numbness that allows him to do what has to be done. He knows that Thompson and Jeff are grappling, and no way in hell will Billy let Jeff lose. Soon the police and the ambulance will come, and they will rush their way down that long driveway marked with caution, where a dilapidated mobile home does indeed house a poisonous snake, the father that seeded a dangerous human being.

His leg sings shrilly as he follows the voices, bursting into and pulling his way through tall grass and wildflowers, strangely dry but damp at the same time from the autumn and the dew. He wishes he had a machete to cut his way, but a weapon like that in his hand, as he approaches the man who dared to hurt the girls and probably brutalized his wife's mother would not be advisable.

Twenty or so feet from the ruckus he slows down, stepping ever so slowly and quietly, and when he reaches within view, the fucker and Jeff are grappling on the ground, rolling one way and the other as one fights his way to the top only to be tumbled under once again. The piece of shit blubbers about something to do with theft and juvie, coach, and football. Finally, Jeff pins him down, his face red as blood, his arms shaking like sails in the wind, and the fucker throws him over again, pins Jeff, lifts his large fist, and draws it back to punch. Billy moves forward with the lightest of steps he can muster. He pulls his gun out of the back of his jeans, switches the safety off and places the muzzle of the gun against the back of Thompson's head.

The son-of-a-bitch stops and slowly raises his hands, as Jeff scurries out from under him, blood running from his nose and a cut just above his left eye.

Billy states through those clenched teeth that have left his jaws sore, "You son-of-a-bitch. Stand up slowly and know that shooting you would be the highlight of my life."

The big man stands slowly but far from smoothly, holding his hands in the air.

"Turn around," Billy commands.

Thompson slowly turns and asks, "Who the fuck are you anyway?"

"I'm your worst fucking nightmare. I'm the father of one of the girls you kidnapped and attacked, and the son-in-law of the woman you murdered."

Thompson looks at the two of them. "What are you talking about?"

"You mentioned the girls back in the house. You admitted that you got Coach back," Jeff clarifies, then bends over to spit out blood.

"I was just fucking with ya."

Jeff continues, "When they arrest you for what you did to the girls, you could come clean, Eric. The cops are on their way now. Aren't you tired of looking over your shoulder all the time? Never knowing when they are going to catch up to you. You could clear your conscience."

"This isn't about my conscience. This is about yours. I don't have one."

"That's probably true, but think about those girls and the people living in pain that were affected by you killing that woman. Like this man right here." He nods his head one time at Billy, then swipes blood off his eyelid.

"I don't care about their pain. Besides, they aren't going to catch up with me about any of it, especially that other thing. If they had anything on me, I'd of been arrested a long time ago."

Billy clarifies, "So you piece of shit, you admit to killing her. You attacked the girls and you murdered a woman."

"I'm not saying one more word."

Billy steps up and places the gun against Thompson's temple. "You will serve some time for what you did tonight. If you don't come clean about the other deal, I will be watching, and when they let you out, I will track you down and finish what we started here."

"Then you'll serve time."

"You and I both know how easy it is to get away with murder." Billy steps up and speaks an inch away from Eric's face, still holding the pistol to his head. "I will hunt you down and kill you. Don't doubt it for a moment."

Eric spits into Billy's face.

Billy kicks out like a mule, knocking Thompson's right leg out from under him; the big man loses balance as Jeff tackles him down onto his back. Jeff starts wailing against his face with his fists as Billy repeatedly kicks him in the ribs. Billy sticks his pistol back into the rear of his pants and begins to throw punches at him too. The fucker laughs and laughs in between all his grunts and groans, rolling over from side to side and pulling his legs up to ward off blows to precious organs. Billy catches himself and pulls at Jeff's shoulder too. "Stop, Jeff. Stop! We can't fuck him up too badly."

Jeff stands up, rubbing the knuckles of his right hand, and out of nowhere, probably because his frustration has hit a breaking point, he begins to cry, something Billy never expected in a hundred years, and he listens as his friend takes a new and unexpected tactic.

"I know that he treated you like shit, Eric. I know he beat you down. I could see it tonight, and I remember how it was in the old days. And he let you get away with everything. He never told you or taught you the difference between right and wrong." Billy watches as Jeff slowly stands, the snot running from his nose and the spittle spraying from his mouth. "I know it. And I had a shitty childhood, too. And in some fucked up way I understand you and I...I...feel sorry for you, Eric. But you have to do the right thing now. You have a chance to do what's right..."

Thompson mutters, "The bitch didn't even try. She died without a fight. It was so easy, man. But those two cunts tonight, they did fight..."

Billy bends quickly and delivers two more heavy punches into the fucker's face.

Once the fucker recovers from the last two blows, he continues, "...and they got away. I wanted to kill them. I wanted to. I have nothing to lose, and I will never, never confess to the cops. In the end, I will have the last laugh. I know people. And I know the laws. You watch."

Jeff pulls on Billy now, and the two men step back away from Thompson, who lifts his head to spit blood but continues to laugh maniacally in between. Jeff kicks him one last time in the kidneys, shaking his head from side to side. He looks over at Billy as they both emit deep sighs. The shrill of sirens fills the distance.

33
Under

Sunday 6:20 a.m.

Jesus, his arm throbs as he holds the long gun on the old man and the woman. Jeff counts the minutes and waits as the shrill of the sirens grow louder. She plops down on the couch and slumps into defeat, or so her body says, but her eyes dart. The old man tries to converse him into some kind of ally, but that wasn't going to happen. The makeshift tourniquet helps with the bleeding, but still the blood runs from his arm. He thinks about Debbie and Jimmy, and sure hopes he sees them again. Sitting propped up against the wall, he begins to feel drowsy and knows he cannot fall asleep, so he takes deep breaths and forces a hyper alert, which the pain assists.

The old man says, "You could put the gun down. What do you think we're going to do?"

Jack just snorts his answer through his nose and shakes his head. That yah right kind of thing.

"I didn't ask the kid to come here. He threatened me. I protected myself. Who the hell do you think beat him up?"

The woman speaks up, "And I was protecting him," and she points to Thompson's father, sitting on the floor with his back to the toppled chair.

"Yeah, you two innocent as lambs," Jack says sarcastically.

When he finally hears the sirens turn down the drive, he lets out a deep breath. He feels miserable sitting in the aftermath of violence once again. He doesn't want to be anywhere near it anymore. He just wants to see Debbie and Jimmy. Just wants to be home in his bed. With her. Close.

At the same time, he thinks about Jeff and Billy out there in the dark, chasing down an animal, not one who loses control and acts out in a moment on a bad day, but one of those who plans, conducts reconnaissance, whose poison ferments and festers, until he carries out his revenge on the world without a flinch. The true savage. What will they do when they catch him? God, he hopes they keep it cool.

Soon police and EMTs will be swarming the house. He holds his breath now, hoping that the two he has at gunpoint don't do anything stupid at the last minute. He figures that they will arrest the old man and the woman – him for harboring a criminal and her for shooting him. Hopefully, his own involvement won't cause future issues. He hears gravel spray as the cars speed in. He imagines doors thrown open, and he hears footsteps crackling as they head for the shack.

The woman stands up as if to head towards the door. Jack commands, "Just fucking stay where you are."

Throwing the door open, four police and two paramedics enter, all of the officers armed and aiming. Five hands spring into the air, including Jack's one.

—ᴍ—

Jack spots Debbie and Jimmy waiting outside by the doors of the emergency room, as the ambulance pulls in; she and the boy are by his side in moments. When she bends over him, he wraps his good arm around her shoulders and holds her closely. She fairly falls on him and begins to cry. The paramedics tell them that they need to get him into the trauma bay, so he grabs Debbie's hand, who holds Jimmy's, and the three hold fast all the way there. They usher wife and son out, as a medical team takes over.

The pain hurts like a son-of-a-bitch now, since the shock wore off, but they tell him he won't feel much in a minute or two. Take a deep breath they say, as they cut away his shirt in short order, pull off his shoes and strip him of everything in between.

They take his vitals and start IVs, as they dress him in a gown. A doctor comes in and asks if Jack feels ready for surgery. He nods and the doctor adds, "Being built like a brick shithouse doesn't make our job any easier."

Jack smiles a bit, as the pain begins to ease. Debbie and Jimmy walk along as they wheel him to the OR, saying their goodbyes at the door. He memorizes their faces in that last glance.

He wakes up back in the joint. It's either after the three inmates jumped him in the shower or maybe something hit him like a semi, but he feels banged up, run over, weak as a kitten. They, meaning the Department of Corrections, decide to send him to a hospital. The ambulance ride blurs by in running colors of yellow, green, and red, but mostly white. They don't put the siren on. The Department tells them to take it easy. Doesn't matter if he lives or dies. One less inmate saves the Department money. But he makes it, and once in the ER, enclosed in a curtain, the nurse, a redhead, says four cracked ribs, a ruptured spleen, two sprained fingers, one sprained arm, a dislocated knee, and hairline fractures in the left foot, over and over like a 33 needle caught in the groove. The same nurse tells him that the dudes that jumped him look worse, or does she say that the semi cab held an engine by Volvo? They wheel him down a hall, clickety-clack, clickety-clack, and he sees photos, paintings, and head busts of famous criminals lining the walls. He doesn't bother to look for his own; it won't be there. He is not a criminal. Not one of them. Just a misunderstanding. One moment of fury that stretched too long. Not his fault that he almost beat to death the man that molested James. The pedophile asked for it. He begged for it. Really.

He feels the needle go in and suddenly he's under. It feels like a dream, as he hovers above the bed watching the team as they scurry like mice. Is he inside his body? Outside his body? As he watches, he wonders. Will he feel the cut of the knife? Will he feel them tie the rubbery muscle tissue together? What will they do if the bullet blew away pieces of his bones?

No, wait. He's in here for four cracked ribs, a ruptured spleen, two sprained fingers, one sprained arm, a dislocated knee, and hairline fractures in the left foot, over and over like a 33 needle caught in the groove.

—⁂—

Then his mother sits before him an arm's length or two away, but her head springs out from the neck, and suddenly she looks him straight in the eyes. Truthfully, something he never experienced before, unless, maybe, she connected to him differently when he was a child. The eyes unnerve him, at least for a count or two, but even in this state, maybe sleeping, maybe dreaming, probably under, waiting for the cut, whether it be in his spleen or his shoulder, and now his mother or an apparition of her offers an opportunity. What he sees in those eyes surprises him.

Tears.

His little boy. He has a little boy inside of him, the one he once was. Before the drunken mom that left them alone so many nights. James and Justin sleeping with him half the time. Before his mother brought the men home, and his suspicions began to mount. Before he beat Sisko a fraction from death when his hunch proved correct.

Then.

When he was that boy.

Maybe then, she looked him in the eyes, and maybe she even showed him when she cried, because somewhere he remembers this. She touched him, she held him, he remembers. Could he conjure this tenderness so clearly in his mind if she hadn't? In the dream, while sleeping, probably under, everything is possible. Right? In the real world, this can happen, too. He feels sure of it at this moment.

He remembers these eyes now, and right at this moment, they are begging for forgiveness. Wet with saltwater from the internal sea, they brim with emotion, and she confesses, "I always loved you and your brothers. Always. Somewhere along the line, I forgot how to show it. The booze washed away any ability I once had. I'm sorry."

Then she stands in front of him and reaches out to hold him. He melts into her and they fly into the air as one, that boy and she. The one he once was.

—⸫—

There and not there, hovering above that bed, as they stand in a circle around him, blood running, nurses mopping, and muscles like strands of red licorice glistening. So it is the shoulder, not the four cracked ribs, a ruptured spleen, two sprained fingers, one sprained arm, a dislocated knee, and hairline fractures in the left foot.

No, those are the injuries from the jump in the shower. Three against one. They look worse than he does. He would like to see that, as they staple the wound in his shoulder shut.

—⸫—

He sits in a ten-by-ten-foot room painted white, and the three inmates who jumped him enter. They step in time to a beat they keep with a click of fingers on their right hand, as the left taps another rhythm on their thighs. They mean him no disrespect, just conjuring the chain gang blues to orchestrate their confessions. One, the tall one, with the ink sleeves and the black tattooed tears beneath his eye states, "Bro. We did you wrong. We saw your charity, how you sheltered those who were weak."

Another one, the one who shaved his head and beat everyone in chess concurs, "Yeah, bro. Your physical strength inspired, but we were jealous. We wanted to lead."

The third one, the one that weighed 350 pounds, finishes, "They still talk about you man," as he mops his brow of sweat. And they click their fingers and they slap their thighs. "You're a legend."

He and the three high five.

—⸫—

As he hovers on the ceiling, the doctors and the nurses make comments about his ink. They are looking over his body, studying the designs, speculating what they all mean. Could he be a biker? Military veteran? Ah, a convict, one says. Now

I'm sure. It all makes sense. Those dudes just can't stay out of trouble. Jack begins to feel suspicious. How could this be real? A doctor would never use the word "dude."

—◊—

Finally, the backyard sits in shade after a blistering day of heat and humidity. He pounds on Sisko, listening to the bone in his face crack. As the blood sprays, a voice begs him repeatedly to stop the attack; he's not worth it, just walk away. We can call the police and press charges, just stop. This time he does. He does stop because he sees the terror in the molester's eyes and realizes that what he set out to do, he did. Frighten the shit out of him, and he knows that because he can smell it. He stands up, rubbing his hand, which no doubt will be black and blue tomorrow, and Sisko raises his torso and braces with his forearms and his elbows. He avows, "I'm sorry. Please don't call the police. I will never do it again."

They do call the police, and in this version of the story, Jack remains a free man. As they cuff the predator, Jack thanks his lucky stars. He can continue to protect his brothers, and just maybe, Jordan wouldn't be shot one cold fall day as he sat drawing in the woods. Maybe, just maybe, Jeff wouldn't have begun to steal, run away, and ink up his body with incendiary words and signs. Maybe James wouldn't have taken up with his best friend's wife and die in a crash when the car rolled like a tumbleweed across the fields. Maybe, just maybe, all of their lives would have looked different. Maybe.

—◊—

Clickety-clack, clickety-clack, down the hall they wheel him. He opens his eyes to see art on the walls, not the headshots, busts, and facsimiles of convicts from the present and the past. Instead, watercolors of lilies on ponds, flowers in vases, golden fields of wheat against blue skies decorate the walls. Then he slips under again.

—◊—

James' cheekbones could cut glass, and his full lips draw in all the girls, as he sits with Jack on a bench on the outer edge of a carnival.

The Ferris wheel goes around and around, and they can see Jordan up on top now, smiling broadly. His black clothes stand out, as he always will, with pierced ears, silver rings, and a haircut that looks like the razor went wild. Over by the gaming section, Jeff shoots repeatedly to win a stuffed bear for a little black-haired girl that stands beside him. They, too, smile broadly. Their mom walks arm-in-arm with a tall gentleman that leans over from time to time to whisper some witticism in her ear. She giggles like a child, returned to something innocent now and safe, so very safe.

James states, "Life is good."

Jack agrees, "Yes, it is."

—⋘—

He opens his eyes again to see Debbie and Jimmy sitting in chairs beside the bed. The walls of the small room are pastel in color, and he can see the bright sun rising through a window to his left. He reaches out his right hand to Debbie, and she reaches back with both of hers. The dream has ended. He's no longer under but awake with an ache in his shoulder that feels like a saw cutting. Jesus! Debbie leans in and gently kisses him on the lips, staring into his eyes.

She asks, "How ya feeling?"

He tries to form words, but at first, they don't come. He tries again and weakly stammers, "Th...this shoulder is killing."

At that moment, a nurse walks in smiling broadly like Jordan, Jeff, James, and he in the dream, while under.

Debbie states, "He needs something stronger for the pain."

"Sure, let me check with the doctor," the nurse says, as she adjusts one of the tubes hanging from a bag.

"But not too much," Jack clarifies. "I don't want to lose consciousness just yet." He looks back at Debbie and asks, "How are you?"

"Better now."

He looks at the kid, his kid. "How are you doing, Jimmy?"

Jimmy moves in closer. "Did you get him?"

"Who?"

"The guy in the black truck."

Jack looks at Debbie, who shrugs, and back at Jimmy. "I didn't, but I'm hoping someone else did. You were right. You do know bad guys."

"When will we know if they got him?"

"Last I knew, your Uncle Jeff and Billy were chasing him. Then the cops got there." He looks at Debbie. "Do you know?"

She shakes her head. "Jeff and Billy are out in the hall, though. They're anxious to see you."

"How are the girls?"

Debbie shrugs. "As good as can be expected." She turns to Jimmy. "Why don't you run out and tell Billy and your Uncle Jeff to come in."

"Okay!" The boy runs out of the room.

Debbie touches Jack's face gently, and he doesn't turn away. She murmurs in a voice smooth as silk, "I think that we woke up spooning this morning."

Jack laughs a little. "Yeah. I think so."

"That sure felt good."

"Yeah, it did."

"We've come a long way, baby." Jack smiles and nods, as Debbie kisses him gently on the lips again. "And…I promise to do better about that other thing."

"I know you will, baby."

Jeff and Billy walk into the room; they look exhausted, and Jeff sports what looks like a stuffed broken nose and a stitched cut above his eye; both have battered hands.

Jack remarks, "Jesus, you two look like shit."

The two nod.

"How's that shoulder feeling?" Jeff asks.

"It hurts like a mother fucker, but I'll live. So what happened?"

Billy answers, "They took him away in cuffs."

"Did they read him his rights?"

"Not from what we heard."

"That's not good."

Jeff continues, "We're supposed to go down to the station and make a statement."

"What the hell are you doing here?"

"Making sure you're okay."

"Jeez! Get going! Finish what you started. Get this guy!"

Billy finishes with, "His father might call him shit bird, but he's far from dumb."

34
Angles
Sunday 9:00 a.m.

They throw him into the back of a squad car, and he begins to slip and slide. No upholstery here. The seat feels hard as a rock, and his clothes wet from rolling around on the earth. A chill rapidly sets in. He would never admit it to anyone, but an anxiety rises as he contemplates incarceration again, and he holds off the teeth chattering with a jaw clenched tight as a vice. He should have just left. Fuck! He could be miles away right now, heading south for the border. He could have lived without rounding up the chicks for a little fun. He could have lived without sticking his father. But he didn't. The cunts got one over on him, and his father could end up behind razor wire sharing a cubicle. Now that would be hell. Here he sits, sliding around, his cuffed hands bowing his back, making it impossible to feel comfortable. It didn't help that the two assholes in the front seat, though muffled through the glass, are talking about the most mundane shit every minute, from the weed patch where they caught up with him and the two pricks all the way back to town. On a positive note, they never read him his rights, which means he's not arrested. Yet. He doesn't know if Tillman and the other dick made their statements yet. Could be they told the cops about his involvement in the murder; his teeth squeak as he clenches and a tremor rises.

"Yeah, the kid hit a homer last week. He was happier than shit."

"Man, I wish I had a son. Don't get me wrong, I love my girls, but..."

"Yeah, my girl's what...thirteen now? I think. She's moodier than the wife sometimes."

"I know what you mean. I can't fucking wait until we get up in those woods. I don't even care if I get a deer. I just want to drink and eat without someone harping on me."

"Hell, yeah!"

When they turn the focus onto him strung up like a turkey, sitting behind glass, slipping and sliding, his hands numb now, the chill transforms into a fireball.

"You know, that fuck in the back seat, the girls they say he attacked tonight were just a bit older than our girls."

"Well, if they convict him, he's going to get his in the joint."

He didn't even do anything to those girls except discipline their bad behavior. It's not like they were five. If they had just done what he wanted, he wouldn't have hit them. All they had to do was suck him off.

Not really.

He planned to kill them. Just like he'd kill these two assholes in the front seat if he could. "He'd get his." Bullshit!

One prick continues, "It's the other bit that's got me going. Wouldn't it be something if he is the one?" So Tillman and the other prick already opened their mouths; he's sure now.

"Hell, yeah!" the other one answers.

The clench slips and his teeth begin to chatter, this time not about the chill, and even his held breath doesn't squash what he feels. He opened up his big mouth to his old friend, Tillman, and who could believe it, a family member of his victims. If they bring Lola into the mix, and she remembers what he told her, they just might have something, at least enough to re-open the case. He confessed to all three, just like the wiser ones warn will happen. Eventually a perpetrator opens his or her big mouth, and he did. He might never be free again. A sob starts rising. He can't believe it, but it's true. He fights the panic back with everything he has.

—⁂—

The snake beat his mother, too, from what he can remember. She left when Eric was seven, and he hasn't seen her since. His brother, eight years older, left soon after she did. He hasn't seen him either. That left good old Dad and him, and Eric served as reluctant witness to the gambling, the drugs, and the women.

Shortly after she left, his father went on a two-week binge, he and his buddies shooting up speed balls of coke chased with heroin. How does he know? They told him while he watched. The stereo pounded day and night with the likes of the Rolling Stones, The Animals, and Mitch Ryder, all music Eric despises to this day. What started with a few close friends became who the fuck wanted to get fucked-up showed-up, and the double-wide mobile home almost tipped over twice. Foundation or no foundation, that puppy swayed from side to side. Eric hid in his room most of the time, or split out into the night for solace, only to return and slide back through the window of his room. If he went out into the group, he knew the girls would coddle him and coo over his cuteness, making comments about what a big hunk he would be someday. Once, a woman teetering on heels, wearing a short black leather skirt sat just right, allowing him to see up there, and she did not wear panties. That one, the one on the heels, reached out and cupped him, announcing to the other girls standing around that he had a pants full. She kept her hand there a few beats too long and he reacted; she grew red, sucked in a breath, then pulled the wandering appendage away. One time he went out for food, something this group never had much of, so fucked-up, smoking cigarettes and pot, dozing in the corners, needles rolling in ashtrays, drips of blood drying where they fell, the makeshift tourniquets laying around like discarded socks. Maybe in a cupboard he could find a box of crackers, some dried meat, something to feed his young belly. Even his dad dozed, mouth open, legs spread, drool rolling out of a corner of his mouth. Eric walked through the crowd marking the ones he knew in his mind, the only ones awake or at least conscious, or those he had never seen before. Four in the last category sat positioned in the four corners of the living room, as he stepped over bodies, his feet clinking against bottles and cans or smooshing plastic bags, some empty and some full of brown powder, white powder, pot, and who knows what. He watched as the four creeped their fingers across the floor to body parts, doing what he doesn't know, but sometimes he heard groans. They eyed him, and when he came near enough, one grabbed him.

He told his father the next day that they had touched him, but he didn't tell him everything, like how they laid him down on his belly.

They touched me, Dad!

His dad acted pissed, but the four molesters were long gone. They left smiling. They left Eric sore.

So his dad taught him to fight. Dirty. From then on, the girls that touched him received a twisted tit or a pinched pussy. The dudes left cussing, while grasping their balls. At ten, large for his age, people often guessed his age at fourteen, he could fight with a knife, shoot the eye out of a bird sitting on the beam of a barn, punch like a boxer, and kick like a mule. Yeah, there were animals, along with the birds, and his dad just looked the other way. As long as Eric kept out of his sight, his dad remained happy. Eric didn't particularly feel joy when he tortured and killed; he felt pain, and this created a change from the usual day-in and day-out numbness. Cruelty made him feel alive.

On some level, he knows what he missed. Something he came close to a couple times with girls. Even Lola. A bit of tenderness. A bit of feeling like someone cared. Here it comes up now, crawling out of the tunnel. The sob. He can't sob. If his hands were un-cuffed, he would hit himself in the face as he has done a thousand times. Stop it! Stop it! Fairy, pansy, fag. The worst of all, shit bird.

—⁂—

The white room looks sterile and empty, containing one table and two chairs. The one-way glass guarantees an audience. Who watches? He hopes it isn't Tillman and that other prick. A detective Holder sits across from him now. The cop un-cuffed him, and the fucker even offered him a pop. He asked Eric if he wanted a lawyer, and Eric answered that he didn't need one. He hadn't done anything wrong. Eric knows that the two girls could cook his ass, but he has already concocted an approach. As for the murder rap, he's already found an angle on that too. He studied a lot of law while serving his bit. He knew he had to find angles, if they ever reopened the murder case. The events of tonight seemed to complicate the situation until he thought about it more. In the time that it took them to bring him into the station, and after what seemed like an eon into this little white room, he found a way to thoroughly review what he knew and put on the face. As they were walking him down the hall, he saw Tillman and the other prick, no doubt there to make a statement. All three glared at each other, until Eric broke out into a smirk that he saw riled the shit out of the two. What a laugh. He felt ready, and the chattering teeth, the inner quaking, and especially the self-pity were quelled, completely at bay now. Oh, yeah, quell? Another one of those words.

The detective states, "You're in some deep doo-doo, buddy."

Eric flashes a smirk, on the face. "Why's that?"

"You match the description of a man who kidnapped and accosted two girls in the wee hours of this morning."

"Really? You must mean the two girls that I picked up hitchhiking after the party. They willingly climbed into my truck."

"That may be, but it's what they claim you did afterwards that we're concerned about."

"What did they say I did?"

"You know exactly what you did."

Eric leans forward and addresses the cop straight in the eyes. "Shouldn't we be talking about what they did?"

The detective leans in towards him. "What exactly did they do, Mr. Thompson?"

"Five minutes in the truck, and they're begging me to turn down a farm lane. The one sitting next to me, the brunette, she reaches over and cups my cock. Now what would you do in a situation like that? They were willing and of age. I was willing. I turned down the lane."

"Why did the girls turn up in the hospital injured, Mr. Thompson?"

Eric sits back in his chair, takes a deep breath, and lets out a dramatic sigh. "When I said they were nice girls, I was being facetious." Yeah, another one of those words. Who knew they would come in so handy? "I parked the truck, and before I knew what hit me, they were punching at me and kicking at me, in the cab. Man haters. I shouldn't have been surprised. I saw blondie in a middle of a catfight at the party. I guess they hate girls too. She's got some tight moves, that little blonde, let me tell ya."

"You're telling me that those two girls were punching and kicking you?"

"That's right. I've got the bruises and cuts to prove it. Look at me!" Eric pulls up his sleeves to reveal scratches and welts, then lowers his head to show the head wounds from blondie and the tree limb. "Of course those two assholes that chased me out of my father's home also got in a few licks. The bruised ribs," he lifts up his shirt, "those are from kicks. And the facial bruising? That one dude must have landed a couple dozen blows. They worked me over real good."

"Let's talk about the girls right now."

"I pushed the brunette away and she fell forward, knocking her head a good one on the dashboard. She went out. Before I knew it, blondie was making a run for it. I couldn't let her run out into the dark alone. I ran after her, but she wouldn't stop. I punched her and carried her back to the truck. I laid her on the ground and turned to see how the girl inside the cab was doing. Before I knew it, blondie banged away on my head hard as shit with a good-sized piece of wood, and I fell forward. Before I knew it, both of them were taking off across the field. I sat there dazed for I don't know how long. I worried about them out there in the dark, but by the time my head stopped spinning, they were long gone. Still, I tore off, ran after them for a long time, but I never did catch up. How are they?"

This time Detective Holder takes a deep breath and sits back in his chair. "Mr. Thompson, a Lola Ramirez came here to the station yesterday to file a restraining order against you. She claims that you have attacked her on numerous occasions. Do you know this woman?"

"Of course I know her. She's my girlfriend. Has been for a couple of years now."

"Did you attack her? You told the officers yesterday that you did not. Maybe she attacked you, too?"

Eric looks down at the table, sighs and shakes his head slowly, then looks back up at the detective. "Her father has been abusing her since she was a little girl. She went over to visit him yesterday. I remember her telling me that she was going." He pauses, making some disgusted sound, from the corner of his mouth, "That son-of-a-bitch beat her again? That's why she didn't come home..."

"I saw that you served some time as a youth and even spent a year or so in adult corrections..."

"I was a thief and dealt a little weed, not a violent offender."

"Just coincidence, Mr. Thompson, that three women in a twenty-four hour period accuse you of attack?"

"I swear, sometimes I wish I were born queer. Don't you?"

"What do you know about Martin Becker's wife being murdered twenty years ago?"

"That was a terrible thing. Becker was my coach back in the day."

"Two men wrote a statement tonight that you confessed to murdering Jeanine Becker."

"Whoa!" Eric dramatically sits back in his chair. "I was just horsing around with those two guys. Three of them showed up to my father's house and harassed us in the middle of the night. Said they came to visit me. I knew one of them back in the day..."

"Jeff Tillman?"

"That's right."

"Why did they come to harass you?"

"Tillman was holding a grudge from the old days. All of a sudden, one pulls a gun out, the blonde guy, so we pulled our guns, too. What were we supposed to do? We thought they were going to kill us. Carrie Joe fired in self-defense, when one lunged for my father's shotgun. I took off out the back door, and two of them chased after me. What those two girls didn't do to me last night, the two of them did. I should be getting checked into the hospital, not sitting here having to defend myself."

"We found some journal entries in your garage this morning. In there you state that you wanted to get back at Martin Becker for ratting on you and calling you out in front of the team..."

"That doesn't mean that I killed his wife. As far as I'm concerned, you can look through everything I own."

"We have your permission to look through your house, your truck, your garage..."

"Sounds like you were already in my garage. How did that happen?"

"We were tipped off."

Eric's mind races, wondering who it was. Lola? She didn't know anything about those journals. Maybe Tillman and the other two pricks? "Since no one else has a key to my garage, I'm thinking that someone broke in. I sure hope that wasn't the police. Maybe it was the pricks that are trying to do me wrong?"

The detective stands up and walks slowly around the table to stand behind Eric. Suddenly, Eric feels an excruciating pinch on his left shoulder that shoots up into his neck and skull, and Holder leans in and speaks softly in his ear. "You're a fucking liar! You attacked that Ramirez woman, the two girls, and twenty years ago, you murdered that poor woman out in the middle of a field. I know it. You know it. Now that we are on to you, we will find what we need."

Tears rush as the pinch virtually paralyzes him; the cop eases up and roughly shoves his shoulder. The detective walks slowly back around the table and drops into the chair. "If you confess to that murder, we'll work with you."

Eric puts on his best face, his I'm so charming you could kiss my ass face. "Detective, I have nothing, absolutely nothing to confess."

Around 2:00 p.m. on Sunday, the two female police officers came for Lily's statement. Finally, around 4:00 p.m. they released her from the hospital. Shortly after, Brenda, Billy, and Lily headed for home, the girl half out of her mind on meds and her right arm in a sling. A light rain fell, plastering the red, orange, yellow, and brown leaves into a slick, mottled carpet. The steel gray sky did nothing to lift spirits, and neither did all the Halloween decorations gracing homes, businesses, and yards. They were a sad lot, the Bagwell family.

They picked up Christopher on the way home, and though he tried to engage with his sister, excitedly telling her about a movie he'd seen at Grandpa's, she only turned to look at him shortly then back to gaze out of the window, her forehead pressed up against the glass.

They pulled into the driveway and Lily climbed out of Brenda's wagon like a zombie, although quiet random giggles occasionally rose up out of nowhere, breaking her vacant stare and slack-lipped mouth.

Brenda wondered where the anger was.

Where the sadness, disappointment, and fear were.

Once home, she dragged up the stairs to her room and quietly closed the door without a word.

Hours later, Brenda wondered what she was doing upstairs. Sleeping? Reading? She dreaded thinking that Lily Rose might be sitting at her vanity, staring at her face. When Lily finally looked at herself in the bathroom mirror of her hospital room, she gasped, then quickly turned away, walked out of the room, laid back down in the bed, and remained quiet. Already, no tears came because the meds had turned the water off. When a social worker came around and asked her how she felt, she answered, "Fine. I'm fine. Ugly."

Brenda and Billy sat on the couch watching TV, with Christopher lying in between them asleep exhausted from worry. They hadn't told him yet about what happened. No doubt his active imagination played with him. After a couple of hour ticked by, the phone rang. Their young son didn't even stir, his little snores occasionally breaking the drone of TV voices. After Billy hung up from the call, he hauled himself back to the couch, his face drawn with tension. She quietly asked, "What's wrong? Who was that?"

Billy wiped his hand across his mouth, looking ready to scream. Brenda stood up and pulled his arm to follow her into the kitchen. She leaned against the counter as he snorted out breath from his nostrils in little streams. She demanded, "What?"

"It was Bobby Ellis. He was on duty at the station today. The son-of-a-bitch told them that the girls were willing, that they tried to seduce him, then beat up on him. He turned everything around!"

"Of course he did. What did you expect? He's lived twenty-one years with the fact he murdered someone. He's incapable of remorse. You said that yourself. And don't forget, I met him, too. He never touched Lola either. He denies all of his bad behavior. That's how he lives with himself. That's how he survives."

"Brenda, there are witnesses from the party that saw Lily beating up on another girl. The girl came forward."

"What?"

Billy hurries towards the stairway leading to the kids' rooms, "I've got to talk to her..."

"No! Let her be!"

"He might get away with this. Get away with everything."

"How can he? It's the word of two girls against his. And Lola's. Plus he confessed to you guys!"

Billy paced back and between the kitchen and living room, Brenda by his side. Christopher finally woke up with a start, lifted his head and exclaimed, "What's wrong?" He looked up at her, then rubbing his eyes, looked up at Billy.

"Son, your mom and I need to talk. Why don't you go up to your room and play with your Game Boy."

"Did something else happen?" His little voice cracked, as he jumped up from the couch. Brenda caught him with one arm as he headed for the stairs, hugged him tightly to her and kissed him on the head. "It's okay. We just need to talk for a bit."

As he ran from the room, he cried tearfully, "It's not fair! It's not fair!"

Billy sat back down on the couch exasperated. He stated through gritted teeth, which no doubt would be ground down to stubs before this whole thing ended, "We should have killed that son-of-a-bitch..."

"Then you'd be in jail now." Brenda dropped onto the couch beside him and reached over to grab his hand. "It's going to work out somehow. I know it will."

"Jesus, Brenda! He's claiming we assaulted him..."

"You and Jeff did beat up on him, didn't you, after you caught up with him?"

Billy kept talking as if he didn't hear her, "That we went there last night with the intent of doing him harm. He could press charges against all of us!"

"Wait! What?" Brenda jumped up from the couch, throwing her long hair over her shoulders. "I thought that this fucking nightmare was going to end!"

"He could press charges for us breaking into his garage..."

"Wait a minute. When the hell did you do that?"

Suddenly, the muffled sounds of little cries and a ruckus echoed down the stairway. Brenda and Billy sprinted up the stairs and down the short hallway that separates the two bedrooms. The sounds came from behind Lily's door, which Billy threw open without a knock.

Lily reached up to tear the last remaining poster from her walls. She used both hands, her right arm free now of the sling. She turned as if in a trance, tears rolling down her cheeks. Brenda looked around the room. Lily's boom box laid on the floor overturned and possibly broken. Her makeup: lipstick, eye shadow, mascara, and powder strewed the floor too. Across her mirror, in bright pink lipstick were the words: Fairy tales are for children.

Both Brenda and Billy moved together as one to encircle their daughter with their arms. Out of one corner of her eye, Brenda watched her small son walk into the room and then run toward the three of them, entwining his strong little arms into their legs.

—⁂—

The four slept as if they had never slept before. The house, where ghostly echoes of laughter, joy, and tears filled the spaces stood still. All four members of the family shared the king-sized bed. Occasionally, a groan, a mumble, a short cry sounded, as one shifted to their other side, or rearranged their entangled legs, or snuggled in tighter to ward off worries.

When they awoke, one by one, stretched and yawned, their eyes caught a glimpse of a bright morning sun, which generally harks in hope for a new day, but a heaviness continued to permeate. Lily and Christopher stayed home from school, and Billy headed for his shop, seeking work as a solace. Brenda thought about her husband, the warrior, who had always fought for what's right, but this time took it a step too far. He now faced a formidable foe. Brenda begged him to remain calm, be patient, though she barely maintained center herself. She thought about that voice that seemed to come out of the sky, to say that the pearls would find the killer. In her weakest moments, she took on the emotion she knew all too well: guilt. In her strongest, she convinced herself that the voice came from her and her alone, the pearls nothing more than a broken string of beads found one dark night in a shallow hole.

—⁂—

Later in the morning now, Brenda drives to the shelter to check in with Grace and complete a bit of bookwork. Brenda tells her about Eric Thompson and what transpired in the wee hours of Sunday. Visibly upset and sympathetic, Grace encourages Brenda to take a few days off and tend to Lily Rose. To her surprise, while Brenda packs up to head for home, in walks Lola, her facial cuts now scabbed, but the rainbow of colors that cover her face still hideous.

Brenda jumps up from the front desk. "Lola!"

The petite woman quickly approaches Brenda and throws her arms around her. "I wanted to come by and thank you, again!"

"Thank you for filing a restraining order."

"Yes, and it must be working because I haven't seen him!"

"Actually," Brenda begins, as she breaks the embrace and walks back behind the desk, "he's been detained for questioning by the police."

"What? Why?"

"I do wonder, Lola, why you didn't press charges against him."

"Well, I…"

"He attacked two teenaged girls." Brenda catches her breath to hold down a sob, and though she succeeds, tears do spring in her eyes.

"He what?"

"Kidnapped and attacked two teenaged girls, and it's possible he may have murdered…a woman years ago."

Lola's eyes widen, and she shakes her head, "No…then it's true?"

"What's true?"

"He told me once he had killed. I didn't believe him."

Brenda scoots quickly around the desk again and grabs one of Lola's hands, "He did? Lola, please, please go to the police and press charges for what he did to you, and tell them about what he told you. Please!"

"He'll come after me. He'll kill me too."

"No. If you go now, they will have to detain him longer…"

"When will he get out, if I don't?"

"Maybe another two days. Seventy-two hours altogether, if you don't go…"

"I don't know. I have to think about it…"

"One of the girls…was my daughter…"

"Oh, *mi dio!*" She covers her mouth with one hand, turns and heads for the door.

"Lola! Please!"

"I…I will think about it." Lola opens the door, turns once to look at Brenda and says, "I do thank you for what you have done for me." She pulls the door closed behind her.

Brenda knows in her heart that Lola will flee for so many reasons, including the fact that she's undocumented and that Eric Thompson has left his indelible mark.

Brenda grabs her purse and heads down the long hall to the back door, her face dropping, her heart breaking, her hope hanging by the thinnest thread.

—⁂—

As she drives home much faster than usual, she's fifteen again. It's the day after her mother's murder, and the sun has gone down. She and Peter sit in her bed, blankets up to their noses. Their dad slouches in his easy chair in the living room drinking whiskey. They hear him throw one empty bottle away with a series of clangs in the garbage, and the cracking of the seal of another. They know that their father will not allow anyone to take them away in the night, while he's awake, but what happens if he passes out? Falls asleep? Though he locked the windows and the doors, what prevents the monster from breaking the glass and reaching in? She tries to be strong for her brother, but she trembles, then fights for control, trembles, than fights again. They begged their dad to let them stay at Grandma Martha's but he refused. She sees the dark beyond the windows shield everything from her sight. For the next ten years, that darkness taunts her.

Now she's twenty-five again. She has never felt safer than she does with Billy, but he's gone, deployed in the distant and foreign Arabian Desert, which stretches out into eternity, or so her husband described. She's with James now, but even though he swears he'll protect her, she knows he's as changeable as the wind, and one whiff of another woman could draw him away.

She pushes up against her fear and ventures out that night she finally found her strength and the pearls hidden in the small womb in the earth. Together with their dog, Jake, she made her way home, swearing that never, ever, would she allow the dark or anyone who used the dark, to prey upon her or the innocent again.

She pulls upon that feeling now with all her might. Eric Thompson will not defeat her and her family. No way. Not ever!

—⁂—

As she turns into the driveway of the house, she spies Billy standing in the long, open doorway of his shop, cigarette in hand, his face so long, she imagines his chin upon the ground. He stares off into the distance and nods to her as she pulls her wagon into the attached garage. She climbs out of the car and walks over to where Billy stands; he glances at her from the corner of one eye, inhales deeply and stares off into the great unknown once again. No hello. No kiss. Nothing.

"Guess what?"

"What?" he says without turning.

"Lola came into Grace, while I was there. I encouraged her to press charges against Thompson. She also told me something that might be helpful."

"What's that?"

"He told her that he had killed."

"So what? Did he tell her that he killed Jeanine Becker? He could have killed a dog, a skunk, who knows..."

"No, he meant a person."

Billy flicks his cigarette into a pail of sand and looks at her.

"Doesn't matter, Brenda. That's not enough. None of it's enough. None of it."

"You're giving up…"

"We broke laws. I could go to jail. Then what?"

"We wait for you." She takes his two hands in hers. "He's going to slip up. I know it. He's smart, but he's not that smart. They are onto him now…"

"Bobby told me that the son-of-a-bitch knows the prosecutor. They're related somehow."

"That doesn't mean that he's going to let him get away…"

"Doesn't it? If they let him out after seventy-two hours, he will run. He'll be out of here so fast… "

"Then maybe he will go away forever, and it won't matter."

"It will always matter."

She wraps her arms around him tightly; at first, he stands coldly, but after a few beats, breaks down and wraps his arms around her too.

"I'm sorry, Bren…" His voice breaks. "I'm sorry I didn't handle it better…"

"You did your best at the time. I know that. I know you, and that's who you are. I don't blame you." They cry together, an exhausted soft cry, chests in slow heaves, almost a whimper, injured animals moaning, the last coos of the dove before night falls.

—◊◊◊—

Sitting quietly side by side in their red Adirondack chairs, Billy and Brenda gaze out upon the fields that stretch down to the creek and up again into a woods. Billy takes his last inhale off his third cigarette, since Brenda arrived back from Grace and flicks it into that pail of sand just inside the doorway of the garage. She's counting. She wonders when he will quit again. She wonders when life will quiet again, when their torment will fade into a distant memory.

They watch as Lily steps slowly and diligently through the tall dried wildflowers, making her way up from the creek. She told them that she wanted to think. They wait for her now, breath held, knowing that she will ask questions. She will want to know what's going on with the man that locked the door of the truck, that punched them, ran after them, changed their lives forever. What will they tell her?

It's a cooler day, although the sun shines, drawing out all the vibrant colors of fall. Brenda wonders if this is what it feels like to take some exotic drug, where the surroundings look too bright and colorful to be real, an imaginative world where anything is possible. In this world, fairy tales could come true, a world where adversaries are distinctly evil but good always wins out in the end. Not a world where even nature transpires to undo the good, bringing in a storm that saved Eric Thompson from paying for his crime, a world where synchronicities work against, rather than act as crumbs on a path to paradise. A world where lies and truth become so intertwined that one cannot be deciphered form the other, a world where two girls must look behind their backs forever because unbridled danger lurks.

Brenda watches as Lily travels closer, clearing the flowers and tall grass, walking freely now. Their daughter looks up from her deep reverie to spy them and come join them where they sit. "Did you have a nice walk?" she asks her strong, courageous daughter, whose face looks like a split mask, one side so sweet and pretty and the other stained with otherworldly colors, that psychedelic world where evil exists but does not conquer.

"What's wrong?" she asks.

Billy sighs, turns his head and looks to the ground, so Brenda speaks up, not quite ready yet to share concerns. "Nothing," she says very softly.

"There is something wrong! Tell me! I have a right to know! I'm not a child anymore. He's been arrested, so why are you so sad?"

"He hasn't been arrested!" Billy outbursts.

"What do you mean?"

"He's been detained. They can hold him for seventy-two hours."

"And then they will arrest him, right? They can't let him back out, right?"

Brenda looks up at her, hesitates for beats on end, then spills, "They can."

"Why? How?"

Brenda drops her head into her hands and begins to cry.

Billy jumps up from his chair. He gently grabs Lily by the shoulders, "He says that you and Kristen asked him to turn down the lane, that you tried to seduce him, and then beat up on him..."

"That's not true! You don't believe him..."

"Of course we don't. But you need to know what he's saying."

Brenda looks up to see Billy searching into his daughter's eyes. He asks, "Did you fight with another girl at the party?"

"Yes. I did. I drank, and I smoked pot, and I became so angry...," she says tearfully.

So pot was the other smell, Brenda couldn't quite identify, lingering upon her.

"She came forward..."

"What do you mean?"

"It supports his story. It's his word against your word. There's no proof."

"Look at me! Look at Kristen!"

Brenda wipes her eyes with the back of one hand. "He has injuries, too. From you, he says, and also from your dad and Jeff."

"You beat him up, Daddy?"

Billy releases Lily's arms and walks over to lean against the outside shop wall, shaking his head, exasperated.

"I'm glad you beat him!"

Brenda speaks emphatically, "You have to prepare yourself, Lily. They might let him out. He might even walk free."

"No. No! It can't work that way. He was going to kill us. I know he was. And you said that he might have murdered Grandma, too."

Billy speaks up, "There has to be proof, Lily. Or a witness. That's the way it works."

They all turn when they hear the back door slam and watch as Christopher run towards them.

Billy breaks into a strained smile, "Hey, Buddy."

Christopher crawls up into Brenda's lap. "Is everything okay now?"

Lily sits down onto the edge of the other chair. She scoots back into it and sits up tall. "No, little brother, things are not okay."

Brenda sniffs her nose and quickly wipes her tears away one last time, for this day at any rate. She states confidently, "No matter what, we will be okay. We have each other, and we are strong." She watches Billy turn his gaze out onto the fields, and that cold ruthless determination she has come to know possess his eyes.

Epilogue
American Heartland – October 2002

Two Weeks Later

36
Evergreens
6:00 a.m.

The sunrise looks beautiful, the first golden rays fingering their way across the landscape. Jeff leans back into a cushy, green upholstered chair, lacing his fingers behind his head; he props up his feet on the round wooden table by the motel window. He keeps one eye on the open fields as those beams illuminate the land and crawl toward him; his other eye he glues to his phone.

Make the call. It's time now. You can do it.

Minutes pass as the sun climbs and highlights the dry fallen leaves, blowing slowly toward piles, where they will add bulk, crevasses where they will fill the shallow, and fences where they will dress wire and wood. The landscape looks rather barren, devoid of leafed trees, but the evergreens stand out as the guardians of all seasons, strong and tall, able to withstand the most frigid of winters, sway in the most tempestuous of storms, and remain green in the most arid of summers. They stand as testimony to nature's strength. But what about mans'?

He watches as two young children stand at the roadside, waiting for the school bus; they are dressed in Halloween costumes, one a ghoul with green skin, black clothes and red gloves, the other a superhero with a fluttering blue and black cape, half mask and boots. They yell at passing cars, muffled voices through the motel glass, and laugh with open mouths, white teeth catching those early rays of sun, and he's betting, if he could see them more clearly, mischievous eyes.

307

Desiree has called him three times since he left California. He has not returned the calls, but he did listen to the messages.

She said his mail has grown into a pile, and one piece is marked urgent.

She said his boss called twice wondering if he could come back early.

She said two fish have died in his aquarium, and the filter seems plugged.

She never said she misses him, but he can read in between the lines, can't he?

He does miss her. He misses her more than he ever thought he could.

The last two weeks feel more like two months since he returned to the Midwest. He came to put his conscience to rest, make his final amends, meet his young nephew, and bond with his one remaining brother. He departs as a man humbled by the good intention of individuals and inspired by what a person will do for another he or she calls family or friend.

He also departs as a man world-weary. How could they release Thompson? How the hell could they? How can he help raise a child in a world like this? Many dangers abound, including himself, he fears.

—⁓—

That part of him he thought he had under control turned out not to be. That part of him he thought he had left behind, he had not. Jack told him later that he couldn't wait to be out of that trailer, out of that den of decadence, away from any semblance of violence. While Jeff felt the old him, that part of him that feasted on the adrenalin of force, move him through the woods after Eric Thompson, like a man on fire. His heart pounded, his palms sweat, and when he felt Eric's flesh give way to bruise bones, if not crack or break them, he could not stop. Thankfully, Billy pulled him back, or god knows how far he would have gone. Now maybe in those minutes that felt like hours when he and Eric grappled, he pounded out every last residue of anger, frustration, bitterness, and regret that he still held. If it hadn't been for this. If it hadn't been for that. All the excuses lined up like pitiful worn out soldiers, standing on a shelf, always there, holding him back from doing good, encouraging him to turn his back on everyone and everything. In those minutes, he didn't care because he beat upon a man he felt ashamed to know. He didn't care because the violence felt familiar, some perverted and stable friend he knew all too well. Did the incident deplete the angst, well did it? Can he go back to California and commit a healthy man to Desiree, and a wise, guiding, and loving force to a child?

Because he's not sure, he leaves the phone on the table.

—m—

She discovered his real identity in the first few weeks. Although sober at the time they started to date, he ran into an old friend about two months in, one who had shared the mosh pits, the attacks on people of color, the shaved head, tattoos and eight-inch Doc's. What began with arm wrestling in the back of a bar, drinking down Mountain Dew, grew into a twenty-one hour drunk, ending in a fistfight with six bikers. He dragged himself up the stairs of his house and onto a brown leather couch, where he passed out with several broken knuckles, no doubt a few cracked ribs, multiple abrasions and bruises, clothes torn and sprinkled with blood.

Desiree dropped by because he had invited her to dinner, hoping to prove himself, as more than a former brute. Sure, he owned the house, two cars, dressed in button-ups and khakis, but what would happen when she saw his tats and scars? He forgot her during the binge, when he poured Bourbon down like water, and even smoked a little coke. She looked through a front window, when he failed to come to the door, to see him disheveled on the couch and decided to try the door, see if he laid alive or dead. He awoke with a start to find her cleaning blood from his face with a warm wet towel. He glanced down to see a pan of pink water and back up to see her face full of concern.

"What happened?" she asked.

Lies flew through his mind, because he knew the truth would repulse her. He liked this woman. He liked her very much, but knew he wasn't good enough. Yes, he had told her about his past, and still she agreed to spend time with him, but truthfully, though he had succeeded in holding himself tall and strong for months, it took little to topple him.

Jeff sat up abruptly, knocking the pan of warm water out of her hands, sprung up from the couch and said, "Run like the wind, baby. Run!" He remembers the shocked look on her face, as she stood up slowly, glancing down at her soaking wet shirt, a white shirt, now pink, and she turned on one heel and strode toward the door. With her hand on the doorknob, she turned; he could see the tears in her eyes and for one moment he did...he wanted to fall upon his knees and swear it would never happen again, but he just wasn't sure.

She said, just above a whisper, "I guess you are an animal."

—⁂—

The Tuesday after Thompson attacked the girls, Doug Holder called Billy and him in for questioning. The same man interviewed Jack in the hospital the day before. Of course, the three chose unanimously to tell the truth and take their chances. After all, isn't honesty always the best policy? Holder directed Jeff and Billy into a small white room, where three chairs and a table sat, and nothing more. The detective kept giving Billy the stink eye, not only in those early hours after Thompson's attack, but from moment one when they gave their statements. Billy shrugged it off.

"Why did you go out to Rick Thompson's place?" Holder began.

"We wanted to confront Eric Thompson about the murder," Billy stated.

"The murder of Jeanine Becker," Holder clarified.

"Yes."

Holder looked at Jeff. "If you suspected Eric, why didn't you come forward at the time?"

"I lived out of state. I had no proof."

"So you three boys decided to 'take things into your own hands.'"

"I knew him back in the day," Jeff said. "I thought I could appeal to his better self. I forgot that he didn't have one."

"Did you also suspect him of kidnapping and attacking the girls?"

"We put two-and-two together after Billy's daughter shared details about the attack."

"So you deny that you and your brother went out with the intention of doing him harm?"

"Absolutely. Jack and I weren't even carrying. They pulled guns on us," Jeff clarifies. He noted his right hand shaking more than usual and stuck it down under one thigh.

"Why did they pull guns on you?"

"Eric said some derogatory things about the girls, and I lunged at him. Jack pulled me back, but it was too late; they grabbed their guns and put a bead on us."

"So he confessed to harming the girls?"

"Yes, he did. You have all of this in our statements..."

"I want to hear it again directly from you." He turned to Billy. "So how did you get involved again?"

"I showed up to support Jack and Jeff, and saw through a window that the two Thompson's had them at gunpoint. I pulled out my pistol, kicked the door open and all hell broke loose."

Jeff remembers gazing off, as Billy described what happened, lost into that moment again, when his heart and mind raced with the adrenalin of force. He remembers the nausea rising as he sat in that room, with Billy and the detective, as the regurgitated images hammered down. The flesh giving way beneath his fists, the blood splattering, the moans and groans of a man, even if a beast, filled him with dread and shame now. At that moment, he did feel a ray of hope. He felt no pride. He felt no triumph. He felt only fatigue and disgust. Maybe he could join Jack and walk away from violence forever.

He came back to focus, as Billy continued, "... the woman shot Jack, and Thompson made a beeline for the door. Jack held them at gunpoint, as Jeff and I went after him to make sure he didn't flee."

"He claims you assaulted him."

"We did beat on him," Billy stated. "He and Jeff were grappling, when I finally caught up, Jeff was doing everything he could to hold him until the police arrived. I won't lie, we pounded on him for a while, but nothing that would harm him too badly, and certainly not kill him."

"You claim he confessed to you that he killed Jeanine Becker."

"He did! The fucker told us that she didn't even fight, that she went down easy. I had the chance to hurt him a bit for all that he'd done. I couldn't pass it up." At that point, Jeff heard Billy grind his teeth, and noted from a side-glance how his new friend's eyes grew darker.

Jeff spoke up, "And I couldn't either."

"You understand that breaking into the garage was trespassing and destruction of private property?" the detective asked.

"Yes," Billy acknowledged. "We felt desperate to find something to connect him with the murder."

"He could press charges for that."

"Don't tell me that you won't use what we found as evidence, if needed."

"He gave us permission to go through everything he owns."

"So, are you arresting us for something, or not?" Jeff snarled.

"At this point, no. Actually, at this point, we won't be arresting anyone."

"So you're going to let him walk?" Jeff asked incredulous.

"Lola Ramirez has disappeared. There is no concrete

evidence or witnesses regarding what happened in that truck or what happened twenty-one years ago in the field."

Billy slapped his hands down on the table and said defiantly, "So you can add the attack on my daughter to your long list of failures to prosecute."

"When it's all said and done, Mr. Bagwell, you and Mr. Tillman might be the only ones serving a bit."

—❧—

After his binge that sent her running, he went to the gym every other day to work out; Desiree worked there as a personal trainer, but not his. She was studying to be a physical therapist at a nearby university. He stayed sober, and would say hi to her, but beyond that left her alone. He figured he blew it with her, so he had no hope that she would ever date him again.

After two months passed, one day while working out on the machines, she walked up. "How you doing, Jeff?"

He stopped his rep and turned to her. His heart beat like hell; why did this woman have such an effect on him? "I'm doing good. How are you?"

"I thought maybe we could go out for a cup of coffee."

He couldn't believe his ears. "I'd...I'd like that."

They started dating again; she was very cautious, and he went to meetings every day. Hand holding moved into hugs, and hugs into kisses, and kisses into sleeping side by side without sex. When they finally made love for the first time, she took control, running her fingers over his scars, studying his tattoos, teaching him what she liked, and when he sped up, she slowed him down, and when he entered her, she searched his eyes. When he came inside her for the first time, he cried and she held him closer. But all of it held a caveat. After all, this woman was anything but stupid.

"If you fall again, it will be the last time you ever see me."

Two years passed without another fall or the lure of violence. He thought sure that he had conquered his demons, or at least had them under control. That was until the adrenalin of violence drove him through the pines, through the hardwoods, through the dark on that night just two weeks before, when he and the symbol of his past, a man named Eric Thompson, set out to kill each other in the middle of that field of dried grass and battered wildflowers.

—⦈—

The sun has climbed higher now, as people in cars race off to work, and drivers of trucks begin their day of deliveries; Jeff takes a big swig of coffee, lights a cigarette and thinks about what occurred the night before, one act by a smug and victorious man to seal the deal on a family's torment.

Billy and Brenda invited him, along with Jack and family, over to their home for dinner. Jeff swung one last time through Willis, not to say goodbye because he knew he would be back but because one part of him wanted to absorb the small town life, one he believes will eventually fade away forever.

The town was busy with people celebrating the night before Halloween, Devil's Night for some, and the Day of the Dead for others. They shared dinner at the diner and made stops at the Dollar Store for last-minute accessories to costumes, replacement bulbs for strings of lights, and plastic pumpkins with funny faces to collect candy. Earlier in the day, he had taken Jimmy to the gaming store and bought him something he didn't have, and thought about his own child, already growing, although not a part of this world yet. This world where killers run free and the innocent pay the price. This world where good and bad run together in a darker shade of gray, and he still questioned where he fell on the spectrum. He found some comfort watching as Jack and Debbie touched and interacted in a way that left him envious, and realized that he could have that, too, if he just let go. Debbie apologized for what she did that first night, and he recognized in her the demons they both fought. He looked at her skin and thought of Desiree's cocoa color; he looked at her hair and thought about how Desiree's ran like a black river down her back. He thought about his girl's smile, yes, his girl.

As he sat at the dining table in the old farmhouse, he noted that even with all of the drama, the tragedy of this lovely girl, Lily, accosted, a young woman really, and a confessed murderer allowed to walk free, this family held intact. He felt a deep respect for them. Billy knew as Jeff knew that once released, Eric would slip away, and he did. Where? Who knows? But far away, probably over the border into countries south, where even if evidence was found or a witness surface, he would be difficult to find.

After dinner, Brenda asked Christopher to run out to the mailbox for the mail, because she had forgotten. The kid ran out and back like a power pack was strapped to his back. Jeff thought about his child, the one still inside the woman that he loved, and he wondered if it were a boy, would he be an athletic little guy like this one? Or maybe a quiet, shy kid like his nephew, Jimmy. He smiled to himself. A girl would be fine too.

Christopher handed Brenda a manila envelope, which she stepped into the kitchen to open. Jeff figures he will never forget the screams that exploded out of that adjacent room. Everyone sitting around the table, including Lily and the two boys all ran into the kitchen, eyes wide, mouths open.

Brenda stood, with her back against the kitchen counter, holding a small piece of paper in one shaking hand. The manila envelope just carried in laid on the counter beside her. She glanced up as everyone now stood around her in a half circle. "That son-of-a-bitch! That mother fucker! How fucking dare he! How fucking dare he!"

Billy exclaimed, "Honey, what the hell?"

Lily, "Who?"

Little Christopher covered his ears with his hands. "Mom!"

Brenda stretched her arm out to Billy, the small piece of paper clutched now between two fingers, "Look!"

Billy took the piece of paper and read it to himself, his lips moving as he did. "What is that supposed to mean?"

"It's from him!"

"How do you know?"

"Because of what's in the envelope!"

Lily stepped forward and grabbed the envelope, turning it upside down to shake the contents out. A string of pearls coiled like a snake in her hand.

"I don't get it," Billy said.

"Lily wore them that night," Brenda stated.

"Jesus Christ!" Billy clenched the paper into a small ball and tossed it across the room.

Brenda screamed, "No!" She walked quickly over to where the ball of paper laid in a corner, picked it back up, and then smoothed the crinkles out with her fingers on the top of the counter. "We might need this. Someday. Who knows?"

"What does it say?" Lily demanded.

Brenda enunciated every syllable, "We are even now."

—⁂—

When the rays of morning light strike him in the eyes, he stands and begins to pack his last few things into the suitcase. Along with his clothes and toiletries, he also places the gifts recently given: a framed photo of Jimmy, the boy picked out especially for him, a book by Lao Tzu from his brother, a baby toy carved from wood that Billy made, and Debbie's first chip from meetings.

He still cannot say with certainty that he will remain sober or neutral to the lure of violence, though his brother, who also struggled for a long time, who exhibits an enviable sense of peace now, gives him hope. After all, the same blood flows through their veins, or at least part of it.

He imagines Eric down south basking in the sun, alone now, alone forever always on the run. Jeff imagines him making one mistake that tumbles him down into a fall. They will probably never know, but they can hope.

Some days the world looks dark, with little separation between good and bad, and he can't lie, he feels anxious about bringing another life into it. But that life has already begun and he determines to do the best he can. After all, if everyone does their part, their very best, won't the world we live in become better?

He zips his suitcase closed, picks up his phone, and with that shaky right hand, at once a stark reminder of the past and his will to become stronger, he presses the numbers with vigor.

"It's about time," she says, in that soft, sultry voice that makes his heart beat faster.

Yes, he thinks. It is about time. He clears his throat and says, "I'll be home in a few days." As he pulls the motel door shut behind him, he nods with reverence to the evergreens.

Acknowledgements

I would like to thank the lovely Dawn A. Hall for sharing her knowledge about the laws and practices regarding domestic abuse. She helped set the stage for the scenes involving Lola.

I felt it imperative that I realistically capture the hospital and emergency room scenes in the novel. I sought experts and found one through my cousin Nikki Schultz, Angela Graham RN. Angie patiently and thoroughly informed me of the practices, so that I could bring authenticity to this important aspect of the book. Thank you.

Even though David Jankowski stated that he didn't think that fiction needed to be spot on with criminal law, I wanted to make sure that this aspect of the book also rang true. We shared long discussion, as he graciously shared multiple layers of law. I dare say he also helped shape the unfolding of events in the last quarter of the book. Thanks, Dave!

I am starting my ninth semester of teaching in the correctional facilities of Michigan. Simply put, I have seen and heard a lot, but I could never claim to accurately replicate the inmate experience. Yet I tried, and with the help of Nicholas Ashmon, I think I succeeded in doing a fairly good job. A big thanks, Nicholas!

Over the three years it took to write this novel, family and friends tirelessly supported me. You know who you are. I could never have done it without you. At times the support took the form of a pat on the back, or a hug, and at others, a kick in the butt. Every bit of it kept me going.

Finally, a big thanks to Marti Smiley Childs and Jeff March of EditPros LLC. Their continuous support has helped to materialize this dream come true, with a little help of a guardian angel, Dawn Smiley.

About the Author

Author S. L. Schultz's body of work includes poetry, prose, plays, screenplays and novels. Her plays have been staged in San Francisco and Chicago, and she has published short works. She lives in Michigan, where she teaches English Composition and Creative Writing. *Cradle Crow* is her second published novel and book two of the *Little Shadow Trilogy*. Visit her website at www.SLSchultz.com.

S. L. Schultz (photo by Alyssa Grant)